The
Dionysian
Alliance

The Dionysian Alliance

A Novel of Sex, Religion, and Murder

Jack Rinella

Rinella Editorial Services

Published by
Rinella Editorial Services
4205 North Avers Avenue
Chicago, IL 60618 USA

www.RinellaEditorial.com

Book and Cover designs and Illustrations
by
Michael Tallgrass

Contact him at mtallgrass@aol.com

Library of Congress Control Number:

ISBN 978-0-940267-23-7

Printed in the United States of America

Table of Contents

Chapter

Strange Letters

1

C hicago, 1988

It came as no surprise when Mom announced she was
selling her home and moving. Since her retirement two years
earlier, she had found life in rural Ohio less and less tenable and
saw no reason to fall in line with the blue-haired ladies who lived
in her neighborhood.

So my brother John and I pitched in to help her sell things,
haul them to the trash dump or parcel them out as gifts and mementos
wherever they best fit. Forty years in the same house is a lot of time
to accumulate almost as much junk as the Collyer brothers could fit
into their trash-filled mansion. That's how I ended up with a box of
old books, never thinking that they would lead me to a sex cult and
a murdered priestess.

The box attracted me because the title on the top of the
stack was a theology book that Great-Uncle Jonathan had given
me when I was in high school some 25 years earlier. I hadn't read
it then, but now I was curious as to why he had given it to me and,
by the way, whatever happened to him? So I stashed the box in the
trunk of my car, went back home to Chicago and put the box on the
dining room table.

Since I was still single, the dining room didn't get used
very often. The extent of my home cooking was hardly more than
to make coffee in the morning before I went off to my job at the
"ad agency." Well, it wasn't really an ad agency. To be honest, it's
a front for a detective agency, but there were few people who knew

that since our client list was select, wealthy, influential, and very demanding of discretion. Our payments from them were always handled discreetly.

Moving Mom was a slow process as she had to sort through the trash and the treasures, find a place to live in the summer, sell the Ohio property, and decide whether what she was going to keep would to be sent to her new place (wherever that was) or to the winter house in Florida. In either case, John and I spent a lot of time last spring piling boxes in the barn until Mom was ready to call the movers.

I didn't get to that box of books very quickly. I had spent a good deal of time in Ohio, so when I returned to work the stack of papers on my desk was a strong distraction. Two weekends later, March weather being what it is, I thought I ought to see what was in that box. I put the theology book on the stairs to my bedroom, thinking I'd read it when I went to bed. If nothing else it might help me fall asleep.

The box held a collection of other old books, mostly about theology, philosophy, and Eastern and ancient religions. Since our family hadn't been especially religious, it seemed strange that my parents would have had such a collection in their home, though it really must have been more my mother's collection, since Dad had died when I was young.

What I hadn't expected was the pile of letters in the bottom of the box. They were still in their original envelopes and neatly bound with a very faded red ribbon, postmarked Louisville, Kentucky, and dated between 1930 and 1962. The return address simply read PO Box 2187, Louisville, KY 01.

"Kentucky?" I wondered.

I pulled out a chair from the table and sat down to see what the letters contained. There were seventy letters in all, and whoever had assembled the package had done so with care. They were in chronological order and most, except for one or two, had been written by Uncle Jonathan.

Uncle Jonathan wasn't really my uncle. He was my mother's uncle and I had only met him on the occasions of a family festivity and the times he had spent with us on vacation so I really didn't know him very well. Mom had a sweet spot in her heart for the old man, but was about the only one in the family who did. The others wouldn't listen to news about him and generally seemed to despise his rumored lifestyle. I'm not sure if the feelings stemmed from his religious life or the hint that he was queer. Whatever the reason, I hadn't heard enough stories about him to draw any serious conclusions. Reading the letters soon changed all that.

Most of them were simply breezy hellos that Jonathan had written to various members of our family. Some were to his grandmother Sarah (my great-great-grandmother); others to his brother (and my grandfather) Ben, and many to my mother.

The ones with some real news in them revealed a religious monk, schooled in his religion by his grandmother in some strange, small, and secretive fertility cult. As I read them I decided to take notes.

The PO Box return address on the envelopes attested to the fact that he lived in a monastery called Eagle Ridge somewhere near Louisville, Kentucky. He was in an organization called the Alliance that seemed to be quite wealthy and to have influential connections around the world.

The last of the letters, written to my mother in 1962, was about me and said:

> I've finally finished the series of journals for Ben. It'll be in safe-keeping for the day when he's ready to seek his place in our holy fraternity.
>
> I know it's hard for you not to share our secret with your own two sons but they must come to Dionysos in their own time and their own way. Be at peace, my dear niece, for come they shall, when they are ready.

At the end of some three hours of reading I had a list of clues leading to my great-uncle. I folded the list and decided to talk to Robert, the agency's manager, on Monday. If our agency couldn't find out what had happened to Uncle Jonathan, no one could.

"Why don't you just ask your mother?" Robert asked after I had told him my Uncle Jonathan story.

"Honestly," I said, "I don't know. First off, of course, I feel strange about asking my mother if she is a member of a secret fertility cult. If she wanted to have told me by now, she certainly had enough chances. From what I've read about this Alliance outfit, she'd be put in a difficult position if she blabbed all their secrets to me.

"Besides," I went on, "I'd rather she not know that I know. That way, if it's something I want to avoid, she won't have any incentive to try and talk me into it."

The Appointment

"Well, Ben Kramer. How interesting to finally meet you. Tell me, what brings you to my office, here in Cincinnati?" the lawyer asked. His question took me off guard. After all, I had expected that he would be answering my questions, not I his. I would have guessed he was in his early sixties, with more gray hair than black, a closely cropped mustache and receding forehead. He was some six feet tall and rather trim for his age.

The paneled walls of mahogany, the obviously old tomes on the rows of shelves, and his large desk cleared of the usual businessman's papers made me feel as if I were before a judge, rather than a man who had invited me to visit him in order to answer my questions. He seemed a gracious enough guy, though "guy" is hardly a word that would have suited his demeanor. Rather he was more the gentleman, kindly and older than I would have expected, with both the slight airs of a college academic and the stern manner of a federal prosecutor.

Indeed, the building to which I had been invited appeared to house law offices, though the small wooden plaque outside of his office read only "Richard Ceznat, Esq." I assumed this man simply worked for my uncle's religious order, but it was a bit disconcerting to think that this place was their representative's office. It seemed more appropriate as an office for some agent representing the Rockefellers, Mellons, or Carnegies, rather than a monastery.

Our research on Mr. Ceznat, on the other hand, revealed that he had few clients; his name only occasionally appeared in a court filing. However, he was a member of several prominent and highly selective social clubs and served on several corporate boards and trusts, most of which were involved in high end real estate and holding companies.

I knew very little about Uncle Jonathan but it did seem that Mr. Ceznat was knowledgeable about the monastery; ostensibly he was their lawyer of record, though I found no paper trail to have proven it. We had found his name in searching the ownership of the post office box. His firm paid the yearly rental fee. The post office box had led us to Ceznat, though the records showed a long list of names that had used the box over the years. Even at that we wouldn't have ferreted out Ceznat's name if we hadn't been able to pull in a favor or two from friends in Washington.

"Well," I answered, "as you might know, my great-uncle Jonathan was a monk on Eagle Ridge. Many years ago he gave me a book of rather esoteric theology. I was in high school at the time and didn't pay much attention to it. Last spring while my brother and I were emptying Mom's house because she was moving, I found it in a box of books in the basement.

"It's strange for that book to have reappeared some twenty-five years later, but now I find it interesting, even alluring. It's taken me nearly five months to track you down, and the truth is that I want to find out more about my uncle's life."

"I thought that might be the case," he replied. "When I received your letter I researched your uncle and found your name in our archives. Your uncle had listed you as a next of kin in his will with the instruction that if you ever came seeking him, you were to be given this packet. Whatever is in it is written, I can assure you, in his own hand. He would be pleased to know that you have finally received it."

With that, he handed me a leather pouch inscribed with the words: "To my great-nephew with love, Uncle Jonathan." It certainly could contain the journals that I had read about in those letters. My curiosity was piqued by this little surprise. "Was it the journals?" I asked myself. After all, Uncle Jonathan, as far as I knew, had been dead for many years. I wondered why the contents hadn't just come to me when his will was probated.

"For now, Mr. Kramer, that's all I can tell you. I suggest you study the materials your great-uncle has left for you and if your desire for more information remains, feel free to call me and we can arrange for a more enlightening meeting."

At that my host rose, came around his desk and offered me his hand, obviously meaning to end the meeting and show me the door. I was taken aback by the shortness of the visit and at how little I had learned. On the other hand, that was not unwelcome, as I wanted to head back to my hotel room and see what I had just inherited.

The taxi cab ride to the hotel went quickly, my brain buzzing with all sorts of questions. In fact, it's probably no surprise that the meeting had left me with more questions than answers. Originally I had merely assumed that I would have been met by a kindly old monk or a prelate of some sort who would have offered to tell me about Uncle Jonathan, show me around some clerical manse, give me a few religious tracts, and eventually end the meeting with some offer to pray for me to the God of whatever religion Uncle Jonathan had believed in. When I learned that I would be meeting with a lawyer, I became suspicious that there was more to be learned than I suspected. Now I was left with the firm idea that whatever it was, it wasn't very open to the public.

My agency's research had confirmed as much. The boards that Ceznat sat on were all privately-held corporations, many of which were simply holding companies for other corporations. Even at that, their yearly IRS filings showed huge assets, generally of a very conservative nature.

We had found no record of Jonathan's death, though that meant only that he hadn't died in Kentucky or Ohio, the two states where we had looked. On the other hand, he wasn't listed on the Social Security Death Index either.

Uncle Jonathan, as I remembered, hadn't seemed very eccentric to me, but then I was a kid and he was a great-uncle. He was single, which was probably the dubious source of the rumor of his homosexuality, but didn't show any traits of being part of some strange cult. Besides, monks were supposed to be single, weren't they? Sure, he didn't go to church with us when he visited, but he bowed his head for grace, never tried to convert me or my brother, and generally was just a quiet, older guy who liked Claire, his niece and my mother.

I wondered where Eagle Ridge was. Though I had some sneaking idea it was in Kentucky, I really did not know for certain. It did come to me that for all the vacations we had taken as a family we had never once gone to visit him. On the other hand, I guess a monastery isn't quite the place you bring your kids for a vacation, and after Dad had passed away, Mom had to curtail our vacations anyway, finances being what they were.

It was a short ride back to the hotel, up the elevator and into my room. "What," I wondered, "do I have in my hands?"

The leather pouch was handcrafted and kept closed with a few buttons, which I undid, revealing a letter written to me and a stack of notebooks like those I used to use in high school. As the lawyer had promised, I recognized the writing as Uncle Jonathan's. Dated Aug 1, 1962, it read:

> Dear Ben,
>
> There's a good chance that I will be long gone from this earth before you see this package but when you do, let me begin by saying that I'm pleased you've arrived thus far. I will be among the first to admit that we in the Brotherhood don't make it very easy to find us, but as you'll soon learn there are good reasons for our secretiveness. After all, we have suffered no small number of burnings at the stake in the past two millennia -- and that from a religion founded on the premise to love one

another as well as to love your neighbor as yourself. But this communication is not about them, it's about us.

Your mom assures me that you're open to the material I've gathered here for you and, having watched you closely during my visits over the years, I believe I can safely say that I agree with her. Nonetheless, I will warn you that learning about our fraternity is no easy task. Even Uncle Jonathan's great-nephew will have to prove his trustworthiness. Now don't let that scare you off if, as your Mom suggests, you find our faith-life attractive.

By now you're probably wondering just what this old man is talking about.

I remember how much you groused about your parents' insistence that you take Latin in high school when all your friends were taking Spanish. There was a reason for that (your attendance I mean). Your folks wanted to be certain that your education included a strong basis in classical languages and literature. Your struggle over "Arma virumque cano" and the like was not without purpose.

You see, your Mom and I follow the ancient faiths of Greece and Rome. That pantheon of gods means something to us. It's not just a bunch of fairy tales made up by primitives waiting for the Christ child. I expect that having said that much you see why we keep this fact a secret. From the time of the Roman Senate's decree in 163 B.C.E. which outlawed the Bacchanalia, the systematic eradication of people of our faith has been nearly all too successful.

In fact, archeologists believe that, except for a few fragments, the mysteries we celebrate are long gone. Fortunately the gods don't disappear that easily. Little do they know that the Bacchanalia is still celebrated by the monks of Eagle Ridge.

There, my dear nephew, you have the gist of our

9

secret. Having passed it into your hands, I trust you will honor the memory of your mother's uncle and not put my brethren in peril with loose talk.

What I am passing on to you are my journals, though they can be called that only in the loosest of terms. They are more a mélange of my musings, assorted clippings, quotes that meant something to me, and an occasional diary entry. There is no rhyme or reason to their compilation nor to the order in which they appear, except that they reflect my thoughts and feelings, as well as the books I was reading at the time of each entry and the musings I was having that day.

I didn't actually write the journal with you in mind, but over the years it slowly became my legacy to you. I hope you will study these pages. They are my effort to shed some light on the subject. If your heart wishes to follow this path, these books will help. If not, destroy them or return them to the brotherhood as you see fit.

Fare thee well, nephew.

Your loving uncle,

Jonathan Caminsky

Well, that was a mouthful. Just as the letters had indicated, the old man was no pious Christian at all. It's no wonder that my uncles and aunts didn't like him. Their one-way Jesus path left no room for those with other ways of thinking. My Mom, on the other hand, hadn't cared for their form of intolerance.

So he was a pagan. Until I had read those letters, I'd have never guessed that. After all, who ever heard of a monastery of pagans? Stonehenge, the Parthenon in Athens, even primitive tribes in Asia, I suppose, but a monastery full of pagans sounds strange to me. On the other hand, since some folks think that Buddhists are pagans, it is a reasonable idea.

But now that book he had given me when I was younger made a

little more sense, as did the other books that Mom had packed in the basement. I guess if I wanted to know more I'd have to dust them off and see what they had to say.

Jonathan had left me seven notebooks in all, many of them bound in cardboard which was printed with a black and white design, with lined pages sewn together, like I used in high school. Other, older ones were simply packets of sheets, numbered and quite orderly. Some entries were hand written, others were copies of quotations, or handouts of some sort. Each book was simply numbered, without any other title. The first entry in Book One read:

> September 14, 1933   The novice master suggested today, though his demeanor was hardly that of one making a suggestion, that we begin our lives under his tutelage with the keeping of a journal. He said it would be ours in which to write, copy, or quote whatever we wished and that we would find it of great value as we made progress in the mysteries of which we wished to gain knowledge.

Thus began my study of my uncle's life and faith.

He was living at the time in a place called the Lodge, part of Eagle Ridge, and a retreat center of some sort where he attended classes and ceremonies devoted to his ancient gods. The most important one was obviously Dionysos, who was called Bacchus by the Romans.

From his writings the lodge seemed like a large well-appointed cabin hidden away from regular traffic and easy notice. There was a small staff dedicated to the indoctrination of applicants to this Order of which Jonathan eventually became a life-long member.

I knew that he had been born in 1905, and from the journal entry that he had joined the monastery at the age of 28. It didn't take too much reading to learn why the Order was so secretive. As a clipping pasted under that first entry explained:

Dionysos, the Greek god and son of Zeus, called Bacchos (Bacchus) by the Romans, was a popular god with incredibly diverse forms of worship.. Thought to have originated in Thrace, he also had connections with Phrygia and perhaps Crete. He had numerous forms: a mighty bull, signifying animal maleness or more effeminate, as man with fair skin and long curls. His followers sometimes clothed themselves in fawn skins and carried thyrsi (the long poles, topped with ivy or vine leaves) and roamed forests and mountainsides. His rites also included theater as he was the god of drama.

Myths about Dionysos were numerous, including his birth from the thigh of his father Zeus, his mutilation and death at the hands of the Titans, and his descent (twice) into Hades to redeem his mother Semele and then Ariadne, who become his wife.

The Dionysian rituals included eating the raw flesh of wild beasts, drinking goblets of wine, a phallus hidden in a winnowing basket, and (among the Orphics who also worshipped Dionysos) in the immortal human soul. Those who were confronted with the vision of Dionysos and possessed by him felt his power in various ways: in ecstasy, in drunkenness, in sexual activity, and in spiritual bliss. Followers of Dionysos became one with the god and were called Bacche (feminine) or Bacchos (masculine) after the god himself.

Knowledge of the actual mysteries of Dionysos has long been lost but seem to have been as diverse as the manifestations of the god, usually included eating and drinking. In the archaic and savage mysteries of Dionysos, as portrayed in Euripides' play The Bacchae, those initiated into the cult were said to tear animals to pieces (sparagmos) and eat the flesh raw (omophagia) as a way of assimilating the Dionysian power embodied within the animal. In more serene Bacchic rites, such as those held in Athens, the rite was reduced to a simple banquet. The holy drink that initiates of Dionysos drank was wine, the special gift of the god. Sexual practices were also a part of Dionysian ritual.

Jonathan then continued the thought with his reflection that "Little do they know that a great deal is known of the 'actual mysteries of Dionysos.'"

If that entry wasn't enough to pique my interest, the one written on the second day at the Lodge was.

Today our classes began in earnest, yesterday having been taken up with unpacking and a general orientation of the Lodge and the surrounding property. It seems the Brotherhood owns a great deal of these lands, the rest of which are primarily federal forest reserves. It must be quite the estate, as the ride up the driveway took more than 45 minutes.

There are three of us applicants: myself, an older man named Karl, and a young woman named Stephanie. I guess I might better stop calling this a brotherhood, in deference to the maiden who is my classmate, but I rather think that Brotherhood as a general term is quite acceptable. On the other hand, it is well-known, even by the mundane world, that the most notorious worshipers of Dionysos were women.

This fraternity takes no time in asserting itself in an applicant's life. Frater David, the novice master, told us that tomorrow begins our week of abstinence. We are to have no sexual activity, either with one another, a fellow Brother or Sister, or even alone. I can't believe that masturbation is off-limits. An idea like that is enough to send me home, though since it's only for a week, I'll do my best to manage it.

13

F.D. then went on to talk about the First Gift. It seems that our first official rite has something to do with offering seed to the gods. Well, after a week, I'll certainly be ready for that.

The entries that followed were all rather short and non-descript until:

September 22, 1933   Tomorrow   is   the Autumnal Equinox and the Rite of First Gift. I hope I can hold out until then. I'm not cut out for this abstention thing. After all I was raised to know that sex is a healthy exercise and ought to be readily enjoyed.

F.D. took time today to explain the rite to us and to finally answer our questions about it. This past week has been filled with way too much theology about Father Zeus and the Pantheon of gods.

During the week, each of us was interviewed by small groups of monks, as if they hadn't grilled us rather incessantly at meal times, in the gardens, or at any other opportunity for that matter. I feel like I've been under a microscope ever since I arrived here. I guess that's to be expected, inasmuch as the Order is very uptight about admitting an ill-suited candidate to its most sacred inner circle. I've actually had an easier time of it than Karl since my grandmother Sarah was rather well-known by several of the older members and she had taken me under her wing from a very early age, teaching me the way of the craft at her kitchen table.

All in all, I'm looking forward to one Hell of an orgasm tomorrow night, though doing so publicly, and in front of women for that matter, feels awkward.

As you can imagine, I was more than intrigued by those paragraphs. Unfortunately there was no entry for the next day, nor for several days afterward. That turned out to be the case with most of the notebooks. Though there were hints of what was going to happen, the Journal turned out to be more a book of pre-Christian Theology than a graphic, or should I write pornographic, treatise. It took me about two weeks to read through them all and another month or so to scan the books I had inherited from my mother. They weren't very enlightening either, though they obviously dealt with witchcraft, spells and potions, and all sorts of psychic phenomena.

When I got through my reading I certainly had a different opinion of Uncle Jonathan and of my mother as well. I resolved to pay a second visit to that lawyer and find out more. This time I would make sure I had a chance to ask my questions. I got really busy at work for the next few weeks, so I wasn't able to schedule a return trip until mid-October.

Introductions 3

My second visit with Richard Ceznat was quite different from the first. This time he greeted me more warmly, invited me to join him in a sitting room adjacent to his office and offered me coffee and tea. He had also scheduled the meeting earlier in the day and began with the assurance that he had kept his date book clear of any other appointments in order to devote his full attention to me.

He then asked me how I had enjoyed my uncle's gift.

"I found it fascinating," I admitted, "though it only left me with more questions than answers. I hadn't realized that my mother and he were so involved in a pagan religion, but the materials they've left behind sure point in that direction. All in all, I find myself greatly attracted to their faith. To be straight-forward with you, I really want to know more."

"I had thought and indeed hoped that such would be the case," Richard replied. "Your uncle was an important and influential member of his Order. His hopes for you were rather well-known by his friends. It is only because of his high standing among them that you were permitted to receive his bequest. Even at that he assured us that nothing he was giving you would compromise their integrity or their safety."

"That's for sure," I said. "His writings gave no clues as to his whereabouts whatsoever and there were damn few descriptions of anything having to do with rituals or celebrations."

"As I hope you can well understand, we have maintained

the highest degree of reticence about revealing ourselves. Even now, to you, I can only speak in guarded terms. There are those, to be sure, who think that the times are sufficiently changed that we can relax our guard and expand our numbers. Tradition, of course, says otherwise."

"How then does your group grow?" I asked. "I mean, how do you get new monks?"

"Well," he said, "it's not my Order. I am only one of its representatives. I will say though that I consider myself a member of their faith. You can find believers such as me spread across the face of the planet, though to be sure few are as Dionysian as the members of your uncle's Order.

"You will know, I presume, that there has been a significant growth in what is contemporarily called neo-Paganism, mostly espoused by the likes of Gerald Gardner and Anton LaVey. In terms of enlightened sexuality, both Gay Liberation and the rise of swingers and of those in what they call the 'Alternative Lifestyle' have proven fertile venues for the liberation of mankind from the onus of Jehovah and his anti-sexual monotheism. However, I digress, Mr. Kramer, and need not bore you with my personal opinions on the matter."

"Please call me Ben," I answered, "and certainly don't worry about boring me with your opinions. I have found the reading materials that Uncle Jonathan left me quite tantalizing. When you join them to mother's collection of books on the subject, my interest only deepens."

I wondered if he knew how much I really knew already. After all, our research had shown that this was no petty cult of a few hundred people. At the same time it dawned on me that perhaps they knew more about me than Richard was letting on. "They can play this hide and seek game as easily as I can," I thought to myself.

"What pledge of trust do I have to vow in order to be let in on the secret? Quite frankly, I find this information coming to me at the most opportune time. At the age of 41 I think it's time I did a bit more reflecting about what I am to make of my life."

"To your first question I can only answer that one has to prove himself to the fellowship in order to gain entrance. I am not in a position to interview you for admission, though with the proper kind of entreaties from you I can facilitate the initiation of the process. The actual path to the monks, though, is through the broader fellowship that we call the Alliance. It is composed of those Dionysians who live openly in the world as do the practitioners of most of the world's religions.

"As for your readiness, may I ask some personal questions of you?"

"Of course you may," I answered. "I fully expected you to, once I understood what Jonathan was about. What do you want to know?"

At that Ceznat reached into the drawer of a small table next to his chair and retrieved a pen and a pad of paper. Once again I had the idea that he would learn more today than I would. He turned to me with a hint of a smile and remarked "I had hoped such would be the case, Ben. I would be pleased to help you surmount the difficulties, if such is the will of the gods. So let's begin. And please, call me Richard."

I took a sip of the tea that had been poured for me, sat comfortably back in the overstuffed sofa on which I found myself, and said, "Go for it, Richard. What do you need to know?"

With that he began a laundry list of biographical questions. As I told the attorney, I'm 41 years old and was born in Ohio. I'm healthy, and have a graduate degree in Business Administration. I work for a small advertising agency in Chicago, where I do marketing research and help develop sales plans for a broad range of clients. I'm financially comfortable, though by no means wealthy, and own a home in a quiet and solidly middle class neighborhood in Chicago. In case you're wondering, I'm five foot eleven and weigh 178 pounds, clean-shaven with light brown hair that is just beginning to show signs of gray.

The interview felt more as if I were applying for a job than seeking information about a religious sect. Certainly no street evangelist had ever sought this kind of information from me. Eventually, though, the line of questioning turned to sexual activity.

"What is your marital status?" Richard asked.

"I'm single," I answered and immediately wondered where this line of questioning might go, given the fact that my life, in its own way, was no more traditional than my uncle's. I decided that it would be best to be truthful and admitted to being bisexual with strong homosexual feelings, which is one of the reasons why I had found my recent reading material so appealing.

Over the years I had short and rather sporadic relationships with several different men, while at the same time I dated women and in fact at one point had been engaged to one. Fortunately for both of us she broke it off. So I had gone through life a bachelor, one whose family had a firm resolve not to ask what might prove to be embarrassing questions.

Richard didn't bat an eyelash over any of my revelations.

"Why," Richard asked, "are you seeking your great-uncle now, after all these years? What can you give as your motivation for this quest?"

"Honestly, I can't say for sure. Yeah, I'm curious about Uncle Jonathan and certainly more so now that I've read his journals, but what really got me wondering was that theology book. I live with this gnawing question about what my life is really about. What does all this mean? I'm comfortable and have what should be a happy life. I've friends, a nice home, a stable job. Every so often I get into a satisfying relationship and though they don't seem to last long enough, they dispel loneliness for a while But I feel this emptiness about the utility and futility of life, Richard, that leads me to wonder if Uncle Jonathan knew something that I ought to know.

"I'm sorry if I can't pinpoint it more than that for you, since if I could I might not be here asking you for help right now."

"Yes, Ben, at one time or another we all sense that quest. Don't think we don't understand it and often enough feel the same way." He paused for a long moment, looked over his notes and continued. "Well, Ben, it seems everything points in an orderly and acceptable direction. I'm satisfied that at this point we can continue our conversation by hearing some of your questions."

"Quite frankly," I admitted, "I don't know where to start."

"Anywhere is fine," Richard commented. "I will merely tell you what I can and refrain from broaching topics that the monks would prefer I not discuss."

"Is the Order's lineage as old as Jonathan implies? Are we really talking about ancient mysteries?"

"The monks of Eagle Ridge trace their heritage back to most ancient times. Here in America we only have documents copied from those in Europe and Asia, but let me assure you that scholars among us have access to parchments and papyri that would be the envy of the world's most renowned archeological institutions. In due course, if accepted into their ranks, you would undoubtedly learn much of the Order's history."

"I suppose that's why my parents made me take Latin in high school," I said.

"Yes, that's right. Many have had high hopes for your future. For better or for worse we can only influence your free choice so much, and must rely on the beneficence of the goddess for the rest."

"Can you tell me what my uncle's life was like? How do the monks support themselves? His journal was rather devoid of any of that kind of information."

"That's not unexpected," replied Richard. "The monks' caution would not have allowed you to receive a gift that was anything more than philosophical in nature. If your great-uncle had given you a more extensive diary, it would not have been allowed into your hands. I am sure that he was well-cautioned early on as to what was acceptable information and what was not. I trust you understand the need for discretion. Our celebrations would not have been tolerated as recently as twenty years ago. There seems indeed to be a gaining acceptance of our practices, or rather tolerance I should say, but the centuries have proven how fragile even that can be and how tragically reversed.

"To answer your question more directly, early on your uncle was a student and scholar, though he too was required to work in the gardens, vineyards, and fields that sustained them. In due time he became a teacher among them and a revered leader, a priest in fact of a very high rank, though his humility and gentleness were as well-known as was his scholarship."

"How large is this order?"

"I'm sorry, Ben, but I cannot divulge secrets such as that."

"Well, can you tell me how I can learn more?"

"That I can do, at least as far as the initial process is concerned.

"Let's just say that your uncle was part of a more scholarly and somewhat elite group. Just as a monastery is only a small part of a larger religious fraternity, so the order is part of our larger Dionysian Alliance. You'll have to get to know us as friends and intimates well before you'd learn much about the order."

"What might that mean? How intimate?"

"We have learned that our souls speak in many ways and there are those among us who can discern your intentions and your future in the embrace of a kiss. Need I remind you that your reading must have at least hinted about the seriously sexual side of our beliefs, even if they didn't present you with the more erotic events that flow from our faith life. You can hardly be seeking admittance to a community that practices sex magic, to use a very poor choice of words for our sacred rituals, without understanding our need to ascertain your feelings about such intimacies."

So, I thought, my hunch about First Seed being a fertility rite wasn't so far off, after all. These people were more Dionysian than I had dared think and their faith life wasn't anywhere near as other-worldly as I had feared, even if there was a lot of talk about gods and goddesses. I still had a certain skepticism about that, but there was nothing repugnant to me about the drunken celebration of Bacchanalia.

While I was tossing these ideas around, Richard asked if I would join them for lunch. We had been talking for more than an hour and the time had come around to noon. Not wanting to miss a chance to learn more, I quickly agreed to do so. With that he stood up, turned to the door, and suggested I follow him.

We walked back into his office and through a side door, down a short hall and into a well-appointed dining room with a table set for four. "There'll be two others joining us. Thomas is a monk with whom I work, and I have also invited a close friend of your Uncle Jonathan's who has been anxious to meet you. Perhaps you will remember her name from one or two of your uncle's stories."

"The strange thing about Jonathan," I said, "is that he didn't tell many stories, so I doubt that will be the case."

Almost on cue, a handsome man and an elderly woman came in through another door. Richard immediately went over to the woman and greeted her with a warm kiss. "Mother," he said, "I am so pleased to introduce you to Ben Kramer. Ben, this is Stephanie DiCarlo."

I offered my hand to her, which she took warmly into hers and to my surprise she kissed it. "Ben, dear Ben, how wonderful to meet you. You're just as I expected, with a sure hint of your uncle's genes. He spoke so highly of you. I am sorry he can't be with us."

"It's my pleasure as well, Ms. DiCarlo." She was of an elusive age. I guess maybe 78, but I really couldn't tell. She had alluring green eyes and pale skin that clung to her frail 5 foot 7 frame. I guessed she weighed some 130 pounds but I couldn't tell that either. Her hair was long and silver, so silver you would never call it gray.

"Oh, please call me Stephanie. These titles are just that. I wish I could get Richard to cut out this 'Mother' talk. He tends to be so damn formal."

"Stephanie, I call you Mother because you have earned my respect and I love you as one."

"Phooey," she replied. "You just don't know what to call an old woman, but no matter, I love you too. Now Richard, enough about me. You've quite left poor Thomas out in the cold."

With that the man came forward, offered his hand to me and said, "Welcome Ben. I'm Thomas Murray. It's a pleasure to meet you."

Richard continued, "Thomas manages the financial concerns of the Order in this part of the country, though I suspect I'm going to lose him to more official monastic duties before long. You and he have similar educational backgrounds, though he made himself known to us at a younger age than you have."

"Now, now, Richard," Stephanie interrupted. "Every person has their own path and their own clock. I'm sure that Ben is right on schedule for his life. The world, after all, doesn't follow your plan for it anymore than it does mine. There is a season for everything under Heaven, you know. Now where is that lunch you promised me?"

"Ben, you can sit here, and Mother, please sit there. I am sure George will be in shortly to satisfy your appetites, or at least some of them," Richard replied with that smile again.

"Stephanie," I asked, "is there any chance that you're the woman mentioned in my uncle's journal? Did I read that you were at the Lodge as a novice with him? I certainly can't believe that you're the same person, since that was more than fifty years ago."

"Thank you, my dear. The days have been kind to me as well as has modern science. Yes, I'm the same and, unlike a lot of things about our fellowship, it's no secret that I'm 74. I was graced to have been born into a believing family and so had the opportunity to join the Order at an earlier age than most."

At that Richard picked up a bottle of wine and poised it above Stephanie's glass. "May I, Mother?" he asked.

"Of course, you fool. When have I ever refused to drink of our lord's gift?"

With that he poured a glass for her and came over to my

place. "May I, Ben? This is a bottle from one of the Order's own vineyards. I am sure you will find it acceptable."

"By all means," I answered. "This will indeed be a treat. It's been too long since Uncle Jonathan brought a bottle of the monks' wine to Mom and Dad. My brother and I were only allowed a taste and even then it was mixed with water."

"Ah yes," said Thomas. "Dionysian through and through. You know, it was the god himself who taught us to dilute the wine at the feasting table, a ritual that our Apollonian detractors fail to mention when they accuse us of being drunkards."

"I didn't know that," I answered. "I guess there's a lot I have yet to learn about your religion and its practices."

"In due time, Ben, I hope we'll all be blessed to aid in your education," said Richard, "but for now, let's eat." With those words he put his hand under the table as if to push a button. I heard a soft ring from behind the door and in no time at all, a waiter brought in a cart of luncheon foods.

He first offered the tray to Stephanie and then to me. This Order sure has no lack for people, I thought. "George, this is Ben Kramer. Ben this is George Cardenas, the mainstay of our office. It is true that we live by the power of what we eat, and that's only part of George's contribution to our welfare."

"My pleasure, Mr. Kramer," said the gray-haired man with a grin. I smiled back at him with "And mine too, George. This food sure looks good."

"It's all from our farms," noted Thomas. "The lands of the West have been a blessing to us all. We produce enough to support ourselves as well as the work in the Old Places."

"Ben, please excuse the obscurity of Thomas' references. To us the West is the Western Hemisphere and the 'Old Places' are our settlements in Europe, Africa, and Asia. It is those small oases of our faith that have survived in hiding over the centuries that have afforded us connections that the mundane world has long counted as lost. In return for their planting of seed in the New World, the old ones have begun to enjoy the fruits of our labor as well."

"I'm not sure you're going to answer this question," I said to Richard, "but can I infer from your use of the word 'seed' that you indeed practice fertility rites?"

"Yes we do," answered Stephanie, "even if Richard might be coy with his information, I can risk a bit of boldness, though I trust you won't press for details."

"No, Ma'am," I said, "I think I've learned enough about patience to wait for revelations to come when they will. I just wanted to make sure that I wasn't barking up the wrong tree."

The conversation then moved into less philosophical and secretive topics as the threesome, well-served by George, warmed up to their meal and the company of one another. In what seemed a short time, though in reality there was more than an hour of animated conversation, Thomas asked, "Will you please excuse me? I really do have some pressing business on my desk. And Ben," he said as he turned to me, "I'm going to be in Chicago on business next week. May I invite you to join me for dinner while I'm there?"

"By all means please do, Thomas," I replied. "I think that would be fun." Reaching into my wallet I offered him my card. He took it and with a nod left the room.

"He's such a sweet man," said Stephanie. "I'm so glad he's coming to work at the monastery."

"Yes," said Richard, "my loss will certainly be your gain."

"And how can I learn more about the Alliance?" I asked.

Chapter

Friends 4

"It will take a bit more time," said Richard, "but it need not be an overly long process. Why don't you and Stephanie discuss your question? I'm sure she can more freely explain the process to you than I can. Besides she has been anxious to meet you since word of your inquiry first arrived to her sisterhood."

"That would be wonderful, Richard. Now run along and let me handle Ben's question."

"Yes, Ma'am," Richard replied like a dutiful son. "Ben, I'll be back as soon as Stephanie is done with you. Good luck," he said with a big grin on his face.

"So, dear, let's get to know one another. I'm so happy that you've asked how you can learn about us. Those are the same words I used so many years ago when I learned that my brother was going to join the Alliance. Now how would you like me to begin?"

"Richard told me about the testing and the interview. Does he arrange those things?" I asked.

"Yes, he does. He's so adept at all that paperwork and the technicalities they entail. Unfortunately sometimes he comes off as being so sterile, but believe me he has a heart of gold and one that is quite warm under that official face of his.

"He'll guide you well, I'm sure. For now we'll just get to know each other and become friends. Of course that assumes that we like one another well enough to do so. I know for my part that won't be a problem, as I've had a warm place in my heart for you ever since Johnnie came back from visiting your home and raved

27

about his two grand-nephews.

"How is your brother John, if I may ask?"

"Fine," I assured her. "He and his wife Beth have their hands full with three children, but they're happy and doing well enough so as to have no reason to complain. It's strange to hear you call my uncle 'Johnnie.' Only my mother ever did that and then it was only when he was teasing her and she him."

"Well we do go back a long way and he and I have shared many a ritual and vision with each other. He knew exactly when and how to call the god so as to make a maiden feel the presence of the highest realms."

Not wanting to press her on the meaning of "call the god," I said, "To think that I only knew him as 'a monk.' How do you hide this so well?"

"We do so because we have to. The fires of Salem and the lessons of century-long witch hunts are not easily forgotten. Mostly, though, we remain in small congregations, seldom in covens of more than ten or, at most, twenty believers. We pass because we are free to blend in with our neighbors and are purposefully entrenched in the mundane world so as to belie any suspicion that we exist otherwise. The chameleon lives by his camouflage and his speed. We do the same, not by choice but by necessity."

"I understand but it still amazes me."

"Yes," said Stephanie, "but there are many who have eyes that refuse to see and ears which don't listen.

"Enough of that as you will be fully warned of what we call 'The Necessity' by those whose task it is to guard our safety.

"I've said that if you are willing, and you need not choose now, that you would be given mentors, who would act as your advocates as well. You must also know that there will be others, whose true identities will be hidden from you, who will act as your detractors. Their task will be to argue against your gaining admission. The process is meant to balance the pros and the cons in order that your life may attain its highest potential, while assuring that the integrity and safety of our Alliance are allowed their protection as well."

"Is that why Thomas is coming to Chicago?" I asked.

"Probably not, my dear. I'm sure he has his financial and management tasks to oversee, since a society as old as ours has amassed quite a large number of holdings. There's more, too, or can't you tell? Even a crone as old as I doesn't lose the knack to see a come-on when it happens. My bet is, knowing Thomas, that he wants to get into your pants as much as into your head. That, of course, is a sentiment you'd best never repeat as coming from this old lady or I'll really get a talking to."

I laughed and said, "Let me call you the dear one. I'll never let on that I had the chance to agree with you on your appraisal of his invitation to dinner. On your part you had best not tell Thomas how pleased I am to have the opportunity to let him try.

"How then can I earn your friendship? What do you want to know?"

"Oh, Ben, I know much about you already, but please humor me by letting me hear your story as you would tell it. What was your childhood like? Let us begin there. There's nothing, I can assure you, that you can't entrust me with. I owe that much to your uncle. Besides, I already like you, if only because you remind me so much of my dear Jonathan in his younger days. Come, let's get comfortable and let the tales be told."

She led me back into Richard's sitting room, lounged on one end of a couch and motioned for me to sit on the other. Thus began my story and it wasn't until nearly four o'clock that Richard knocked on the door and came in. "Mother," he said, "it's high time you let poor Ben off the hook. You've likely run him ragged with questions."

"Oh my," Stephanie replied, "you're probably right about that, but this has been such a delightful time. Ben has taken thirty years off my life and practically carried me back to the Lodge."

29

"And the same goes for me," I said, "but I do have a flight home tonight, so I'd probably best be on my way to the airport. What's my next step, Richard?"

"I'll give you some time to consider what you've heard and then give you a call.

Feel free, of course, to call me anytime you like. I'm sure, too, that Thomas will do his best to follow up on the dinner invitation, so you might want to keep your calendar clear for midweek next, if you can."

"No problem." I assured him, "I wouldn't miss that opportunity for anything," I said with a wink to Stephanie.

"Now dear, I'm going to run off, so give me a big hug, and be well." With that she practically accosted me, threw her arms around me, and planted a big, wet, and amazingly hot kiss right on my lips. I could have sworn she wanted to French. With every attempt to remain polite, I thanked them both and allowed Richard to rescue me as he led me to the door.

"I'll help you flag a taxi," he said. "There's nearly always one waiting at the hotel across the street."

So in no time I was on my way, with more to think about than I could have imagined. Had I really suggested I wanted to become a Dionysian? And what the hell did that mean?

There had been something exhilarating about the day, especially the way these folks handled sex, or at least an adult discussion of it. My own sexual experiences in the past ten years had forced me to think about what it was that I was doing and why. It also made me confront any thoughts I had had about traditional religion with serious doubts.

Once I had begun to confront my own bisexuality, I had to reconsider the religious views about sex that surrounded me. If I was right, then all those mainstream Gay condemning religions were wrong. If they were wrong about sexuality then they were just as apt to be wrong about their theology in general.

I remembered now the rare mention in Latin class of

fertility rites and temple prostitution. There had been, too, some talk about mystery cults, though any discussion of them had been quickly followed by their condemnation. I had been taught that such pagan rites had been completely eradicated. What if, I thought, that hadn't been the case? What if?

I found myself looking forward to that dinner with Thomas and what might happen afterwards. He was, after all, a man I could, and did, find attractive. I wondered if sexual contact with me was forbidden. I thought about that question a second time, a mere minute later, and realized how ridiculous it sounded. Perhaps, I thought it might be closer to the truth that having sex with him might actually be a requirement, a sort of getting-to-know you process, a way to become friends. Well, that made looking forward to dinner very interesting, to say the least.

The flight home would have been uneventful except for the fantasies that poured through my mind. I hadn't been so titillated in years. I found myself thinking the same once I got home and went to bed. Slipping between the sheets, I couldn't stop myself from feeling my cock and remembering what I could of Thomas' body. Strangely too, Stephanie's wet kiss grabbed my attention as well. In due time I felt my body seized by a delightful orgasm, which led to a sound sleep, one that held only pleasant dreams of what might come.

On Tuesday morning of the following week, Thomas called as he had promised, and we agreed to meet at Anna Maria's, an Italian restaurant on the north side, for dinner the following evening.

I intentionally arrived there early in order to ask Anna (one of the sisters who owned the place) to seat us around the corner from the main dining room. I hoped to ensure a bit more privacy for us than the popular local eatery usually provided. Taking a seat near the entrance, I quietly tapped my foot in anticipation of my dinner partner's arrival.

For his part, Thomas was early as well, and I rose to greet him as I watched him through the glass of the front door. At about five foot seven in height and thirty-seven years old, he had dark hair, a moustache and trim goatee. His steel blue eyes gave his somewhat boyish figure a bit of intensity. He was carrying a briefcase or satchel of some kind and was dressed in a rather conventional suit and overcoat. He pulled the door open, took a step in and with a huge grin offered me his hand. "Ben," he said, "it's good to see you."

"I feel the same about you," I replied. "Come on, Anna's already picked a spot for us." As I passed by her usual station at the cash register, I nodded and said "Grazie."

She responded with a smile and bright eyes that said "I know what you're doing tonight, Ben," though all she really said was "Buon appetito."

I led my guest -- or was I his, I wondered -- through the front dining room to the back. We hadn't been seated three minutes when a bus boy arrived with bread, oil, and ice water. "So have you recovered from Stephanie's grilling yet?" he asked.

"It wasn't that bad, you know. She really is a delightful conversationalist, though to be honest my head has been spinning with questions ever since."

"I understand, though I can't say I exactly know the feeling," said Thomas, "but I'm ritual-bred so I was raised with ideas that most people would consider heresy, if not worse."

"Ritual-bred?" I asked with a start. "Is that some kind of artificial breeding program?"

"Not at all," laughed Thomas. "It's just that my mother caught my Dad (or maybe it was the other way around) during a festival and I was the blessing that popped out nine months later. As a result, my knowledge of the gods and the mysteries flowed with my mother's milk, so to speak.

"That's not to say that they let me in on all the secrets, of course, but at least I knew the mysteries existed. After my travel years and a few more, I sought to know more and was admitted to the faith."

"Where did you go?"

"The Mediterranean mostly, with a stint in India. Dionysians recognize that children offer special challenges to our faith, both as possible revealers of our secrets and as men and women who need to be given a chance to choose this life. It's not a religion that we want you to be born into, though we certainly are a sect that has, and loves, lots of children. After high school, then, our parents, funded by the Alliance, send us to travel and explore the world however we wish. It's meant to give us time to learn that not everyone lives in the freedom and faith as we do and if we prefer to refrain from embracing the path of our ancestors we are free to do so.

"If on the other hand we wish to celebrate the Bacchanalia, we will do so on the same terms, generally speaking, as all others who seek to join us. We've got to apply and go through the initiations just like anyone else, once we can demonstrate that we're making an adult choice."

"Kind of like insurance against the 'preacher's kid' syndrome, huh?" I asked.

"You got that right. There's no faster way to turn your children off to your beliefs than to force it down their throats. Lots of Dionysian children, in fact, only embrace the gods long after they have spent years in the world. Believe me, it makes for better believers."

At that the waiter came over with the usual index card of specials and asked if we wanted something to drink or any appetizers. Thomas looked at me and I said, "Bring your best bottle of Chianti and a plate of fried calamari." I looked at Thomas and asked, "You eat it,, right?"

"Sure do," he answered.

With that the waiter turned away, only to reappear a minute later with two glasses and a bottle which he showed to me. I nodded and said, "Let Tom here taste it. I'm sure he's more expert than I   33 when it comes to wine."

After the usual wine tasting ceremonies were conducted, Thomas pronounced the wine excellent and the waiter poured healthy portions in each of our glasses. "Yes it is good, I'm happy to say, but the Order's is still better," I told Thomas.

He and I spent the next hour and a half like old friends catching up on a year's worth of news. Not only, did I learn, was he attractive, but he was intelligent and easy to talk to as well. No question seemed to fluster him and no amount of probing into the intimate details of his life could make him hesitate to answer.

He had, as I learned, known he was gay from the onset of puberty and his folks had never tried to persuade him otherwise. During his "worldly days," as he called them, he had had a non-believing lover for some three years. Eventually that relationship paled and grew cold, at which time Thomas talked to his parents about the gods of his childhood.

"Most people see paganism as a simplistic mythology clothed in superstition. In fact, it's a deeply mystical experience wrapped in thousands and thousands of years of study and reflection. Even today we differ from the 'Big Three' in a fundamental way. Our faith comes from our experience. Until you have encountered the bliss, been enraptured, or gone ecstatic, there can be no explanation for why we worship the gods. Once you have that enlightening, there is nothing left to explain.

"That's why children can't join us, adults must seek us out, and we won't seek you."

"I suppose the 'Big Three' are Christianity, Judaism, and Islam?" I asked.

"Oh, sorry," Thomas apologized. "I keep forgetting that my slang isn't yours. Yes, you're right. In that regard we're much more Eastern in our practice than the Western churches. On the other hand, we are deeply rooted in the traditions of Egypt, Greece, and Rome, though those traditions themselves evolved, it seems, from the East.

"But I'm talking too much. Let's look at the menu."

"Good idea," I said, as I poured Thomas more wine. "Anything here is good and the specials are usually even better."

The rest of the evening was filled with a variety of questions and answers as Thomas and I parried back and forth, first asking a biographical question, then a philosophical one, and then on to a political or historical one. It seemed that every answer was followed by "And what about you?" The result of which was that by the time we had finished our bottle of wine, dessert, and coffee, we felt like long-lost friends from the neighborhood.

Thomas insisted on picking up the tab. "My pockets are deeper than yours," he said and I replied, "OK, but only if I can get you into my bedroom."

"The price of dinner is well worth that offer," he smiled, "but I'm not sure you could keep me out if you wanted to. I thought you would never ask."

"Yeah, right," I laughed. "You came to the restaurant with lust on your mind and it hasn't left all evening."

"So?" retorted Thomas. "In my religion lust is a virtue. How about in yours?"

"You've got me there, you satyr." I motioned to the waiter for our check and by the time he delivered it, Thomas had a hundred dollar bill ready for him. He picked up the tab, took one look at it, handed him the bill and said "Keep the change." With a broad smile on his face the waiter thanked him and turned away.

I arose and said, "Come on buddy, my car is just outside and we'll be home before you can say 'The Ides of March,' or whatever it is you say."

It took a little longer than saying "The Ides of March" to drive the fourteen blocks to my home but that didn't dampen our spirits. We joked about which of us was the horniest. I

35

asked Thomas, "Seriously, though, what is it about you folks? Stephanie nearly planted her tongue down my throat just kissing me goodbye last week."

"That old girl is something else," Thomas admitted, "but it's not uncommon among us. The centuries have given us time enough to understand what we physically experience and to pass that wisdom on not only by recreating the experience but also by appreciating it intellectually, emotionally and spiritually. Basically you'll find it a healthy synthesis of eastern Tantra, Egyptian magic, and Greek philosophy. In the meantime, just relax and enjoy it."

"Easy for you to say, Thomas," I retorted. "I don't want to make a fool of myself nor get sucked into some half-assed cult, if you excuse my prejudices for a moment."

"You're excused, I'm sure," he said. "As for sucking you in, let time speak for itself."

With that I parked the car in front of the house and said "OK, welcome to my home." He picked up the briefcase he had been carrying and we left the car.

"Can I offer you a drink?" I asked, once I had closed the drapes and we had settled comfortably on the couch. I didn't want to appear to be rushing him to bed, though that's probably what both of us wanted.

"Only water," he said, opening his case and presenting me with two bottles of the Order's wine. "One for you and one for your mother."

"My mother?" I asked in surprise. "She doesn't know I've been talking to you guys."

"I figured that and thought this would be a good way for you to tell her -- of course that's only when you're ready to do so."

"Are you telling me she's one of you?" I asked.

"No," Thomas said, "I'm only telling you she'll like the wine."

"OK," I answered, "but I'm not promising it will be soon."

"And that's OK with me," he said. "I'm not telling you when you have to give it to her."

I left Thomas in the living room and returned with two glasses of ice water. He lifted his glass as I lifted mine. "To the lord Dionysos," he said.

I repeated "To the lord Dionysos." What was I getting into? I thought as the cool liquid ran down my throat.

Interlude 5

We sat there pensively for a moment and then I ventured to say "I'm glad you didn't ask to open one of the bottles of wine. I apologize if I was a bit too testy in the car, but the wine at dinner seems to have loosened my tongue."

"We Dionysians expect 'in vino veritas,' Ben, so don't sweat it. Show me that bedroom you promised and we'll let words give way to what I hope will be soothing touches."

"Sounds good to me," I replied. I stood up, glass in hand and said, "Follow me." Thomas grabbed his water as well and we walked to the back staircase. As we did, I pointed out the guest room, bathroom, kitchen, and office. "There's a garden in the back, too. City living isn't as sterile as some folks think."

We turned up the stairs to my bedroom. I purposely didn't invite him to see the basement, as I wasn't up to explaining my adult play room to him or to get into discussing any of my "toys." I wasn't ready for him to know that I was kinky and had a dungeon in my basement. Part of me might have been excited to discover this sex-filled religion but some of me wasn't so sure and wanted to put on the brakes or even stop completely.

"Here we are," I said, turning on the small lamp next to the king-sized bed. "Just put your glass on the bed stand. It won't hurt it."

Having done so, Thomas came over to me, put his arms around me and said, "I hope you like this one better than Stephanie's." With that he gave me a warm, tender, and long kiss. It certainly changed my attitude for the better.

"Let's get comfortable," I suggested as I took off my shirt. Thomas did the same, and continued until he was buck naked. In the meantime I managed to take off my shoes as well but not much else. I was pleased at his physique and hoped he would think kindly of my 41-year-old body.

"Nice," he said to my relief, as he gently ran his hands down the sides of my chest. I could feel my cock respond as I leaned forward and returned his kiss.

My arms encircled him and I rubbed his ass cheeks. They were slightly hairy, as was the rest of him. His body showed that he kept himself fit with exercise, something that I only managed infrequently. Our lips parted; he nuzzled my neck and hugged me more tightly. I could feel his heart beating against my chest.

"Lie down on the bed," he said.

"Let me take my clothes off first," I protested but he insisted.

"Don't worry about that. I'll take care of it." So I did as he asked, wondering what would be next, though I suspected that whatever it was would be fun. "Now just relax. Like they say, 'Actions speak louder than words' and I mean to make you feel real good."

I lay there on my back, my head on the pillow and my hands behind my head. Thomas moved to the foot of the bed and took the sock off my left foot, kissing it gently. He slowly moved to the right foot and did the same. Then, grasping my right foot in both his hands, he knelt. His eyes quietly closed for a moment and then he began to gently massage my foot, in a short time adding kisses to the massage. It was sensuous to say the least and inside my pants my male member grew. His kisses turned into a full tongue bath, his hands never missing a beat. I don't know how long that lasted but it sure was nice. This guy certainly knew what he was doing.

Finally he released my foot and moved to do the same with the other. Whatever he did began to melt my tension and my

40

resistance. My now raging hard-on wanted to yell "Stop," so I could aggressively confront him with it. Instead I took a couple of deep breaths and let him continue undisturbed.

When my left foot had received the same treatment and pleasure as the right one had, Thomas moved to sit beside me. "Just rest for a moment," he said. "There's a lot more that I learned in India but all of it is best done slowly."

"Hey," I said, "this is great. You'll get no argument from me."

With that he leaned over and kissed me deeply, taking my head in his hands. As a kiss it was way too short. He sat up and closed his eyes, obviously taking his own advice about going slowly.

"OK," he said in a short time, "Breathe with me. As I exhale you inhale, and vice versa." Once again he leaned near my face but only close enough to let me feel the warm touch of his breath on my face. As his breath moved over my lips I inhaled it, releasing it when he inhaled. He breathed at a long, measured pace. "Breathe more deeply," he said. "Slowly pull the air all the way down to your belly button."

What he was doing was much like I had learned in those few TM classes I had taken years ago. Of course they weren't anywhere as sensuous as this and their effect was no match for what this guy could do.

We breathed together for about twenty times and then he kissed me. This kiss lasted longer, but still not long enough for me. Thomas pulled away and reached to loosen my belt. "May I?" he asked.

"May you?" I countered. "You'd better or I'll shoot in my underwear."

With that he moved back to the foot of the bed, leaned across my feet and undid my pants, pulling them and my underwear off. My prick bounced out of my jockey shorts at stiff attention. "Beautiful," he said. "Just beautiful." I didn't know if he meant me or my cock and quite frankly I didn't care.

41

He placed a hand on each foot. Slowly and gently he stroked his way up my legs toward my crotch. It seemed to take a delightfully long time for him to finish his task. His face showed a quiet intensity, his eyes closed, his body aroused, his cock almost as stiff as mine. Once his hands had reached my crotch, he moved to my side and kissed me. "How you doin', Ben?" he asked.

My lips murmured "Mmmm" and I kissed him back, pulling his head close to mine. He collapsed on top of me and I quickly rolled him off and over, forcing him beneath me, though to be honest, no force was really needed. As my body lay upon his, he spread his legs. Our cocks were head to head and I could feel the dampness of our pre-cum and the moisture of our sweat lubricating our bodies. My dick pushed itself under his scrotum, itching to enter his hole.

I moved my right hand behind his chest as I cradled his head with my other hand. We kissed and kissed; each of us returning one kiss with another. His hands caressed my ass; his fingers played at my ass hole, tickling my anus softly. It sent pulses of electricity up my spine and my breathing, in sync with his, gained speed. What is this? I asked myself, only to hear my inner self say shut up and enjoy it. I lost my sense of self for a bit in the passion of a timeless moment, until Thomas asserted himself by pushing me off of him.

"Slow down, Ben," he said. "Slow down for a minute or two." He sat up and reached for his glass of water. Taking a sip, he handed it to me. Suddenly I realized how thirsty I was, sat on the edge of the bed and took the glass.

"Thanks," I said. "I think I need that." The ice cubes had melted some, making the water refreshingly cold. I felt it calm my thirst as I drained the glass. "You're something else," I said to Thomas. "That trip to India must have been remarkable. Where did you learn to have sex like that?"

"We don't practice fertility rites only for the sake of a good harvest, you know. Let's just say Dionysian priests of both genders teach their faithful how to enjoy their bodies."

42

"I guess there's a lot I don't understand about you guys," I said. "You're certainly a different kind of religion. Sometimes your language and what you say about the 'gods' is really weird. But when you throw something like those kisses at me, the theology becomes unimportant."

"You're right about that, Ben. We try not to be dogmatic. We've learned to be cautious, as I'm sure is obvious, but by and large we are a free and loose group of people. We're more about celebrating life than ritual and about selfhood rather than structure. That's not to say that there aren't differences among us, but by and large they all have to do with superficialities, not substance."

With that he pushed me back down on the bed and straddled my cock with his ass. "Come on, guy. You've made it clear you want in. Fuck me, buddy, and we'll both go for a ride."

"Wait a minute," I said, awkwardly trying to sit up. "Grab a towel from the lower drawer. You'll find some lube and condoms in the drawer above it." It took a few minutes to rearrange ourselves, as Thomas lubed up his fuck hole.

"On my back or stomach?" he asked.

"Back, of course," I replied. "I want to watch the smile on your face as my dick fucks the hell out of you."

I knelt between his legs, his handsome chest and beautiful eyes making me hotter and hotter. I stoked myself to make my prick stiffer, then quickly rolled a rubber onto my shaft. "Here I come, buddy. Ready or not."

Thomas laughed. "Ready or not? Of course, I'm ready," he said as he lifted his legs and laid them on my shoulders.

It was the easiest fuck I'd ever given, as my cock slid into his waiting hole. Before I knew it he had clamped down on it with his ass muscles and began to massage my shaft. It was as if he was sucking it with his man cunt. For my part I tried to thrust in and out but only managed to rub my pubic hair against the rim of his hole. I leaned forward to kiss him and he pulled me to his face. Our lips met; his tongue entered my mouth. I wrapped my arms around his 43 chest and together we rocked in a passionate beat.

"Breathe with me, Ben," he said and so we did until he said, "Now be still, breathe deeply but slowly and quietly. Don't move." I did as he suggested and for a wonderful moment we hung there as one.

Slowly Thomas began to breathe normally again. "Sit up slowly," he said, "then lean back so I can straddle you. But do it slowly so I don't lose having your cock in me." I did as he said and with slow gymnastics I moved onto my back as he rearranged his legs. When we had accomplished the move he pushed himself even further onto my cock.

He moved his hands forward to tease my tits and I reached up to do the same with his. I closed my eyes in delight as I began to pump my hips into his butt hole. He matched me move for move and I felt a surge of lightning rush up my spine as my prick let loose with a torrent of jism. The orgasm thrust me into a deep sense of nothingness, an abyss filled with light and love and pleasure, as my body jerked in ecstasy and my mouth let out groans of intense pleasure. Then there was quiet. Thomas held me within his hole but ceased to move. I knew something special had happened but could only lay in silent awe at the intensity and majesty of it all.

I began to breathe slowly and quietly again as I returned to what could only be called consciousness. Thomas, for his part, gently lifted himself off my man meat and waited patiently in silence for me to return to reality. When I recovered he was there with a big smile on his face. "Wow," I said," you're something else."

"No," said Thomas, "you are." I smiled, closed my eyes, and took a deep breath. I didn't want to move. I didn't want to lose this moment. Yet in spite of my efforts it slowly passed.

With a sheepish grin on my face, I turned to Thomas and said "Thanks, man. That was great."

"I could tell," he answered in return and he lay next to me on the bed, putting his arm on my chest. I turned to nestle into him and fell asleep.

44

Sometime later I heard Thomas get up. I tried to do the same but he said "I'll let myself out. I'll call you in the morning. Pleasant dreams, buddy. Sleep well."

Chapter 6

The Day After

The next morning I found that Thomas had left his business card on the kitchen table along with a note that read "Drake Hotel, room 2109. I'll call you at 5. Love, Thomas."

I made some coffee and reflected on what had happened. Not only had it been the hottest date of my life, I was still basking in the sensations. Thomas had been right about actions speaking louder than words. No fuck had ever been as satisfying as that one. Now I really wanted to learn his secrets.

My mind turned to the day as I got ready for work. I took a couple of steaks out of the freezer just in case I'd get lucky two nights in a row and in no time at all I was on my way to the "L" stop. It sure would be hard to concentrate on today's reports, I thought, as I rode the train to the Loop. I decided to call Thomas as soon as I got to the office.

He wasn't in his room when I called, so I left a message that simply said, "Thanks. I hope you're free for dinner tonight. I owe you one."

All through the day I waited for his call, arguing with myself as to whether this spiritual investigation of my uncle's life had instead turned into an adolescent love affair. By three o'clock I decided to calm down about it and not to worry. After all, the note in my pocket said he'd call after five. By four I had cleared my desk of the day's mail, and told my assistant that I had to leave early for an errand. As I was doing so, I decided to try the Drake one more time. That time when the hotel operator put me through to his room,

Thomas answered with a bright hello.

"I called to say 'Thanks' and see if I could talk you into a steak dinner. I've got a great bottle of wine to go with it." I said.

"Sure," he answered. "What's your address?"

I gave it to him and said, "Tell the taxicab driver it's near Pulaski and Irving Park."

"OK," he answered, "I'll get there about six."

"Great, see you then," I said.

The commute home was filled with all sorts of thoughts: of wonder at what would happen next, at the foolishness of having acted so boldly, at the excitement that I had finally found something meaningful, and doubt that there really was any substance to it at all. I wondered, too, what my mother would think of all of this, and the fact that Thomas kept saying to slow down. Well, time would tell, that was for sure.

As I set the table, put two potatoes into the oven and made a salad, I thought about everything I had learned since I had found the book my uncle had given me. Pretty heady stuff, but then I really was ready for some adventure in my life. If Dionysians could answer some of those lingering religious doubts and improve my sex life, I was all for it.

Thomas wouldn't be arriving for another half hour or so, so I hopped into the shower and put on some clean clothes. That done, I turned on the grill to get it hot, as the clock seemed to take forever to get to six.

About five minutes after the hour, I saw a Yellow Cab pull up in front of the house. "Here goes," I thought. "I wonder what Thomas is thinking about all this."

I opened the door before he had a chance to ring the doorbell and welcomed him in. He was dressed more casually than he had been the night before. "Have a seat," I said, pointing to the couch. "Ready for that glass of wine?"

"Like Stephanie said at Richard's," Thomas answered, "'Dionysians never say no to wine.'" I left him on the couch and went to the dining room table where I filled two glasses with the wine he had brought the night before. I lifted both of them, walked back to the couch, and handed one to Thomas.

"To the gods," he said.

I replied "Amen" and sat next to him. "Do you always salute each other that way?" I asked. "Sometimes you sound like a Baptist except that your god is plural instead of singular."

"Well," said Thomas, "I don't want to offend you but our beliefs are just as important to us as theirs are to them."

"No offense is taken," I answered. "I'm just curious about what all the polytheism really means. It seems strange to me that someone as educated as you would in fact hold to such a primitive view of theology."

"Yes, I understand your surprise. After all, western culture is dominated by monotheism. It's not that I don't believe in a unified Deity. In fact I do. My language reflects my experience of God as a manifestation of divinity in the appearance of many forms, each but an aspect of that which is in its entirety unknowable. There are philosophical and theological underpinnings to my faith, just as there are for Catholicism, Judaism, and all the other religions of the world. Unfortunately there are not very many well-known theologians who understand us outside the circle of those who believe as we do. If you continue with us, you'll get a lot of answers, I'm sure."

"I don't mean to be critical," I said. "I'm just trying to understand all of this."

"Like you said a minute ago, 'No offense taken.' If you choose me as your mentor, it will be my pleasure to help you understand, at least until the scholars in our midst take over your formal education."

"As long as mentoring doesn't eliminate fucking, I'm all for that," I said.

"No need to worry about that, Ben. A good fuck is a sacred responsibility where I come from."

"Amen to that," I said. "Now come out back," I said, 49

"while I grill the steaks. How do you like yours done?"

"Rare's fine," he answered. I was lucky that the weather hadn't yet turned cold, though it would probably do so any day now. We stood there on the patio and chatted about work, the weather and an assortment of other non-crucial topics. In no time at all the steaks were sizzling and dinner was ready. I put them on a serving dish and we headed inside. "Grab our glasses," I said, "while I put the rest of the food on the table. Sit anywhere you like, I'll be right there."

When dinner was served, I refilled our glasses and said to Thomas, "I'd really like to hear about your trip to India. How did you ever learn those techniques you used last night?"

"It's quite a story, really," said Thomas. "Now when I answer it, don't blame me if I sound theological. You're the one who asked the question."

"You've got me there, Thomas. I'll remember I asked for it."

He began by telling me about his trip to Europe after high school and his late adolescent sabbatical, as they called it. Since he had some knowledge of his folks' beliefs he decided that he would travel to places where the ancient religions had been celebrated and lived. He went to Stonehenge, Delphi, Rome, Athens, and Egypt, in search of his past. Eventually he ended up in an ashram in India.

A guru there taught an eclectic form of Tantra, called "the left hand path," with a special emphasis on what Hindus call the chakras, or energy centers in the human body. I had read something about them recently in both the book my uncle had given me so many years ago and in his journal. I commented to Thomas that what he was telling me was vaguely familiar.

"That doesn't surprise me," he said. "Your great-uncle is well-known for his abilities with chakras. Our understanding of the universe rests heavily on our understanding of energy and what is called the power exchange. It's a course all in itself so forgive me if I don't try to explain it all to you.

50   "In short, what I can say is that our faith holds truths

from many paths. In this case we have a more eastern approach; at other times, it reflects the experience of millennia in the west. We understand, for instance, the value of scientific materialism while at the same time we acknowledge that as finite beings we are limited in our ability to comprehend the infinite."

Our conversation was so engrossing that in no time we had finished dinner without even realizing we were eating. "Want some ice cream for dessert?" I asked.

"No, thanks, I'll pass," said Thomas. "I want to ask you something and then see if I can have you for dessert," he said with a wink.

"Of course, you can," I replied. "I can hardly refuse an answer when you have been so generous in satisfying my curiosity."

"I just want to check in with you that nothing that happened last night was upsetting or disturbing. We usually don't get so intimate so quickly, especially with people who are just getting to know us."

"Disturbing or upsetting? You've got to be kidding. I loved every minute of it. In fact, I was worried that I had pushed you too fast. To be honest, I hope we go on like this for a long time. On the other hand, I certainly don't want you think that I'm being impetuous or foolish," I said.

"No problem," he replied. "We'll take it a day at a time. Hey," Thomas said, getting out of his chair and coming over to mine, "get up. I have something to give you."

As I stood he put his arms around me, drew his face close to mine, and kissed me long and deeply. "I feel the same way, so don't sweat it. This will work out fine."

I filled our glasses with what was left of the wine and raised mine to Thomas. He picked up his as well. "To us and what may come," I said.

"To us and what may come," he repeated as our glasses clicked.

"Come on. Let's get comfortable," I said as I moved to the couch.

"You know what I'd like?" he asked.

"Another fuck?" I joked.

"That too, but before we do, can I see one of the journals?"

"Sure," I answered, "let me get you one." I went back into the office where Book Four was perched on a shelf to the right of my desk. In no time I handed it to Thomas.

"Thanks," he said. "You don't know how lucky you are to have gotten this. What a beautiful gift," he said, slowly turning its pages.

"'The abbot asked tonight at dinner that we devise a plan for our city brethren. Economic conditions continue to worsen,'" he read. "Talk about having history in your hands," Thomas said. "This is great."

"When was that entry?" I asked.

"1930," Thomas answered. "Seems like another world, doesn't it?"

"Yeah, it does. Do you know what the monks did?" I asked.

"I only know that they increased the size of their gardens and sent food to the covens in the city. Some city folks joined the country covens for a time as well and some sent their children to live on their brethren's farms. It's long before my time, of course, but my folks always said that the Great Depression proved that their faith was more than just words, though they never gave me any more details."

With that he closed the book and handed it back to me. "Thanks," he said. "I hope someday I'll have the time and opportunity to read all of them."

"I'm sure you will," I replied. "I've been thinking that they really ought to go back to the monks. They'll be safest there."

"I agree," said Thomas, "but make sure you're done with

them first. For now let me help you clear the table."

Together we made short work of the mess left from dinner. All in all, Thomas had made me very comfortable and it just wasn't the wine. He was so easy-going but with an amazing wisdom for his age. It was strange to think that he was younger than me when he acted so much older.

Chapter

Florida 7

Thomas left Chicago the next morning. Our second night together proved to be as exciting as the first one and he promised to stay in touch. "The phone number on my business card will usually put you in touch with me. Leave a message if you want. I get back here twice a month so don't think I'm going to be gone too long."

I wasn't sure where this search was heading and I sure hadn't expected to find a lover, but I was old enough, when I thought rationally about it, to not get too carried away. At least I hoped that was the case.

Over the next few weeks, what with all the hints I had had about Mom and this pagan faith, I changed my mind and decided that having a good talk with her could help set things straight, so I called to see if she wanted a house guest for Thanksgiving. Mom and I had a friendly and open relationship, one where we shared freely and honestly with each other. I felt that there wasn't anything I couldn't tell her or ask her. We were, after all, a close family, though I have to admit that the discovery of this family secret about Uncle Jonathan made me wonder if I was correct in feeling that way.

I called my mother on the first of November to announce that she needed to set her Thanksgiving table for two. "That's wonderful, Ben," she said. "I'll be so happy to see you. I don't have to set the table, though, as I'm having dinner with Jack and Estelle O'Malley. They'll be so pleased to know that you'll be coming with me."

"Who are they, mom?" I asked.

"Friends I knew up north. They moved down here about 25 years ago. Since I've had the Florida house, we've reconnected. You met them when you were younger and have just forgotten about them."

I made airline reservations with a bit of difficulty and had to pay through the nose since I hadn't made my plans sooner.

"I'll arrive on the Tuesday before Thanksgiving, Mom, and have to wait until the next Tuesday to fly home. Is that OK?" I asked her two days later.

"Of course it is," she answered. "Just because I'm in Florida doesn't meant that you're not welcome in my home."

I put in for vacation time from work.

In the meantime I searched through Jonathan's journals a second time, looking now for his writings about chakras. In September of 1926 he had written:

> Frater David gave a lecture today about the energetic composition of the human body. To be more precise, he spoke of all bodies being made of energy, but his purpose was to teach us about our own. Taken from Vedic scriptures and millennia of interpretations by Tantric masters, the topic explains the relationship between our physical organs, the energy of which they are composed, and what is called the Kundalini or Coiled Serpent, which lies at the base of the spine until it is aroused, whence it rises up the spinal column and brings enlightenment to the mind of man.

His notes then followed in both English and what appeared to be a foreign language. The latter being the names of the centers, which he called "chakras," though their pronunciation totally

escaped me. I decided to ask Thomas, the next time we talked, to refer me to a decent contemporary text on the subject, if such a book existed.

During the second week of November Thomas called to say he was returning to Chicago and I invited him to stay with me. He was happy to do so, but warned me that he had to get his business done while there, so he hoped I wouldn't be disappointed if he left the house rather early every morning. I reminded him that I had a job as well and certainly understood.

I really didn't want a long distance relationship, so having him close for three or four days would be a welcome relief. This time he showed up without any wine. Instead he gave me a copy of a small volume called Eastern Thoughts for the Western Mind, written by someone named Brother Michael and obviously printed on a monastery press in 1947.

"What do you think about my going to Florida for Thanksgiving?" I asked him while he was visiting.

"To see your mom?" he asked.

"Yes," I answered.

"Well, you hardly need my permission to do that," he replied.

"I know that, dummy. Do you think I should ask her about the monks?"

"She's your mom," Thomas said. "I bet she has some opinion about her Uncle Jonathan. Asking her might just help clear your confusion, though I may be entirely wrong on that count."

"Well, is she one of you or not?" I asked.

"I can't say because I don't know. You'll have to venture your own questions and come to your own conclusions," Thomas replied.

Once again I was beating my head against this secrecy stuff. I couldn't believe that I had lived my whole life with a mother that practiced what most people would call an occult religion. In simple terms it boiled down to witchcraft when you looked at it. Hadn't Richard called their rites "sex magic"? In asking about the

57

Great Depression, Thomas had used the word "coven." What were they hiding?

I had, of course, come close to falling in love with Thomas but that could have been -- and perhaps was -- a natural result of great sex, a handsome man, and that fact that we had a lot in common. In my more doubting moments I worried that he might be using wine and sex to seduce me into an occult organization.

After he left, the days moved slowly until the night before I was to fly south, when all of a sudden it seemed I had everything to do. I worried about bringing the bottle of wine and one of Jonathan's journals to Florida with me and then realized how foolish I was. "Of course you should bring them," I thought. Mom has always said that the truth would set you free. A good dose of real information from her just might clear this fog. I had never hidden my life from her before, I thought. Why am I thinking about hiding it now? Still something said to me that no matter how good the sex was, I had no intention of involving myself in a clandestine sex ring of drunks.

I wondered why my mother had hidden this family history from me and what would I do if now, after I had brought the subject up, she denied it all.

In spite of my feelings I made it to O'Hare in plenty of time, got to Sarasota and Mom's without a struggle, and spent the next few days relaxing around her neighborhood pool, catching up on news about the family and not doing much else. I had decided to lay low with the news about Uncle Jonathan until after Thanksgiving dinner.

Dinner was extravagant, entertaining, and pleasant. The O'Malleys were nice enough, though for the life of me I didn't remember them. Their daughter, Cynthia, didn't remember me either, though she admitted that my mom had talked about me. Moms are that way and you can't stop them.

I found Cynthia attractive. We actually hit it off quite well. She was, for me at least, the highlight of the party and a welcome distraction. Though the cooking was good and the nine of us (three

O'Malleys, Mom and I, and two other couples) had a good time, to be honest I was a bit pre-occupied with the talk I had planned to have with my mother when we got home later.

In spite of that, Cynthia did a good job in engaging me in conversation and made it clear she would like to get together with me while I was in town. She had moved south with her parents and had become pretty much a native. On the other hand, she complained about the fact that Florida was full of what she called "snow birds, none of them my age." As we were leaving she said "Call me," and I said "I will."

It was a short but quiet ride back to Mom's place, and the silence was not unexpected after five hours of food and chatter. I was going to have this talk, I thought to myself, as soon as we get home.

So when we arrived there, I said, "Mom, wait for me in the living room. I have a surprise for you." She did so and I ran to the guest room to get my suitcase. I was flooded with feelings as I returned to the living room, one of them being apprehension.

"What do you have for me, Ben?" she asked.

"A bottle of wine," I answered as I reached my hand into the suitcase and pulled it out. I felt like a magician pulling a rabbit out of his hat and, at the same time, Pandora opening up her famous box. I handed the gift from Thomas to her.

"My god, Ben," she said. "Where did you get this?"

"It's a long story, Mom, and one I came here to tell you." With that I recounted my finding that theology book in her basement and my meeting with Richard. When I got to the part about the journals, I reached back into the suitcase and handed her Book One.

She held it like a long lost family heirloom and tears welled up in her eyes. "I can't believe it, son," she said. "Uncle Johnnie's journals. How wonderful. I've always wanted to read them. It's a miracle that you have them."

"So you know about them?" I asked, though from the

letters I knew perfectly well that she did.

"Of course I do," she admitted, "though I had no idea that you had gotten them."

"Johnnie?" I asked. "That's what Stephanie called Uncle Jonathan."

"Who's Stephanie?" she asked.

I went on with my story, telling her about my second appointment with Richard and meeting Stephanie and Thomas. I didn't go into many details about Thomas except to say that we were seeing each other once in a while to talk about the monks.

"But Mom," I said as my story came to a close, "I don't know what to make of all of this, especially that this has been such a family secret all these years. How could you not have told me? After all, I am your son."

"Come sit here, Benjamin," she said. I did so and she took my hands in hers.

"We all have stories to tell but some of them can only be told in due time. Like most Dionysians, your Dad and I had to raise our children 'mainstream.' There really wasn't an alternative, since living in the fifties as a pagan was much more difficult than you might think. In any case, after your father passed away, I had too much on my hands to be really involved religiously so it became a moot point. But yes, dear, I am what you think, a believing and practicing pagan who honors Dionysos."

I sat there dumb-founded, questioning everything I knew, or thought I knew, about my mother. "What else was there to ask?" I thought and then answered myself with the word "plenty." I was flooded with emotions and every idea I ever had of my mother was changed in those few words. It was one thing to think of her uncle as being an eccentric old man who lived in some strange and hidden monastery. It was another to have discovered an outlandish group of people, Richard and Stephanie and Thomas, who held antiquated and sexually-deviating ideas about god and religion. I could even accept Thomas as an avant-garde and off-the-charts kind of queer who held to a theology that helped him get laid, but my own mother? That hit too close to home.

I took my hands away from hers and stood up. "I've got to catch my breath, Mom," I said. "This is a bit too much to handle. Do you mean that you believe this stuff? That Zeus and the rest of that mythological bunch is real to you? How can you say that?"

"I say it because I believe it, Ben. But I need to add that I believe it because I have experienced the power of my faith. Now sit down here and listen to me. I think you owe me that much."

With that she told me about her gods and the roles they played in her life. It was more about her secret faith and what it meant to her. She saw the gods as Jungian archetypes, as symbols that help explain human motives and emotions. In everything she said, she was actually coherent and her usual down-to-earth self. More than anything else and her story was filled with peace and contentment. You couldn't ask more from your mother than that, so I didn't press her for details.

I woke up the next morning feeling better about this Dionysian stuff, even though I had few facts and many questions. After all, I asked myself, why or how should a twentieth-century American espouse a 500 B.C. faith life? Still her appeal to joy, her recognition that reason was an important partner with her faith, and her insistence on a lack of dogmatism among her fellow pagan believers all added to increasing my comfort level with the combination of wine, sex, and ecstatic experience.

"She is, after all is said and done," I said to myself, "my mother. In the forty-odd years of being her son, she has never given me cause to think she was crazy, so why should I think any differently of her now?" I still wondered why she hadn't told me of her earlier but I guess she had her reasons and I probably wouldn't have been ready to listen before now anyway.

After coffee and the paper I decided that retreating to the

pool would be the best way to sort this out, so I put on my trunks and grabbed a towel and that book on Eastern thought that Thomas had given me. At the pool I found a lounge chair in a sunny spot away from noisy children and neighbors who might want to talk. I settled into the sunshine until boredom set in, when I opened the book and began to read it.

"Perception," began this Brother Michael, "is the root of all knowing, for what you perceive of an object will form your knowledge of it. What it actually is, in so far as your perception differs from its reality, will have less effect on your idea of it than what you perceive it to be." He went on to discuss perception and reality, his obvious premise being that all human perception is filtered by physical, experiential, emotional, and psychological factors inherent in the perceiver. "The best we can do," he wrote, "is recognize our perceptual limitations and find ways to mitigate their effect."

As I progressed through the book, I found that he relied heavily on the writings of psychologist and philosopher Carl Gustav Jung. He also made a transition, new to my thinking, from these Greek gods as beings who sit in the clouds around Mount Olympus to archetypes resting firmly in what he called the "Ground of Unconsciousness."

Just as a small light had gone on about why my folks had insisted I take Latin, I now saw the same subtle push in college, when my mom had once or twice asked about my choice of electives and suggested that I might find a class on Jungian psychology interesting. Little had I suspected her motivation. Now it appeared as a small piece to a puzzle that would fit somewhere, though I only had a few pieces and no idea of what the completed puzzle would look like.

Cynthia 8

"Eastern Thoughts" turned out to be a surprising book. Whereas I had expected it to be either a heavy tome of esoteric theology or a pastiche of some kind of erotic evangelism, it turned out to be neither. It was just a short, highly readable explanation of why Easterners perceive things differently than we do. Fundamental to their perception is the belief that we live in a universe of energy, much as Thomas had tried to explain to me, and expanding upon the notes that I had found in Jonathan's journals.

Though such explanations were out of my realm of experience, they were generally not so outlandish as to be immediately rejected. After all, it wasn't so different from the explanation of energy in those TM classes I had taken.

Like Thomas, the author stressed the experiential aspects of what he knew. Like my mother, he made it clear that his discussion relied a great deal on allegory and storytelling, rather than on pure logic or dogmatic creeds. "Still" wrote Brother Michael, "I can only tell you what I know and even then my speech fails as much as does your hearing and understanding. Let me end, then, with our fundamental tenet, repeated from time immemorial. 'Know Thyself and be true to the One you know.'"

I closed the book and reached for my wrist watch. It was nearly two o'clock and I suddenly felt hot, sweaty, and hungry. I picked up my stuff and walked back to my mother's.

"There you are," she said. "I wondered if you had fallen into the pool. It's after two and your lunch has been ready for more than an hour. Sit down and I'll pour you something to drink. What would you like?"

"Thanks, Mom. I'm sorry I'm late. I lost track of the time while I was reading the book that Thomas gave me. As for a drink, I'll get myself a soda."

"No matter," she replied. "By the way, Cynthia called and left you her phone number."

"She did, huh? I wondered if she'd have time for me while I was here. What do you think?"

"I think that any woman who calls to give a man her phone number will make time. Why don't you ask her yourself?"

"OK, Mom, I get your point. Would you mind if I took her out to dinner?"

"Not at all and you know that. I hope you didn't come all the way down here just to coop me up for a week waiting on the likes of you," she said with a laugh.

After lunch I called Cynthia. She was happy to hear from me. "How about I take you to your favorite restaurant for dinner?"

"Sure," she answered.

"Tonight or tomorrow night?" I asked.

"I'm going to some friends' on Saturday so would you mind if we made it tonight?"

"Fine with me," I answered. "You just name the time and the place."

"Come on over here at about six and I'll make you a drink. What kind of meal would you like? Italian, Greek, Mexican, Thai?" she asked.

"They all sound fine with me. You pick; my treat."

"Well then let's try this new place near the beach. Everyone's talking about it."

"You're on," I said and after getting directions closed with "See you at six."

"Well, Mom," I said returning to the kitchen. "I hope I can borrow the car." I know I sounded like a teenager when I asked that, but there hadn't been any reason to get a rental car. Now I thought twice about not having done so.

"No problem, Ben, I hadn't planned to do much tonight anyway."

I had gotten a bit more sun than I needed so I took a shower and a nap, not really having a better way to pass the time.

By 4:45 I was up and getting ready. Cynthia had said it would take about 45 minutes to get to her place, Friday afternoon traffic being what it was. By 5:15 I was backing Mom's car out of the driveway and wondering what the evening would be like.

Cynthia lived in a gated complex of townhouses and single family homes. It was obviously a better neighborhood and the landscape was luxurious, the palm trees well-cared for, and flowers bloomed everywhere. I pushed the code to open the gate and entered one of those Florida Edens. "Some class," I thought, and wondered how a single woman could afford such a posh location.

In no time at all I parked in her driveway and saw Cynthia standing on the front walk to greet me. Her dress was an interesting mix of casual and alluring; her hair flowed easily onto her shoulders. She wore only a hint of make-up but her smile and eyes radiated enough beauty that she didn't need any cosmetics at all.

"Welcome to my home, Ben," she said as she led me into her living room. The air was comfortably cool, the lighting relaxing. The room was dominated by a large stone fireplace that reached up into a high, vaulted ceiling. In front of it were a large black leather couch and two side chairs. The living room was actually a great room, with a dining area and a kitchen around the corner from where I stood.

A hall led back into other rooms, but Cynthia simply said, "Have a seat and make yourself comfortable. What would you like to drink?"

"What do you have?" I asked.

"Most anything. Beer, wine, soda, juice, hard stuff."

"What are you having?" I replied, not wanting to be

different.

"Oh, I usually stick with red wine."

"That'll do for me," I said, thinking "When in Rome do as the Romans do."

"I'll be right back then," she said as she went into the kitchen area. I sat on the sofa and thumbed through a magazine on the end table to my right. It was a copy of Archaeology Monthly. "Surprising reading material," I thought.

In no time at all Cynthia returned with two glasses, a bottle of Zinfandel, and a cork screw. As she did the honors, I said, "Pretty interesting magazine you have there. Is that a hobby or a profession?"

"Oh, it's only an interest. Actually I only have that issue because there's an article in it about the ruins of Pompeii that I wanted to read. Have you ever been to Italy?"

"No, my traveling has been mostly stateside with a few trips to the Caribbean."

"Mom and Dad sent me to Europe after college and I spent most of my time visiting museums, churches, and ruins. I loved it but I wish I hadn't gone alone."

"What was your major in college?" I asked.

"Art, with a minor in the classics. And yours?"

"Business. I'm afraid I'm not as sophisticated as you when it comes to culture."

"I don't know about that. The way your mom brags about you there mustn't be anything you couldn't deal with."

"Well, don't believe everything she says, though I can be somewhat of a bookworm. So tell me, what did you like about Pompeii?"

By then the bottle was open and the wine poured. We picked up our glasses and I went to click hers against mine and said, "To a fine night with a beautiful woman."

"And a handsome stud," she added. "I got the magazine to see what they had to say about Pompeii, since I had visited the ruins and the visit had clarified a great deal for me."

During the next quarter hour we talked about ourselves and our folks. It was obvious that our parents had been friends for a while. When Cynthia talked about her former home up north, I could tell that she hadn't lived too far from us.

Still, she had moved away early enough that I didn't remember her. I was certain that Mom had shared a lot about my brother and me. By the way Cynthia spoke I could tell that she knew my mother well and seemed to consider her a family member. "We treat your mom like family because she is. I hope you don't mind sharing her with us," she said.

"Not at all," I answered. "I'm happy to know that someone is looking after her."

"No worry about that down here. She has lots of friends."

"That's what I'm learning. Mom has been really quiet all these years and only now am I learning what really makes her tick."

"More wine?" Cynthia asked.

"Not now," I said, "maybe later. Do we have reservations?" I asked, looking at my watch.

"Yes," she said, "at 7:30, but the restaurant isn't far from here."

"I'm curious, Cynthia. Does your family have anything to do with my Mom's religion?"

"Why, Ben, I thought you'd never ask. Of course we do. That's what makes Claire so important to us."

I'd say another light went on but that would be an understatement. I wondered if I was being seduced, if sex had been planned, if Cynthia was some kind of witch, if Mom had arranged it, if Thomas knew what "going to Florida" really meant, and if I was ready to have my questions answered. I hoped that Cynthia might shed some light on this cult but I feared that all I would get was polite secrecy or discover how outlandish it really was under its façade.

67

"Well, I have to admit that all of this is a surprise to me," I confessed.

"I understand," she replied. "My parents kept me in the dark about Dionysos as well and I was pretty upset when I found out about their hidden pagan life. I actually gave up on them for a few years during college and only accepted the offer to fund a trip to Europe because I thought turning it down was a stupid idea. As a matter of fact it was an even better idea than I had thought. The trip helped me to make up my own mind, to learn my own truths about the world, and to come to terms with history in my own way."

"So what did you find at Pompeii, if I may ask?"

"Nothing really new, and nothing I hadn't seen in Art class, but the mural in the Villa of the Mysteries took on a new meaning for me."

"Which one was that?" I asked.

"This one," she said, opening the archaeology magazine and showing me a picture of the mural. I had seen it before but hadn't ever thought much about it.

"It depicts Roman rites associated with an initiation of a woman into the cult of Dionysos. I was drawn to study it since it represents a spiritual path that favored feminism."

"How's that?" I asked.

"The followers of Dionysos were predominantly women and the biennial feast that the Romans called Bacchanalia was a celebration of women's liberation. The women of ancient Greece were known to leave their homes and families for a raucous celebration in the forest, without men and without the constraint of male domination."

"You don't strike me as a feminist," I said.

"I'm not, that's for sure, but what I am is a person who has found a way to freely express my femininity while recognizing that we all must balance the male and female energies in the world."

"So do your men have their own god as well?"

68

"Certainly. Dionysos' half brother Apollo reflects the

masculine in the world, but that's not to say that both forces aren't important. It is not a choice of either one or the other. The Greeks recognized the place of each, as do we, even if our Dionysian rites are more exciting than our recognition and worship of Apollo. On the other hand, it is the order and structure of an Apollonian approach that gives us continuity and endurance. Dionysos brings liberation and creativity. It's Apollo, after all, who reminds us that we have dinner reservations."

"You're right about that," I said. "Shall we go?"

"I would say so. This is supposed to be a date, not a philosophy lesson." With that we got up and headed for the door. "Shall I drive?" she asked.

"No, you don't have to, but don't worry. I won't mind taking directions from a woman."

"Really?" she laughed. "Be careful what you commit to."

It was a good thing Cynthia had made reservations, as there was a line of people waiting to get into the restaurant. Its décor was subdued, plush with foliage and lit with little more than candles and torch-light. Nevertheless the Thai menu was interesting and had a great deal of variety. I asked our waiter how hot was hot and she pointed to a pepper chart. At least mild was a choice. Cynthia and I discussed our culinary preferences, made a few selections, and agreed to share what we ordered so we could sample a larger variety. In the meantime, our waiter returned with a small tray of appetizers and asked if we wanted anything to drink.

"How about a bottle of wine?" I asked Cynthia.

"Sounds good to me," she replied.

"I know,"" I said. "Dionysians never refuse a glass of wine." I returned with a smile.

"Oh some of us do," she assured me, "lest it hinder our performance later."

When the wine was poured I lifted my glass to hers and toasted, "Here's to a performance later."

69

Cynthia smiled back, "You rogue. You'd better be careful or I might decide your brashness needs to be corrected," a comment the possible significance of which I didn't miss. Frankly, I would have expected that response from a professional dominatrix but not from Cynthia.

The conversation turned to getting-to-know you kinds of questions. Even without the Dionysian intrigue Cynthia was an amazing woman and I wondered where knowing her might lead, though I had no idea the answer would be so forth-coming.

"What do you do for a living?" I asked and she broke into a broad smile.

"In secular terms, I'm what's called a professional dominatrix, though in the Alliance I'm known as a priestess," she answered without the slightest bit of hesitation. Her answer jolted me into a new curiosity of where this date might go.

"That's a surprise," I said, trying to subdue the torrent of questions that flooded my mind.

"I'm sure it is," she answered, "but I always think it's better to put that topic on the table sooner rather than later. I hope I haven't offended you."

"Not at all, there's definitely a kinky side to my life as well, though I have to admit that I'm not as forth-coming about it as you are."

"Well, it's certainly not a subject one brings up lightly. After all, it does raise all sorts of social and legal problems with anyone except the most tolerant of friends," she replied.

"That's true, "I added. "As liberal as most of my friends might be, they still have a certain superior and intolerant attitude about S&M, probably because it makes them nervous."

"I hope I haven't made you nervous, Ben. If I have, please forgive me, as I hope tonight is a completely social event. I certainly don't want it to become professional in nature. Even pro dommes have to have fun once in a while."

"Well, that's good," I replied. "When you said 'professional dominatrix' I half expected you might be looking for a new client."

"I understand you might feel that way, but I promise that's not the case."

I shook my head and smiled broadly. "God, you folks have a new surprise every time I turn around. No wonder it's so hard to figure out what's going on with all of you. I am, sad to say, pretty confused about all of this. The secrecy of your cult is often starkly contrasted by your willingness to share details of your lives that most people rarely venture to mention. I find the company of Dionysians very inviting and the sexual possibilities are certainly attractive, but that still leaves me wondering what comes next."

"What comes next, Ben, is dinner but, more than that, I hope we can be friends. Some of us might be free enough to share our lives rather openly but that doesn't mean that the person next door is going to accept us for who we are and how we live."

"You've got a point there. I've certainly known prejudice in my life. With what little I've learned about your religion I can see that your secrecy is probably appropriate."

"Not only appropriate, Ben, but unfortunately necessary."

Cynthia picked up her wine glass and raised it to mine. "To friendship that wipes away secrecy," she said.

I raised my glass and said "I'll drink to that."

Fortunately just as we finished the toast the waiter arrived with a second round of appetizers and the tidbits sufficiently distracted us that we were able to move on to lighter topics. Even though the conversation might have shifted, I was left pondering this last bit of information. It's not that any of it was new to me. Rather it was that this sex cult was appearing ever more extensive, primitive, and, yes, attractive. My playroom in the basement, after all, proved I was no stranger to whatever Cynthia had to offer.

As dinner progressed I couldn't help but think about Cynthia's profession. I hadn't been entirely forth-coming in my response to her admission. After all, I had started my own venture into S&M by paying dominatrices in Chicago to help me experiment

71

with spicy sex. I guess we all keep some secrets, I told myself.

Still I found myself very attracted to my dinner partner and horny for some hot sex as well. I decided that I'd broach the subject on the way back to her house. Cynthia had, after all, given me a lot of encouragement in that regard. Even my mother had said that.

I wondered, too, if Cynthia was as good at intimacy as Thomas had been. On second thought I had to admit that the answer was probably yes.

It was after ten o'clock by the time I drove into Cynthia's driveway. I quietly took a deep breath and said "This has been a wonderful night, Cynthia. I hope you've enjoyed yourself as much as I have."

"No worry there, Ben," she replied. "I certainly have."

"Well," I replied, "there's something I should have said and didn't. When you spoke about your being a dominatrix I was less shocked than you might have expected. The fact is that I rather enjoy playing the submissive role with a woman."

"Really, Ben? That could make a wonderful night spectacular."

You have to admit that there are times that these Dionysians don't beat around the bush. In spite of my hopes, the direction of Cynthia's response was a great deal more than I had expected. It caught me off guard for a second.

"Well, Ma'am, how may I serve you?" I asked, lapsing into the jargon several mistresses had taught me.

"I'll tell you what. It's 10:15. Wait here until 10:30 and then ring the doorbell. We'll start the festivities when you come in the door. I'm sure we'll find our way to a good time. Or would you rather we discuss a more detailed experience?"

"Not at all," I replied, "I'm perfectly at ease with following your lead in this matter."

"Excellent," she said. "I'll be ready for you in fifteen minutes." With that she got out of the car and left me to ponder what might come next. After a few minutes it dawned on me that I might not actually be "perfectly at ease" with what might come next. On the other hand, my time with Thomas and the fact that my mother was involved in all of this led me to feel I was probably in good hands. Besides I knew that I could always just say "No" and get the hell out of here.

I waited the fifteen minutes in a mixed state of curiosity and sexual excitement. I knew enough about mistresses to ring her doorbell at precisely 10:30.

Cynthia opened the door and stood before me smiling. What had been alluring at dinner was now downright seductive. She had put on a black corset which accentuated her bust and had changed her flats for high heels. Her hair was now drawn back and held with a thin silver band. Hanging from her neck was a silver chain; a horn dangled from it.

"Come in, Benjamin, and we shall begin," she said, pointing the way the down the hall. What had begun with a dinner date was taking on a whole new direction. Indeed there was something of priestess about her, her demeanor, and her attire. I wondered what she had in mind -- I knew what I had in mind.

We walked toward the rear of the house and entered a large room. It was part boudoir, part dungeon, and part sanctuary.

At the wall opposite the door was a high-backed chair of fine teak and lush cushions. On each side were poles of wood, entwined with carved garlands of grape leaves and topped with clusters of grapes. On the right side of the room was a large and similarly ornate St. Andrews Cross, with manacles dangling from its extremities. The wall adjacent to it was lined with whips, riding crops, and paddles. It was as well furnished a sex room as I had ever

73

seen. Across the room was a four-poster bed, luxuriously laden with silks and furs.

In the center of the room was an altar-like table draped with a cloth embroidered with nymphs and satyrs.

Cynthia adjusted the lighting and turned on some music. Then she sat in the large chair and told me to stand facing her.

"Well, this is a pleasant turn of events. We've progressed a bit faster than one might have expected, but I am sure no harm will come of it. Tell me, Benjamin, what do you wish of me?"

"I'm not sure where to begin," I said.

"You can begin by calling me 'My Lady.' I think that will set a proper tone, don't you?"

"Yes, My Lady. I understand."

"You are familiar, then, with the protocols of dominant women in situations such as this?" she asked. I thought of all the times when I had served a woman. None matched the intrigue of this encounter.

"Yes, My Lady. At least I hope so, though none have seemed to offer as much as you. I am here to learn and to serve. My desire is to please you, My Lady, and to worship you as befits your status and mine."

"Well said, Benjamin. I see that Claire's son comes to me well-prepared. Strip, my minion, and we shall have our pleasure."

I did as I was told. That was, after all, the whole point of my being there, wasn't it? As I unbuttoned my shirt, I looked for a place to put it. I knew that most women would want my clothes neatly folded. There was a space on the floor near the door so I walked to it and laid my shirt there. Then I put my shoes next to it, followed by my socks, each of which I put into one of the shoes.

My cock began to swell as I thought of being naked in front of my dinner partner. I loosened my belt, undid the clasp on my pants and lowered the zipper. In no time, or so it seemed, my pants and underwear were folded and atop my shirt. I walked back to face my lady.

"Well done, Benjamin. I see you are indeed aware of a woman's desires."

I stood there tense and nervous, yet proud of my 178-pound body. I am moderately hairy and well-proportioned for my 41 years, as I had worked (if not actually worked out) to make sure that I was still physically desirable. My few days in Florida had added a rosy glow to most of my skin and the tan line around my waist and thighs made that even more noticeable.

Cynthia stood up and walked to the wall of implements, choosing a short black riding crop. She approached me and caressed its length with her left hand while holding it in her right one. Presently she brushed one of my tits with its tip. "How pretty, my minion. I am pleased with your offering," she said. The brushing continued and my prick got stiffer.

"Oh," Cynthia said with a smile, "I see your mansex enjoys the attention. That is very good. Are you familiar with pain as a doorway to ecstasy, Benjamin?"

"Yes, My Lady," I answered. "There have been times, though not often, when a good flogging has sent me sailing into the heavens."

"Yes, even the secular application of our ancient rituals is known to bring joy to the hearts of those who have no hint of our Dionysian pleasures."

The crop's speed and intensity grew slowly as Cynthia applied its force to first one, then the other of my nipples. The skin around them began to turn pink. While applying the crop, she began stroking my torso, my cheeks, my arms. Her tenderness and sadism merged into a flood of sensations that only increased my excitement. I found myself melting into a state of surrender to the woman who stood before me. Though we were silent, her ministrations and my reactions spoke volumes.

In time, she paused and stroked my cock. "I see by the

dripping of your pre-cum that you take readily to domination. Kneel."

I gently fell to my knees as ordered and she stroked the back of my head. I found myself facing her waist and imagined her womanhood awaiting me behind and under her clothing. I wanted to smell and taste her, though I knew by experience that most likely the reward of sexual contact would come only when she was ready, if at all. Her next comment confirmed my suspicion: "It is for you to please me, Benjamin. Is that your wish as well?"

"Yes, My Lady," I replied.

"And how do you intend to do so?"

"In any way you wish, My Lady. Please teach me to do so."

"That is good," she said. "For the moment, your pain will be my pleasure."

"As you wish, My Lady," I answered.

"Undo my corset," she ordered.

I quickly unhinged the clasps that ran down the front of her garment and she let it drop to the floor behind her.

"Stand facing the cross," she directed. I did so and Cynthia spread me against its wood, fastening the restraints so that they stretched me upon its surface. She leaned into my body, rubbing her clothing against my nakedness while caressing me with her fingers. I felt her kisses on the back of my neck and knew that the kiss of the whip would soon replace them. She took a blindfold from the wall and put it on me. It was a sweet darkness that was one more step into my feeling of helplessness, another way of making it harder to say "No" if she went further than I wanted.

There was no concern in that idea. I wanted her to take me as far as she liked, to consume me, overpower me, dominate me. I wanted nothing less than to surrender to this woman and to discover her mastery, feel her priesthood, and worship the goddess that I knew she would reveal.

76   The brush of a flogger interrupted my reverie, calling me

back to the reality of my position. She pelted my back with a steady cadence, beginning with a simple caress of leather on my skin. In time she increased the intensity of the whipping and then I could tell that the first whip had been replaced with one that held more sting as it scratched my back. I felt real pain and began to cringe.

I took several deep breaths in an attempt to cope with it. I would take what my lady gave me. I knew the rewards of surrender and hoped that I could earn them. More than one dominatrix had told me that the pain she gave me would wipe away my male arrogance and prepare me to render to her the adoration she desired.

I found myself desiring, lusting, craving to satisfy my lady's wishes. In the short time between dinner and this moment, Cynthia had aroused the masochist in me, pulling from some depth in my soul a will to submit that only surfaced in the most special of circumstances.

The second flogger gave way to another one with fewer strands and more pain. I could sense that my back was turning red with its stripes. It became increasingly difficult to refrain from movement. It took more of an effort to remember to breathe and relax, to allow Cynthia her pleasure, no matter its cost. I lost track of time and the number of lashes. The blindfold's darkness began to fade as my mind's eye transformed the pain into a revelation of points of light, starry and distant, that gave me the illusion of travel into the heavens.

Cynthia stopped the whipping and I hung there in silence, waiting to see what would come next. I heard her undressing and then felt her weight leaning against me again. This time her bare breasts rubbed my back while her fingers reached to my nipples. She gyrated her body against mine and dug her fingernails into my tits. My cock was forced against the cross, bulging and aching for attention.

The touch of her skin and the warmth of her body relaxed my mind and excited my cock. She moved away and I felt her releasing my ankles from the manacles. She freed my wrists and removed the blindfold. "Follow me," she said and moved to seat herself on the bed. Pointing to a spot next to her she bid me "Sit" with a simple click of her fingers.

"I am loath to proceed further with someone as new as you, Ben. I certainly hope for more but for now let's not rush either domination or worship. Let's get to know one another as we are. Come lie with me and let us sample the beauty of each other's bodies."

"Yes, My Lady," I replied.

She laughed and said "For now, Ben, let me be Cynthia. There is plenty of time later for entering into the depths. It has been a long and lovely evening; let's not push ourselves too hard, lest we miss the sweetness of the night."

With that she pushed me onto my back and rose on top of me, straddling my thighs. Her naked beauty flooded my sight. She leaned into my face and began kissing me with passion, a passion I hungrily returned.

Chapter

Home 9

The Tuesday morning flight back to Chicago gave me ample solitude to reflect on the whirlwind of events I had experienced in Florida. The revelation about the extent of my mother's involvement in paganism, the time spent with Cynthia, the reading I had done, and the idea that such an Alliance actually existed made my head spin. I was at a loss to understand it all, even if much of what I had experienced had been delightful.

Was there, I wondered, a group of Dionysians that met in Chicago? How would I find them and, if I did, what would I learn? I faced the idea of fertility rites, temple priestesses, and drunken orgies with mixed feelings. Were they sincerely religious rites and practices or were they merely an elaborate cover for lewdness and debauchery? I was no prude and enjoyed a good time as much as the next guy, but there was something about it all that seemed clandestine, even blasphemous.

It's not as if I was Christian or even religious for that matter but at least the mainstream denominations were generally accepted and predictable. The idea of a fringe cult on the other hand held all sorts of weird possibilities akin to James Jones in Guyana or the Manson family in California.

Those musings were merely background noise, really. Whatever confusion or curiosity I had about this cult had been overpowered by my feelings for Cynthia. I had fallen in love like some acne-faced teenager who knew that he wanted more of her dominance and her affection. Nevertheless the ideas of priestess and prostitute nagged at my feelings, accentuating the fact that I had no idea what I might be getting myself into, and then my mind brought up the thought "What about Thomas?" I really was spinning, after all.

On Wednesday I plunged myself into the pile of letters on my desk at work and tried to rein in the strong emotions that both Cynthia and Thomas had aroused. By Thursday I had calmed down enough to put the questions about this cult to rest, at least for the time being. I decided that time would tell and that hurrying things wouldn't help. So I put my Dionysian explorations to the side for a couple of weeks. With the Christmas holidays fast approaching, there was certainly enough to keep me distracted.

In spite of the approaching holidays, work kept me busier than usual, so I was surprised when I came home one evening and found a message from Thomas on my answering machine. "I'll be in Chicago next week," he had said. "Give me a call and let's get together." He had left a phone number so I called him and we arranged to meet at the Drake Hotel for drinks after work on the next Monday.

Thomas greeted me with a warm hug and we took seats in a private corner of the bar. He was in a jovial mood. When our drinks arrived, he lifted his glass and said "Well, Ben, here's to a raucous Bacchanalia. You know, it is getting near to that time of the year."

"I didn't," I replied, "but I guess you ought to know. I've kind of put my Dionysian quest on hold since I came back from Florida."

"Something go wrong at your mother's?" he asked.

Now it was my turn to laugh and I did. "No, not at all. In fact just the opposite. I had a really good time. It's just that it all became a bit overwhelming. I met a woman named Cynthia -- the daughter of two of my mom's friends -- and we went out to dinner for what I thought would be a quiet date. It turned out that she was the most fascinating and attractive female I've ever met. I came back to Chicago feeling like a teenager in love."

"And what's wrong with that?" he asked.

"I suppose I should say 'Nothing,' but quite frankly I have too many doubts and too many unanswered questions. I guess I just can't believe that all of this talk of pagan worship is for real. This is, after all, twentieth century America, and temple priestesses and fertility rites belong in pagan Rome, not civilized Chicago. I'm afraid that the next thing I'm going to learn is that you sacrifice bulls at the dark of the moon."

"I'm sorry to hear you say that, Ben. I had hoped your trip to Florida would have eased your doubts about us and it obviously hasn't. How can I help?"

"To be honest, I don't know. I've just got to sort these feelings out. I guess that'll just take time. I did learn a lot in Florida and, quite frankly, none of it was bad. The real problem is that I'm not sure where all of this leads. After all, this did start out as a rather benign search to find my great-uncle. Little did I know it would lead to a secret Greek cult."

"We're only secretive for our protection. If you want to know more about us, that can certainly be arranged, even right here in 'civilized Chicago.'"

"I thought that would be the case. After all, the truth of the matter is that I wasn't at all comfortable with talking to my mother about her religion. It was different, of course, with Cynthia, but I'm wary of getting emotionally involved with a priestess and professional dominatrix."

"Well, if you spent time with Cynthia, you probably learned a lot in Florida," Thomas said. "You know we are a small group so you'll not be surprised to hear that I know her and her family. Let me assure you, first off, that I'll keep our conversations strictly between us."

"I'd appreciate that. I'd hate to be accused of kissing and telling."

"Secondly, hard as it might seem, don't let all the religious titles screw up your thinking. Yeah, we've got a coherent theology and a functioning structure, but for the most part this is about having a good time, not slaughter, rape, and pillage."

"For the most part, huh?" I asked.

"Yeah, for the most part," he answered and his grin grew wider.

He took a sip of his drink and asked "So tell me, Ben, what did happen over Thanksgiving?"

With that I leaned back and said, "It's a long story. I guess we'd better find some dinner while I tell you."

"You talk and I'll buy," he said and so I began my tale.

When I got to the part about reading at the pool, Thomas stopped me and suggested we move to the restaurant. So we finished our drinks, paid the waiter, and went across the lobby to the dining room. Once we had ordered, I continued my narrative. By the time after-dinner coffee arrived, I had told him just about everything and said "So, how can I meet some Dionysians in Chicago? I really don't want to commute to Florida every weekend just for theology lessons."

"Easy. There's a study group that meets in Rogers Park once a month at the home of a woman named Stacie. The group meets on a first name only basis and is part lecture and part discussion. It's one of the very few newcomers' groups that we have. Most people get their Dionysian education on a one-on-one basis. In that regard Stacie's group is rather controversial among us. For that reason it's rather secretive as well. If you're interested, I'll have Stacie contact you, since I can't give out her address or phone number."

"Might as well do that. But will they mind a skeptical visitor?"

"Not at all. Given the chance, some Dionysians like to show off their theology. Don't expect much more than that from this group, though. Unlike most Dionysian gatherings, these folks keep their clothes on and their meetings are very formal. Stacie will want to know more about you before she'll invite you, but I think if you give me and Cynthia as references, you'll not have much of a problem."

"Is she a priestess, too?" I asked.

"Well, Ben, here's where I have to keep silent. It'll be up to Stacie to tell you what she wants you to know about her life in the Alliance. It's one thing for me and Cynthia to talk about ourselves. It's another for us to talk about a third person.

"One of our codes is to protect one another's identity and respect each other's privacy. I can only say that Stacie opens her home for a discussion of classical literature. Whatever else she wants you to know, you'll have to learn from her."

"I guess that's OK," I said. "Have her give me a call."

"Will do, Ben. Now shall we go back to the bar for more talk or do you want to call it a night?"

"Call it a night?" I asked. "Don't I get an invite for a private lesson in your hotel room?"

"You sure do. I just wasn't sure if Cynthia had turned your head so much that you might have lost interest in my tutoring," Thomas replied.

"No," I answered. "If it's anything like our last time together, I'm ready for another lesson."

"So be it," Thomas smiled. "My place or yours?"

"Hell, we're at yours now. Let's go for it."

When we got to Thomas's room, he motioned for me to sit on the bed facing him. "Are you serious about a lesson?" he asked. "There's more to the Alliance than just sex, you know."

"Yes, I know. In fact my problem is that I feel I know too little about your cult. Everything I've experienced with you folks has been good, but doubts linger and make me cautious."

"Let me suggest three things, then. First, get yourself to a library and read some books about primitive cults, especially those by Günter Hirschberg. He's a professor at U of C and has written some pretty incredible studies about shamanic religions. Secondly, when Stacie calls you, try to attend at least some of her lectures.

She's knowledgeable and friendly and will help your intellectual side catch up with your libido. Lastly, let me give you an introduction to our rituals. You'll find the techniques we use are helpful, even if they seem a bit strange."

"Like I said in the dining room, I'm game."

"Kiss me, then," Thomas said, "and we'll begin."

Kiss we did and then we stripped. He went to his suitcase and unpacked two leather kilts and a couple of armbands. They were made of black leather with inlays of spotted fur, leopard or jaguar or some such animal . I couldn't tell if the fur was real or synthetic. He had me put on a kilt and tied one of the armbands on my upper right arm, the other on his left.

"Our celebrations begin and end with rather formal rituals that have their origins in antiquity, even if they have evolved over the years. We use them to create an atmosphere, a feeling of devotion, that lets us put aside the mundane thoughts of our everyday life and helps us to focus on the supernatural. The rituals act like bookends to the sexual celebration that comes in the center of the service.

"The opening and closing create what is commonly called a 'sacred circle.' It's a common practice among Pagans and is practiced by a wide number of aboriginal and native cultures. It's also been popularized by neo-Pagans and Wiccans, especially through the writings and teaching of Aleister Crowley, though that's not to say that Crowley has a very good reputation among followers of the Alliance.

"So what I'll do is create that space and then we'll have sex. I hope you don't mind if I give a running commentary as well. That's the usual way we mentor. 'Preach and practice' we call it."

"Go right ahead," I said. "I'm as ready as I'll ever be."

Thomas laid out four candles, one at each of the points of the compass, explaining all of it as he did so. With each candle was a symbol: east was incense; south had an extra candle for fire; west was a dish of water for life; and north was a bowl of salt for earth. He turned out the lights, leaving the room in darkness that was only broken by the city lights that filtered in through the drawn curtains, and lit four of the candles. He then invoked an eagle, a lion, a serpent and a bull to create a circle "to teach and protect."

Finally he recited a long prayer that began with an invocation to some supreme unknown God and was followed by calling Zeus, Hera, and Apollo, and ended with a prayer invoking the presence of Dionysos. It was somewhat churchy, even if it wasn't at all Christian. On the other hand, you could tell that Thomas was dead serious in what he was doing. It did put me into a rather calm state of mind, even if the garb we were wearing was a bit theatrical.

"And now," he said, "come to bed with me. Sit like we did before, facing one another and I will show you how we do what we do."

Thomas had me think about light and energy and to imagine rays of love moving from his heart to mine and back again. In no time at all we were kissing and fondling one another, rolling on the bed as impassioned lovers. When he took off our kilts, our pricks were rock-hard solid. He massaged my anus with lube and put on a rubber. It was obvious that it was my turn to get fucked and I wasn't going to complain about his doing so. He told me to straddle his dick and I guided his cock into my ready and waiting hole.

That done, he said "Imagine the power of the earth surging up from the ground below us, through the bed and into me, from me through my cock to you, and from you to me as we kiss. He put his arms around me and drew me close. It was as it had been before, an incredible feeling of comfort, warmth, security. There was even a tinge of electricity between us. I fell into a state of passion and desire, his thrusts matching the rhythms of my ride on his man-shaft.

"Come, Dionysos, come. We seek your presence, oh holy god of lust," he quietly prayed, even as we were having sex. It was a strange mixture of religion and sex, spirit and flesh acting together. It was unlike any church service I had ever attended, yet had so many of the characteristics one expected: prayer, candles, even

85

incense. Devotion and passion merged. I felt light-headed, as if I were floating. I closed my eyes as Thomas kissed me, his tongue probing my mouth, his arms holding me as close as he could.

We slowed our tempo and I rested quietly upon his prick, impaled by a new god; not a new sensation but certainly a more intense fuck than usual. Our breathing slowed and he gently maneuvered me into a prone position on the bed. My legs encircled his neck as he leaned his shoulders against them and pressed himself down to kiss me again and again.

His kisses ceased and he slid out of my fuck-hole, took off the condom, and moved back from me. Laying his head in my crotch, he began kissing my dick and rubbing my thighs and testicles with his fingers. It was a heavenly massage. I could hear him whispering. Then his voice grew louder, more discernible. I heard him worshipping my cock, praising and loving it as he kissed and fondled it.

"I praise you, holy prick," he said. "I worship and adore your manhood, your godliness, your divinity." He worshipped me as one would worship God or Jesus or Allah, but there was something mystical, and right, about it. I knew that this was the secret of their cult. It was a blasphemous revelation that they worshipped not some abstract spirit in heaven, not some Jehovah who sat upon the clouds on a throne of gold, but one another.

I had felt that in my desire to worship and serve Cynthia and now I knew that what Thomas felt for me is what I had felt for her. I lay there intoxicated with the feeling of godly power until my genitals could take no more and emptied themselves into a passionate burst of cum and light. It was ecstasy like I had never imagined. It was then that I knew why I had been so attracted to these strange worshippers.

We lay there in silence as the impact of my orgasm passed. Thomas then rose, said some kind of prayer as he extinguished each candle, and returned to cuddle next to me. We began kissing again, but not for long, as I quietly drifted off to sleep.

Chapter

Stacie 10

The following Thursday evening I got a phone call from Stacie, who told me that she was a friend of Thomas' and had heard from him that I was interested in classical literature. She asked if I wanted to attend her little discussion group. "Yes, I would," I responded, my curiosity and my courage bolstered by my last encounter with Thomas.

She suggested that we meet first, "To get to know each other," she said, and arranged for us to have a drink at Big Chicks, a bar on Sheridan Road just south of Rogers Park. We set a date for the following Monday evening, right after work.

Stacie was waiting for me at the bar and smiled when I came in. She had been reading what looked like a small notebook and put it away. She asked if I were Ben and I said I was. She then suggested that we move to a small table near the vacant dance floor. Dressed in a neat suit with a lacy blue blouse, her hair was graying and she appeared to be in her mid-to-late fifties. Her attire made her look a bit matronly but her demeanor was certainly not academic. I wondered if she, too, were a temple priestess.

"I'm so glad to meet you, Ben," she said. "I've heard about you from Thomas and Cynthia. I'm also an acquaintance of your mother's, though I haven't seen her in years. How is she and what is she doing these days?"

"Mom's fine. I saw her at Thanksgiving. I don't suppose you know she's got a winter place in Florida and lives not too far from Cynthia's family."

87

"Well, I'm not surprised to hear that," Stacie said. "She and the O'Malleys have always been close. In that case, I'm sure she's doing well."

"Seems so to me," I added.

Stacie asked about my interest in the classics and about my education. She seemed pleased to know that I had taken Latin in high school and had a college degree. She asked how I had met Thomas, though she seemed to shy away from any discussion of the Alliance. Our meeting was remarkably short. The interrogation I had expected never really materialized. She gave me a card with an address on it and wrote on it the date and time of the next group meeting. I was surprised that she also included her phone number.

"Tomorrow night, huh?" I asked.

"Yes, I apologize for the short notice. Can you make it?"

"I think so. I'll certainly try, anyway."

"Good," she said and added that she hadn't time to get to know me better but that since both Thomas and Cynthia had spoken so highly of me, she was sure I would fit in really well. "I look forward to having you join us," she said, "but now I must rush off to another appointment."

"No problem," I replied. "I have some things to do tonight as well." With that we left the bar and walked together to the Argyle CTA station. I took a train south and she took one north. I hadn't really gotten any information, but did look forward to what her group had to offer.

The next day I took a trip to the library that didn't turn up a whole lot of information, as there weren't a lot of books on ancient cults. Still, I did look through Primitives to Zen (Mircea Eliade), The Religion of Ancient Greece (Thaddeus Zielinski), Dionysos At Large (Marcel Dteinne) and Rites and Symbols of Initiation (Mircea Eliade). All to no avail, I might add.

A rather scholarly book by Walter F. Otto, entitled *Dionysus,*

Myth and Cult, had this to say about Dionysos:

> All of antiquity extolled Dionysus as the god who
> gave man wine. However, he was known also as the raving god
> whose presence makes man mad and incites him to savagery
> and even to lust for blood. He was the confidant and companion
> of the spirits of the dead. Mysterious dedications called him the
> Lord of Souls. To his worship belonged the drama which has
> enriched the world with a miracle of the spirit. The flowers of
> spring bore witness to him, too. The ivy, the pine, the fig tree
> were dear to him. Yet far above all of these blessings in the
> natural world of vegetation stood the gift of the vine, which has
> been blessed a thousand fold. Dionysus was the god of the most
> blessed ecstasy and the most enraptured love. But he was also
> the persecuted god, the suffering and dying god, and all whom
> he loved, all who attended him, had to share his tragic fate.

There was one book that was more helpful, *The God of
Ecstasy* by Arthur Evans. Evans presented an excellent and detailed
study of Euripides's play, *The Bakkhai*.

Though the term Bakkhai has several different connotations
(well explained in Evans' book), in general they were women who
worshipped Dionysos with their biennial celebrations in the woods,
celebrations that were rumored to be filled with drunken ecstasy,
orgies, and the eating of raw flesh. Still in all of my reading I found
little about actual Dionysian rites and practices and certainly no
indication that the cult had survived the two millennia since the
birth of Christianity.

I also found a book with quotations from Livy where he
recounted the Roman Senate's proclamation banning the Dionysian
cult. Dionysos was called Bacchus in Rome.

> Hispala explained the origin of the rites: at first it was
> a rite for women, and it was the custom that no man should be
> admitted to it. They had had three fixed days per year in which

89

women were initiated by day into the Bacchic rites; married women were customarily appointed priests in turn. Paculla Annia (she said), a priestess from Campania, had changed everything, allegedly on the basis of divine instructions; for she was the first to initiate men, namely her sons Minius and Herennius Cerrinius; and she transferred the ritual from day to night, and established five days for initiation per month, in place of the three per year. Ever since the rites involved the admission of men among the women, and with the added liberation of darkness, absolutely every crime and vice was performed there. The men had more sex with each other than with the women. Anyone who was less prepared for disgrace and slow to commit crimes was offered up as a sacrifice. To consider nothing wrong was (she continued) the principal tenet of their religio. Men, as if insane, prophesied with wild convulsions of their bodies; married women in the dress of Bacchants with streaming hair ran down to the Tiber carrying burning torches, which they dipped into the water and brought out still alight (because they contained live sulphur mixed with calcium). People were said to have been carried off by gods; they had been strapped to a machine and snatched from sight to hidden caves. Those seized were people who had refused to join in conspiracy or participate in crimes or engage in sex. It was (she said) a great crowd, almost a second state, including some nobles, both male and female. Within the last two years it had been resolved that no one aged over twenty should be initiated; people of this age were sought as being inclined to both erroneous ways and sexual indulgence.

Needless to say, my research left me with more questions than answers. I was left wondering why there was so little known about the cult but since the penalty for disclosing mystery rites was death, according to at least one author, I guess that was good enough reason not to be caught writing anything down. I also supposed that the Christian church probably destroyed a lot of anything that might have been written. Was there material in the fabled Vatican Library? Now there was a question that I certainly couldn't answer.

Most mysterious of all was how could such a mystery cult, outlawed by the Roman Senate in 186 A.D., survive for more than two thousand years and still be hidden? Might it not just be a newly-invented hoax? Now there was a question to ask Thomas. On the other hand how could I know if he really knew the answer? Or that the answer he would give me was the right one?

There was one idea that I thought I could pursue. Thomas had mentioned that I should talk to Günter Hirschberg, a professor at the University of Chicago. I wondered if he could shed some light on these Bacchanalian rites and the cult of Dionysos. It was worth a phone call. In the meantime I decided I had better spend a little less time worrying about the Alliance and a little more time on getting some work done at the library.

That evening I grabbed a quick supper in the Loop and took the "L" to Stacie's. I was looking forward to the meeting of the book club. As I descended the stairs at her stop, the air was filled with the sound of police car sirens and as I rounded the corner onto her street, I saw that the police were going to the same address as I. In fact, the closer I got to her place, the more I could tell that the police were already there. I paused several houses away, wondering what was happening. As I watched, two men carried a stretcher out of her three story brownstone and put it into a waiting ambulance. Minutes later, the ambulance sped away. I decided that whatever meeting was being held there had probably been cancelled, turned around and walked back to the train station. It was obvious that this was no time to get involved.

The search for my great-uncle had just taken another very puzzling turn.

The front page of Wednesday morning's *Tribune* blared "Grisly Murder in Rogers Park." I knew at once that reading further would only confirm that the classical literature group I was going to attend had been the scene of some very ugly violence. It did.

As I read the story, I stood dumbfounded to think how close I had come to danger, while worrying about what I should do next. The article lacked detail, citing that the police were reluctant to release details pending an autopsy and investigation. They did say that the victim's name was Stacie Sherman and that she probably knew the murderer since there was no sign of forced entry nor of violence, except on the victim's body.

I was at a loss as to what to do next but I was certain that the last thing I wanted to do was to go into work, so I called in a personal day. About ten a.m. I decided that I had to talk to someone about what had happened and figured out that Thomas was probably the only "someone" I could call. I wasn't sure if I could reach him at the last number I had for him but I gave it a try anyway. He answered.

"Thomas?" I asked. "This is Ben."

"Boy, am I glad to hear from you," he replied. "Did you go to Stacie's meeting last night?"

"I tried, but there was trouble so I came home. Have you heard about Stacie?"

"Unfortunately, I have," he answered. "News of a tragedy like this doesn't take long to get spread about among members of the Alliance. I take it that's why you're calling?"

"You're right about that. It's got me a bit shaken. I can't believe this happened."

"I can't either," Thomas said. "From what we can tell it was pre-meditated, cold-blooded murder. It must have happened Monday night. Two members of the Alliance called the police late on Tuesday afternoon since Stacie didn't come to the door when they rang her doorbell. The door was unlocked so they figured she had to be there, preparing for the meeting, so they opened the door, knocked loudly and yelled for her. They found her body in her private dungeon and called the police."

"By the time I got there for the meeting the place was crawling with cops, so I went home," I interrupted. "It's front page news in the Trib this morning."

"Look, Ben. I'm sorry I can't talk right now. I'm about to leave for the airport. Richard and I are coming to Chicago for the funeral and to try and help out where we can. The police will be asking a lot of questions and someone with expertise needs to answer them."

"Do you think they'll want to talk to me?" I asked.

"It depends on whether they know you were with Stacie before she was killed. We'll have to see," he answered, "but I bet they will. If you're worried about it, I'm sure that Richard will give you good advice. I don't think you have anything to fear. If the police ask you anything, just tell them what you know. There is nothing you can tell them that they probably won't already know."

"I'm surprised," I said, "to hear you telling me that. After all your warnings about secrecy, I would have thought you'd want me to keep quiet."

"That wouldn't work with the police. They'd see through your lack of cooperation and only make matters worse for you. Trust me. In this case the truth is our best tactic. Anyway I'll see you in Chicago soon enough. I'll be at The Drake again. Hang in there. It'll work out OK for you. Now I really do have to go."

"OK," I said. "Goodbye."

"Goodbye," he echoed and hung up, leaving me wondering where this would lead.

On Friday after work, as I turned onto the sidewalk going to my front steps, a well-dressed man got out of a car parked nearby and followed me to my door. He was about six feet tall, with slightly graying hair and a short mustache. He carried a satchel with him. I turned to face him and he came up the stairs to my door.

93

"Are you Benjamin Kramer?" he asked.

"Yes, I am. Can I help you?" I answered.

He pulled a police badge out of his coat pocket and slowly showed it to me. "My name is Mike O'Connor and I'm a detective with the homicide division. I would like to ask you a few questions."

"Here?" I asked, "Or would you like to come in?"

"I'll come in, if you don't mind."

"Not at all," I answered, opened the door, and held it for him. "Make yourself comfortable on the couch. It's about Stacie's murder, isn't it?" I asked.

"Yes, Mr. Kramer, it is. Let me say that this is no more than routine questioning. We're trying to trace Stacie's whereabouts in the hours before her death. You have nothing to worry about."

"I'm sure that's the case, so just ask what you want to know."

He asked me a number of what seemed like routine questions about myself and about how I knew Stacie. "I really didn't know her, Mr. O'Connor," I told him. "I only met her on Monday. My friend Thomas Murray suggested that I attend a monthly study group she hosted and she called to arrange to meet me prior to the meeting.

"So I met her at Big Chicks. It seems that she was an old friend of my mother's so she didn't hesitate to ask me to join her group. She gave me a card with her address and the date and time of the meeting, which was the next night. I have it somewhere if you want it," I offered. "Our meeting didn't last very long as she had to excuse herself because she had another appointment. We left the bar together, walked to the CTA and she took a north-bound train and I took one that was going south."

"What did you do after you left Stacie?"

"I took the 'L' to Montrose and then transferred to the Montrose bus to get home."

"Did you see or meet anyone on the way?" he asked.

"As a matter of fact, a neighbor, John Scots, was on the same bus and we sat and talked on the way home. We both got off at Hamlin and walked over to Avers together."

"Did you go to the meeting, Mr. Kramer?" the detective asked.

"Yes, I did, but when I got there I saw the ambulance and the police cars and thought it best to just come home. I read what happened in the Trib on Wednesday morning."

"Well, Mr. Kramer, as I said, you have nothing to worry about. Everything you've told me fits in with what we have learned so far. Can you tell me how we can find this Thomas Murray?" he added.

"Sure. I can give you his phone number, though he won't be there this week. He's come to Chicago for the funeral and is staying at The Drake, as far as I know, and he's probably still there, though I haven't seen him this week. Let me get the number for you." With that I went to my desk, wrote down Thomas's phone number, and returned to hand it to him.

"Thanks," he said and handed me his card. "I'm done for now. If you think of anything else, just give me a call."

"Will do, Sir," I replied. We shook hands and he left.

The interview had been easy enough so I figured I had earned myself a drink. I poured a glass of Absolut on the rocks and sat in the sun porch, wondering what to do about dinner and mulling over the week's events, when the phone rang. I answered it and heard Thomas's voice. "Hi, Ben. What are you doing?" he asked.

"Just thinking about this week," I answered. "A detective just left."

"How did it go?"

"Fine, I guess. He kept telling me that I had nothing to worry about. The interview didn't last very long. Still, it does give a guy a reason to pause. Anyway, how are you?"

"Busy," he answered. "That's for sure. Richard and I were wondering if you'd join us for dinner? I want to take him to that

95

Italian restaurant we went to. Will you join us?"

"Sure," I said. "I was wondering what to do about dinner and can always use some company."

"Great," he responded. "Shall we meet there at eight?"

"OK." I agreed. "See you at eight."

Richard and Thomas were standing outside Anna Maria's when I got there. I was glad to see Thomas. He was, after all, slowly gaining a foothold in my life, which I supposed just added another complication to this whole Dionysian mess.

Once we were settled, Richard ordered a bottle of wine and three glasses. He turned to me and said "You will have a glass with us, won't you?"

"Of course I will, Richard. Just remember that I have to drive home."

"Or you can leave your car here," Thomas volunteered, "and come back to The Drake with me."

I smiled at Thomas's comment and said "Do you ever think of anything besides sex and booze?"

"What else is there to think about?" he joked.

"OK. You've got me there," I responded.

When the wine was poured, Richard lifted his glass and said "To sex and booze, and to Dionysos, the Lord of both." We toasted our glasses to his words. Richard had chosen a very fine wine and it went down well.

"So," he said, picking up a menu, "shall we consider something besides sex and booze? How about food, for instance?" he asked.

"Or basketball," I added, "This is Chicago, after all."

"To Chicago," Thomas replied, as he tilted his glass towards me and took a sip of wine.

"Have you had a busy week, Richard?" I asked, trying to make conversation and find out what he might know about the murder.

"Very. I was the lawyer who prepared Stacie's will and I've had to deal with the police about her affairs. They've been combing her home for clues. She was a rather meticulous person and kept a somewhat cryptic notebook. They hope it just might have some lead to her killer in it."

"Whoever it was knew about her Dionysian connections," Thomas added. "In fact the murder looks like the work of some religious fanatic."

"Why do you say that, Thomas?" I asked.

"Well, I don't want to ruin your dinner, but the murderer used a knife to scratch a reference to a Bible verse on her chest. It was Ezekiel chapter 16, verse 40, about using a sword against a harlot. The whole chapter is a not very veiled Hebraic threat against pagan cults such as ours."

"Yes," Richard added. "More fuel for the secrecy debate. This will certainly give the faithful reason to stay under cover. Just as many believers say, the days of witch-hunts aren't over."

"I agree," said Thomas, "but after the events of this week it's inevitable that we'll get more publicity than we want. Once the police let out the details of this story, pagan fertility rites will seem like Sunday school material."

"Why do you say that?" I asked.

"Well," Thomas continued, "it may look like some Christian fundamentalist decided to kill a heathen prostitute, but I'll bet there are also those who want to picture it as some satanic sacrifice. Stacie was, after all, murdered on an altar in what was a well-decorated prayer room, though definitely not a prayer room of the Christian sort."

"Then why didn't I get asked more about the Alliance?" I said. "The detective didn't bring up the subject at all."

"He didn't have to," Thomas answered. "He already knew about it from the questions they had asked Casey and Ariadne, the two people who had called the police in the first place. By the time they talked to you, they had already talked with Richard. You were

97

only involved because you had been seen with Stacie before she died and your phone number was in her appointment book. My guess is that they hoped you knew who her next appointment was. Unfortunately Stacie hadn't put that appointment in her book."

"Why not?" I wondered out loud.

"Because," said Richard, "he was probably a paying client, not a seeker like you."

"Are all temple priestesses prostitutes?" I asked.

"Well not really," answered Richard, "but many do earn other income as professional dominatrices. I know that seems to be a semantic difference but it does keep them on the legal side of the law.

"Oh," I said, not able to think of anything more astute. There was, it seemed, a lot more to Stacie than classical literature, just as I had suspected.

"Yes," said Thomas, "and the scandal ought to hit the papers right after the funeral."

"When's that?" I asked.

"On Monday. It had to be postponed until after the autopsy was complete. Now, I think, we should change the subject to basketball."

Dinner progressed at a lighter tone after that. Richard was much less of a stiff shirt than I had thought when I had met him in his office in Cincinnati, and it turned out he really was a basketball buff.

For my part I let the two of them do most of the talking. The more I watched and listened, the more fascinating these two guys, and the cult they represented, became. I wondered, for a moment, if Richard were gay as well, then put the question out of my mind. I couldn't, after all, fuck with everyone in the Alliance, could I? Or, I thought, did they expect just such a thing to happen? While the two of them discussed the pros and cons of major league sports, I

wondered what a three-way would be like with these two guys. I had to admit that this sex and booze thing might not be a bad idea.

After dinner Richard paid the tab and we walked out the front door. As we did, Thomas asked me if I was going to take him up on his offer to go back to The Drake with him. I turned to Richard and said "If you don't mind, Richard, I'd rather take Thomas back with me."

"Be my guest, Ben. I'm sure you two will get along quite well without me. Besides, I have a pile of work to catch up on in the morning." With that he hailed a cab, leaving Thomas with the easy choice of riding back to my place.

"I'm glad to have this time to talk you, Thomas," I said on the drive west on Montrose to my place. "I find myself with more questions than ever, even as I am becoming more comfortable with the whole idea of your Dionysian cult."

"I'm glad to know you trust me enough to ask," Thomas replied. "What's on your mind?"

"It's not easy to start this conversation as I am flooded with questions. Are all your women pro dommes? How do you handle love in all of this? With this AIDS epidemic raging, how do you all stay healthy? How do you handle the emotional roller coaster that wild sexuality can cause? What about too much alcohol and alcoholism? See, I told you there was a lot going on. And those are the starters."

"Whoa, Ben, I'm not sure I can get to them all at once."

"I know you can't," I replied, "but quite frankly it is more than overwhelming, especially since now there's murder in the picture."

"You're right about that. Stacie's death is going to echo through the Alliance like the roar of a cannon in the Grand Canyon. Whether her experiment in hosting that classical literature meeting back-fired, or someone infiltrated her defenses as a client, isn't going to make any difference at all. We'll be battening down the hatches and keeping a tight lip for many years to come. Quite frankly, if someone came to us today looking for a great-uncle he wouldn't be given the time of day, mother or no mother in the Alliance.

"But enough of that, let's see if I can at least answer one or two of the easy questions. For starters, you'll notice that we use disease prevention quite readily. What you don't see is that our fellowship is filled with doctors and nurses and all of us get tested regularly for disease. On the other hand, there's probably not as much sex going on as you might think. A lot of it is simply voyeurism or mutual masturbation. The fact that a hot man like you has hit a sexual watershed is rather rare. After all, bisexual switches aren't that common, even in a group like ours."

"OK," I granted, "but how do you handle the roller coaster of love and intimacy?"

"Mostly," Thomas answered, "we don't. I mean it's still a human organization. What happens, really, is when folks find us, as you have, there is often a kind of 'kid in a candy store' feeling, but you'll find that after a while new folks settle down and find their comfort zone with it all. For some it's some sort of swinger's lifestyle and for others it's just as monogamous as it can be, especially with the married-with-children set.

"Like some other gay men, I've always been shy of promising some kind of monogamous relationship, but that doesn't mean that someone can't still have a special place in my heart."

As he said that I pulled into my garage. "Well, Thomas," I said, "I guess I'll just have to figure it all out. Come on into the house, I could use a good hug."

"Honestly, Ben," he answered, "I could too."

And that's what happened in my bedroom that night. There were no special rites, no mention of gods or goddesses, no mention of temple priests, just kissing and hugging and stroking. I knew then that I really was falling in love, even if I didn't know how far I would fall and, for that matter, with whom.

100   I chose not to go the funeral on Monday, though I had

thought about doing so. After all, I had only met the woman once. I threw together a quick dinner for myself and watched a Star Trek re-run as I ate it. Thomas and I talked on the phone that night and he apologized that he was too busy to get together. Nevertheless we did make plans for him to come over on Friday night.

On Tuesday I was surprised to get a call at work from Richard. "I'd like to meet you sometime soon, if I may," he said.

"Sure," I answered, though I was caught off guard by his calling me at work. "When?" I asked.

"Can you come over to The Drake this afternoon?" he said. "It's a business call."

"Let me look at my calendar," I answered, while I wondered just how much he knew about my business. "This afternoon is fine," I said. "How about two p.m.?"

"That works for me," he answered. "I'm in room 543. See you then." With that we hung up.

I left the office at 1:30, grabbed a cab, and was at the Drake in 20 minutes. I had purposely not brought much with me, except for a small notebook that fit in my shirt pocket and a pen. I had already decided to play this visit close to my chest, though I was pretty sure that Richard, and God only knows who else, knew I was a detective.

Richard's room was hardly "a room." It was the Presidential suite on the fifth floor. He greeted me with a smile, handshake, and a gesture to come in. I stepped into an elegant 1,000 square foot room with royal blue carpeting, beige wainscoting and gray wall paper. French doors looked out onto the north side of the city and Lake Michigan. The room itself was furnished with a Louis XIV sofa and side chairs, several small tables, and a collection of floor and table lamps. A large painting of a pastoral scene hung over a white marble fireplace.

One corner held a large mahogany and inlay desk. It was 101

obvious that Richard had been working, as the desk was neatly stacked with papers and folders.

"Thank you for coming," Richard said.

"My pleasure, Richard," I answered. "I'm surprised, though, that you called this a 'business' meeting. How can I be of service?"

Richard picked a large folder off the desk and walked over to one of the side chairs. "Have a seat, Ben," he said. "May I get you something to drink?"

"No, thanks," I answered, "not just yet, at least."

When I had sat on the sofa, he continued. "To answer your question rather bluntly, the Alliance has investigated you just as thoroughly as you have us. We are quite aware that advertising is simply a cover for your real work and that you do your real work quite well. We want to hire you to investigate Stacie's murder."

"Well, that's quite a mouthful, Richard. Why me?"

"As you know, it is highly unlikely, given Stacie's occupation as a Dionysian priestess, that the police are going to put very much effort into finding her murderer. After all to them she's no different than a prostitute. At the same time, the Alliance can ill afford to let the perpetrators go unpunished.

"As is often the case, we have to take justice into our own hands in order to see that the task of solving the murder is done correctly and discreetly. To be quite frank, Ben, we've learned a lot about you since we first received your letter about your great-uncle and have come to the conclusion that you are the best man for this job."

"Well, thank you, Richard, for saying that. When I last left your office in Cincinnati, I wondered how much you had researched my background and if you suspected that I had done the same in learning about the Alliance."

"Trust me, Ben, and I don't say this lightly, but Jonathan's great-nephew or not, we would have never given you those journals unless we thought you could be trusted. The times you spent with

Thomas and Cynthia were more than enough for both of them to give you high praise, as we have learned how important discretion is when it comes to protecting our interests. Additionally, you and your firm come highly recommended for thoroughness and discretion, else I would not be broaching this subject with you today."

"I'm certainly interested in helping on this case, Richard, and I find it interesting, as you can well imagine, for more than one reason. On the other hand, I'm concerned that my personal involvement might pose some conflict of interest here. Perhaps it might be better if we ask Robert Manning, one of our managing partners, to join us in this discussion."

"I understand your concerns, Ben," Richard replied, "but the Alliance will have to insist that as few people as possible, outside of our own operatives, be brought into this affair. Rather than seeing your, shall I say, intimate knowledge of our practices as a conflict, we rather think it gives you a very helpful insight into the culture you are going to have to investigate.

"There are some happy coincidences here that we want to exploit. First off, you are already in some measure part of the Dionysian family, both by your family heritage and your recent dating patterns. Secondly, whereas you've had intimate experience with some of our membership, thankfully you are not yet known to any Dionysians in Chicago. It is quite fortunate that you became involved with us only in Cincinnati and Sarasota; therefore, you are virtually unknown to any of the Brethren here."

"Why," I asked, "is that of concern?"

"Quite frankly," Richard answered, "there is some probability that Stacie's murder was either done by a Dionysian or that she was at least betrayed by one who helped the murderer gain access to the temple."

"Yes," I said, "Thomas mentioned that possibility on Friday night. Nevertheless," I continued, "Robert will have to be let in on my working for you. I can't afford to endanger our partnership by outside freelance work."

103

"We fully understand that, Ben, and are prepared to compensate your corporate entity for allowing you to take a leave of absence. With your consent I'll meet with Mr. Manning and arrange a liberal financial incentive for your services."

"That's fine with me," I said, "I'm sure that if there are enough shekels in the hopper, Robert will be amenable. As for my services, I expect that you'll compensate me at our firm's usual billing rates both for time and expenses?"

"Most certainly, Ben. We would not expect otherwise. Will you write up a contract or shall I?"

"Richard, I'll just use our standard contract and messenger one over to you tomorrow, if that's OK with you."

"It most certainly is, Ben. I am pleased to see that you are willing to aid in our search."

With that, he leaned over towards me and stretched out his hand. "May we begin with a handshake, my friend?" he asked.

"Most certainly," I replied. I took his hand in mine and the deal was done.

Richard met with Robert (who also acted as messenger to bring over a copy of our standard contract) on the next day and when he returned, all smiles to be sure, he came into my office and said, "Well, Mr. Kramer, I don't know what you've gotten yourself into with this Richard guy, but it sure is lucrative. As of now, you're on leave with full pay and benefits. And I'm not supposed to ask you anything about it."

"Full pay with benefits, huh?" I asked. "That is more than I expected but I won't turn it down. Let's just say that my search for Uncle Jonathan has a great deal more to it than family genealogy. When the job's over, I'll fill you in on what details I can."

"No need to do that, Ben," Robert said, "I've been in this business long enough to know that I probably don't want to know. Good luck hunting, so to speak, and if we can be of any assistance, don't hesitate to ask. In the meantime, Richard wants you to call him ASAP. He certainly is in a rush to get started."

"OK, I'll do that. Thanks."

"And with that, I'd better go and see who I can get to cover for you while you're gone."

"It shouldn't be a problem. The way work has been coming in, having the Alliance pay my salary will help keep the bank account humming until I get back."

"That's true," Robert agreed. "Still, someone's going to have pick up the slack when you're not here."

"If you can't find what you need in the files, ask Laurie. She's a great help and will probably know what little you'll ask. If not, you've got my number. After all, I'm just going on leave, I'm not leaving the company."

"OK," he said, "but in any case, I'd better find out what's going on here. If I don't see you soon, good luck." With that he held out his hand to shake mine, we said goodbye, and he left the office. For the first time in a long time I suddenly wondered if I had bitten off more than I could chew.

"No matter," I thought to myself. "Just dig in and see what comes of it." With that I called Richard and he asked me to meet with him the following morning. I answered in the affirmative and decided to pack up a few essentials from my desk and take them home.

It was four o'clock anyway and I was ready for a drink.

Chapter

Plans 11

Wednesday morning came rather early. The day was cloudy, damp and threatened snow. It was just the kind of day that made me want to stay warmly nestled in bed. Instead Richard had asked that we get started at 8:30 with a working breakfast at The Drake. I could hardly say no.

So the alarm jangled me awake at seven. I showered, dressed, skipped the coffee and was on the "L" by 7:30. I took the paper with me since *The Sun-Times'* headline was all about Stacie's murder. It was filled with gruesome coverage of her murder, with words such as "ritual sacrifice" and "religious fanaticism." The quote from Ezekiel was splashed on the front page, implying that some right-wing Christian was the culprit. On the other hand there was more than a hint that it could have been an "inside job" by cult members who were trying to protect the sect's secrecy or who had bungled a "ritual in preparation for the celebration of the Bacchanalia." All in all, it confirmed what Richard had said about the end of Dionysian secrecy.

I knew that any rational man would probably distance himself from these people as far as possible, but something in me propelled me forward. I couldn't tell how much of it was love, lust, or just the excitement of investigating a murder. Was it the intrigue, the desire to learn more about my mother's religion, or the hope that finding out the truth would somehow make my life more complete? In any case, curiosity was certainly getting the best of me and I had already thrown my lot in with Richard *et al.*

I got off at Chicago Avenue and grabbed a cab from there

to The Drake. "You'd better get used to this commute," I thought to myself as I paid the cabby his fare.

Since I arrived 15 minutes early, I decided to wait in the lobby and took a seat where I could watch the passers-by while not being too noticeable. I didn't see anything out of the ordinary, though I did see Thomas come in the front door and walk in the direction of the elevators. I supposed he'd be at the meeting but I really didn't know for sure. It didn't make any difference, anyway, since I'd find out who was going to be there in the next seven minutes.

I waited another three minutes, stood up and grabbed an elevator to the fifth floor. It was a few steps to the suite. As I stood in front of the door, I took a deep breath, thought "Here goes," and knocked. In no time at all, Thomas was standing in front of me.

"Ben," he said, "come in. This is a surprise."

"Hello, Thomas," I answered. "I guess that makes two of us. I'll let Richard fill you in on the details and I hope he'll do the same for me." With that I walked into the suite.

"Good morning, Ben," Richard said. "Make yourself at home. Would you like some coffee?"

"Sure would. Double sugar and cream."

"Have a seat, Ben," Richard said and he went over to a push cart with a coffee urn and all the fixings on it. As he did, there was a knock on the door and Thomas went to answer it. He opened the door and said "Hello, Sebastian. Come in."

As he did so, I looked over this guy and was impressed. Somewhere in his early fifties, he certainly looked like he could handle himself. He wore a polo shirt and well-fitting slacks. His black skin was accented with a mustache, deep brown eyes, and short, cropped hair. He obviously worked out regularly.

"Ben," Thomas said, "this is Sebastian Cleveland." I stood up and offered him my hand, which he shook. "Nice to meet you, Ben," he said in a confident voice. "I've heard a lot of good things about you."

108 "Thanks," I replied. "I'm happy to meet you, too."

"Sebastian's from the thiasoi in Atlanta," Richard said. "He's a security specialist and, like you, a private investigator."

"What's a thiasoi?" I asked.

"Oh, sorry," Richard said. "That's Greek for congregation."

"OK," I said.

He turned to Thomas and said "Just so you know, Thomas, Ben's a private detective as well, and the Alliance has hired him to solve Stacie's murder. Sebastian is going to be working for him for as long as Ben needs him."

Turning to me, Richard said, "The Abbot has asked that Thomas be on your team as well, Ben. He may not be a very good detective but he's very familiar with the Chicago Brethren and, of course, will be helpful in answering most of your Dionysian questions.

"As of now, only the Abbot and the three of us know of these arrangements. I am sure Ben will need more help in the next few weeks, but until he does," he said, turning to Sebastian and Thomas, "I hope I don't have to remind you that none of this is to get out to anyone and I mean anyone." The inflection in his voice was very clear.

He paused a moment and continued. "Gentlemen, we've a lot of work to do but don't let that stop you from enjoying whatever you might find on the breakfast tray.

"Ben, I've got a few thoughts on how we might proceed, so if you don't mind we can start there, unless you have some questions for us."

"I'm sure I have lots of questions but why don't you begin. It seems to me, Richard, that as usual you have matters well in hand."

With that both Thomas and Sebastian smiled. "Looks like you've got Richard pegged pretty well," Sebastian said. "I've never known him to call a meeting and not have the agenda already printed in triplicate."

109

"As a matter of fact, my dear Sebastian," replied Richard, "for your information I have four copies of it, not three." With that he went to the desk, picked up his briefcase and brought it back to the sofa, setting it on one of the end tables. He opened it, took out some papers and handed one to each of us. Just as Sebastian had joked, it was an agenda and labeled so at the top. Dated for this morning, it listed "Contract, Office, Credentials, Dossier, The Mansion, The Police Report, and New Business."

"Looks fine to me," I said to Richard. "Are you sure you don't want to conduct this investigation yourself?"

"Now, Ben," he said, "give me a break. The Alliance fully intends that you're to be the lead here. If you want to tear up my suggestions just do so."

"No need, Richard. It really does look fine. Let's start."

"First things first, Ben. Here's your contract, signed, sealed and now delivered. I trust that the check accompanying it is a sufficient start for you."

I look over the check which was paper-clipped to the back of the contract. I took a minute to check the signature on the contract. There was only one, Richard's, drawn on a bank in Louisville. It was made out payable to me in the amount of $10,000.00. I thought, "This is no fly-by-night organization," and said "Everything looks fine to me," as I opened my briefcase and slid the contract and the check safely into one of the pockets.

"So, Richard, since that's taken care of, what were you thinking when you wrote 'Office'?"

"Well, I thought a quick discussion about office logistics might be helpful. You are, after all, going to need some place to work. Of necessity it needs to be rather private. What do you think?"

"Yes, you're right. I certainly can't use my office at the firm and keep my doings secret from them. I could use my home, but an off-site location would certainly be more discreet."

Sebastian chimed in with "I agree. We ought to have a spot that's easy to get to and away from Ben's home, The Drake, and

Stacie's. It also ought to have lots of local foot traffic nearby so it will be harder to know who's coming and going from it. Since I'm not all that familiar with Chicago, Ben, where do you suggest?"

"There are lots of offices to be had in the Loop. I'll find one in the next day or two. Do you want the office expenses to come through me or do you want to handle them directly, Richard? "

"It's your call, Ben, but why not just make it easy on yourself and when you find a place, have Thomas sign the contract. I can assure you that he'll handle those details very well."

"That would be fine with me," Thomas said. "I was hoping there'd be something for me to do in all this besides teach Ben our theology."

"You're on, Thomas. I'll make some calls this afternoon and, if you're available, we'll go office hunting tomorrow. That OK with you?"

"Do I have any choice?" Thomas asked. "It looks to me like the Abbot has given me over to you lock, stock, and barrel. What do you think, Richard?"

"Yes, Thomas," Richard replied, "though I hardly think that it's an assignment that you're going to refuse, much less dislike. Here, read the Abbot's letter."

With that he handed Thomas an envelope. Thomas opened it, read it quickly, and said, "It's pretty clear. Ben, forget about that lock, stock and barrel stuff. This letter gives you my body and soul to boot. I'm yours, it seems, for the duration. I'm to move into the mansion as well, so I guess I'd better plan on getting back to the monastery to fetch some more clothes. Frankly," he said, looking at me with a twinkle in his eye, "this is a very pleasant turn of events, as far as I can see."

"Just don't forget that it is a business turn of events," Richard warned.

"Don't worry about that, Richard," I said. "This is, after all, about solving a gruesome and horrific murder. It seems to me that if we keep that in mind, we'll all be better off."

111

"You're on the mark there," Sebastian said. "From what I can tell so far, we're not dealing with amateurs. The police report made it clear they didn't find much to go on, though to be honest, I'm not about to trust the thoroughness of their work."

"Yeah," I said. "I wouldn't trust it either. It's not as if they really care about what happens to a woman like Stacie. Let's move on. Richard, what do you have in mind with Credentials?"

"We've got you covered there," he said, reaching into the briefcase. "Here's some ID for you. It will make it a lot easier for you to get around. You'll also find the name of our contact at the FBI. He knows what we're doing and will make sure that if anyone asks, he'll back up your credentials. He'll also make other assets available to you as you need them. Feel free to call him. In fact, you might want to schedule a quick trip to Washington so you can get to know exactly how he might help us."

"OK, Richard," I said, "it's time for one of those questions. How did you manage this badge?"

"The Alliance, shall we say, has friends in high places. What makes this murder of special interest to them is that several prominent political figures were especially close, shall we say, with Stacie and they most certainly don't want their names linked with her or any other part of this investigation."

"Well, that explains a great deal. Do you think that one of them might have arranged her death?" I asked.

"We don't have a clue," said Sebastian. "As far as I can tell, most anyone is fair game in this plot: a Dionysian, a right-wing crazy, or a politico. Your guess, Ben, is as good as mine."

"Unfortunately," Richard added, "Sebastian is right on the mark with that statement. We just don't know who pulled this off. What the Abbot and his advisors are sure of is that the four of us are the least likely suspects. Ben, you didn't get to know Stacie enough to pull this off. Thomas has been too busy, as well as too supportive of her, to do it either. Sebastian has no affiliation with the Chicago thiasoi and has already proven his abilities on behalf of the Alliance.

I guess that leaves me, and no one thinks I would be able to have done it, for whatever that's worth."

"Don't worry, Richard," Sebastian said, "I can't speak for the others but I'm sure your hands are clean."

"Thanks, Sebastian," Richard replied, "and I agree with you."

"OK," I said, "let's see what the rest of this agenda holds for us. Richard, what's this dossier about?"

"Well," he answered, "Thomas and I have done our best to put together a list of Chicago Dionysians and those from elsewhere who have had frequent contact with Stacie, a list as best we can tell of who attended Stacie's book club and a list of Stacie's clients. When you read that, you'll see why the FBI was willing to get involved. We don't need to go into it now. It's just to give you a place to start." With that he pulled another package out of his briefcase and handed it to me. I didn't open it. Instead it went into my briefcase.

"Thanks, I can see I have some reading to do this afternoon. So what about the mansion?"

"First," said Sebastian, "we'll want to redo the forensics that the police did. I'm just not comfortable with thinking they were as thorough as they could have been."

"You're probably right, there," I said.

"And secondly," Richard added, "we have to make sure the mansion is secure and safe for us to use. We can't ignore the needs of the Chicago Brethren, we can't retreat from the necessary pastoral work of the Alliance, and we have got to find a priestess ready and willing to take over Stacie's work. The Abbot has some ideas about that but he and his counsel are waiting to see how things develop over the New Year. By then, they will have probably found Stacie's replacement. The idea is that she and Thomas will move in, unless that proves to be un-advisable."

"I guess that means that we'll be busy this week at the mansion, Sebastian. How soon can you get a start on the forensics with me?"

"I came to Chicago expecting the worst, so I'm ready now. I would like, though, to be able to get back to Atlanta for New Year's. With some diligence I think we can get most of the on-site work done by then."

"I agree," I said. "In fact, I've been thinking about going to Sarasota for New Year's. Richard, do you have any hesitations about that?"

"Not at all," he answered. "As a matter of fact Cynthia is on the short list to fill in for Stacie, so getting to know her might be a help for you. If the Abbot does give her the assignment, she'll have to know some of what's going on. Besides, whoever takes over as priestess for the Chicago thiasoi will have to help you contact the local Brethren for interviews. On the other hand, don't tell her we hired you until we are sure of who's taking over as priestess."

"OK," I said, while thinking about how concerned, and rightly so, Richard was about the covert nature of this job.

"So let's see," I continued. "That means we find an office, search the mansion, read the dossier, and develop a plan. Thomas, let's you and I meet this afternoon and figure out the office search. I'm going to ask you to find the place without me. OK?"

"Sure," he said, "I can handle that. In fact I'm sure we can find an Alliance realtor to help. We just won't tell him what it's for. He'll not ask anyway."

"And that leaves us with one last thing. What does the police report say?"

"Not much, I'm afraid," said Sebastian. "As I said, forensics found nothing and the interviews were poorly done."

"No surprise there," I said. "I was certainly unimpressed with the questioning I got from Detective O'Connor. It really is back to square one on all of this. I just hope they haven't done too much to obliterate what little evidence might have been there in the first place."

"That wraps up what I have," Richard said. "Anyone got anything else to add?"

"Not now," I said. "Sebastian, can you get us into Stacie's OK?"

"Yeah, I've got the keys. I've been working in the house to make sure that whoever is the next priestess is never out of sight and is well protected by cameras. If I've done my job right, you'll never see them and neither will any murderer. Like the rest of you, it's important to me that we find out who killed Stacie and see that justice is done. If we Dionysians don't do the job of protecting ourselves, nobody else will, that's for sure."

"And I'll be moving out of The Drake and into the mansion as soon as you guys give me the go-ahead."

"All right, team," I said. "It looks like we've got our work cut out for us. Thomas, can you come to my place at about three this afternoon?"

"Sure thing, boss," he said as a big grin spread across his face. "In the meantime, if you give me some travel dates, I'll get our agency to book you flights to Sarasota."

"OK," I said and pulled my calendar out of my briefcase. "See if you can make them for December 30th with a return on January third. Thanks."

"And Sebastian, can you come over as well?"

"Sure," he answered. "Just give me an address." I did and Thomas said, "We can go together, Sebastian. It's an easy ride on the Blue Line."

"If we're going to get a good start before the New Year begins, we'd better plan on working late tonight," I said.

"Looks like that to me," Sebastian said.

And so ended Richard's agenda, but not our work.

I spent the early part of the afternoon at home, reading the dossier and the police report. Richard was right; the list of Stacie's clients read like a who's who in City Hall, the State House in Springfield, and Congress. No wonder the police wouldn't do a very

115

thorough job, pagan priestess or not. This was one murder they'd want to forget about quickly.

As for the Dionysian list, there were some 103 brethren in and around the city and 27 people were listed as having attended the book club. I didn't recognize any names on either of the lists, but that was no surprise. Out of Chicago's population, 130 people would hardly be a noticeable number. Still I wondered if I could con Robert into letting Laurie join me or if Richard might have some other suggestions for clerical assistance. No matter how we worked it, there needed to be someone we could trust to keep the investigation's paperwork organized, the schedules synchronized, and the minutia of information collected and accessible.

I grabbed a pad of paper and began listing what needed to be done. Murder was hardly one of our agency's strong specialties, but there was really nothing new here that we hadn't tackled before. Just because it felt like looking for a needle in a haystack didn't mean the needle couldn't be found.

Thomas and Sebastian arrived at two, right on the dot. By then my list was rather long, but the three of us managed to organize it well enough that it seemed we'd at least be able to scope out the mansion. Sebastian suggested that I call my contact in Washington. I did and before I had hung up the phone he had arranged to have two forensic experts from the FBI at Stacie's the first thing on Monday morning, December 28. He expected that they'd be there two days and have a full report done by January 12. I couldn't ask for anything better than that. It was obvious that the Alliance had a lot more influence than I had ever guessed.

When I asked Thomas and Sebastian for their opinion on getting clerical help, Thomas was quick to chime in. "What do you think the Abbot assigned me to you for, Ben?" he asked. "That kind of work is just up my alley. Besides, what the Hell do I know about investigating murders? Tell me what you need and I'll get it done."

"Sounds good to me," I said. "Grab a notepad. Here's what I need now." With that I described creating a database of names from Richard's dossier and writing a short bio on each entry for the people he might know on the list.

With that taken care of, Sebastian and I agreed to meet at Stacie's the following morning. He'd give me a detailed tour of the mansion and a run-down on his security enhancements. By the time the cocktail hour rolled around, I have to admit that I was feeling quite good about our progress and Sebastian's abilities.

We ended at about 6 and I broke out the drinks, followed by a hearty meal at La Villa, an Italian restaurant on Pulaski just south of my house.

New Year's

The flight to Sarasota was uneventful and I decided it wise to rent a car. I hadn't found Cynthia's phone number, but I did call Thomas and ask him for it. "I might as well call Cynthia when I get to my mom's for New Year's," I told him, not volunteering that I was really making the trip to see Cynthia.

"Great," Thomas replied. "Be sure that you give them my love."

"To my mom or to Cynthia?" I asked.

"To both of them, you ninny," Thomas scolded. "To both of them."

When I had driven the seven miles from the airport to my mother's, I could see how devious mom could be. Who was there with her, but Cynthia? God, I thought, is this a conspiracy or what? I got a warm kiss from Mom and a wet one from Cynthia. Then I was informed that the three of us were having dinner at the O'Malleys' that night and that they hoped I didn't mind. I didn't, of course.

During dinner I asked what kind of plans there were for New Year's Eve. "Well," said Cynthia, "the older crowd is going to be at Reggie and Ann Franklin's for a party and the younger set will be at my place. Which is it for you, Ben?"

"Since I have no intention in throwing my hat in with the 'older crowd' I guess I'll have to ask you for an invitation to your place."

"OK," Cynthia said, "I guess we'll make an exception and let you join us."

"What do you mean by 'an exception?'" I asked.

"It's a joke. It's a joke," Cynthia protested.

"I hear there's been big trouble in Chicago," said Jack, Cynthia's father.

"Yes, you could say that, to put it mildly," I admitted.

"Ah yes," Jack replied. "If Stacie had known what was good for her, she'd have made less of a target of herself. All this proselytizing, even if it is cloaked in the guise of classical literature, is going to lead to no good."

"Now, Dad," Cynthia chimed in, "it was only a discussion club. Give her a break. You know, this isn't the Middle Ages."

"Middle Ages or not," he replied. "There are still plenty of fundamentalists who think that we're witches and that witches ought to be burned at the stake. Stacie's murder proves my point."

"Jack," his wife Estelle said, "it's the holidays and we have guests. It's no time for arguing. Have another glass of wine and forget it. Besides, it's hundreds of miles away. Nothing's going to come of it down here."

"Easy for you to say, Mother," said Jack, "but I knew these new tactics in recruiting would lead to no good, and I was right ." He picked up his glass and my mother changed the subject to Chicago weather.

Mom and I had a light dinner on New Year's Eve, since we were both headed out to parties. She gave me the directions to Cynthia's and the code for the gate to her subdivision, warning me not to drive home if I was going to be drinking. For herself she volunteered that she'd probably be staying in the Franklins' guest room since New Year's was no time to be out on the road.

I didn't ask "Staying in the guest room with whom?"

Half-way to Cynthia's there was a police road block. They were checking licenses, obviously looking for booze in the cars and people who had alcohol on their breath. I got through easily enough

120

but it did highlight Mom's warning. In any case I got to Cynthia's subdivision at 9:30 and used the code to open the front gate. Her driveway was filled with cars so I parked on the street, walked the short distance to her door, and rang the bell.

To say I was surprised when Cynthia opened the door would be an understatement. She was dressed, or should I say half-dressed, in a white leather corset that lifted and exposed her breasts, nipples and all. She was absolutely stunning and captivating. A long white skirt, parted in the front to reveal the insides of her thighs and her womanhood, flowed from her waist. Her hair tumbled down onto her shoulders and she wore a sparkling tiara and necklace to match. At the foot of all of this she wore thigh-high white boots. She was dressed to kill, to put it mildly.

"Don't just stand there gaping, Ben," she said. "Come in."

"My god, Cynthia, you look ravishing," I stuttered.

"Thank you, Ben, but isn't the proper word 'goddess'? In any case I fully intend to feed on you later. Welcome to a Dionysian New Year's." With that she closed the door behind me. I felt like my fate was happily sealed for the evening.

She immediately grabbed me, planted a big kiss on my lips, and said "I'm so glad you're here. Now please don't be shocked. You've caught us off guard at the height of our revelries and you're just going to have to go with the flow. Now don't forget our two rules: first names only and use protection when you fuck."

"Yes, Ma'am," I grinned, though I really wanted to say "OK, Mom," instead.

She led me through the living area and over to the kitchen where the breakfast counter had been set up as a bar. "Vinnie," she said to the guy who was obviously bartending, "this is Ben. Give this guy anything he wants. Just make sure I'm nearby when you slip him a mickey."

"Yes, Ma'am," he said and asked me "What'll you have?"

121

"Vodka and Seven," I replied.

"Is that vodka with Seagram's Seven or vodka with Seven-Up?" he asked.

I smiled and said, "Seven-Up, please. I think I had better keep my wits about me, at least for now."

Vinnie was even less-dressed than Cynthia, stark naked except for the black bow tie around his neck and the starched white cuffs with gold cuff-links at his wrists. I turned to Cynthia and apologized, "Gee, Cynthia, I wish you had told me it was formal attire."

"It's not," she explained. "It's formal non-attire. Now have fun and introduce yourself. I've got to keep an ear on the door. There's still about half a dozen more people who'll be here soon. After 10:15 we lock the door and no one comes or goes without my saying so. Now, dear boy, give me your keys and wallet so I can make sure that you and they are safe for the rest of the night."

I did as she asked and she handed them to Vinnie, who pulled a small paper bag out of a drawer, wrote my name on it and dropped the wallet and keys into it. With that he put it under the counter and said, "Thanks, now go party."

There were about a dozen people milling around the house and it was obvious that they were all dressed for sex. I felt really uncomfortable, though I'm not sure whether it was because I was over-dressed or intimidated by all the flesh. I guess it was both.

I took my drink and went to sit on the sofa. A woman came over to me with a man on a leash. She sat next to me and he knelt at her feet. "You must be Ben," she said. "I'm Rebecca and this is my slave Joseph. I've been wanting to meet you. That Cynthia always keeps the most eligible men to herself."

"My pleasure," I said. "May I call you Rebecca?"

"Of course, you can. After all, I hope we're going to become close friends." With that she put her hand on my thigh and rubbed it gently. "Now why don't you get comfortable and take off that shirt?" With that she unbuttoned the top four buttons and pulled it aside to reveal my chest. "How beautiful you are, under all of that," she assured me, and moved her hand to stroke my chest hair and brush a nipple.

I thought, "I really wish I had known what I was getting myself into. I wish that Mom would have at least warned my about how I should dress." On the other hand, I wondered if the silence was meant to ensure that my only recourse would be nudity. "Another 'Do as the Romans do' thing," I thought, and took off my shirt.

"That's better," Rebecca said. "Joseph, give Ben's shirt to Vinnie so he can put it somewhere safe."

"Yes, Ma'am," he answered and did as he had been told.

"That Joseph can be so good sometimes," said Rebecca. "I don't know what I would do without him."

Rebecca started to quiz me on the who, what and where of my life. She knew my mother, of course, and knew that I had met both Thomas and Richard. I remarked about that and she assured me that "There aren't any secrets in this group, honey. We just love our gossip."

Cynthia walked by escorting two more guests, looked at Rebecca and warned, "Now, Rebecca, you can enjoy Ben all you want, but remember he sleeps with me tonight."

"Sleep?" asked Rebecca, "Who's worried about sleeping tonight?" and then she laughed and added, "Cynthia, didn't your momma teach you to share and share alike? What kind of selfish person are you?"

"No more selfish than you, my dear," Cynthia said with a big grin and walked away. I wondered who the men with Cynthia were and figured that I'd have to get out of Rebecca's arms to find out, but that right now wasn't the time.

About twenty minutes later I heard the clanging and ringing of a tambourine from the other side of the house. Its sound came closer and then Vinnie appeared with the instrument and a woman I hadn't yet met. "Come 'round the fireplace," she announced. "It's time to light the season's fire." With that the crowd moved to the

123

fireplace where a pile of kindling and logs had been arranged. Vinnie knelt in front of it and the woman recited a short poem:

Assemble Brethren, one and all.
Answer when you hear the thrice-born's call.
Gather round his holy fire.
Let him fill you with strong desire.

Drink deeply of his vine's gift
And let it your spirits lift.
For he who has conquered death
Would ne'er leave you here bereft.

Be like the Helmsman of old
Of whom the poet Homer told
That he knew the god in human form
And urged that the god be not scorned.

He found favor with Semele's child
And found our god to be mild,
Unlike the pirates whose taunts and cries
Brought anger to the god's fiery eyes.

Let us now praise our king
That he may grant us these four things:
Joy and sight and heav'nly delight
And make us gods this very night.

With that Vinnie lit the fire, which burst into flame with surprising quickness. He and the woman turned to the assembled guests, bowed slightly, and walked away to the sound of the tambourine. The party resumed its chatter and the guests dispersed to whence they had come.

"Anna does that so well, don't you think, Ben?" Rebecca

asked.

I figured that a simple yes was all I needed to say.

"Well, in any case, we'll leave you to your own devices for now," she went on to say. "Don't be shy, dear. You're among friends, you just haven't met them yet, so go and do so." She stood up and left me alone to watch the action. I have to admit that I still felt out of place, but figured it would work out all right.

Cynthia spotted me on the couch and came over to sit next to me. "There," she said, "now that the invocation is done, I can relax. This crowd can take care of itself, that's for sure. I see that Rebecca has managed to get your shirt off. Follow me, Ben, and we'll see what I can find to help you fit in." We rose and I followed her into her dungeon, where one of the guys I had just seen with Cynthia was tying the other to her two-by-fours. Another couple, oblivious to what was happening in the rest of the house, was making out on the bed.

Cynthia opened a cupboard and found a leather jock strap, harness, boots, and cock ring. "Here," she said, "this'll have to do for now. I hope the boots fit OK. I'm sorry I didn't give you better warning, but I was sure you could handle it. Give your clothes to Vinnie and he'll put them away for you." With that she kissed me again and walked away. I stripped, donned what she had given me and, at least for the moment, I no longer felt out of place.

I gave Vinnie my clothes for safe-keeping and he offered to refill my drink. "Big improvement," he said, giving me the once over. "When I go off duty I hope you'll let me make you feel good."

"That can be arranged," I said, taking my drink from his hand and giving him a kiss.

With that I walked back to the dungeon to see how those two guys were progressing. The top had his bottom restrained and had begun flogging him lightly. I figured it was OK to watch, so I sat on that decorative chair and did so. The scene on the bed, in the meantime, had gone from necking to nudity to passion. I couldn't remember the last time I actually saw a guy fucking a woman in real

125

time. It seemed like it should be pornographic, but it wasn't. To be honest, the flogging was hotter.

I sat there and began stroking the jock strap and my cock beneath it. "Quite some party," I thought. "You've come a long way since finding that theology book. It's been some ride." The flogging became more intense; the bound boy groaned. Across the room, the woman groaned louder, as her partner pumped himself into her with wild abandon.

I sat there taking it in as my cock grew. "Hey, dummy," I thought to myself, "go get some action." I rose from the chair and moved towards the door. As I did, the guy with the flogger turned to me and asked "You next?"

I smiled and replied, "Could be. I'll see you in a bit." It was obvious that shyness was in scarce supply with this crowd.

Once out of the dungeon I decided to scout out the rest of the house. Two bedrooms were each being used for sex. The larger of them, the master bedroom, had sliding glass doors that led into the back yard. I quietly made my way past the three folks screwing on the bed and onto a patio. The rather large yard was enclosed in a privacy fence and obviously well-protected from neighboring eyes. To my left was a hot tub and near it a small bar, without a bartender, had been set up. The yard also had a swimming pool, a cabana , and lots of lush foliage. There was a three-way going on under some large tropical plants.

Rebecca was sitting alone in the hot tub and motioned for me to come over. I did. "Now, Ben, don't be shy. Take off that leather and come on in. Momma wants to get to know you." I doffed the gear and slid into the tub next to her.

"That's better, cousin," Rebecca said.

"Cousin?" I asked. "I haven't heard that term in this crowd before."

"No, Ben, you won't, though in many cases the Alliance is very much a family organization."

126   "How so?" I asked.

"Well," she answered, 'it's probably no surprise that all this sex does lead to some marriage, creating a crazy web of in-laws. More to the point, since it's necessary we keep our religion to ourselves, the safest place to find new members is within one's family, though even our own kin aren't always very receptive to our theology.

"In our case," she continued, "you probably don't know it, but we are cousins, second cousins to be exact. My grandmother was Margaret Caminsky McNulty, your great-uncle's oldest sister."

"Really?" I asked.

"Really," she grinned. "Now let's seal the relationship and become kissing cousins."

With that she leaned over and planted a deep kiss on my lips, her tongue doing its best to invade my mouth. I parted my lips for her. After a long mouth-to-mouth encounter, she stood up, straddled my thighs and sat on my lap facing me. Her breasts were full, her areolas large. Her arms encircled my neck and she pulled herself even closer to me. I had no choice but to put my arms around her, not that I was going to complain. I could feel her genital hair rubbing my dick and, in spite of the bubbling water of the tub, she began to arouse me.

"Come on, Cuz'," she said. "Let's go somewhere more comfortable." With that she stood up, took my hand and we walked to the cabana. There she picked up a towel and began drying me off, licking my face as she rubbed my torso, hair, and arms with the terry cloth. Then she dropped down and began licking the water from my crotch, while using the towel to dry my legs and ass. Quite an experience, to say the least. Finally she stood up, gave me the towel and said, "Here, you finish the job while I dry myself off."

In short order we were both dry and she told me to sit in a lawn chair. I did. She knelt in front of me and began sucking my cock. Her hands rubbed my thighs and torso. Out of what seemed nowhere, Joseph appeared and stood behind me. His fingers began caressing my tits and my cock stiffened even further. I tried to fondle 127

Rebecca but she stopped me, saying "Not now, Ben, let us do you. Consider it a welcome to the family."

Rebecca's ministrations to my prick were as good as any guy had ever given me. She kept her tongue licking my shaft while her head bobbed up and down on my dick head. Both her hands fondled my nuts and inner thighs. "Joseph," she paused just long enough to say, "go find me some lubricant and some condoms."

"Yes, Ma'am," he replied, left his place behind me and in no time at all put the items on the ground next to Rebecca. She stopped her sucking and put some lube on her left hand.

That done, she resumed her efforts on my prick and put her left hand under my crotch. I could feel her lubricated fingers tickling the rim of my asshole, then gently enter my anus with a soft wiggle. I groaned. "Relax and breathe, Ben," she said. "I don't want you to blow your load this soon." I leaned back, closed my eyes, and did as she said.

In a few minutes, though, there was another sensation. Someone's mouth was licking my foot. I opened my eyes to see who it might be. It was Vinnie, come to add even more excitement to my physical sensations. I was sure this would put me over the edge, but he didn't last long down there. Instead he stood up and returned the kiss I had given him in the house. His kiss was no peck, to be sure. While Rebecca kept up her cock worship, he began French-ing me in earnest.

I went to move my arms and Rebecca said, "Don't move. We know what we're doing," then paused, turned to Joseph and said "Make sure he can't move." Joseph left his post again and took slightly longer to return. This time he carried two lengths of rope and a blindfold. He covered my eyes and secured each of my arms to the chair. I wasn't going anywhere with this crowd in charge, and I didn't want to, either. It sure was one hell of a way to spend New Year's Eve.

Without the distraction of sight, I became ever more aware of the sensations on various parts of my body. Someone began some

128

kind of low volume chant, as much as humming as chanting. I heard several voices join Rebecca's, and even those whose mouths were arousing me joined in on the singing, their mouths acting like small vibrators on my tits, lips, and prick. Someone pushed my legs apart and the tongue of a second person joined Rebecca's. Her mouth, at least I think it was a woman's, sucked at my testicles, washing them with spit.

"Come on," a woman's voice said, "let's do this right." It sounded like Cynthia's. "Untie him and carry him to the bedroom with the sling." With that the ropes were loosened and arms lifted me out of the chair. I could feel them holding me tightly as we moved into the house. Within a short matter of time, they put me into a sling, fastened my legs high into the air, and tied my hands behind my back.

Someone's fingers applied even more lubricant to my anus. Someone else offered a glass of wine to my lips. I heard a tambourine being gently tapped and the chanting increased in volume. Numerous lips planted kisses on my face, my tits, and my feet. Two people were giving my thighs a tongue bath. Some male stood between them and rubbed his swollen cock against my now wet hole. He teased my ass open and entered me, pounding it to the beat of the tambourine. Two or three others began clapping in time to the beat. Someone said "Fuck him, fuck him with your holy phallus."

Someone else whispered in my ear "Let the god enter you. Let Dionysos penetrate you." The fucker withdrew and someone used a dildo on me for a short while, followed by another man or maybe the first. Then there was another drink of wine, another fucker (I could tell it was a different man, as he was much larger where it counts), and another dildo, another dildo, and on and on. Between the fucks and the drinks I found myself getting drunk and my ass exhausted. The crowd, at least it felt like a crowd, kept me on edge, never letting me come, as the intensity of the sex and frenzy of the tambourines and chanting grew. It was revelry and orgy. New Year's 129

Eve had turned into an ancient Bacchanalian frenzy.

I grew dizzy. I lost my sense of time and place. I saw demonic faces drifting in and out of my field of vision, faces that stared at me, faces of demons and angels. Dionysos, his beautiful cock at my asshole, appeared to me. It was he that was fucking me. The voices around me demanded that I let the god enter me. I saw him and said, "Fuck me, my Lord. Fuck me,"

The crowd said. "Let the god come in. Let the god come in."

And he did.

Chapter

Back to Work 13

The flight home on Sunday was crowded, uncomfortable and noisy with families, but at least the weather didn't delay us and I got home at a decent hour. I was certainly ready for my own bed and a chance to recover from the New Year's trip. Needless to say it had given me a lot to think about, but frankly the investigation was enough in itself. I decided I had to plunge into the work on Monday morning, so before I went to bed I called Thomas at The Drake. "Come to the house at ten am," I said. "No sense starting too early," and he agreed. I called Sebastian, who had just gotten back from Atlanta, and told him to come over in the morning as well.

The late start gave me a chance to gear up for the day with coffee, the paper and a chance to collect my thoughts. Most of what I wanted to do was to finalize the office, get a run-down from Thomas of the people on the lists, and then Sebastian and I had to decide whom I should interview first.

Thomas had done his job well, with short bios on almost everyone and the requisite contact information as well. He had also found a two-room office in the South Loop's Monadnock Building on West Jackson Boulevard. "The Alliance will have it furnished by Tuesday afternoon," he said, handing me keys to the small suite. "The phones will be turned on by then, and the number will be listed as 'Benson & Hartcliffe, Brokers.'"

Thomas spent the rest of the morning giving Sebastian and me his impressions of the who's who he had compiled. We decided to start the interviewing on Wednesday evening. We'd start with the

131

leadership of the thiasoi and Stacie's closest friends. Doing so would help us test our interviewing techniques, refine our questions, and (hopefully) gain us some trusted allies to support the investigation.

That left us with a short list for starters: James Friedman, Casey Bronson and his wife Ariadne, and Michelle Stanislov were all leaders in the Dionysian community, and three more people-- David Mantzios, Christine Davis and Marjorie Cummings-- were Dionysians who had attended Stacie's book club meetings. Thomas would contact them that evening and arrange for me to meet with each of them individually. Sebastian would make sure I was wired for sound. We decided that Stacie's home would be a good place to hold the interviews with the Dionysians, but the office would be better for the book club attendees. We hoped we wouldn't have to talk to the politicos, since that would increase the risks of their scrutiny.

We spent the rest of the day writing a questionnaire to guide the interviews, and talking about the progress Sebastian had made with security, as well as his reaction to the forensics the two guys from the FBI had done. "All in all," he said, "they were quite thorough and very tight-lipped about it all. They did a lot of fingerprint collecting. They scraped up a lot of blood and are going to see what the DNA might tell us. Only time will tell whether they found anything worthwhile."

"But it's only Stacie's blood, right?" asked Thomas. "Just her DNA?"

"Well," I said, "if the murderer got excited it might contain some of his or her sweat. You'll never know what they find until the lab reports come back."

By five we were ready to call it quits. Sebastian was ready to head back to the hotel and I asked Thomas if he wanted to have dinner with me. His answer, of course, was yes, but he added "I'd better not, if I'm going to catch anyone on the phone tonight." That left me alone for the night, and frankly I was glad to have some time to myself.

The next morning I called the University of Chicago and asked for Dr. Hirschberg's office number. The operator gave it to me and then transferred me to his secretary. "Dr. Hirschberg is retired," she said, "so he isn't in the office every day, but I can give him your phone number."

"Will that bother him?" I asked.

"Not at all," she replied. "In fact he likes to keep his hand in things, as he is fond of saying. I'm sure he'll talk to you." I gave her both my office and my home numbers, thanked her, and hung up.

To my surprise the phone rang not more than five minutes later. The voice on the other end was heavy with a German accent and asked for me. "This is he," I said.

"Good morning, Mr. Kramer. My name is Dr. Günter Hirschberg and my secretary said you called. How may I help you?"

"Well, Doctor, I was hoping you would be kind enough to answer a few questions for me about the Bacchanalia. Would it be possible for me to meet you in Hyde Park sometime?"

"Well," he said, "I am sure that could be arranged. When would you like to do so?"

"Are you free anytime this week?" I suggested.

"Yes," he replied, "at my age one has lots of free time. When and where would you like to meet?"

"I'm afraid you'll have suggest a time and place, Doctor," I said. "I'm not really familiar with the campus, since I live on the Northside. Would the library do, or do you have a favorite coffee shop?"

"I tell you what, Mr. Kramer. Is this afternoon OK with you?"

"That would be good, Doctor. Where?"

"Come to my office in the Department of Classics. It's at

133

1115 E. 58th Street and I'm in room 311. Is one p.m. a good time for you?"

"Certainly, Doctor. Thank you so much for your time. I'll see you then."

It was a clear but very cold day in the Windy City. I reviewed the bios of those on the short interview list and took a few minutes to write down a list of questions that I wanted to ask Dr. Hirschberg. I had a quick lunch just before noon, drove south on the Kennedy, crossed to Lake Shore Drive at I-55, and arrived at the University and Dr. Hirschberg's office right at one. I knocked on his open door and he bid me "Come in," and rose from his desk to shake my hand. He pointed to a chair where I could sit and said "Have a seat, Mr. Kramer. How may I help you and what makes you interested in the Bacchanalia, if I may ask?"

I wasn't sure about how much I wanted to reveal about the Alliance, so I skirted the real answer with the reply "I went to see my mother in Florida over the holidays where I had a discussion with a cousin about the rites of Dionysos, including the Bacchanalia. She had been reading Euripides's play and suggested to me that there are secret cults that do the same thing today. Now I've got a smidgen of education about the classics and found her premise intriguing but difficult to believe. I was hoping a scholar such as yourself might throw some light on the subject.

"I know that according to Livy the Roman Senate outlawed the Bacchanalia in 186 B.C. If that is the case, was the cult eradicated or could it have survived?"

"Ah, yes," he said, "there are always rumors of hidden cults and secret rites. If they are hidden and secret, how is one to know of them?" he asked. "But as for the decree in 186, the textbooks often fail to mention that the Bacchanalia was revived around 50 BC, during the reign of Julius Caesar, who repealed the Senate's ban."

134   "Oh," I said, "that explains how ruins in Pompeii could

have been decorated with Dionysian rites a hundred years later."

"Mr. Kramer," the doctor said, "you jump to the simple conclusions of the uninformed, though since your statement merely reflects the sentiment of more than a few, you ought not to feel ashamed. Those ruins of which you speak certainly point to a revival of some kind in the worship of Dionysos, and Caesar's repeal of the ban implies their survival at least into the Christian era, but we cannot tell what the mural in the House of the Mysteries really demonstrates. It could illustrate for us some point of belief on the part of the owner of the home, but it could just as easily have been an artistic endeavor with little religious meaning. In any case we have little information to aid in deciphering exactly what the artwork is meant to portray."

"So you don't think the cult survived the Fall of the Roman Empire and continued into the Christian Era?" I asked.

"Hardly," he answered, "though that is not to say that fertility rites, phallic worship, and religious-motivated orgies haven't been found on occasion over the centuries. The Knights Templar, after all, were accused of such practices in the late Middle Ages."

I fumbled for the note that held my questions, unfolded it and asked "What would a Dionysian initiation have looked like?"

"Now, Mr. Kramer," he said with a grin, "you remind me of my class in Classical Roman Religions. There was always at least one student who sought that answer.

"We know that the postulant took an oath of secrecy concerning all that he would see and hear in the course of the ceremonies," he said. "He then most likely learned the cult's sacred history. The myth was probably already known to the neophyte, but he was now given a new, esoteric, interpretation of it—which was equivalent to revealing the true meaning of the divine drama. The initiation was preceded by a period of fasting and mortification, at the end of which the novice was purified by lustrations."

"What is a lustration?" I interrupted.

"Oh, it's a purifying ceremony, such as baptism in a Christian Church, or penance.

"At a certain time in his initiation the candidate partook of a ritual banquet. At the period with which we are concerned, this immemorial practice had chiefly an after-life meaning. It was by virtue of his initiation that the neophyte became the equal of the gods. Apotheosis, deification, 'de-mortalization' are concepts that are familiar to all of the Mysteries, including those of Dionysos.

"By Caesar's time, the public cult of Dionysos had been 'purified' and spiritualized by the elimination of ecstasy, so that in fact we find two parallel Dionysian liturgies, the public ones and the secret ones, which we call the Dionysiac Mysteries.

"The mythology, the sites of the cult, and the monuments, all pointed to Dionysus' twofold nature, born of divine Zeus and a mortal woman, persecuted yet victorious, murdered yet resuscitated. At Delphi his tomb was shown, but his resurrection was depicted on many monuments elsewhere. He had succeeded in raising his mother to the rank of an Olympian; above all, he had brought Ariadne back from Hades and married her. In the Hellenistic period the figure of Ariadne symbolized the human soul.

"In other words, Dionysus not only delivered the soul from death; he also united himself with it in a mystical marriage. Gaining this immortality was the heart and soul of the Mystery.

"In Euripides's play, " Dr. Hirschberg continued, "The Bacchae, Dionysus proclaims the Mystery structure of his cult and explains the necessity for initiatory secrecy:

'Their secrecy forbids communicating them to those who are not bacchants,' says Dionysos to the King.

'What use are they to those who celebrate them?' Pentheus asks.

'It is not permitted thee to learn that, but they are things worthy to be known'.

"In the last analysis, the cult's secrecy was well-maintained. The texts referring to the liturgical service have almost all disappeared, except for some late Orphic hymns. The archeological documents from the Hellenistic and Roman periods are numerous enough, but the interpretation of their symbolism, even when it is accepted by the majority of scholars, is not enough to throw light on what took place during the initiation.

"There can be no doubt of the closed structure of the Dionysiac congregation or community. The texts refer to sacred dances and ritual banquets in front of Dionysiac caves; on the other hand, they also state that the ceremonies take place at night to ensure their secrecy. As for the rituals themselves, we are reduced to guessing.

"The central act of the initiation was to invoke some feeling of the divine presence, probably through music, chanting, dance, and perhaps drugs to induce ecstasy, an experience that engendered belief in an intimate bond established with the god.

"In the modern Western world such a religious experience is, of course, inaccessible. For, unlike the mysteries, Christianity has ignored the sacramental value of sexuality. The same could be said of the Dionysiac ritual meals, when the initiates, crowned with flowers, surrendered to a joyous intoxication, regarded as a divine possession. It is difficult for us to grasp the sacredness of such rejoicings as they anticipated the otherworld bliss promised to initiates into the Mystery of Dionysus."

"So the orgy and the drunken-ness led to revelation of some kind?" I asked.

"Yes, that is exactly the case. Induce ecstasy so that the candidate has a vision of the god and an experience, fleeting though it might be, of immortality. We suspect that the wine was spiced up with herbs and mushrooms to induce visions and hallucinations. It is certainly what some would today call 'false spirituality.'"

Dr. Hirschberg was certainly both wordy and academic, but shed no light on Dionysians in America.

I was left with one last question. "Is it possible the cult is still to be found?"

"It has, my friend, been extinct for centuries," the doctor replied, "and of that fact we can be certain."

The simple fact, I thought as I left his office, was that whether Dionysians were directly descended from the ancient Greeks or some neo-fabrication didn't make much difference. They were here, had wealth and power, and one of their priestesses was dead.

On Wednesday night I interviewed the first local Dionysian. His name was Casey Bronson and he was one of the elders of the thiasoi. His bio said he was 53 and married to Ariadne, another local Dionysian. He and his wife had both joined the cult in their early 20s, which is where they had met and after several years married. Both had been steady, devout and active Dionysians ever since.

During the interview Casey, ruggedly handsome with dark but graying hair, was friendly, relaxed and obviously concerned about the brethren in the city. Though he hadn't been to any of the book club meetings, he was generally supportive of Stacie and was visibly shaken by her death. As an elder he had easy access to the mansion and actually lived just around the corner from it. Talking with him made it clear that he wasn't a suspect.

He spoke freely to me about his involvement in Dionysianism, he said because I had come "highly recommended by both Thomas and Richard and someone, God damn it, has to help us get to the bottom of this. Until the murder is solved, we'll be walking on pins and needles and, quite frankly, none of us is going to feel safe." I checked him off as a safe ally and asked him to help us when he could.

"I sure will," he said. "I'll do anything I can to safeguard my Dionysian family. Good luck, Ben. I think you're going to need it."

Next I had a similar talk with Ariadne and, as I expected, concluded that she was on our side. No evidence so far. "These interviews," I thought after Ariadne had left, "are going to take a lot longer than I expected."

In the meantime Thomas arranged for me to interview the remaining members of the top list, and he and Sebastian began to get the mansion ready for the new priestess, whoever that might be.

We planned for Thomas to come over to my house on Friday for a drink, and then we'd head somewhere for dinner. With high expectations I was looking forward to seeing him socially. I made sure the house looked OK and took a peek at the dungeon as well. No time like the present to spring that surprise on him, I thought.

Did I think "surprise?" Right on time the doorbell rang and I went to open it. Well, Thomas had pulled a fast one on me. You can hardly imagine the look on my face when who should be standing there but Cynthia. "Hello, Ben. How nice to see you again," she said.

With that, Thomas looked around from the side of the front door, handed me two bottles of wine, and said, "It sure is, buddy. I hope you don't mind that I've invited a mutual friend to dinner."

In spite of my amazement I somehow managed a "Not at all. Come on in."

I set the bottles on an end table, left them in the living room as I took their coats and threw them on the bed in the guest room, and returned to two of the biggest smiles in the world. "Sorry, Ben, but when I heard that Thomas had you all to himself tonight I couldn't resist crashing the party."

"Well," I said, "after I get over the shock of your being here, I'm sure it will all work out well. But what the hell are you doing in Chicago in January? I thought that was something that a resident of Florida would never do."

"It's a combination of events that made the decision to come to the Windy City in winter unavoidable. Someone needs to help Richard with the estate as well as counsel the brethren who are reeling from this tragedy. We're approaching Bacchanalia and with Stacie's murder the Dionysians in Chicago were left without a priestess, and when the Abbot asked me to fill in I said yes. And how could I not take advantage of this chance to see you? I can't just sit idly by and let Thomas have you all to himself now, can I?"

"If you put it that way, I guess you had to come up. It may be a surprise and all the circumstances might not be agreeable, but seeing you certainly is," I responded. "Now I promised Thomas a drink before dinner. What would each of you like?" I asked.

"Make mine a Scotch, neat. It's been a tough week," said Thomas.

"I'll have the same," said Cynthia.

"OK, guys, make yourselves at home and I'll see what I can do," I said as I headed to the kitchen. I poured myself a vodka on the rocks and yelled into the living room "Dewars or Glenlivet?"

They both answered "Glenlivet" and Thomas added "Make mine a double."

In no time at all we were sitting comfortably in the living room. I looked at them both and wondered what would happen next. I decided that an innocuous question would be most appropriate. "How's my mom, Cynthia?" I asked. "What's she doing these days?"

"Fine, as usual," she replied. "I tried to talk her into coming north with me but she said she had had enough of winter to last the rest of her life. 'Besides,' she told me, 'you don't need me to be around when you and Ben have a chance to be together.' I guess she thinks we're hitting it off."

"God," I said, 'if she could only see the three of us now. How does all of this fit into the scheme of things?" I asked, forgetting that I might be opening a real can of worms with that kind of remark.

"Don't sweat it," said Thomas. "We Dionysians are used to all kind of strange arrangements. Your mother would be surprised if we didn't get together, at least for dinner, and it's well-known in the Alliance that two's company and that three is never a crowd."

"Now Thomas," Cynthia chimed in, "don't rush Ben's education. You know I'm perfectly able to take a taxi back to the hotel alone, if that's what's best. Far be it from me to weasel in between two handsome men and their tryst."

I think I blushed at that idea, but if I did, either no one noticed or they were both polite enough not to point it out. In any case, Thomas chirped right back with "And what makes you think that these two handsome men might not want to take you on together?"

I thought she would have slapped him right there and then, but she didn't. Instead she raised the ante, so to speak, by saying "As if you two could."

"Wait a minute. Wait a minute. Don't I have a say in this?" I asked.

"Don't worry, Ben," said Thomas. "Cynthia and I are used to this sort of banter. It happens all the time. Nothing will go on that's not agreed to, though it might be that a couple of drinks and a good dinner might just make agreeing that much more easy. I did say, didn't I, that Dionysians are mostly in it for the fun?"

Before I could answer, Cynthia chimed in with "Dinner? Did someone say 'Dinner'? Now there's a novel idea. Where are you two studs taking me?" It was a welcome change of topic.

"What would you like, Cynthia?" asked.

"A good steak" was her quick answer.

"There's a place over on Milwaukee that I think you'll both enjoy. Great ribs, good steaks. It's a local hangout so tourists like you will get a real taste of Chicago cooking."

"Sounds good to me," said Thomas. "Just let me finish my drink in peace and I'll be ready to go."

That calmed some of the sexual tension for a moment but it sure didn't keep my libido from reminding my mind that there just might be more to come.

We drove to the Gale Street Inn on Milwaukee and dinner was up to my usual expectations. Thomas and Cynthia were pleased as well. We started with another round of drinks, though this time

I opted for a soda. I used the excuse of "designated driver" but in truth I wanted to keep my senses about me. No sense getting wasted, I thought. After all, I didn't want to agree too easily.

Of course I didn't need alcohol to help me agree -- and I suspect that my dinner partners didn't either. The problem was all about my feelings for them. I knew that sex with Cynthia would arouse my desire to serve her, to worship her, and yes to love her, even while I worried about how doing so would affect my feelings for Thomas. I kept thinking that I couldn't have my cake and eat it too, while that is exactly what I wanted to happen.

I sat there with a list of questions a mile long and decided that I had to have some answers. It was just possible, wasn't it, that they were using my lust to seduce me into their insanity? Or worse, were they using it to lure me into murder? What exactly was the group about, I wondered. Where did their wealth come from? Were they serious about temple priestesses and Greek myths? Even as I thought that, I hoped that such thoughts were utter nonsense. And then my conscience reminded me that Stacie was dead.

As pleasant as dinner might be, as friendly as Cynthia and Thomas seemed, Stacie's death hung about us. Not just death but murder, and not just murder but murder by some bizarre ritual. As the flood of fear and doubt rolled over me, Cynthia turned and asked "You're awfully quiet, Ben. Are you all right?"

I paused, caught between a polite "Sure" and the torrents of thoughts that flooded my mind. The pause grew longer and I knew that its length was an answer in and of itself. I took a breath and confessed. "There are just too many questions and Stacie's murder doesn't help answer any of them. To be honest, I've spent a lot of time researching what the experts say about Dionysians and what little I found marks Dionysianism as a dangerous cult, filled with anarchy, debauchery, and murder.

"But when I think of the accusations that Livy wrote about this cult, I think of the two of you and my mother. You're all such decent people, liberated and fun-loving, with a secret life that any man with healthy hormones would envy.

"OK, I'll let it all hang out, even if I don't know what it means. I want you both, but those words fill me with terror. How can I not be quiet? You saw *The Sun-Times*. You went to Stacie's funeral. You know why you have to keep the Alliance's secrets. I'm sorry to have ruined dinner for you, but you asked and that's the answer."

Now it was their turn to pause. We three sat there in silence. After all, as much as this was difficult for me, Stacie's death was a much more deeply personal tragedy for them.

"We understand you, Ben, and we're sorry all of this has involved you," said Thomas, "but before we go any further, let me put my cards on the table too. Cynthia and I love you. We've talked about you more than once and want you in our lives. I know that sounds sudden but you are family to us. The Caminskys have been family to us for as long as we can remember and it would be a shame for you not to be part of our history. But mostly it's about real love, godly love, even if some right-wing bastard calls it harlotry."

"Look, Ben," Cynthia chimed in, "we'll do our best to answer your questions. Why don't we try to do so when we get back to your place. You fire away and we'll answer. No booze, no sarcasm, no sex, just answers as straight as we can give them."

"Well," I answered, "that sounds good to me, as long as the no sex part doesn't count after you finish with my list."

That took off the pressure, at least for the rest of dinner and for the ride back to the house. When we were again settled in the living room, Thomas asked "So what do you want to know, Ben? We're all ears."

"Well, Thomas, I took your advice and researched texts in the library. This week I met with Dr. Hirschberg. There wasn't much that I could find, but let me start with some of what I did find. The most damning piece was from Livy. Give me a minute and I'll find

143

the quote."

All of what I had collected was actually sitting on the dining room table so I grabbed the stack, found the pages I had copied at the library and read him what Livy had to say about Dionysian murder and secrecy.

"Sounds pretty straight-forward to me. Is this the kind of religion you have?"

"No," Cynthia said rather bluntly. "Livy was using the same kind of lies that people have used against us for centuries. He was writing and quoting lies that were cooked up because the establishment couldn't face the idea of a religion that was out of the Senate's control. Don't forget that the state was the established religion and the oligarchy that ran Rome was a mixture of noble families and priests that were in cahoots with each other. Of course they had to condemn the Bacchanalia. It was outside their control and they couldn't abide that.

"You see, Ben, the basic conflict is one of power. Hierarchies of priests, rabbis, ministers, and imams think they have got to maintain their power and control over revelation. Let the common people have visions and let them prophesize, and the power of the religious hierarchy is over, caput, the end. You can see the same thing with Luther and the Church of Rome. Rome opposed Luther because he threatened its power. Of course Rome didn't want the Bible translated, because if it were, the Pope would lose control over the faithful."

"OK," I said, "I get that. But what about these drunken orgies and the ripping apart of animals to eat their meat raw. Sounds too far out for me."

"And it is far out," said Thomas. "It's far out because you think we take myth seriously. On one level, of course, we do. Myth teaches. Myth explains. Myth reveals secrets in ways that mundane language can't. But myth is myth. It is story meant to do just those things. But do we think that some god named Zeus appeared to Semele, got her pregnant, and then later caused her to burst into flame? Hardly. It's just as much a myth as a snake telling Eve to eat some apple. In its day and its context it worked. In the twentieth century, I don't think so, even if the truth it tries to teach still has meaning.

"Those meanings, of course, have to be interpreted in light of the times in which they are found. There are eternal truths, to be sure, but that doesn't mean that we can't and don't see truth in different lights at different times.

"Face it," said Thomas. "When Christianity took over Europe, what was left of the nature-based religions--Druidism, the worship of Baal and Astarte, Mithraism, and the like-- were doomed to extinction. But of course it wasn't only Christianity that did them in. Patriarchy and urbanization had their hand in the demise of fertility rites and the role of priestesses as well."

"We don't mean to preach at you, Ben," Cynthia said, "but fundamentally it's a matter of power and who has it. Religions such as ours encourage personal empowerment and the freedom that goes along with it. When you meet the gods in ecstasy, you realize that you are, in fact, one with them."

"Not only one with them," interrupted Thomas, "but one of them. In that way Christ was one of us when he said 'The Kingdom of God is within you.' In fact Christ's message isn't so far different from ours. It is the power structure of the Church that distorted his message. It was the betrayal of the Gospel to subjugate the faithful, not the Gospel itself, that created popes, cardinals, and yes even priests to rule their congregations, to come between them and the gods they love."

"Whoa," I said, 'you've got priestesses. What makes you so different?"

"We've got priests, too, Ben. But our priests are only facilitators that help us to know the gods when the gods possess us. And when you know the god in us, you meet the god in yourself and know that just as we are both human, we too are both divine."

"After all," said Thomas, "what is that desire you have to   145 worship the one you love if it's not the desire to love and worship yourself? Sex is the natural vehicle for true worship and that's why the monotheists, in the final analysis, are so anti-sexual. They know that sex is worship and they cannot allow that to be so, because if you don't worship the god they use to control you, they lose their power over you."

"OK," I admitted, "so you've got a radical theology of personal empowerment but to get right down to it for me, do you or do you not sacrifice -- you know, kill animals on an altar and eat their flesh?"

"You mean like we did tonight at the restaurant?" asked Cynthia. "Of course we do, Ben. Do you mean do we murder children and those who oppose us? Of course we don't. The other thing that we don't do is take the fact of sacrifice -- that is to make something holy -- and sanitize it and repackage it into a mere shadow, a simple, rote activity devoid of passion and reality.

"You do know, don't you, that Catholic priests perform the sacrifice of the Mass? They've taken the power of life-blood and diluted it into a parody of its former self under what they call the appearance of bread and wine. That's not to say that we don't have rituals of bread and wine, because we do. It's an historical fact, though, that our bread and wine festivals are at least 300 years older than theirs."

It was a lot to think about. It made sense to me but they had flooded my mind with a torrent of new ideas. I knew that they had presented a new way of thinking to me that actually helped to make sense of what I had learned since my first trip to meet Richard in Cincinnati. For now, though, I had had enough talk.

"I think," I said, "it's time for a drink."

With that I got up, got three wine glasses out of the china cabinet in the dining room, a corkscrew out of the kitchen, and opened one of the bottles that Ben had given me.

"Let me pour it, Ben," he said. With that he took the bottle out of my hand and filled the three glasses. As he handed one to

Cynthia and then one to me, he said, "Let the party begin and let the gods come in."

It was delicious monastery wine. As I drank it, I realized that these two believers really did make sense, even if they were the most counter-cultural couple I had ever met. The truth is that my own sexuality had made me counter-cultural years ago, a struggle I had been living with ever since I found myself attracted to the guys in the locker room. Only now was it beginning to make sense and explain why, beneath the disguise of a successful account executive, I was so different.

I held the glass in my hand and looked into the blood-red liquid it held. A certain peace came over me, one I hadn't felt since the day I had discovered that I was different, a day long buried in my childhood, a day without a date, but with a feeling that I had lived with ever since. Only now did that day begin to make some sense.

I was no longer the only one who thought that there had to be more to sex than breeding, that there was something inexplicable sacred about sex, that the mainstream religions that surrounded me, though in the majority, had their theology of sex all wrong.

I took a sip of the wine and smiled at my friends. My eyes misted. I raised my glass to them and said "I love you both. Now what the hell do I do?"

Cynthia stood up, put her glass down and came over to me. She took my glass out of my hand and set it down as well. Putting her hand on my shoulders she planted a wet kiss on my lips. As her tongue poked its way into my mouth, Thomas moved behind me and surrounded me with his arms while he gave her as much of a hug as possible. We stood there in that comforting embrace for as long as we could but eventually Cynthia nudged Thomas away and backed off a bit from me. "We love you, too, Ben. Now take us to your bedroom," she said.

"I've got something a little better," I said. "Come with me." I led them into the kitchen and down the stairs to the basement

147

where I took them into what I called my dungeon. "It's not very fancy," I said, "but it's all I've got."

"It's wonderful," said Cynthia.

"Just like home," smiled Thomas.

The room was dimly lit with track lighting and I had painted the walls a dark gray. One wall had a few hooks from which my small collection of floggers hung. Another wall had an assortment of two-by-fours with eyebolts screwed into them. Nearby hung about a dozen lengths of rope.

"You rogue, you," Thomas said . "You never let me in on this secret."

"Dionysians aren't the only ones with secrets," I replied. "Give me a break. It takes a while to spill all the beans. Where should we start?"

"Thomas," said Cynthia, "be a dear and run upstairs and get those bottles of wine. We're gonna have a party." By the time Thomas returned, Cynthia and I had taken off our clothes and were making out on the bed near the floggers.

"No fair," Thomas complained. "You've started without me."

Chapter

The Covenant █14█
Church of the Holy
God

T he next morning I realized that in spite of being a
man who lived alone, buying a king-sized bed had been a good
idea. Here I was sprawled on the mattress with Thomas on one side
and Cynthia on the other. It had been a wild and crazy night in
the basement. I'd had one or two three-ways with men before but
last night certainly took the prize for spice and variety. Perhaps this
multi-partner thing could work. Oh, well, I thought, the cat's out of
the bag now. No use worrying about it.

I debated as to whether I should crawl over Thomas or
over Cynthia to get out of bed or just lie there until one of them
woke up. My bladder suggested that I get up now and my early
childhood training suggested that I should do it soon. We had had,
after all, more than one bottle of wine. I took the gentlemanly route
and mauled my way over Thomas, who woke up, said "Hi" and
went back to sleep.

I grabbed a robe as quietly as I could and answered nature's
call. From the bathroom I went downstairs to the kitchen to make
some coffee. It was nearly ten a.m. While the pot was brewing,
I went to the front porch, grabbed the paper, and settled down at
the kitchen table. In a short time I had a cup of coffee in hand and
began my Saturday morning read-the-paper ritual. By the time I was
half-way through the local news section, Cynthia came downstairs,
kissed me good morning, said "I must look like the wreck of the
Hesperus," and asked where I kept the coffee cups.

She took a cup out of the cabinet, filled it and sat at the 149 table. I noticed she drank it black. "Want sugar or cream?" I asked, just in case she didn't like black coffee.

"No thanks," she answered. In another gesture of manners, I folded up the paper and smiled at her.

"You know, you're as good looking in the morning as you are just before dinner."

She smiled at me and asked "You OK, Ben? That was a pretty intense night."

"As a matter of fact, I'm surprisingly fine. A little dazed at the turn of events, but no worse for the wear."

"I'm glad to hear that. I can imagine that Stacie's murder would make anyone wary of getting involved with us now. I just hope it doesn't start another round of witch-hunting. I know the brethren I've talked to this week are walking on pins and needles. Whoever did this dropped horrible memories of the Dark Ages squarely into the psyches of our members. It will take us years to get past it all and back into some semblance of feeling safe. Several of the believers even went so far as to tell me 'We told her so.'

"As you well know, more than one Dionysian was against her book club. They thought she was all too ready to invite in people who could easily be up to no good. Unfortunately, it seems like they were right."

"Perhaps," I said, "unless it was done by an insider, someone who wanted to prove to the Alliance that Stacie was wrong, dead wrong."

Just then we could hear Thomas walking down the stairs. "Started again without me, huh?" he smiled. "Where's my cup of coffee. Someone should have served it to me in bed."

"You chauvinist pig," Cynthia replied. "Quite the contrary, you should have offered me coffee, while dutifully kneeling at the side of the bed."

"Yes, Ma'am. I'm sorry, Ma'am," he said jokingly. "Shall I get you a second cup, your majesty?"

150   "No thanks, minion," she said. "You're not good enough to

do that for me. Besides, it's nearly 10:30 and we have a lot to do today."

"How about I treat you both to breakfast at IHOP?" I asked. "I'd cook something for you here, but this bachelor refrigerator isn't used to being filled with eggs."

"OK," said Thomas, "as long as we get to it sooner rather than later."

"No problem," I said and then added, "I'll even save you cab fare and drive you wherever you need to be."

"That sounds good to me," said Cynthia. "I've got to meet Richard in Rogers Park at one. Sebastian told me that we can clean up the house now that the detectives have made a complete mess of it."

It was nearly 12:15 when I paid the IHOP bill, giving us just the right amount of time to drive up to Stacie's home. One interesting development did come out during the breakfast: Cynthia invited me to opening night of *The Bacchae*, Euripides's play about Dionysos in Thebes. Coincidently the script they were using was the same as the one I had just read in Evan's book, *The God of Ecstasy*. I assured her that I would be there and wrote myself a note so I wouldn't forget the date.

As we neared Stacie's we couldn't but help but notice the church message bulletin board outside The Covenant Church of the Holy God: "'and thrust thee through with their swords' Ezekiel 16:40." You could feel a shiver go through the car.

"My god," Cynthia said. "Did you see that?"

"I sure did," answered Thomas.

"It's just some pastor using *The Sun-Times* headline to get some publicity," I said.

"Maybe," Cynthia shuddered, "but it sure is weird, not to mention exploitive."

"Well, let's pay him a visit in the morning," Thomas said. "It might be interesting to hear what he has to say."

"Yeah," said Cynthia, "as interesting as putting your hand

into a hornet's nest to see if they sting."

"I'm game if you are, Thomas," I said.

"Give me a break, guys, will you?" Cynthia chimed.

"Oh come on, Cynthia, maybe we'll learn something about how those fundamentalists think."

"I know how they think, Mr. Murray. No thank you."

By then I was parking the car on Stacie's street. Cynthia asked if we wanted to come in and Thomas and I both declined, so she kissed us both good-bye and walked up the stairs and into the brownstone.

On the drive down to the Gold Coast, Thomas apologized that he would be busy that night, since there were a lot of things he had to do for the soon-coming Bacchanalian festivities. He also apologized that even as well as he and Cynthia knew me , there were still Dionysian secrets that he couldn't share with me until I had been initiated. I told him that I understood, though his admission only stoked more of those damn doubts.

By the time we had arrived at The Drake, it was obvious that Thomas was serious about going to that church, so I said I'd pick him up at 8:15 the next morning. I kept my fears to myself, wondering what those folks would think when two guys walked into their church together. Then I remembered that they would probably be glad to see us, thinking that their message board had lured some poor souls from the brink of Hell into their Bible-based salvation. Sometimes, you know, curiosity gets the best of you and this certainly seemed like one of those times. I hoped they wouldn't get the idea to stone two faggots right after the sermon.

I spent the afternoon interviewing Dionysians. Nothing came of it except that I met a few more very likeable people.

The next morning Thomas was waiting for me outside The Drake and we made our way north to the church in record time.

I had forgotten that Lake Shore Drive would be nearly devoid of traffic on a Sunday morning in January, so we sat in the car for about 15 minutes, not wanting to walk in early enough to let rabid evangelicals ask us any questions.

By the time we ventured into this den of Christians, the organist was playing a classic hymn. The congregation was surprisingly young, I thought. The church was a rather simple Baptist-type structure. No statues, non-descript and cheap-looking stained glass, and no kneelers. At least the pews were more comfortable than I would have expected. But then what did I know? I had only been in a church for the few times that friends had gotten married and once for a funeral of an older guy from work.

I winced when some guy from the congregation walked up to the pulpit and read the complete quote from Ezekiel:

Wherefore, O harlot, hear the word of the Lord: Thus saith the Lord God; Because thy filthiness was poured out, and thy nakedness discovered through thy whoredoms with thy lovers, and with all the idols of thy abominations, and by the blood of thy children, which thou didst give unto them; Behold, therefore I will gather all thy lovers, with whom thou hast taken pleasure, and all them that thou hast loved, with all them that thou hast hated; I will even gather them round about against thee, and will discover thy nakedness unto them, that they may see all thy nakedness. And I will judge thee, as women that break wedlock and shed blood are judged; and I will give thee blood in fury and jealousy. And I will also give thee into their hand, and they shall throw down thine eminent place, and shall break down thy high places: they shall strip thee also of thy clothes, and shall take thy fair jewels, and leave thee naked and bare. They shall also bring up a company against thee, and they shall stone thee with stones, and thrust thee through with their swords. And they shall burn thine houses with fire, and execute judgments upon thee in the sight of

153

many women: and I will cause thee to cease from playing the harlot, and thou also shalt give no hire any more.

That was followed by a short hymn of praise, sung by a rather good tenor. In spite of the music, I shuddered to think about what was coming next. I looked at Thomas and got the idea that he felt the same way I did. In short order the minister, garbed in a choir robe and with a purple sash around his neck, went over to the pulpit.

"My brothers and sisters," he began, "it is not very often, in fact it is seldom, that *The Sun-Times* puts words from the Bible, which you have just heard, on its front page. The horrific tragedy that our neighborhood has been forced to face gives us all reason to pause. I need not, I am sure, recount to you the details that the Times printed in Thursday's paper. Surely this house of God is no place for such language. Yet lust and violence, it would seem, have reared their ugly heads just down the street. I know that many of you, just as I, cannot fathom such danger and depravity so close to home. What makes it all the more insidious is that whoever has brought the evil of murder so near to us has done it, it would seem, in the name of our Lord.

"And yes, it is true that those are words from our Holy Scriptures. True, also, is that the Old Testament speaks of such wrath more than once in its pages. What are we to learn from all of this? How can we find the love of God in such writing? 'They shall stone thee with stones, and thrust thee through with their swords,' Ezekiel says. Harsh words. What shall we make of them?

"Let us remember, too, that fire and sword were not only used by the Hebrews against the Canaanites. The Romans used them against our forefathers in faith, the Christians of their time. The Spanish used them against the Jews during the Inquisition. They were used against witches in Salem, Massachusetts. Even in our time, Hitler used them against Jews, homosexuals, and even the retarded and handicapped. As you see, these are not words that come only from the prophets of the Old Testament."

With that he paused. I wondered where he was going. After all, I wasn't getting the brimstone I had expected. Soon the pause ceased. He went on.

"Let me continue, Brethren, by reminding you of our Lord's path: 'And as you would that men would to you, do so them.' And in Matthew, 'Then Jesus said to him, "Put your sword back into its place; for all who take the sword will perish by the sword."' Let us be guided by the words written to the Galatians, 'For the whole law is fulfilled in one word, "You shall love your neighbor as yourself."'

"I know that some of you who are here today might have expected another reading of the Gospel, one that says 'Stacie got what was coming to her,' but that is not the Christ I know, nor the God who knows us

"I do not know who brought this evil to our neighborhood. I do know that the Father of us all reminds us of his deep and unfailing love. I implore you today, I exhort you today, I remind you today that no matter the depth of the tragedy, no matter the severity of your fears, God is love. Just as we know he loves us, our divine Father loves Stacie and the criminal that killed her. It is that, my dear brethren, that you need to remember today.

"It is hard to remember such a truth when *The Sun-Times* blares a story that reeks of hatred, religious or otherwise, from its pages. Take your lesson not from the front page of a newspaper, but from the word of God. I cannot explain to you what took place down the street, nor will I try. I have no rationale for such violence, nor for such hatred. I have only the comfort of my faith in God. 'For now we see in a mirror dimly, but then face to face. Now I know in part; then I shall understand fully, even as I have been fully understood. So faith, hope, love abide, these three; but the greatest of these is love.'"

With that he turned and walked away from the pulpit. I don't know what Thomas thought but I was left dumbfounded. 155

Once the service had ended we did our best to leave the church with as little fanfare as possible. We were no sooner in the car than Thomas said "Well, I guess that sermon showed a different side of Christianity. It reminds me that I need to be careful about painting pictures with strokes that are too broad."

"Yeah," I agreed, "that minister certainly didn't conform to my expectations. My treat for breakfast?" I asked.

"Thanks. That sounds good to me, but Richard insisted I come back to the hotel after our excursion this morning. I'm not sure what the crisis is, but I'd better not disappoint him. He is really in the center of this storm, and I think it just may get worse before it gets better."

"OK, back to The Drake it is. When can I get you alone with me again?"

"I'm not sure but I'll call you later this afternoon and we'll see what works. Is that fair?" Thomas asked.

"Sure," I replied and drove him back south. The rest of the ride was relatively quiet as each of us got lost in our own private thoughts.

When I got back to the house I remembered the note about the play and marked the date, February 17th, on my calendar. It was a Wednesday and the dark of the moon. I wondered what the significance of that might be. I'll have to ask Cynthia or Thomas, I thought to myself. The sky was clear and the weather had turned cold again. There wasn't much to do, except those usual weekend chores around the house, so I put on a load of laundry and read through another of Uncle Jonathan's journals. I also called my mother to see what she was up to, as I hadn't heard from her in a while.

Mom, as usual, didn't have much to say except that everything was fine. She asked a few questions about the funeral and such and we talked about my seeing Thomas, whom she knew only in passing, and Cynthia, whom, of course, she knew well. I made it a point to leave out the details.

By three o'clock I was bored as hell and wondered if I could track down Cynthia. Then I remembered that Stacie had written her phone number on the card she had given me. I wondered if Cynthia was still at Stacie's and figured she had to be there or at the hotel. I tried the hotel first and left a message with the front desk after she didn't answer her room phone. However, she was at Stacie's and glad to hear from me. We chatted a bit and she asked about the church service.

I replied "I'll tell you what. Let's do dinner and we'll talk about it."

"That would be wonderful, Ben," she answered. "I need to get out of this place for some fresh air. What do you suggest?"

"Well, if it's fresh air you want, there's a nice Mexican place in Boys Town that you might like, if Mexican is OK. They have lots of windows that face on to Halsted. It's as close to outside as you want to be in Chicago in February. What do you think?"

"You're on. Shall I meet you there?" she asked.

"No need for that," I replied. "I'll pick you up. Can you be ready by 5:30?"

"Sure," she said. "I'll clean up here at Stacie's and be ready for you then. See you at 5:30."

"OK, see you in a while," I said.

As I hung up the phone I wondered what I would tell Thomas if he called. I certainly saw that this swinging lifestyle, if that's what you could call it, would take some getting used to, but I wasn't up for a three-way every time I turned around. Besides, having to juggle two lovers felt a little overwhelming,

I left the house at 4:40 and Thomas hadn't called, which meant I didn't have to tell him about dinner with Cynthia.

As she came down the brownstone's front steps, I re-experienced the passion that had surged through me in her dungeon. "God, you're hot," I said as she and I planted a "welcome" kiss on

157

each other's lips.

The ride to Las Mananitas, the Mexican restaurant with windows on Halsted, was filled with idle chit-chat: my phone call to my mother, February in Chicago, the rehearsal schedule for The Bacchae. It was as if we were old high school friends simply catching up on the week's news. You'd never guess that we had spent all of Friday night together, much less together with Thomas.

The traffic on the Drive was heavier than it had been that morning, but the real problem, as usual, was finding a parking spot. I landed one not too far away and we walked hand-in-hand to the restaurant. "What if some of the guys see me?" I wondered. Oh well, bisexuality has its risks, I reminded myself. If anyone demanded I turn in my gay card, I'd offer them a blow job. That would earn it back.

After silently laughing at my own joke, I turned to Cynthia and turned my private joke into a mutual one. She laughed at the ridiculousness of a gay card, then asked how she could get one. "Got to lick some pussy, girl," I said, "or move in with a woman the day after your first date."

"I'd rather move in with you and Thomas," she admitted.

"You'll never get a gay card that way," I warned. "On the other hand it might get you the Fag Hag of the Year Award."

With that we entered the restaurant, were seated, and, ignoring the peril, I ordered a pitcher of margaritas. "Want your glass salted?" I asked.

"Sure," Cynthia said, "'cause that will make me thirstier for more." In no time at all we had our drinks.

The big smile on her face only turned me on more. I wondered how she'd handle edgy language, then decided that was a stupid question, and gave her a typical faggot response. "Don't fret about that, Cynthia, I'll satisfy your thirst with a nice big load later."

"You cad," she retorted, "that's no language for polite company. Lucky for you, I avoid polite company. You're on, fucker,

158

if you think you're man enough."

"Hey," I said, "I bet you're woman enough to make me man enough." I raised my glass and she raised hers. "Here's to later, you sex goddess, no matter what the Fates have in store."

"Amen," she said.

"Speaking of amen," Cynthia continued, "what did I miss this morning?" With that she got a full rendition of the Covenant Church's Sunday service. "Well," she said at the end of my story, "that doesn't mean that some other right-wing bastard didn't do it."

"You're right about that," I said. "I'm sure there's more than one church where that sermon would never be heard."

Our waitress came back to see what we wanted to eat. I picked up a menu and asked her to come back in a few minutes, handing the menu to Cynthia and picking the other one up for myself. "It's all good," I assured her. "I do my best to avoid bad Mexican."

We sat there in silence until we put down the menus. As if on cue, our waitress returned, we ordered, and I added more margaritas to each of our glasses. "So how's the clean up going?" I asked.

"Shit, it's hard work," Cynthia admitted. "I mean it's not hard like in heavy labor. It's hard because of the sadness of it all. Cleaning up blood is no fun, especially when it is one of your best friend's blood.

"But it's more than that. It's harder than that. I probably ought to keep this to myself but, Ben, I have got to tell someone and you're the someone. What really scares me is that Stacie wasn't murdered in her first floor dungeon, the one she would have used with a paying client. I probably ought to change the subject but Stacie's body was found in the basement."

"Why does that mean you should change the subject?" I asked.

"Because we don't tell the uninitiated about the caves in which our rites are performed."

159

"Caves in Chicago?" I asked. I felt bad that I hadn't told Cynthia that I already had seen every inch of the house, but I thought I had better heed Richard's warning about silence. He was, after all, still the client paying for all of this.

"Traditionally," Cynthia explained, "Dionysians have worshipped in underground caverns both for secrecy and because Dionysos descended into Hades."

"Yes," I said, "I remember some reference to rituals in caves and Dr. Hirschberg spoke of them. I guess I never gave it any thought that you all might still be using them."

"Well," she went on, "'cave' isn't exactly the right word. The word 'cavern' is better. If we can locate a hidden natural cavern, so much the better, but these days what Dionysians usually do is dig out a cavern under a hospitable house. In fact, Stacie's house has had a man-made cavern underneath it for more than 60 years."

"So why is that a problem?" I asked.

"It's a problem because as far as we can tell, the only people who would have known about that subterranean dungeon would have been initiated Dionysians. The detectives would have learned that when they questioned any Chicago members of the Alliance."

"I still don't understand why," I admitted.

"Why?" Cynthia said. "Because the entrance to the cavern was pretty well hidden and no mere client would have any way of knowing about it. Thomas, Richard and I have strong evidence supporting the fact that we were a long distance away the night the murder was committed, but each and every local Dionysian is a suspect. Hell, even the three of us might be suspected of having hired the killer.

"The web of trust among us all has been shredded." Cynthia closed her eyes and breathed deeply. Her face was distraught with fear and grief as tears welled in her eyes. I watched as the strong and confident professional melted before my eyes.

I reached across the table and took her hands in mine. "I'm sorry. I am so sorry," I said, not knowing any other words.

"You need not be sorry, Ben," she insisted. "You are a breath of fresh air, even fresher than a February breeze off Lake Michigan." With that she wiped her eyes with her napkin, took another breath, smiled, and raised her margarita. "Here's to a happier time, as it will surely come."

"Here, here," I said, tapping my glass with hers. "I tell you what. After dinner come back to my place and have a good cry on my shoulder.

"No thanks," she smiled. "I'm coming back to your place for deep kisses and a good fuck."

"You're on, you sottish hussy. You're on." And then the waitress brought our appetizers and the food helped us forget about the blood in Stacie's basement.

Halfway through my enchiladas I wondered if Thomas had called and what he would have thought when I didn't answer the phone. There was more than a touch of guilt about my not being home. Either it showed on my face or Cynthia could read minds because she looked at me and said "A penny for your thoughts."

Now I felt even more guilty. How could I tell her that I was thinking about Thomas? Then I decided that if I didn't, I'd make matters worse so I let her in on my thoughts. "Thomas," I said, "and I feel guilty about doing that."

"You really needn't," she replied. "He knows where we are and told me to say he was sorry he hadn't called you."

"What?" I asked.

"Well, he called to see if I was all right and I told him we were going out for dinner. What's the big deal about that?"

"None. I guess," I admitted.

"Look, Ben. This three-way stuff is just that. You're going to have to get used to it. Whereas the Christian world cheats, or wants to cheat, all the time, we don't, and we don't because of the simple fact that you can't cheat if nothing's hidden. You see, sex

161

isn't something we ration. In fact, not only is it not rationed, it's not forbidden, it's not hidden, and it's not a reason for shame or guilt.

"I know that's hard for you to imagine but think of it this way: for us, lust is a virtue. I mean it's a celebration of the most beautiful entity in the universe -- ourselves -- and the most sacred act in all of history -- sex. Thomas isn't worried about what we're doing. Ask him. You'll see. And don't be disappointed because he isn't worried. He knows that what you're doing with me is a kind act of love and caring. After all, I really did have to get out of the house.

"As for the sex, Thomas loves both of us. He really loves both of us and that means he wants both of us to be happy. He wants us satisfied. You see, Dionysian love is liberating. His love won't let him pin you down, make you his, or demand that you restrict yourself, your pleasure, or your love only to him. We Dionysians feel sorry for someone who thinks they can love only one person, because the truth is you can love and have sex with as many people as you like.

"What you can't do is use your love to control them and make them limit their love only to you. And, yes, sometimes it's not about love at all. Sometimes it's just about good old-fashioned lust, pure, animal desire, the rutting and the fucking that comes from the fact that we are flesh-bound animals just as certainly as we are spirit-filled beings. We are who we are and to pretend otherwise is the real deception, the real cheating."

"God," I said, "there sure is a lot to this Dionysian stuff."

"Yes, dear, there is, but you'll get the hang of it. Now enough of your guilt. Eat your refried beans. They're getting cold."

Of course, now I knew why Thomas hadn't called and, if nothing else, at least I didn't feel bad about missing his call. I did, on the other hand, feel good about the woman I was dining with. I hoped it wasn't some kind of Dionysian sin that I would have her all to myself tonight.

We skipped dessert and drove back to my place. I parked the car in the garage and we walked up the back steps into the house. Once inside I asked "Upstairs or downstairs?"

"That depends on how well you know how to use your whips on a woman," Cynthia said, which is the last thing I thought she would have said.

"Well," I answered, "I'm certainly no slouch with them, but why does that matter?"

"Because I don't want to cry on your shoulder. I want to cry on your wall and you're going to help me to do it with a really nice flogging." With that she slithered up to me, put her arms around my neck, slathered me with a kiss and said "Now you will do that for me, won't you, big boy?"

"I guess I will if you want me to, but that does seem like a strange request. Wouldn't you just rather get naked and put that lust you spoke about to good use?"

"Of course I would, you nit-wit. It's just that a good catharsis will make us both horny, or don't you know anything about sadomasochism?"

"You win. The basement it is," I said.

"Now, now," Cynthia chided. "You watch. We're both gonna win in this round." She took my hand in hers, turned toward the stairway and led me to the dungeon. I tell you that woman was some piece of work, to be sure, and the more I knew about her, the better I liked what I knew.

When we got to the dungeon I lit candles and asked her what kind of music she liked. "What do you have?" she asked and came over to the stereo cabinet. She began picking through my small assortment, found a cassette of Mozart's music and handed it to me. "This'll work," she said, handing it to me and began to take off her blouse. I started the music and took off my shirt and undershirt. Then I grabbed her by the waist and began kissing her. "Your flogging can wait. I want to warm up first," I said.

"I know that. After all, we've got all night," she said.

163

"Well, not really all night," I corrected her. "After all, I do have to be at work in the morning."

"Now, you're not going let something like work get the best of you, are you? After all, one night without sleep won't kill you at your desk in the morning."

"OK," I answered, "you win," pushed her down on the mattress and we pulled off our clothes.

By the time I had her tied to the two-by-fours on the wall, my cock was raging stiff and dripping pre-cum. Fuck my gay card, I thought, and chose a deerskin whip from the collection hanging nearby. I hung it about her neck, put my arms around her, massaged her breasts while standing behind her and rubbed my raging hard-on into the crack in her ass. Then I moved back about three feet and caressed her back with the flogger, slowly at first, and building up the intensity. The strokes of the whip began to bring a little color into her flesh so I chose a flogger with a little more bite to it. I could see her body move into the beating as we both moved to the music and the pounding of the flogger. I paused to touch her back and kissed the nape of her neck. I rubbed my chest against her spine and dropped the flogger to the floor.

I moved my right hand into her crotch and gently rubbed her labia. "Hurt me. Hurt me," she whispered with a subtle plea. I moved back again, picked up the flogger and let her have twenty hard strokes. This was some broad, I thought, as her back turned from pink to red. I turned to the wall where the whips hung and chose an old buggy whip. I began to let it sting her slowly and then intensified its impact. I knew from experience that the red lines it drew on her flesh would hurt.

I was right. Cynthia began to moan. I took that as a sign to lay it on harder and her sounds moved into screams. She instinctively tried, to no avail, to pull away from the whip's impact. Soon she began to cry. I slowed down my pace a little, hoping to extend the tears without drawing blood or welts. Her tears turned to sobs. I kept

164 up the slow beating until she was silent, a sign that she had met her

limit and the sorrow in her heart had been touched.

I untied her, led her to the mattress and held her tight as she cried in my arms. I began licking her tears with my kisses and she returned the kisses with passion. My fingers penetrated her pussy and I rubbed her clit with my fuck finger. She began to writhe in pleasure and moaned that she loved me. I rolled her onto her back, grabbed a condom from the table next to the bed, and rolled it on to my raging cock. It took no time at all for her writhing to turn to bucking in an intense moan-filled orgasm. God was she fun to ride.

I pushed myself off her chest and savagely pumped my dick into her. She was helplessly spread before me and the god within me ravaged the victim under me with the thrusts of my cock. My body became that of Dionysos, the avenger, and he roared his divine majesty into the universe.

Then I fell again on top of her and pulled her closer and securely under me. Her arms reached around me and her tongue probed my mouth. Her body tensed in another violent orgasm. I had to do my best to not come myself. I knew that if I shot, I'd be useless for at least an hour and I had no intention of not prolonging this moment as long as I could.

Cynthia slowed her movements and I lay quietly on top of her, my prick nestled inside of her. Neither of us dared to speak as a serene peace filled the air. When my hard-on subsided, I rolled off of her, and she cuddled up next to me. Her breasts rested on my side and one of her legs straddled mine. "Thanks, Ben," she whispered. "That was exactly what the doctor ordered."

"Let's go upstairs," I suggested. "I bet there's more where that came from."

"You're right about that," she said. "Besides, mister, all that humping made me really thirsty. I want to drink that load you were bragging about at dinner."

Strange Mail 15

In spite of her threat of making me pull an all-nighter, Cynthia and I actually got a good night's sleep. We shared a pot of coffee the next morning, cleaned up, and walked to the "L." We rode the O'Hare line to the Loop and parted. She took the Howard-Dan Ryan back to The Drake and I went off to work.

Thomas was already in our new office and Sebastian arrived soon after I did. We reviewed the interviews I had done on Saturday, increased the number of names to be scheduled and planned out the rest of the week.

Richard dropped by later that afternoon to see how things were going. He got a full report, seemed assured and told us to keep up the good work.

Since it had been on my mind, I asked him how much or how little I could tell Cynthia about the investigation. "Don't worry about it, Ben," he said. "The Abbot decided that it would be impossible to keep what's going on from her so you're free to talk to her about it. Believe me, she'll be discreet, and helpful as well."

When I got home that evening I called the hotel so see how Cynthia was doing, only to be told that she had checked out. So I called Stacie's and there was no answer. Worried, I called Thomas and didn't reach him either. I thought about trying to reach Richard but didn't like that idea very much. Besides, I thought, there's a good explanation for what's going on and there's probably nothing wrong. Knowing them, there's another meeting or a rehearsal for the play or dinner on the town. They are, after all, here on business.

I took a deep breath, made myself a vodka on the rocks with olives, and began hunting in the kitchen for what might be dinner. I didn't find anything that looked appetizing so I decided to chill out with my drink and find another journal to read.

After the first ten pages or so, I decided that I was hungry after all and went back to the kitchen to get some cheese and crackers. Fifteen pages later I had polished off the snack and made myself another vodka. I guess it was about seven pages after that that I fell asleep on the couch. I hadn't planned it that way, as I had only set the journal down to rest my eyes.

It was about two a.m. when I woke up and went upstairs to my bedroom. I was a little miffed that no one had called but not angry enough to stay awake. I made sure the alarm was set, doffed my clothes, and fell back to sleep rather quickly. This time, at least, it wasn't on the couch.

The good long sleep wiped away both my worry and my anger. I took the "L" down to the Monadnock office to review more bios. At about three in the afternoon, Thomas called. "Where've you been?" I asked. "Oh, sorry, Ben, but I've been swamped with one meeting after another. Busy tonight? Richard gave me the night off."

"Sure," I answered. "Is Cynthia all right? Why did she check out of the hotel?"

"She decided that Stacie's place was more to her liking, now that it's almost back to being inhabitable. It's closer to the place where they're rehearsing and she has to be up there for meetings with the Brethren anyway."

"That makes me feel better. I was worried."

"Yeah," said Thomas, "I guess we really should have clued you in on what we were doing, but I forgot. I'm sorry. Can I make it up to you with dinner?"

"You sure can," I said. "My neighborhood or yours?"

"Doesn't matter to me. You're the boss, so you decide."

"Well, if you put it that way, then I'll meet you at my place.

Plan on spending the night."

"Sure will," Thomas replied. "Want another lesson?"

"OK," I said, "but only if it includes something more than theology."

"Don't worry, Ben, Dionysian lessons always include practice with the preaching. I'll see you at 6:30. Is that a good time?"

"I'll be home before six, so make it at six," I said.

"Will do, guy. See you then." With that we hung up and I turned my attention to the papers on my desk.

The doorbell rang at six and I opened the door for Thomas. The way he smiled at me said a great deal about his feelings. He stood there with a sheepish grin on his face, his briefcase in one hand and flowers in the other. He handed me the flowers.

"Gee, Thomas," I said, "what will the neighbors think when they see a man bringing flowers to a man?"

"I guess they'll think it's true love; don't you?" he asked. "What's wrong with that?"

"Nothing," I said, giving him a kiss right there at the front door. "I just wanted to make sure it wasn't a bribe."

"Whatever it takes, cutie pie," he grinned. "Whatever it takes." With that he came in and we had cocktails. By now I knew not to ask. It was Glenlivet neat for him and a vodka for me.

"So what's new in the cult world of Dionysos?" I asked.

"God, we're busy. Let's see. I guess the big news is that the autopsy came back. The police gave it to Richard and he gave it to me to give to you." Thomas handed me the report. "In a nutshell," Thomas said, "it says that Stacie was drugged with Flunitrazepam."

"A mickey, huh? That explains how the murderer got into the Temple. With Flunitrazepam, Stacie would have told him anything, including where the altar was."

169

"Other than that, the report just said she was knifed to death, but we all knew that. Not even any sexual molestation. Murder, pure and simple, pre-meditated at that. No unusual fingerprints, no dirty or broken glasses, no blood or skin under her fingernails. Whoever it was came in, not even leaving a fingerprint on the doorbell, had a drink with Stacie, knocked her out, did her in, and then washed the glasses and put them away before he or she left.

"I wonder if the Feds will tell us the same. Their report is due this week, too, isn't it?" I asked.

"Yes, tomorrow to be exact. Let's change the subject."

"Fine by me," I said. "So what were you all doing last night? I tried to call you and Cynthia and all I got was that she had checked out of the hotel."

"Over the weekend members of the thiasoi demanded a meeting so we called it. They wanted to know what we knew. We told them what we could and that the Abbot had sent Cynthia to act as their priestess until a permanent one could be found. They liked that idea and it became very clear that at least some of them wanted Cynthia to take over Stacie's role for good."

"Cynthia said she'd think about it, especially since there are several priestesses in Sarasota and now there are none here, at least none with her level of expertise. Besides I bet she wouldn't mind being closer to you, even if she had to put up with Chicago weather.

"So what are our plans for dinner?" Thomas asked.

"Let's just walk down the street and bring home some Chinese," I said. "Is that OK with you?"

"Sure. It'll give us more time for sex and won't ruin my expense account for the week."

After dinner Thomas wanted to know where my head was at when it came to the Alliance. We had talked several times since I had gotten back from New Year's, both about the gang fuck and my visit to Dr. Hirschberg. "You know, Ben," he said, "you're getting closer and closer to knowing the god within you. Cynthia told me about your roaring like Dionysos while you were fucking her. That's pretty close to knowing how we feel, when the god enters us."

"I didn't feel any god enter me," I said.

"I know you didn't, buddy. It's just an expression. It really means that you experience your own godliness, your own divinity. Didn't you feel like a god when you were plowing Cynthia? Didn't you feel like Dionysos was plowing you when you were in the sling in Sarasota?"

"Well, if you put it that way, yes," I admitted.

"Then I think it's time we made you an anazititis, a seeker."

"What does that do?" I asked.

"It means that you've begun the process of becoming one of us. You'll take vows of secrecy and be given the first of several initiations. It also means that the members of the thiasoi will meet you as not just a detective but as one of us. You'll be given the chance to get to know them as real people, not just suspects. Two people will be named your friends, to guide you in the process, and two, who will remain unknown to you, will be appointed your detractors. It'll be their job to try and find reasons not to allow you in the thiasoi, that is, to not allow you to learn the deeper mysteries of our faith.

"With Bacchanalia so close, this is a good time to proceed because you'll be able to party with us."

"Will Cynthia stay in Chicago for good?" I asked.

"Cynthia said she'd stay here but wanted it to be on a temporary basis so that everyone, herself included, could reconsider their options in six months. I think she really doesn't want to leave the thiasoi in Sarasota but knows she's needed in Chicago for a while. The fact that you're here and that I'm here as well makes it easier for her to stay."

171

"When I met you I thought you were leaving Cincinnati for the monastery."

"Yeah, you're right about that, but Stacie's murder has changed everyone's thinking about my future. I'm going to move into Stacie's with Cynthia. No one, myself included, wants her living alone in that house. On the other hand, it is Alliance property and we can't easily walk away from it."

"Alliance property?" I asked.

"Yes," he said. "They may look like regular homes from the outside, but the fact is that taking on the role of priest or priestess for the community means that you get to live in what for all intents and purposes is a Dionysian temple."

I wondered if every house, then, was the entrance to a cavern-- but something told me not to ask. Instead I said, "So will the Bacchanalia be celebrated at Stacie's?"

"Only partly," Thomas replied, "as it includes all kinds of celebrations: theatrical, festive, and religious. We'll have a modified Bacchanalia, as it's too cold to go romping in the woods. Are you ready to join us?" I took a deep breath and paused for a moment. I think it was more for dramatic effect than from a delayed decision. Thomas waited. There was a bit of the imp in me and I enjoyed watching him wait and sweat. I finally broke my silence.

"Yes, Thomas, I am. I'm ready to become a Dionysian," and I smiled.

He broke into a broad grin as well and wrapped his arms around me. "That's great. Welcome to the family," he said and planted a big kiss on my lips. We sat there and made out on the couch for a few minutes and then Thomas came up for air and said, "This calls for a special bottle of wine. Go get some glasses and that corkscrew of yours."

At about 11 am on Thursday morning I wondered what

Cynthia was doing and on the spur of the moment called her from the office. "Hi, this is Ben," I said when she answered. "What have you been up to?"

"God, I've been busy," she replied. "Between rehearsals and Brethren coming over to convince me to stay in Chicago, it's been one hell of a week."

"Well, can you find time for me?" I asked.

"As a matter of fact I can. How about I cook dinner for you tonight?"

"That would be great," I said. "What time?:

"Oh, come over about 6:15. I've got a five o'clock appointment that will end by six. You can watch me cook while we have drinks and catch up on the news."

"Sure thing," I said and we ended the conversation on that note.

Later that day, Fedex delivered the FBI report. I read through it and learned that indeed there had been two kinds of DNA in the samples. One was Stacie's. The other belonged to a man. Until we could test a suspect's DNA, we wouldn't whose DNA it was, but at least we had one more clue to persuade a jury.

After work I took the "L" home and drove over to Stacie's. I parked the car near the front door, went up the steps and rang the doorbell. Out of curiosity I tried the door knob to see if it was locked. It was. In a few minutes Cynthia opened the door for me and I went into the foyer, where she gave me a warm hug and really good kiss.

"Honey," she said. "Did you drive over?"

"Yes," I said. "Why?"

"I'm sorry to bother you, but can I cook for you at your place? I've really got to get out of here."

"Sure thing, Cynthia," I replied. "Are you ready to go now?"

"I sure am. Just let me get my things for dinner and I'll be out the door." With that she practically ran back to the kitchen and reappeared with a picnic basket and a bottle of wine. "Take me

173

away, Ben," she said, "I'm all yours."

I broke into a big smile, said "Yes, Ma'am" and we were in the car in no time at all. Once the car was moving, Cynthia closed her eyes, folded her hands in her lap and took a deep sigh. I could tell something was wrong but decided that silence was the best course of action for right now. She'll talk when she's ready, I thought, and was just glad to be with her and that she trusted me enough to want to be with me.

The 25 minutes or so to my place were quiet and uneventful. When the car finally pulled into my garage, Cynthia turned to me, smiled, and said "Thanks, Ben. I needed that." She bounded out of the car and I grabbed the basket while she carried the wine into the house. Once inside she said "Make me a drink, will you? I need one."

"Sure," I said, "but only if you'll tell me what's up."

"Of course I will, Ben. You know that. Just make it a double."

I went to the cupboard and got two glasses, filled them with ice, and then decided that I had better ask her what she wanted. "Got any more Glenlivet?" she asked.

"Of course I do," I answered. "How else can I keep Thomas coming back?"

She smiled broadly and said "Right, as if the only thing Thomas gets from you is expensive Scotch. Give me a break. I know what part of you he likes best and it doesn't yet come in a bottle."

I grinned back, empted the ice from one of the glasses into the sink, and poured her a neat double. I stuck with my usual Absolut. We clinked our glasses together and toasted "To Dionysos."

"OK, cutie," she said. "you sit and I'll talk and cook. Just watch how domestic I can be."

"Yeah," I replied, "like a lioness," and took a sip of my drink. For her part she pulled an apron out of the basket and put it on. Then she said "Do I look like June Cleaver, or what?"

"Yes," I answered, "you look like 'or what,'" and smiled back, set down my drink and said "I love you," just before I gave her another big kiss.

174   With that, she shuddered and started to cry. I held her for a few

minutes and then she pulled away, wiping her eyes with the bottom of the apron. "I'm sorry, Ben," she said.

"Now don't go apologizing about a few tears," I said. "You've probably earned them. What happened now?"

With that she opened the basket and pulled out an opened envelope. "This came in the mail this afternoon," she said and handed it to me. It was a plain envelope with Stacie's address on a mimeographed label and a PO box return address. I pulled the contents out of it and found a church bulletin from the Broadway Community Church, which wasn't the church that Thomas and I had visited. It looked like any other church bulletin. The outside was a message full of Bible quotes and the inside was the Sunday's service and announcements.

"What do you make of this?" I asked.

"I don't know," she said, "but I do know that Stacie would never have joined a Christian church, nor have signed up for their bulletin. Someone at that church was out to convert her and I find that very scary."

"Yeah," I agreed. "Sometimes even a church bulletin can be hate mail. What do you want to do about it?" I asked.

"I'm going to see what Richard thinks, but I bet he'll say to give it to the police detectives, and then they'll just file it with the rest of their notes and that'll be the end of the story."

"Do you want me to go with you when you see Richard?" I asked. "We can call and see if he's busy tonight."

"No," she said, "I'll talk to him tomorrow. Tonight I just want it to be you and me."

"That's fine with me," I said. With that I sat on the kitchen stool and she began pulling steak, salad, and potatoes out of the basket. In five minutes, the potatoes were baking and she had set the table. "You know, Cynthia, I think you'll make someone a great wife."

"Well," she replied, "don't get any ideas Ben-boy. I plan on making you a great wife." She handed me two glasses and said

175

"Now fill these with water and ice and put them on the table."

"Yes, Ma'am," I said, and did as I was told.

Dinner went well, We had coffee afterwards and Cynthia looked at me and said, "Ben, you do know, don't you, that my being in Chicago is going to strain our friendship?"

"How so?" I asked.

"Well, on the one hand we'll see a lot more of each other, but on the other I'm going to have to build up a clientele list. I'm worried about that on two fronts. First, will you be OK with my seeing men for hire, even if sex isn't part of the deal? That's always the problem that pro dommes have to face with their boyfriends. Secondly, by doing so I run the risk of meeting Stacie's murderer and becoming his next target."

"That is a mouthful," I said, "anyway you cut it. I guess I hadn't thought about it in those terms. To be honest, I was more concerned about what would happen to me when Thomas moved in with you. I chalked that up to my insecurities about Dionysian relationships and this poly stuff."

Cynthia reached over and took my hand. "Ben, dear, "she said, "I know it's tough to get this all into perspective but believe me it will work out for all of us. As for Thomas, sure I love him, but having him move in is more a matter of safety for me and less a matter of sexual convenience."

"Are you afraid the murderer will aim for you next?"

"It's that, certainly, but mostly Stacie's death has ripped apart our ties of trust. We just don't know who did this and why, even if this envelope gives us another clue. The Alliance has survived by being covert for centuries and it's obvious that someone has infiltrated our Chicago community and is out to destroy us, if only one person at a time."

"As for me, I'm glad Thomas moved in so you're not alone in that house. As for the client thing, I'm not going to let it bother me, as long as I don't have to become a client to be with you."

"That's being a good sport, Ben. Thanks. Now let's talk about other things. Thomas said you wanted to become one of us."

"Yes," I said with a grin on my face, "the two of you have done a really good job reeling me in, even if I didn't find my great-uncle. So what's next?"

"I think," she said, "that Richard is trying to arrange an official interview for you on Saturday."

"What happens at the interview?" I asked.

"Oh it will be mostly pro-forma. No surprises there. Thomas and I have agreed to sponsor you, and Richard will gather four local Dionysians to meet with the three of us. They'll ask the usual questions about why you want to join us, how you found out about us, and who you are in general terms. Your family connections make you a shoe-in, but we still have to follow the rules. Quite frankly, this mess with Stacie means the rules will be followed even more closely, but it's obvious to us that you have nothing to sweat."

"So do you really think I have nothing to worry about?"

"Not at all. Hunks like you are on the top of our most wanted list," she said with a laugh.

"What's after that?"

"You'll become an anazititis, which is Greek for seeker. That happens in an initiation ceremony. I think the plan is to get you initiated as soon as we can so you can join in at least some of the Bacchanalian celebrations. After all, the highest feast of the year begins less than two weeks from now."

"Is this some kind of fraternity hazing?" I asked.

"Hardly, Ben. Dionysians work on an eastern model of religious education.

"Like ancient societies we depend on an oral tradition. Like eastern gurus we practice experiential learning, letting the actual experience of our rites demonstrate the truths of our doctrines. The experiences are followed by doctrinal lessons of explanation. You've already have some of those experiences, with both Thomas and me, and certainly with the New Year's crowd in Sarasota."

"How so?"

"If you think back on your experience in the sling, you'll remember that you said 'Fuck me, my Lord. Fuck me,' and the 177 crowd said 'Yes, yes, yes. Let the god come in. Let the god come in.' What happened to cause you to say 'Fuck me, my Lord. Fuck me?'"

"I think," I admitted, "that I saw Dionysos fucking me."

"Exactly," Cynthia said, "and that's why we know you're ready to become one of us."

Chapter

Ritual 16

On Saturday afternoon we met in Richard's suite. "We" were Cynthia, Thomas, Richard, four of the local Brethren whom I had met when I had interviewed them about the murder (Casey and Ariadne Bronson, Michelle Stanislov, and David Mantzios), and me. Richard acted as facilitator and the four quizzed me about my past, my family, and my motives. They threw an occasional question to Cynthia and Thomas as well. Just as Cynthia had said, it wasn't really very tough, though I did have to tell the story about my Great-Uncle Jonathan and all that had transpired – not including the detective stuff, of course -- since then.

After nearly two hours, they asked me to step out of the room and in a very short while, Richard invited me back in. Each of the four said, rather seriously, "Ben Kramer, I find you ready to join our brotherhood and in the name of our lord Dionysos, I welcome you." With that formality over, they all applauded and there was a round of hugs and kisses.

Richard asked me if I was willing to be initiated as an anazititis on Saturday, February thirteenth, and I said I was.

"Cynthia," Richard asked, "will you prepare our candidate for the ceremony?"

"I sure will," she answered and broke out into a big smile. "I'll make sure he has his lines down pat."

"Lines?" I asked.

"Yes, lines," Cynthia said. "All five of them."

By now it was close enough to cocktail time that Richard

suggested we all go down to third floor for drinks and dinner. No one objected to that idea and off we went. Once we got there, I thought "Leave it to Richard." He had arranged for a private dining room and a bar had been set up for us. "Who pays for all of this?" I wondered, and made a mental note to ask Thomas when I could. I couldn't imagine that religion paid all that well, but the way I saw money being spent, even if Thomas did poor mouth his expense account now and then, I obviously had to change my mind about the amount of income one could derive from a collection basket.

Booze flowed freely as a handsome waiter served appetizers and took our orders. There was lots of monastery wine during dinner. The menu was straight out of Bon Appetit and the waiter was smart enough not to interrupt very often. As the evening progressed I wondered what would happen after dessert, half-expecting that this horny crowd would segue into an orgy.

When the after-dinner coffee was served and we'd all been offered an amazing array of liqueurs, Richard excused himself for a few minutes and returned. Must have paid the bill, I thought, and I might have been right. Meanwhile Casey said, "Well, this has been a long day. I'm ready to call it a night."

Thomas leaned over and whispered "I don't know about you, Ben, but I could use a good fuck." I smiled and whispered back "Count me in."

Cynthia had obviously heard Thomas's proposition. She tapped me on the arm and said "Not without me." And so the night was set for another three-way.

On Monday, Sebastian, Thomas, and I met with Richard to update him on our progress. The house was secure and well monitored, as he already knew. Cynthia had given him the bulletin, which he had then given to me. The three of us then worked out a plan to infiltrate the church, though to do so would take some time, and recruitment of Dionysians able to pass as fundamental

Christians.

On Tuesday I had a three-hour appointment with Dr. Marian Fortis, who gave me a complete physical, including several blood tests and a short battery of psychological tests, followed by an interview. On Wednesday, Thomas and I had dinner at Cynthia's, where they taught me the five lines I would have to know for the initiation.

"We're not sure when or where your initiation's going to be held, Ben. Richard doesn't want you to be seen coming here when there are religious events going on. He thinks you need to be somewhat aloof from the Temple and the Brethren until the murderer is behind bars. We'll figure something out soon, so just hang loose." So ended my preparations for becoming a Dionysian.

Thomas picked me up in a rented car at my place on Saturday, since it was decided that he could drive me to Cynthia's, and I could go in through the garage and not be seen. He was dressed in his Dionysian kilt. I went in the back, through the house and into the foyer where he hugged me quickly and said, "Everything is ready, Ben. Now just relax and we'll take over from here." He picked up a tambourine that was on the small table in the foyer and banged it once. Casey and James, dressed as Thomas was, walked down the hallway to me.

Casey was about five nine and a little pudgy, his gut and torso covered in dark hair, his head balding. Nevertheless there was something handsome about him, a sense created by his exposed upper arms, sturdy thighs, and fair complexion. "We'll take him from here, Thomas," Casey said.

Thomas then said, "I love you, Ben," gave me a kiss, turned to the men and said, "He's all yours." Each of them grabbed me by an arm and walked me down the hall and into the basement.

181

Hooded and bound, my senses of hearing and touch had to supply my mind with the details that my eyes could not see. It was early evening, at sunset to be exact, when they had led me down the stairs and into an antechamber, undressed and washed me. Next came the hood, one with an open mouth, but the rest of my head was sealed in leather. The restraints were of leather and chain, tight but not constrictive. After putting that all on me, they walked me into another room and made me sit in a chair. A woman prayed:

> We, the faithful, join our voices with the maenads of old, with the women who nursed the young Dionysos and with those who long ago traveled with him from the Phrygian woods. Come Lord, thrice-born son of the mighty Zeus, and let thy holy will be known. Call forth, mighty man-god, the powers of the heavens and of the underworld. Let us justly judge this mortal so that according to thy ways he may enter into the rites that bring immortality.

Several voices spoke "amen," followed by the same woman who said, "Ben Kramer, you sit now before the five Protectors of our temple. It is only by their judgment that you may be admitted to our altar. First, though, I must ask you the questions that have come down from ages past. Do you wish me to proceed?"

"In the name of the great Dionysos, I do," I answered, just as I had been taught.

"It is well, then. Who speaks first?"

"I do." I could tell that it was Richard who was speaking, the first to befriend me in my journey to this moment.

"And what, wise brother, do you say?"

"This man comes to us from the Caminsky line, his mother being our sister Claire, his great-uncle our reverend brother Jonathan. He is 41 years old, a marketing executive by trade. He is unmarried but well-known by several in our Alliance who have seen his progress in our ways."

"Why does he come now to us?" a voice asked.

"He comes," said Richard, "because he seeks a holy bond with our Lord and the promise of immortality that the man-god bestows."

"But why now?" asked the voice again. "He is older than many who are family-bred in our midst."

"This is true," said Richard, "but his mother hid the mysteries from him because his father, Jordan, had wanted his sons to come to the Lord in their own way. Though his father died before Ben reached the age of manhood, our sister Claire kept her promise to her husband, with the hope that our lord would call him in due time."

"How, then, does he now come to us?" asked another voice.

"By the grace of a book given him by Jonathan when his great-nephew had come of age," answered Richard. "Ben found the book in his mother's basement last summer and was prompted by it to seek his great-uncle. This search led to us and his search was rewarded by careful instruction and holy revelation."

"Are there any other questions for Richard?" she asked. There was no reply and I heard "There being none, that will be all, Richard. Thank you."

"Doctor," said the obvious leader, "do you have your report ready?"

"I do," said a woman who must have been the doctor who had given me a rather complete physical earlier in the week.

"Proceed, then," the other said.

"Ben, as you can see, is five foot eleven and weighs 178 pounds. He has light brown hair and brown eyes. He is normally clean-shaven and, I might add, rather attractive. His health is excellent and the required blood tests show him disease free. His immune system shows the usual antibodies brought on by childhood disease and vaccinations, including resistance to Hepatitis.

"He is psychologically balanced, an experienced bisexual

183

and appears accepting of both promiscuity and multiple intimate relationships. I found him a very intelligent and friendly man and certainly find no reason that the Protectors ought not to admit him."

"Thank you, Doctor, I am sure your advice will be well-considered. Now, who vouches for this man? Are there the necessary three?"

"I vouch for him," said Richard.

"As do I."

"And I," said two other voices, Cynthia's and Thomas's.

"With what knowledge do you speak, sister?" asked the questoiner's voice.

"We have known one another in the union of our bodies and the sharing of our thoughts. I have been present when our lord revealed his power to him," she said.

"And you, brother?"

"Ben and I have loved well," said Thomas, "and he has often shown me the sincerity of his heart. With Themis, the goddess of justice, as my witness, I swear that he comes in love and devotion."

"Ben Kramer, what do you say of these things?"

"These are my friends who speak and they speak the truth. They have carefully led me to the knowledge of sacred things and I come now to enter more deeply into them."

"You speak well," said the voice.

"Cynthia's a good teacher," I replied, somewhat off script for a moment.

"And Richard, what do you have to add?" the woman asked.

"Only that I agree with Thomas and Cynthia. Ben is ready and worthy," he said.

"And what do the detractors say?" she asked.

"Those who would bar his entrance and thus protect our rites have found no reason to oppose him," said another voice. I think it was Casey's.

"It is well and good. Are the Protectors willing for us to proceed?"

With that I heard several people say "Yes."

"That being so, what say the five Protectors?"

"Let him proceed," said the first.

"Let him proceed," said the second and the rest in turn. Then prayers were said in both English and in Greek and I was offered a goblet of wine from which I drank. It was sweet and thick with a slight after-taste that I did not recognize. Warm hands lifted me from the chair and carried me, though not too far, as I was soon laid on a soft bed of sorts.

Except for dull footsteps there were few sounds. I smelled the burning wax of what I assumed were candles. The temperature was warm and comforted my skin. Stronger than the smell of wax was the incense that filled the air, the smell of which I knew to be thorax, an incense used in ancient Greece.

My studies had taught me that much. It was the Dionysian herb of choice, so that was no surprise. This was, after all my first initiation into the sacred rites of that long-forgotten god, the one called Bacchus in Rome, Shiva in India, and Dionysos in Greece. He was one of the begotten sons of Zeus, whose ceremonies were long ago banned even in a city as pagan as Rome. How implausible, I thought, that I was experiencing them here in the city of Chicago in the twentieth century. Who would have thought?

I hadn't.

As I lay there breathing the perfumes of this ancient cult, I heard the softest of hums, one sound only, then joined by others as it grew into a low chant, gaining volume and rhythm as the minutes passed. It grew into the melody of what I thought was a Byzantine hymn. Though I had no assurance that it was Greek I was hearing, it sounded like it to me.

"Who is this blinded and bound man and why is he here?" asked the woman who had led the prayer. She spoke with the stern voice of a woman of authority.

185

"This is Ben, son of Claire Kramer and a descendant of the Caminsky family, who now seeks to join the brotherhood of his ancestors so he may partake in the worship and blessings of the holy ones." That was the unmistakable voice of Cynthia. The "hidden doctrines," as they were called, had remained that way to me. Only now, I was told, after I had passed through these rites of entry, would I learn of them.

"And who among us befriends this kin of our kin? Who attests that he is ready and a true seeker of the mysteries?"

"I do." It was Thomas.

"It is right and just to proceed," said the woman, "for wisdom need be bestowed on those who truly desire it. Ben Kramer do you seek wisdom?"

"I do," I said, as Cynthia had taught me.

"Why?" she asked.

"For the sake of being made whole and partaking in the fellowship of the initiated."

"That is good," she said. "Let the rites begin."

A touch of dizziness hit me. Strong wine, I thought, or was there something else in it? I felt my body drift. Of course it could have been the incense, or the excitement and anticipation of what was to come.

Musical instruments -- harps, flutes, stringed instruments, and the soft clatter and tap of tambourines -- intoned a melody that was joined by the voices in the room. Beneath the music I heard footsteps and surmised that the singers were circling me. I thought of what it might look like from above. There I lay, naked but for the hood and the restraints, while who knew how many people shuffled around me in what must have been a dimly candle-lit cavern.

Was it merely a cave or had it been built into some magnificent hall of worship? Probably the latter, I surmised. This crowd was high church to say the least, or that's what the chant, the theology, and the elaborate façade that so well hid their existence implied.

My silent query was dispelled as drops hit my body. "I purify you for your journey," the woman said, as I was sprinkled with a cool liquid. "Let the blood of the god wash away your past, returning you to the time in the garden, when no shame was found in the body of the first born.

The liquid dripped off the sides of my chest, arms, and legs. Was it blood? I wondered. No, my senses replied as the smell of the aspersion was clearly wine, confirmed as a few drops hit my lips and my tongue washed them away. It was fine monastery wine. Would there be blood later? I knew from my study of archeology that the Greeks had sacrificed animals in their Dionysian rites. Was it the same now?

I realized how little I knew of what I was getting myself into, though all I had learned up to now had brought me to trust in these people.

The search that had brought me thus far had been slow and steady, my curiosity satisfied enough to make me continue, my fears sufficiently dissipated by the obvious sincerity of those I met, though the word "met" wasn't a very accurate verb. After all, I had begun my search looking for a great-uncle I hadn't seen in years and it had soon led me back to my own mother.

I wondered if she were in the congregation, if you could name a gathering such as this with that word. "Coven," the Christian world would call it, and they would condemn these "witches" to death, usually by fire.

My mind, racing with too many thoughts, was soon muted by the words of the priestess "Unbind his feet," she ordered, "that he may be led for all to see."

Quickly the ropes around my knees and ankles were loosened and I was made to rise. Hands held my arms to steady me. They led me slowly in what seemed like a wide circle and as they did other hands caressed my body -- all of it. Whose were they? I wondered, though the eroticism of the moment quickly pushed out any rational thought. My cock swelled into stiffness and I once again thought, with a bit of warmth rushing to put a blush on my face, of my mother watching the ceremony, if indeed she were there.

I began to feel less steady, as I was led around the room.

Except for Richard, Thomas and Cynthia, whose voices I had recognized, were these people strangers? I assumed that Casey and James were there, since they had led me into the room. Were the others Dionysians whom I had met during the recent interviews?

I was being pawed, fondled, now kissed and groped. My trek around the room was crowded with sensations of skin, of sweat, of incense. The chanting began again. This time the air was filled with a certain chaos, a staccato-like chirping.

The arms holding me now lifted me. I was back on the mattress and the ropes that bound me were refastened. Meanwhile, the tambourines increased their volume. The ceremony, if that's what one could call it, was reaching a fevered pitch. I sensed a beast in the room. Fear--no, terror-- clenched at my stomach. Was I to be the blood sacrifice? Was this the secret that I had not yet been told?

A cacophony of chirps, clangs, and growls filled the air. I flashed back to what the Roman historian Livy had written about this cult: "Anyone who was less prepared for disgrace and slow to commit crimes was offered up as a sacrifice." Was this to be my initiation or my death? I wondered. But I also thought how ridiculous that sounded.

Amid the confusion I felt dizzy, nauseous. I've been drugged, I thought. The classics professor at the University of Chicago had warned me that the ancient cults often used herbs and mushrooms to induce visions and hallucinations. "False spirituality," he had said it was called.

Panic overtook me. I had learned enough about the myths and rumors of Dionysos' followers to know that blood and ecstasy could be too often mixed.

I began to struggle against the ropes at my side, a useless attempt to be sure. My lungs gasped for air, as I writhed in fear and I thought "No. No. Stop," but my voice withheld any scream.

Still the beast in the room roared, drowning out my thoughts. The tambourines began to sound in unison, a martial cadence. As if on cue the other sounds began to subside and when only their sound was heard, they, too, slowed and softened until they were silent.

A quiet flute awoke in my darkness. Faintly and far away. It raised its volume and came nearer. Now it was the only sound, a sweet dawn after the terror.

"Our gods are not trifling, son of man. They have shown you their terror. Now let them show you their light," came the woman's voice.

My feet were spread apart and fastened to the bed; my arms released and likewise fastened; my hood removed, leaving the blindfold on my eyes as restraints were used to anchor my head, thighs, and torso to the bier on which I lay. The sounds of string instruments joined the flutes in a lilting, calming melody. Their sweet music captivated me even more .

I felt silks and furs caress my body and a soft hand rubbed my skin with warm oil. Lips brushed mine. Someone was kissing me. It was a familiar kiss. Was it Cynthia? I hoped so. I had grown to trust her, that was for sure. I had trusted others, too: Thomas, Richard, my mother. That trust seemed so strange after the cacophony I had just experienced.

Still, the lips, the lips and the hands. The sensuous touches. They blurred the memory of the beast as my sexual passion grew once more. The one who had kissed me climbed on top of me, the kisses continuing as I felt breasts brush my torso. My shaft grew with anticipation. I struggled now not to escape but to gain release. Hands softly brushed my body and caressed my crotch. I struggled to rise off the bed, my prick aching to enter the vagina that began to tease it mercilessly. Its erection made it stand tall and someone slid a condom over it.

Soon the woman who had climbed on top of me, mounted me. I became a dildo for her pleasure as she stroked my limbs, face, torso and my phallus. My hips gyrated pathetically, the restraints 189 forbidding any real movement. I hungered for more, more. My sexual drive dispelled every feeling but that of hot passion. This was what I wanted, at least now, in this moment. Her movements obliterated my fear and filled me with desire for what was to come. My breath raced. Yes, yes, I thought and then began to actually say the words. "Yes, yes."

The woman who rode me slowed her movements, her hands now gently resting on my hips. Only the muscles of her cunt moved, pulsing, grasping, releasing and grasping my organ. It was an incredible massage, as only most the skilled practitioners of this cult could give.

"So, Ben, son of Claire and of the family of Caminsky, shall we proceed with our sacred rites? Do you still seek entrance into the holiness of our circle?"

It was the question that Cynthia had told me would come. Now that it had, I saw its great seriousness in a whole new light. It was not just an initiation into fellowship, into orgy, into pleasure. It was more than I could grasp. It was the dark as well as the light, the dangerous as well as the safe, death as well as life. And I knew now what I had known almost from the beginning, that here was more than just dead rituals, Sunday morning pleasantries, or religious services which had long lost their power. It was a risky journey into the unknown realms of gods.

The onlookers were mute. I only heard the sound of my own breathing and the beat of my own heart. The woman lifted herself off of me and I was left with the question posed by the priestess. It seemed a great, long time passed before I spoke but I knew I had come too far to turn back. "Yes," I uttered.

"Then let the vows begin," said the priestess.

Five voices (I think it was the Protectors) said in unison, "Ben Kramer, we have found you worthy of joining the holy circle of Dionysos."

Then someone continued, "But before we can let you become a part of our thiasoi, you must be bound by oaths to protect those who love our lord. These pledges are meant to keep our secrets secure lest the unworthy learn of our doctrines and profane the knowledge that brings immortality. For that reason I warn you not to take our questions lightly nor to pledge that which you will not do. Is this clear?"

"Yes," I said and my mind quickly flashed to what I had seen and heard in the months since I had traveled to Cincinnati.

"Unbind him," she said, "but let his eyes be covered until the vows be said." Someone did as she ordered and I was made to sit up on the couch. "Now, Ben, repeat after me in a voice so that all can hear," and this is what I repeated:

I call upon the directions so the universe may hear my prayer. Come hither, Apheliotes, god of the east wind, and hear my vows. Come hither, Notes, god of the south wind, and Zephyroes, god of the west wind, and hear my vows. Come hither, Boreas, god of the north wind, and hear my vows.

Theia, goddess of sight and shining light of the clear blue sky, and your children, Helios, god of the sun, Eos, goddess of the dawn, and Selene, goddess of the moon, I call upon you to give me sight. Let your lights shine in the skies that I may see clearly and know the truth.

Great Sophia, goddess of wisdom, be present to show me the way of the righteous. Let me walk the right path and give me wisdom to choose the road to glory.

Kratos, mighty god of strength, powerful son of Pallas and Styx, fill me with thy holy strength to make me strong in courage and service.

Aphrodite, goddess of love, beauty, and sexuality, fill me with thy passion. Bring with thee thy twin children, Eros and Himeros, that their divine power may fill my life.

Great Poseidon, god of water, son of Cronus and Rhea, brother of Zeus and Hades, ever cleanse my body

191

and quench my thirst that I may worship purely and with right intent.

Rhea, mother of the gods, grant me to know the eternal flow of time and be counted among the everlasting generations.

Gaia, I call thee mother earth. Ever support me, fruitful mother, ever feed me, and teach me true devotion.

Mighty Zeus, sky father who rules from Mount Olympus, send not the fury of thy lightning bolts but the power of thy kingdom to protect and comfort me as I make my pledge to thy thrice-born son Dionysos.

All ye gods, here assembled, witness my pledge to keep as a sacred trust that which I learn. Let me steadfastly protect the followers of Dionysos with love and devotion, keeping silent in all that is to be hidden. I hereby pledge and promise, on my sacred word, never to reveal the mysteries of the Bacchoi's way, except during a sacred rite to those who are found worthy of instruction.

I make this oath for all to hear, knowing that to betray it will bring the wrath of Dionysos, who drove Pentheus, the King of Thebes, to madness and caused his mad mother Agavë to kill him and dismember his body.

Let me be bound as was Prometheus and may an eagle torment me daily if I fail to keep this oath. Let me be cast into Tartarus, the deepest pit of Hades, to languish forever with the Titans if I fail to keep my pledge. Let death take me slowly and light shine on me nevermore if I protect not my Brethren and keep not sacred my trust.

With all my strength, with all my heart, I call upon Dionysos to make me his. I speak these words in truth: This day and hence forward I worship you, mighty Dionysos, great god, holy Zagreus, hunter and bringer of life. I dedicate, I consecrate, I surrender my life to your service. As you did to the helmsman of old, great god of the vine, have mercy on me and say, 'Take courage, you have found favour with my heart.' Hail, child of fair-faced Semele! He who forgets you can in no wise order sweet song.

"It is done," said the priestess, "Amen."

And "Amen" resounded from all the voices in the cavern.

"Let the initiation begin," the priestess continued. "Thomas, friend of Ben, remove his blinder."

I felt Thomas's hands on my face and then his kiss, as he untied the blindfold. I blinked but all was dark. "Stay here, my beloved," he said, "as our ritual continues." With those words he was gone in the darkness.

In a few minutes, Cynthia stood in front of me and lit a votive candle that illuminated her face. "Welcome," she said, "my beloved brother. It gives me great joy to know that soon you will be one with our lord." She set the votive light at my feet and gave me a long and impassioned kiss and said to those in the darkness, "As you have heard, today the five Protectors declared that Ben Kramer, of the Caminsky family, was ready to join our thiasoi. He is bound to us by vows and so has become our kin." Then she turned to me and said, her face beautiful in the candle light, "My brother Ben, let me be the first to welcome you to our family." Her lips caressed mine with deep passion.

Then she picked up her candle and extinguished it, disappearing into the darkness. Now Thomas appeared candle-lit and gave me a warm kiss, followed by Casey. Casey's kiss was tender as well and I was surprised that he thrust his tongue into my mouth. Then came Michael who, instead of kissing me, gave me a greeting of welcoming and began to suck my dick. All this time, my cock had been growing and Michael only made it stiffer.

I wondered what was next when Richard appeared. The votive light he held was bright enough to expose the epaulets he wore on his shoulders but no more. His broad smile showed joy and pleasure. "I am so pleased to greet you this night, Ben," he said. "I have watched your journey to the light with much joy. It has been an uneasy quest for you and I am happy to know that it is nearing its joyous conclusion." He set down the votive candle, and pulled me off the couch. Now that I was standing he put his arms around me in a warm and close embrace. His lips caressed mine and his tongue began exploring my mouth. His hands worked their way down my back and as he massaged my ass, I could feel his crotch pushing itself into mine from beneath his kilt.

Too soon he backed away. "Sit down, my brother, and let the others greet you," he said, and I did as he requested.

Two lights appeared across the room, illuminating Ariadne and Michelle. They walked together towards me, kissed me quickly, each on one cheek, and said "Welcome, Ben, to our family." With that they put their candles at my feet and retreated back across the room.

Then, Cynthia came forward again, placing her now lit votive candle at my feet. "Let there be light, the gods of old commanded, and now I bid the same," she said. With that, one by one everyone in the room relit their votives and gradually I could dimly make out the room in its entirety. Cynthia nodded to Casey who went over to the door and turned on soft ceiling lights that allowed me to see more clearly who was in the room.

I was surprised to see who else was there: Rebecca and Joseph and Jack and Estelle O'Malley from Florida, as well as Sebastian, George Cardenas, and Clark.

The people who had just greeted me were in all states of attire or lack thereof. Some, like Cynthia and Clark, were dressed in leather. Others were in various garbs of lingerie, jock straps or furs. A few, like Michael, Thomas and me, were simply stark naked. It all reminded me that from now on I had better be prepared clothing-wise, though I had to admit that nudity in this crowd was not all that exceptional.

194   All together there were sixteen Brethren assembled in the

room. Several people in the room wore strips of leopard skin, either as arm bands or decorations sewn into their clothing. There was the usual variety of ages, weights and shapes. Rebecca and Estelle wore toga-like dresses trimmed in fur.

Ariadne and Michelle were dressed like maenads, the women often pictured on Greek vases who worshipped and waited upon Dionysos. They wore singlets of fawn skin, each with an exposed breast and skirts as short as any mini I had ever seen. Their hair cascaded to their shoulders and was decorated with sprigs of grape leaves. They wore sandals with laces that wound their way up their shins to above their knees.

Casey then went to a nearby stereo and turned on some soft music. A few of the assembled Dionysians accompanied the music with small tambourines or castanets. After five or six measures, Ariadne and Michelle stood up and began dancing, stepping, swinging, and whirling like fairies and butterflies. Ariadne began circling within the center of the group, a wineskin was passed around and each person took a swig and passed it on to the person next to him. Round and round the two women danced, and round and round the wineskin was passed. I took a swig each time it came to me and wondered what was coming next. Next was another wineskin and then a third, so that the swigs came faster and faster. A third woman joined the first two, and then others. Someone began a chant and the music became louder.

"Come satyrs and maenads. Show thy love for your god. Call upon him to show himself to Ben, to be present in our revelry, to bless our assembly, to welcome Ben into our midst and his," said Rebecca, who I now realized had been leading the ceremony all along.

Cynthia reached for my hand and pulled me off the couch. "Dance with me," she said, offering her other hand to me. I took it and she began to swing me into the crowd. We made three passes around the room and then she handed me to Richard who did the same. Then he gave me to Michelle who held me in the center of 195 the room as Ariadne hugged me from behind. Together they rubbed their bodies against mine, their flesh enflaming mine, the furs of their singlets caressing me.

They began kissing and fondling me and I felt Ariadne's finger tickling my ass. Thomas joined the duo, kissing my face and stroking my cock. Michelle backed away and Thomas rubbed his ass cheeks against my cock. I could feel the heat of his man cunt and the slickness of the lube with which he had prepared himself for me. "Fuck me, now," he said. "Fuck me now."

With that he rolled a condom onto my prick and guided its stiffness into his anus. I put my arms around him and began squeezing his tits. My hips gyrated into him. I felt sweat on my brow as the warmth of the room and the passion of sex combined their heat.

The dancers slowed their pace as they circled around us. The singing grew louder. "Fuck him. Fuck him," someone said.

My hips began thrusting to the beat of the music and hands began clapping to the same beat. I felt dizzy with wine, sex, and power. Michelle came up to me and wrapped a garland of grape vines around my head. "Dionysos, Dionysos," voices around me called. "Come holy hunter. Come great Zagreus. Come god of bliss. Reveal thyself. Reveal thyself." I grew drunk on the passion of it all, carried higher by a vortex of sexual energy.

I pulled out of my lover's ass, needing to steady myself lest I fall. "Lie on the mattress, Thomas," I said. He did so, raising his legs invitingly. For my part I climbed on top of him, spread his legs even further and thrust my cock back into his waiting hole.

"Come, Dionysos, come," he cried and the call was repeated again and again around the room. Hands stroked me and caressed my back and ass. I could see others pairing off as well. Casey and Ariadne were entangled on the floor. Michael sucked at Clark's cock.

I leaned down and kissed Thomas, pulling myself closer to him. Someone began kissing my ass cheeks and then I felt a tongue tickling my ass hole. It was Rebecca, clad in furs and silks. A well-lubed finger entered me and I backed into it, wanting to be penetrated even while I did

196

the same to Thomas. Now two fingers poked into me, then a dildo.

I heard warbling and chirping from the corners of the room. Loud thrilling sounds, filled with "La" and "Lo," whistling and yelping erupted in the room. "Euloi, euloi," rang around the room. A pandemonium of sound filled the air as kissing, fondling, and fucking went on all around me.

I drifted in pleasure. Someone squirted wine onto my back and head. It dripped down onto Thomas. They shot wine into his mouth. Another hand pulled my head up from his face and said "Drink this. It is from the lord." A goblet was thrust to my lips and the liquid within it ran into my mouth. Sweet wine, warm and thick, swirled into my mouth and I gulped it down. Keeping the last swig in my mouth, I leaned down again to kiss Thomas and spit the last of the wine into his mouth, sharing its sweetness with my beloved.

My body grew alive with the drink. It tingled and I felt recharged by the wine. Joy overtook me and I felt myself lifted. My heart beat quickly, my cock thrusting into Thomas. The dildo left me and I felt a real cock enter me. It was Casey's.

The ceiling lights went dim and half the candles went dark, leaving the room shadow-filled and nearly dark, except for an eerie glow of gold, cast by candle light. The smell of thorax increased; the room grew smoky. I felt lighter and lighter, my head drifting in ecstasy. Nearly in a swoon I fell upon Thomas, my cock pulling out of him. My eyes grew blurry and the room swayed and moved to the tempo and the sounds of the orgy.

Faces darted in and out of my vision. Powerful masks of beauty and fear. Gods and goddesses stared at me and a laughing Dionysos appeared and left, only to reappear again. I was seeing the gods I had called. The winds caressed me, though the air was still. Father Zeus watched me, his flowing beard and the whiteness of his hair making him appear as old as time. Rhea, full-breasted and ripe with milk, opened her arms to me. Dionysos danced around me, laughing, laughing, and gulping clusters of grapes.

Round and round the room encircled me. I closed my eyes

197

but the visions remained. Slowly the world came to a standstill, the music died. Only the vision of Dionysos remained. "Take courage," he said. "You have found favor in my heart." Then the power left and I collapsed into a deep and tranquil peace.

Chapter

The Bacchae **17**

A thin ray of sunlight peeked through the drapes in Cynthia's bedroom. She lay curled beneath the covers next to me and I half-slumbered there, stiff with a hard on and fuzzy as to what had happened. I certainly had no idea how I had ended up here, next to her, since I had some recollection of last being with Thomas. I rolled over with the hope of falling back into whatever dreams I had had.

I remembered them, that's for sure. They were filled with gods and goddesses, a virtual picture book of Greek mythology. First among them was Dionysos, more handsome than I would have thought. His gentle face had been filled with kindness, even feminine-like but not nellie in any way at all. No matter, the peace I felt made everything right with the world, though I was thirsty as hell.

I was amazed that I didn't have a hangover, since I was sure that wine had flown freely all during the initiation. I had certainly lost count of the wine skins. God, these folks knew how to party, I thought. Then I remembered that it wasn't a party, it was a religious service, in fact, a divine ritual. It was no wonder that the Christian churches wanted it banned, since no Bible preacher could ever give a Sunday morning service as good as that one.

I must have fallen back to sleep because the next thing I knew was that Thomas was sitting on the side of the bed gently waking me, and Cynthia wasn't next to me any longer. "Wake up, Mr. Sleepyhead," he said.

"What time is it?" I asked, squinting my eyes towards him.

"Nearly 1:30 in the afternoon," he replied.

"That late, huh?" I answered. "I guess I ought to get up."

"Here," Thomas said, as he offered me a glass of juice. "It's a special next morning Dionysian concoction, mixed just right to bring you back to earth."

"Another drink?" I asked. "I had enough last night to do me for a week."

"No alcohol in this, I promise. Nothing but good old-fashioned snake oil. Drink it." I did. It certainly didn't taste like snake oil, but I was thirsty and it went down easily.

When I set the glass on the bed stand, Thomas leaned over and gave me a kiss, rolling over me and onto the bed. "I'm so glad you're one of us," he said. "It makes my love for you all that more special."

"I love you, too, Thomas," I answered. "That was some ritual last night. What happened?"

"We created a sacred space for you to meet our lord. From everything I could tell, that's exactly what happened."

"I remember ," I answered. "It was an amazing experience. I guess I always thought of mythology as just that."

"There is much we don't know about the gods. In fact, each of us just might have a different take on what's going on. In time, the mysteries will unfold for you and you will be taught to perform the rites. Our goal is to reach beyond what we can find with our five senses, deep into our unconscious selves to find our inner guide. You have taken only the first step. There are many more, my brother. But now, let's get some brunch."

After brunch Cynthia apologized that she really had to go to the theater for rehearsal. "After all," she said, "the play is in three days; you know that, don't you?"

Thomas and I agreed that we did, and said we would clean up the kitchen and get out of her hair. We did so and then the two of us drove to my place, since that seemed as good a spot as any to spend a lazy Sunday afternoon.

On Wednesday I left the office early so I could get home, grab something to eat and be at the theater for the play at 7 pm.

The theater itself was one of Chicago's many small venues where an aspiring actor hoped to get discovered and offered a larger role downtown in a major production. The marquee said "One night only, The God of Ecstasy by Euripides." Theater posters in the front windows featured two masks -- a laughing Dionysos and a horribly tragic one. I wondered who had done the artwork.

Thomas and I paid our seven dollar ticket fees and went into the theater's small foyer. Christine and Marjorie, dressed in fawn maenad costumes (though they wore leotards beneath them) welcomed us at the door and gave us program notes. Michael, dressed in the costume of a Greek slave, served small plastic glasses of wine. The foyer itself was rather simple but clean. About a dozen people stood in small groups chatting. Many of them said hello to Thomas. I didn't really know very many of them.

Two I did know of, though hadn't yet met, Mark and Beth, came over to say hello. Mark seemed to have met Thomas once or twice before and made small talk about inviting him to dinner. Thomas gave a half-hearted assent and Mark turned to me and said "Now you make sure he brings you along too, you hear? That way we'll have an even number at the dinner table." I made some non-committal response and finished my wine.

When I did, Thomas said "Let's get another glass of wine," so we went back and got seconds from Michael and then made our way into the auditorium. As we walked in I said something about having to interview Mark and Beth. "I suppose," said Thomas, "that his wife goes along with this begrudgingly. Stacie used to say she really didn't seem interested in our beliefs."

The theater was in the round and the stage décor was rather stark, consisting of a few Doric columns on one side of the stage and some artificial trees on the other. The fifty or so seats around the stage were well-worn but comfortable. They were only half-filled with spectators.

201

The last play written by Euripides, in about 406 BC, tells the tale of Dionysos and his attendant women, called Bakkhai in Greek and Bacchae in Latin, who have come to Thebes to establish his rituals. Doing so causes the women of Thebes to leave the city to worship Dionysos in the celebration of the Bacchanalia. Patriarchal King Pentheus, played by none other but Clark, rejects Dionysos who, in the first act, finally convinces him to don the clothing of a woman in order to spy on the festivities on Mount Kithairon, the place where the Theban woman have gone.

In the second act, Pentheus, dressed to look like a woman, does so and is discovered by the women, whom Dionysos puts into a state of madness. In the tragic ending, Agaue, Pentheus' mother, thinking that her victim is a mountain lion, leads the woman in a frenzied murder and dismembering of her son. The crazed Agaue returns to Thebes carrying her son's bloody and severed head.

There's much more to the play than this quick description, of course, and I looked forward to seeing how the cast would portray both the comedy of the first act and the horrendous tragedy of the second. With this crowd, I thought, Dionysos would certainly be a grand hero and Pentheus the most vile of evil-doers.

The handout noted that they were using Arthur Evans' new translation, which I had read over the Christmas holidays. The play bill listed a lot of names that I already recognized. Some of the actors, like Cynthia (leader of the Maenad chorus), Casey (the Theban seer Teiresias), and Clark I knew. Others I had only met casually, if you can have a casual meeting at an orgy, during my initiation. A few were strangers.

"Are all the actors Dionysians?" I asked Thomas.

"No, some are hired professionals, some friends, some just volunteers who like to act. The same goes for the audience. We do, though, keep our ears open at events like this to see who might be interested in knowing more about us, though as you can imagine we do it rather discreetly."

With all that had happened since my New Year's trip to

Florida, I found the play both enjoyable and informative. The fact that I knew some of the actors gave it a very personal feeling, almost like watching a high school play put on by your classmates. Still I was impressed by the underlying balance of the script. Tiresias, the seer, had a goodly number of lines that spoke of devotion, proper respect for the gods, and other religious axioms that were often lost in the intense sexuality of the Dionysian theology.

King Pentheus' attitude of disdain for women and his obvious homophobia made it easy to dislike him, though his murder and the fall of his Theban regime did seem a bit much. I had "met" a gentler Dionysos during my fuck-orgy in Sarasota and wine-induced visions in Chicago. Squaring that up with a vengeful and madness-inducing god was tough to take.

The tragic side of the play reminded me of the panic I had felt during my initiation. There was a lot more to this Dionysian story than met the eye. The play brought home the truth of what Thomas had said on Sunday, "There is much we don't know about the gods."

When the play ended and the applause had ceased, Thomas and I made our way to Casey's where there was a low-key cast party. It was Wednesday night and I had to things to do the next morning, so I left early, even if Thomas and Cynthia wanted otherwise.

In spite of all the Bacchanalian revelry, the investigation took a lot of time, planning, and meeting. By the end of the week, I was feeling frazzled. Thomas asked me at work on Friday morning whether I wanted to join him and Cynthia for dinner. I declined because I didn't really feel up to going out. "Are you OK?" he asked, with obvious distress in his voice.

"Sure, buddy," I said. "I'm just tired. How about we make it tomorrow night?"

"That's fine with me," he replied. "Let me check with Cynthia."

He called Cynthia a few minutes later and came back to say "Cynthia's going to bow out for tomorrow and wants to know if you want to go out for dinner on Sunday?"

"Sure," I answered, "but are we still on for tomorrow?"

"By all means," Thomas said. "In fact it'll be nice to have some time alone with you." So my weekend was once again all planned. The rest of the day was quiet and my evening alone was even quieter.

I spent Saturday morning catching up on chores, especially laundry. I spent the afternoon doing more interviews, though I did take a quick break to call Thomas to see what kind of plans he wanted to make for dinner. We decided on Anna Maria's. Having moved his stuff up from Cincinnati, he now had a car, and so I said, "Come over to my place at six and we'll have cocktails, then drive over to Clark Street for dinner."

"I'll see you then," he answered and that was the end of the conversation.

I had the cocktails ready right at six and Thomas rang the doorbell three minutes later. "You're just in time," I said. "I was worried that the ice in my drink would be melted by the time you got here."

"That's why I drink my Scotch neat," he smiled. "That way you don't have to worry about getting a diluted drink."

With that he gave me a warm hug and several kisses, took off his coat, and I gave him his drink. We settled on the couch to talk and nibble at the cheese and crackers I had set out. "What's Cynthia up to?" I asked. "I'm surprised she didn't come over with you."

"Tonight is girls' night in Chicago," Thomas said. "The women of the Alliance are getting together to celebrate Bacchanalia, or at least as much of it as they can in the temple basement.

"Since we're not in the Mediterranean, we can't exactly run off to Mount Kithairon and party naked in the woods. Cynthia and I talked about inviting you and decided that a few more theology lessons might be needed before she asked you to join in the festival."

"Well, if it's women's night, why would I be welcome?" I asked.

"Because you're Dionysian now, remember? We could attend, but only if we did it in drag, like Teiresias and Kadmon did. Would that bother you?"

"Not at all," I assured him, "but I've still got a lot to learn about this, you know."

"Yes, I do, Ben," he replied, "so keep asking your questions and I'll do my best to answer them."

"Will do," I said. "Now kiss me. I think we need to make up for some lost time. We've been so busy with religion and detective work we haven't spent much quality time together." With that, Thomas did as I asked and we started making out on the couch. After a few minutes, we came up for air and he suggested we either get some food or head to bed, so we got in his car and he drove to the restaurant.

After the calamari appetizer, I said "So what am I going to miss tonight? What happens at Bacchanalia? Is it as frenzied as the madness of the Theban women?"

"Not hardly, Ben," Thomas answered. "It's mostly drinking, singing, and dancing with lots of Lesbian sex thrown in. The men get to watch and eventually some of the women get in the mood to have sex with them, but it is more along the lines of the bucolic calm of Dionysian nurses, not the mad women of Thebes.

"Don't forget that the madness was Dionysos' punishment for his rejection by the city. There is a vengeful Dionysos, to be sure, but I would hope he doesn't erupt at Cynthia's tonight."

"That reminds me. What was in those goblets of wine I drank? During my initiation I felt some real panic, early on, and the wine tasted strange."

"Well," Thomas asked, "you know those secrets you promised to keep? One of them has to do with what we call 'sacred libations.' The first goblet contained some psychotropic herbs that induced the panic. It was formulated to last only a few minutes. Likewise the second drink was a different mixture that helped you experience the visions you had.

"The recipes are highly guarded and only the most learned among us know what they actually contain. You do know, don't you, that many Eastern and primitive religions rely on plants to gain access to the spirit world? It's much like the peyote of Native Americans, or even tobacco for that matter. I hope that doesn't bother you to know that."

"So was Dr. Hirschberg right when he told me about using herbs and mushrooms to induce visions and hallucinations and called it 'false spirituality?'"

"I guess that's up to you to decide. It's a question that each of us has to answer. Remember that I said that there's a lot we don't know. Certainly the relationship between the use of hallucinogenic potions and spiritual discovery is one of them," Thomas admitted.

"That's not answer enough, Thomas," I said. "I'm not asking what Dionysians think. I'm asking what you think."

"I think there are many paths to self-knowledge and that herbs and spices, to use a restaurant-friendly euphemism, are certainly both viable and licit ways to extrasensory perception, just as a microscopes, X-rays, and satellites are viable means of discovery. On the other hand, I don't think that unguided, unmonitored, and recreational use of every new chemical that comes along is at all healthy, nor can it be defended on religious grounds.

"Our Western culture has socialized us to ignore the vast spiritual realities that we can experience through proper and proven religious experiences, and I, for one, am not going to discredit those experiences as 'false spirituality' any more than I'm going to discredit saying the Rosary, spinning a prayer wheel, or receiving Holy Communion.

"Sorry for the lecture, but you asked what I thought. Now you know."

206   "I like what you think, Thomas, so please don't take my

questions as being offensive. I just have got to put all this together so it makes sense. You understand that, don't you?"

"Certainly I do. After all, I asked the same questions you're asking in the weeks following my first initiation. We all do. Unfortunately it's at this point that we lose a lot of seekers, since some come to the conclusion that it is a false spirituality. That's why we're very careful about what we tell people and when we tell them."

"So you think I'm ready now?"

"Of course I do, and so did the Protectors. You wouldn't have gotten this far if we hadn't concluded that you were ready to hear the truth."

I smiled at the man facing me across the table, took his hand and said "I love you, Thomas, and I'm very glad you've helped me come this far."

"And I'm glad," he said, "that you have. Now finish your chicken, I'm ready for some dessert and then a go at you in your dungeon."

When we finished dinner we lingered over a glass of Cointreau and then drove back to my place. Thomas parked outside my house and we walked up the steps and into my living room. "Would you mind a suggestion?" I asked.

"Of course not. What's up?"

"I'd rather forego the dungeon tonight and make love to you in the bedroom."

Thomas and I finally got out of bed about 10:30 the next morning. The weather was gray, cold, and damp, perhaps not cold enough for snow but cold enough to make getting up undesirable. We did anyway.

While I made coffee, he got the paper off the front porch. Neither of us was very hungry so we ignored making toast or going out to the IHOP. Instead we sat at the table like an old married couple sitting on a park bench. I read the first section while he read the sports, and in half an hour or so I was reading the entertainment section and he the business.

I looked up at him, smiled, and said "Thomas, what do you do for a living? Here we are practically living with each other all weekend long and I don't even know where you work."

"Well," he smiled back, "I used to work in Richard's office in Cincinnati, but for now the Alliance has me working for you. Usually, I work for the Alliance in two positions. Some of my time is spent doing accounting, monitoring the Alliance's widespread finances and paying its bills. My more important job, though it takes less time, is as a monk in the Order, except that I spend very little time with the monks.

"As you might imagine, most of us monks are anything but cloistered or living at Eagle Ridge. We serve as adjuncts in our temples, assistants and trouble shooters with our priestesses, and teachers of arcane Dionysian knowledge. The teacher part," he admitted, "isn't a big part of my duties since I'm really still more a theology student as far as that goes. My teaching, therefore, is generally limited to seeker's information. There's a small cadre of men like myself who ensure that seekers learn the basics."

"Is that why you see me so often?" I asked.

"Hardly," he answered, "though that is one of the lesser reasons. More importantly, I've liked you from the day we had lunch in Richard's law office, and I've done my best to be around you as much as possible ever since."

"Well, I'm glad of that," I said. "Is that why you moved to Chicago?"

"Yes," he said, "though the Order wouldn't have let me do it if that were the only reason."

"Does Cynthia need that much help with the local thiasoi? It seems to me that things are going along OK, though I can't really say I know that much about everyone's reaction to the murder."

"Honestly, it's not so much about the thiasoi as it is about

Cynthia. Frankly, she's put herself in a dangerous position, since whoever killed Stacie could just as well have her in his sights as the next victim. I'm in the house as a sort of protection, extra eyes, and someone there to keep track of what's going on when Cynthia's back is turned."

"I'm glad to hear that," I said, "because what I really don't need is for some fanatic to do either of you in, much less both of you."

"There hasn't been much to worry about so far, Ben," Thomas said. "We've had a lot of coming and going at the temple and there've been a lot of eyes and ears open since Stacie's death. The holidays and the theater production have meant that no murderer would have shown his hand.

"Quite frankly, now that things will settle back to normal, so to speak, the danger increases."

"What's normal?" I asked.

"Dionysian worship and the usual instruction of our members is most often a one-on-one occurrence. You know, private instruction, and a believer and a priestess celebrating mysteries just between the two of them. Add to that the coming and going of a few money-making clients and you have a lot of opportunity for Cynthia to be in danger."

"She's not going to take over Stacie's clientele, is she?" I asked.

"I'm sorry to say that she is. First off, it is a major means of support for both her and the temple. Secondly, if Stacie was killed by a client, the only way to find him is to meet her clients."

"You mean that you guys are using Cynthia as bait to trap the murderer? I can't believe you'd do that. I thought you loved her as much as I do. You're both playing amateur cops and both of you are way out of your league."

"I know how you feel," Thomas said, "but we can't ignore any possible path to find a way to get to the bottom of this. If we don't find Stacie's murderer, nobody will, and only the gods know who will become his next victim."

"Shit," I said. "I don't like this one bit either. Let me handle it. That's my job, not yours."

"And what are you going to do about it, Mr. Sherlock Ben Kramer Holmes?"

"Well, since you ask, I think it's time we put our plan to infiltrate the Broadway Community Church into action."

"What we need is a family with money to join the church. Two or three people who can pass as born-again believers. We'll have to sit down with Richard and Sebastian tomorrow to discuss it, but I think that's what we need to do. Any idea who might be able to pull it off?

"I do," said Thomas. "I think we should get Stephanie."

"Stephanie? Stephanie? You mean the old lady I met at Richard's?"

"Bingo, Ben. She can move to Chicago and it'll just so happen that she wants to join a Bible-believing church on the north side. It seems to me that her daughter Rebecca and her husband Joseph would be just the people to help her do that."

"Well," I breathed out deeply, "it seems to me that you've been thinking this one out. At least we'll have some ideas to throw at Sebastian and Richard in the morning. That's good enough for now. Thanks," I said, and kissed him.

We hadn't finished reading the paper when the phone rang. It was Cynthia, asking to speak with Thomas. I heard him say "Yes" and "Good" a couple of times and then he put down the receiver and asked "Are you still planning on going out to dinner with Cynthia?"

"Of course I am," I answered.

He picked up the phone and said "Sure, Ben's coming. What time do you want us to pick you up?" There was a pause and he continued "No, we haven't eaten, so an early dinner would work."

Another pause and then he said "OK, we'll see you at two."

At 1:30 I drove to Ann Sather's in Andersonville and Thomas picked up Cynthia to meet me there. I didn't know what to think about this Sherlock Holmes adventure and began to wonder if Dionysians were even crazier than they seemed. Good sex and lots of it were one thing. Messing with murderers was another. How in Hell were they going to pull this off, I wondered. I wasn't sure if a little group of swingers hidden and operating on the fringe of society had what it took to get this job done, and another murder in their temple wouldn't help, that was for sure.

On the other hand, I had to admit that this really wasn't "a little group of swingers." Everything I had seen so far pointed to a well-financed, well-organized, and certainly well-connected establishment. In fact, sometimes they seemed to be more like the Mafia than a church.

In any case, it was a thought-filled 25 minute drive to the restaurant, and I wondered what new surprises the team of Cynthia and Thomas might throw at me next. I loved them both, that I knew, but this was way more risky than either of them imagined.

Richard, Sebastian, Thomas and I met in the office on Monday. I started the discussion about infiltrating the Broadway Community Church and then asked Thomas to give us his take on it. He talked about Stephanie, Rebecca, and Joseph and then ended with "Ben's not sure we can pull this off, Sebastian. I hope you guys can instill some faith in him for us."

"Well," said Sebastian, "he's right to be cautious. Whoever killed Stacie was no amateur. His ability to penetrate our secrets and to murder and leave so few clues does spell trouble. Fortunately I think we can smoke him out, as long as we are careful and attentive."

211

Sebastian, for one, was making sense.

I turned to Thomas and said "Well, Thomas, at least Sebastian is partial proof that you're not completely out of your minds, but what makes you think those three can pull this off? You know, don't you, that they'll be walking right into the hornets" nest?"

"I'm sure he does," Sebastian interrupted. "Thomas tells me that you became an anazititis just last week, so it's understandable for you to underestimate the size and power of the Alliance. You see, Ben, we are part of an ancient congregation that's older than Christianity and even pre-dates Judaism. Think about the resources that an institution like the Vatican has amassed over the two millennia since that cult was founded. Think of the knowledge, collective experience, hell, even the wealth, that they have at their disposal.

"What you probably don't know is that we can match them, if not in numbers, at least where it counts, in hidden power and expertise. Some three thousand years of experience counts for something, and that something is on our side, even if few people know we have it.

"It is that power, whether it be from knowledge or money, that allows us to hide so well and so completely. It is that same power that means we have to protect ourselves even more carefully. There's been some tragic slip-up here and we've got to get to the bottom of it. Make no mistake about it, we will."

"That makes sense, Sebastian," I said. "I've always meant to ask Thomas how the Alliance could seem to live so high on the hog."

"If you had asked me," Thomas said, "I would have told you some of what Sebastian has said. On the other hand, not all of our secrets are about potions and rituals. I would have had to be discreet in my answers until you had taken at least some vows. Now that you have, there's a great deal to teach you. We're giving you a cram course when taking our time would be the more usual route. Unfortunately none of us knows how much time we really have.

212

After all, the murderer could strike again."

I turned to Sebastian and asked "Do you think we can pull off this thing with Stephanie, Rebecca and Joseph?"

"That depends," he said, "if they can swallow born-again preaching and pray to Jesus like it was saving their souls. On the other hand it really is more up to Stephanie, since she'll be in the thick of it. After all, Rebecca and Joseph will just be her chauffeurs, like any good children would do, especially for a mother with money."

Chapter
Progress 18

The Nova Scotia is a brown and beige high-rise on North Lake Shore Drive, just south of Irving Park Road. Unlike most of the "zip codes in a building," it was actually built with some good taste. Stephanie leased a condo on the southeast corner of the 39th floor. It had great views of the Chicago Skyline and Lake Michigan, was newly remodeled, and had two bedrooms, "one for me and one for you and your friends," she said.

Rebecca and Joseph rented a mansion not too far away.

It took the three of them a couple of weeks to get settled into their respective new digs, buy wardrobes that reflected their newly-assumed status, and to get to know each other's stories as mother, daughter and son-in-law. Since they were already familiar with each other, it was natural for Stephanie (who was going to use the last name of DiCarlo) to take on the persona of Rebecca's mother.

We spent several weeks talking about their lives in Ohio and Stephanie's deceased "husband," Jordan, whose life, as Stephanie created it, was spent working hard and making money the old-fashioned way, but "Thank the good Lord he found Jesus before he was called home."

To learn their parts even better, Stephanie dragged Rebecca and Joseph to evangelical churches across the city. In no time at all they knew the words to "What A Friend We Have in Jesus," "In the Garden," and "Amazing Grace." In the meantime I went hunting for a very used King James Bible so Stephanie could go to church well-prepared. I shook my head thinking about what they were getting themselves into.

While the three of them were becoming "born again," Thomas was hoping I'd learn enough about the Alliance to move on to the traveler's initiation (taxidiotis in Greek, if you must know).

Stephanie was adamant they know their parts well. "Besides," she warned them, "if they think you aren't saved, they'll badger you to come to Jesus no end. Get the lingo and the fervor for their Lord down pat and they won't bother you half as much." That meant, of course, that they had to have salvation stories to tell.

I had no idea what they would think of all this religion back at the detective agency, but it was certain that my gay friends would be shaking their heads in disbelief. On the other hand, most them probably were wondering where the hell I had disappeared to. My time, after all, had really been cornered by Thomas and Cynthia. The intensity of the investigation just meant I saw a lot less of them.

On the other hand, having the use of Stephanie's parking space at the high rise would make it easier for Thomas, Cynthia and me to develop more of a social life on Halsted Street and Broadway.

In the meantime Sebastian had spent considerable time beefing up the surveillance cameras in and around the temple, as well as setting up cameras in the Buena Vista apartment building across from the Broadway church. One of the Alliance's realtors had arranged for us to rent a third floor apartment, and I recruited three out-of-work detectives to ID everyone who darkened the door of the church. Richard used the Alliance's CIA connection to get warrants allowing us to wiretap the church's phones.

By Sunday, April third, the three infiltrators were ready to attend their first service at Broadway Community Church. Since it was Easter, we knew it would be a good day for their first visit. The congregation would be larger than usual and therefore they'd be less noticed, at least that's what we hoped.

Stephanie had planned otherwise. When they got to the church she made sure she filled out the guest book, even to the point of checking the box that read "Please have the pastor call on me" and including her phone number.

To make her point even clearer, when the time came, she put a hundred dollar bill in the collection plate. It was obvious to the three of them that the usher had seen her do it, since it lay, loud and clear for all to see, on the top of a bunch of collection envelopes. The pastor, we knew, would find out about that bit of generosity in no time at all.

Later that afternoon the four of us met in Stephanie's' apartment to get their first report. A look around the church, they said, made it obvious that there weren't many people giving a hundred dollars that week. Broadway Community Church was housed in a small storefront with not much more than curtains in the window and a large white board sign that read "Broadway Community Church, Where We Believe in the Word of God, Rev. Jeremy Horton, Minister of the Gospel." A smaller sign gave the days and times of worship, prayer meetings, Bible studies, and evangelism. We could tell at a glance that there would be lots of opportunities for them to get to know the congregation.

Inside there was a rather stark altar in the back of the single room with a plain cross on the wall behind it. Besides that there was a wooden podium (they said they'd hardly call it a pulpit) and rows of used folding chairs. Between the altar and chairs were four kneelers. "That's where you get saved," Rebecca said. The room itself was filled with an assortment of people, diverse to say the least, but generally appearing to be lower-class, working folk.

Stephanie had hardly needed to put that hundred in the collection plate as her attire, recently purchased at high-end retailers on Michigan Avenue, made her stand out in stark contrast to the usual Target and Wal-Mart clothing that surrounded her.

"Mom" had insisted that Rebecca and Joseph buy new 217

wardrobes, too, so they stood out just as much. Joseph's new Brooks Brothers suit certainly looked sharp, but it was going to take some getting used to. Actually both the suit and the church would take getting used to. We hoped it was just a temporary strategy for the three of them to be going there; we didn't feel at all comfortable, since this crowd would hardly be friendly if they knew what we were doing. These were, after all, the kind of people whose religion let them burn witches in Salem.

"Believe me," said Rebecca, "I would have much rather been drinking a glass of wine to Dionysos and not messing with the Broadway Community Church."

"If you didn't know that the Reverend Horton was white, and you closed your eyes during his sermon," Joseph told us, "you would have sworn you were in a Black Gospel-singing church. Hooting and hollering here was just as spirited as in our Dionysian Temple.

"Oh the exact syllables were different," he continued, "theirs being 'Amen' and 'Thank you, Jesus'' rather than 'La,' 'Lo,' and the name of Dionysos, but really it was the same kind of exuberance. Members of the congregation even had tambourines, and though I didn't hear any flutes or lyres, there were two guitars and a piano."

The service was followed by "fellowship" and it didn't take the Reverend Horton any time at all to wend his way to Stephanie.

For her part, Stephanie said she was quick to introduce herself and begin an exposition about how much she enjoyed the sermon and how inspiring the singing was. "The way the silver words rolled off her tongue," Rebecca said, "one could never guess she was a priestess in the pagan cult of Dionysos.

"She introduced me as her daughter, but the minister, thank the gods, was much more interested in her than in me, so Joseph and I were left acting the part of the dutiful daughter and son-in-law. I admit to showing a bit of impatience about wanting to get out of there, and Stephanie picked up on it, So she went on to remind the pastor that 'These young people just don't pay attention to the Lord as we did, you know,' adding 'but they are good to me and that's what matters, so I'd best not complain.'"

Joseph reported that Horton had lent a sympathetic ear to her mild complaint and assured her that "As long as they love Jesus, they'll do fine. Besides Mrs. DiCarlo, there are lots of women who don't have children who'll get them to church."

"With that," Joseph went on, "Stephanie told him 'Yes, pastor, I am blessed that way, so I'll say no more,' And she gave him her card, saying 'We'd better let you tend to your flock, Reverend, but be sure to come by my new home soon. I'm very impressed with what we've heard today and want to learn more about God's work in this neighborhood.'

"With that, she turned to us and said 'Come now, we've already taken much too much of the pastor's time and the Easter ham will need tending to as well.' Thankfully we made our exit, found the car, and were back at the 'Scotia' in a short time."

I spent the rest of the afternoon at Stephanie's mostly reading the paper and staying out of her way. Cynthia, Thomas, and James were coming over to have dinner with us and Stephanie was cooking a full-fledged Easter feast. I had offered to help her, but she would hear nothing of it, except to have me light the candles and fill the crystal glasses with ice water.

The doorman announced that James was here at about 4:30. He was in his seventies, though his exact age was as elusive as was Stephanie's. These Dionysians, one could easily note, did seem to age gracefully. Thin and agile, he was relatively short, balding, and impeccably dressed, dapper even. He appeared much more impish than one might think, though the imp in him was often hidden by his very submissive actions. In fact, it was obvious that he loved to serve women and by the attention he got from them he must have done so very well.

Stephanie immediately recruited him to help with dinner. A few minutes later the doorman called on the phone to announce that our other guests were here and Stephanie said to send them right up. Four minutes later the doorbell rang and I let our friends in. The pair at the door lunged at me and each planted a kiss on my cheek. "Happy Easter, Ben," Thomas said. "We hear you've found the lord."

I was going to respond with "Cut the crap," but instead I smiled and said "You're right and his name is Dionysos."

"You've got it," said Cynthia, as she walked into the living room. At the same time, Stephanie came out of the kitchen and gave Cynthia a hug and long hard kiss.

"What about me?" complained Thomas.

Stephanie moved away from Cynthia and said "You're next, so don't worry." With that she gave Thomas the same treatment.

"Why am I being left out?" I asked.

"Because Thomas and I have other plans for you for later," said Cynthia, "and we want you begging for it by the time we're ready to take you on."

"I'm ready to beg right now, Ma'am."

"First things first," said Stephanie. "You youngsters are going to have to postpone your orgy until after we eat. Now come on, Ben, and serve my guests a proper drink."

"Yes, Mother," I said with a smile on my face. "What will it be, Cynthia? Coffee, tea, or me?"

"That'll be the day when Cynthia chooses coffee or tea over thee," said Thomas.

"In fact, Ben," Cynthia said, "it will be none of the above. Make me a Bloody Mary."

"And Thomas," I asked, "do you want your regular?"

"Yes," he answered, "but I don't think I need a double."

With that I headed into the kitchen to make drinks and Stephanie asked James to take the appetizers out of the refrigerator and pass them around, while she took a cookie sheet of hot appetizers out of the oven and scraped them onto a serving plate. "Come back for these as well," she said.

The five of us sat in the living room admiring the view and chatting away about the weather, the news, and the investigation. We had agreed that the first visit had gone off well, and that if the murderer were in the congregation they could possibly smoke him or her out.

That led into news about the investigation. I had been interviewing area Dionysians for hints, clues, and leads. One by one I was eliminating each of them from the suspects' list, checking their alibis, attitudes, and feelings about Stacie and her murder. Sebastian had also begun canvassing the neighbors to determine if they had seen anyone come or go to Stacie's home on the evening or night of her murder.

Just at that moment, Stephanie put seven servings of shrimp cocktail on the dining room table and said, "Enough chatter, children, dinner is served." None of us needed any more coaxing than that to get to our places. Stephanie joined us and asked me to pour everyone a glass of wine. I did. We toasted to the return of Dionysos from the underworld, and plunged into the first course.

Sometime between the ham and yams I looked around and remembered Easters in Ohio with my real mom, dad, and my brother John. This meal felt every bit as wonderful as the days of my childhood. I realized that once again I was no longer alone and that these people, who had been totally unknown to me early last summer, had become an important part of my family. Likewise, and what even felt better, was that I knew without a doubt that I had become part of theirs.

After dinner we pitched in to help Stephanie clear the table and then all landed on the sofas in the living room. It was as if I   221 had been transported into an episode of "Lifestyles of the Rich and Famous." "Don't get too comfortable," Cynthia warned me, "as I think we had better leave Stephanie and James to their own devices. Let's the three of us head over to your place, Ben."

"That's fine with me," I said. "Did you guys drive here?"

"Yes," said Thomas, "so why don't you take Cynthia to your place and I'll drive my car right behind you." So we said our good-byes and with lust in our hearts, headed west on Irving Park to my house.

"So," I asked Cynthia once we were out of the parking garage, "what have you been up to?"

"Meeting and getting to know the local thiasoi, mostly," she answered, "and slowly Stacie's clients have been calling to meet me as well."

"Are you being careful?" I asked.

"As careful as I can make it. Thomas has monitors in his upstairs office so he can see and record who comes and goes and much of what happens. I'm almost never out of sight. Sebastian is making a photo collection of everyone so that you and Stephanie can see if anyone who comes to the temple also shows up at Broadway Community."

"Whatever you do," I warned, "don't let anyone slip you a mickey while you're with them."

"Believe me, dear boy, there's no need to worry. I'm doing my best and have two wonderful men watching over me."

I was encouraged by Sebastian's obvious thoroughness and professional attention to detail, but that didn't mean I wouldn't worry about this amazing woman who had entered my life via my heart.

Traffic to the house was light and Thomas rang the doorbell just as Cynthia and I were going into the kitchen through the back door. In no time at all we were in the living room. "Drinks?" I

222

asked.

To my surprise, Thomas said, "No thanks, at least not yet."

I looked at him with amazement and Cynthia spoke up.

"Thomas and I want to talk to you, Ben, about your progress."

"Have I done something wrong?" I asked.

They both laughed and Thomas said "Not at all, lover boy. Not at all. We want to talk about your moving ahead with the next initiation and we want to make sure that it's done right."

"What does that mean?" I asked.

"Well, under most circumstances, it would mean that you would participate in the Alliance for six months to a year, be observed by the congregation in general and the Protectors in particular and finally, everything being a 'go,' receive the next initiation, becoming a taxidiotis. Unfortunately, things in Chicago aren't very usual these days.

"First off, your initiation as an anazititis was a bit rushed, and your inclusion in the search for Stacie's murder has meant that you've been thrust into the midst of a difficult time for the thiasoi, and thirdly I'm afraid that we haven't taken the time necessary to assure you know the fundamental doctrines. None of that, of course, means that you've done anything 'wrong.' It just means that we need to recognize our responsibilities to you and take care to see that we meet them."

"OK," I said. "I'm all ears."

"Thomas is mostly concerned about making sure that you understand the Dionysian viewpoint on doctrine," said Cynthia. "Unlike the mainstream denominations, pagans, by and large, are rather non-dogmatic and hold many varying tenets about their faith. Sometimes those tenets are at odds with one another."

"In that respect," Thomas added to Cynthia's statement, "it's like the various doctrinal differences among Jews or Christians or Hindus, to name but a few. We have our conservatives, moderates, and liberals just like anyone else.

223

"It has to do with the many paths that I've talked about now and again. Wine mixed with herbal potions, for instance, is one way to achieve a vision. Fasting, chanting, and pain are other ways, among many, that lead to a successful vision quest. This is just one example.

"Another example is the interpretation of what is a 'god.' Here again we run the usual gamut of opinions. There are fundamentalist Dionysians who believe that the gods exist as entities to be worshipped, perhaps even to the extent that they dwell on Mount Olympus. On the other end of the spectrum there are those who believe that the whole concept of gods is merely a nice myth, an allegory that works for them but certainly holds no status in objective reality. Since the turn of the last century, Dionysians have increasingly seen the gods as Jung did. That is, they are archetypes in the collective unconsciousness of the human race, passed on from generation to generation as a psychological inheritance from parents to children.

"The idea of archetype, then, implies that the vision of the god is an internal experience. The god is already within you as a characteristic of your inner self, as a power that is yours to discover and embrace."

"Yeah," I said, "I read some of that in Brother Michael's book Eastern Thoughts for the Western Mind. I'm slowly seeing how all of this fits in and, quite frankly, I'm impressed by what I'm learning."

"That's good news," said Cynthia. She turned to Thomas and said "I can see we're really underestimating Ben's progress."

"That's a relief," Thomas said.

"There is, though, one point we have to get clear on," he continued. "What our search for a killer at Broadway Community omits is the possibility that the murderer is actually a member of the Alliance, a right-wing pagan who felt that Stacie's book club, among other ideas she held, was a threat to our security, enough of a threat that he or she deemed murder to be an acceptable solution."

"One might even come to the conclusion," Cynthia said, "that the murderer, if indeed he or she was a Dionysian, believed that Stacie deserved death because she had been too free with our secrets, that she had broken her vows of silence and protection. It's a tragic conclusion but not impossible. After all, you heard what my father said about her classical book club, and he's hardly a right-winger."

"So what you're telling me is that no one can be trusted?" I asked.

"It's not as bad as all that," Thomas answered. "The list of trustworthy Dionysians continues to grow, which means that we're increasingly able to make a list of those who can be trusted. On the other hand, first we need to be careful that what we're doing doesn't become common knowledge, even to the point that your initiation wasn't common knowledge. We only invited the Dionysian believers who we thought were clear of suspicion."

"What does all that have to do with my next initiation?" I asked.

"What it means," said Cynthia, "is that your passage to taxidiotis is going to have be another quiet affair."

"I hardly thought that my last initiation was a quiet affair," I said

"Believe me," said Cynthia. "It was. Under normal circumstances there would have been a lot more than 18 people present."

"Really?" I asked in surprise.

"Yeah," said Thomas, "probably closer to 50. Our rites of initiation reflect the many pathways philosophy as well. The first initiation is centered on the path of wine and herbs. The second initiation is devoted to the path of pain."

"Pain?" I asked.

"Pain as in 'It hurts,'" Cynthia said. "Though we don't often talk about initiation before it is given, when it comes to becoming a taxidiotis, we do. It's only fair to warn the initiate that a good whipping is in his future."

"OK," I said, "when does all this happen?"

"We'd like to schedule it for a week from Saturday," said Thomas. "Do you think you're ready?"

"I guess so," I answered, "but isn't that really up to you guys to figure out?"

"Well," said Cynthia, "we have figured it out and fully expect that the Protectors will agree with us."

In the meantime Stephanie, Rebecca and Joseph went to church again on Sunday. This time the congregation was greatly diminished, they said, it not being Easter. The weather wasn't very enticing for getting out of bed, either, but solving the murder was important, at least to us, if not to the police. They were certainly willing to do their parts, even if it did mean listening to salvation preaching.

"Reverend Horton preached about being anointed with the Holy Spirit," Rebecca later reported, "as that was what the risen Jesus had promised before he ascended to Heaven. 'Getting ready to receive the spirit,' said Horton 'was important and we needed to heed the words of the Bible. After all, it was 'spirit-filled' men and women who would change the world for the better, if only by changing all of us sinners to live according to his Lord's will.'

"Here," she said, "you can listen to the sermon yourself," and handed me a small diskette from the tape recorder she had hidden in her hat.

"Thanks, maybe I'll find salvation with the rest of you," I said, putting it in my pocket.

The next morning, Thomas, Sebastian and I listened to the sermon.

Horton began with a reading from the Book of Judges,

where the Spirit of the Lord came upon Samson, who at the time was a captive of the Philistines. He read:

> And when he came unto Lehi, the Philistines shouted against him: and the Spirit of the LORD came mightily upon him, and the cords that were upon his arms became as flax that was burnt with fire, and his bands loosed from off his hands. And he found a new jawbone of an ass, and put forth his hand, and took it, and slew a thousand men therewith.
>
> And Samson said, "With the jawbone of an ass, heaps upon heaps, with the jaw of an ass have I slain a thousand men."
>
> And it came to pass, when he had made an end of speaking, that he cast away the jawbone out of his hand, and called that place Ramathlehi.

Horton continued his sermon thusly: "My brothers and sisters, let us be mindful that knowing the Lord is but the beginning of our holiness. As Jesus promised, the Holy Spirit comes to anoint us with power, the power to live righteously.

"I plead with you to look around. See the beauty of Lake Michigan and the great parks that line its shore. See the glory of the sunset and the peace of gulls as they drift on the winds. Look at the innocence on the faces of young children and love of husband and wife for one another. Yes, we are blessed with God's goodness."

"Amen," a woman voice shouted onto the tape.

"Yes, sister, amen it is."

"But then, I say, turn your eyes to the city, to the profanity and promiscuity that walk our streets. Only blocks away on Broadway, prostitutes shamelessly hawk their bodies, gang members sell deadly drugs, and derelicts languish in entry ways, their clothing reeking of dirt and alcohol.

"Like Samson, we live among the Philistines. Like Moses,   227 we suffer under the sinfulness of Egypt. Like Jesus himself, we walk among the Pharisees and Sadducees, teachers of religion who live hypocritical lives.

"Know ye not," he read, "that the unrighteous shall not inherit the kingdom of God? Be not deceived: neither fornicators, nor idolaters, nor adulterers, nor effeminates, nor abusers of themselves with mankind, nor thieves, nor the covetous, nor drunkards, nor revilers, nor extortioners, shall inherit the kingdom of God. And such were some of you: but ye are washed, but ye are sanctified, but ye are justified in the name of the Lord Jesus, and by the Spirit of our God."

"That, too, deserves an 'amen' from the lips of believers," said Horton, who paused waiting to hear the amens.

Several in the congregation answered "Amen."

"And what do we read in our papers?" he continued. "News of fornication and adultery. What do we see on Halsted Street? The effeminate who call themselves 'gay" and flaunt their pride parades, abusing themselves man with man and woman with woman. The lord will not abide these sinners.

"As in the days of Samson, yes right here and now, the lord wants to send his anointing spirit to you, to bless you with the spirit that comes upon you, to lead you to clean this land of the filth around us.

"Yes, our lord is the god of love. But I say to you that love has limits. There is no love in sexual promiscuity, no love in homosexuality, no love in liars, in the greedy, and in drunkenness. Hear what it says in Deuteronomy: 'Their wine is the poison of dragons, and the cruel venom of asps.'

"Open your hearts, my brethren. Come forward to let the lord anoint you. Take up the call to purify yourselves and your city. Let righteousness live in you and let sinners be cast into the fires of Hell where they belong. To this I say 'Amen,' and what do you say, my brethren?"

228   At that, the congregation began shouting "Amen," and the

small group of musicians began playing "Nearer my God to thee."

"Come forward, I say to those who say 'Amen.' Let the spirit of God move you to do his holy work. Let him come upon you as it came upon Samson. Let the spirit of God anoint you for his holy work of cleansing. Come forward. Come forward and receive ye the holy spirit."

We could hear the congregation walking to the front of the hall, and Stephanie saying "Let's go." I thought they were leaving until I realized she wanted them to go and get anointed with the rest of them. I guess that's what they did and before long I could hear the Reverend Horton praying for Rebecca in words loud enough for God, wherever he might be, to hear them.

"Holy God," he prayed, "we thank thee for causing this woman to come forward. Bless her heart with your holiness. Make her righteous by the blood of our beloved Lord. Send your spirit upon her to do thy holy will. Make her a Samson onto the people, to deliver them from evil. Amen."

I heard "Amen" as I thought, "Lord Dionysos, I'm glad I wasn't there."

Chapter

Journey

I arrived at the Temple on Saturday at 9 pm, as Thomas had instructed me, entering from the garage as I had the last time. As before, when I got to the foyer, he met me there, banged a tambourine once, and Casey appeared to take me downstairs in preparation for my next initiation. In the anteroom to the cavern, Casey stripped and washed me, then told me to wait until I was called into the ceremony. So I sat there quietly, listening to the singing in the next room.

It wasn't long before Casey came out and escorted me into the temple proper. This time it was properly lit and only a few people were in attendance. He told me to sit in a chair that faced Stephanie, Ariadne, Rebecca, Stephanie, and Richard, who were seated in a semi-circle facing me. Cynthia stood between us, dressed in leopard skins, while Thomas and Casey wore those black kilts with fur trim and heavy boots.

The others were arrayed in what could only be called "Dionysian Drag," much like they had been wearing during my first initiation. I felt a little uncomfortable, since this time I was the only one who was naked.

"Brother Ben," said Cynthia, "you are here for your next initiation into our sacred thiasoi. You have spent some nine weeks seeking our lord. Now it is time for these five believers, sworn to protect our gatherings, to question your progress and pass judgment on your readiness to advance in the practice and knowledge of our sacred rites.

231

As you have been taught, we are a people of many paths. The first, that of anazititis, is one entered with the aid of wine and herbs. The second, taxidiotis, uses the path of pain. If you are found worthy, will you freely and willingly agree to undergo the torment of whips?"

"I will," I said, giving the answer that Thomas had taught me, "because I seek to know the Lord Dionysos in all his manifestations."

"You have spoken well," said Cynthia. Turning to the five, she asked "Are the Protectors ready to proceed?"

"We are," said Stephanie. Then standing and approaching me she said "Dear Ben, though we have seen each other often and have become close friends in these few weeks, I still must strive to keep our assembly safe from those who would mock our ceremonies and profane our temples. Tell me, then, what have you learned as a seeker?"

"I have been blessed with joy in the lord's ways and fellowship with holy brethren," I said, again as I had been taught. "If I may speak from my heart as well," I added, "I have found a new and greater family in the thiasoi and have seen remarkable visions of the gods."

"Thank you," she said, and returned to her seat.

Rebecca stood up next and as she did, Richard stood and interrupted her. "Excuse me, sister, but before you pose the required questions, I think it's necessary for the record that I explain to the Protectors why we are seeking initiation now, and to Ben how he should answer."

"Really?" she asked. "OK, if you say so."

"Ben," said Richard to the Protectors, "has undertaken an important and possibly dangerous task, helping a select few from the assembly to search for Stacie's murderer. It is for that reason that there are so few Brethren here today. I am going to advise Ben to speak freely of his efforts and to withhold no information from any of you, as I believe it is important that each of you have full

232

knowledge of our investigation.

"On the other hand, I want to remind all of us of the serious threat we are under at the hands of a murderous intruder, who must be brought to justice. I say that, not only for the sake of Justice, but in order to assure that each and every one of us can worship freely and without threat of harm.

"Remember that we have little or no confidence that we will be safe until Stacie's murderer is found. I will also remind you that we have few clues as to who he or she might be. Unfortunately the fact that Stacie was found dead in this very room is a mystery yet to be solved. We don't know if she brought a believer here to worship or if an unbeliever used drugs to force his way with her in order to uncover the secrets that this basement holds. Therefore, in the privacy and holiness of our temple, I ask you, Ben, to tell the Protectors whatever they ask of you.

"And to everyone I say to remember that great discretion is needed, lest the murderer learn of our search for him or her, and our plans are thus thwarted."

With that Richard sat down and said to Rebecca, "Thank you, dear sister, please continue."

"Richard," she said as she turned to him, "why did you include Ben in this search?""

"Because not only is he a seeker and comes from an Alliance family, he has experience as a detective far greater than any of ours."

"And what, Ben," Marjorie asked, "do you think of all this?"

"I think that the teachings of this temple far surpass the evil messages anyone's heard in the Broadway Community Church. I'd rather be anointed with your wine than their spirit."

"That is enough for me, brother. Thank you. Your secret and your work are safe with me."

"And with me," said Casey. "I have no questions."

Stephanie turned to Ariadne and said "And you, Ariadne,

what do you want to ask?"

"Well," she said, "I have heard enough, but before we proceed, I believe we ought to follow our traditions. Ben," she said to me, "why do you believe that Dionysos is lord?"

"Well," I answered, "the teachings I have learned so far make sense to me, and getting to know several Dionysians very well has added a great deal of both pleasure and comfort to my life. Beyond that, however they were induced, the mystical states I have experienced were powerful and empowering. I believe I have seen Dionysos and in doing so I have come to love him."

"And what did you see when you saw him?"

"Well, it's happened a couple of times, but the most powerful encounter was here, in this room, when I became a seeker. At first, faces seemed to dart in and out of my vision. They were powerful masks like African witch doctors might wear. It looked like gods and goddesses were staring at me. I saw Father Zeus watching me, his flowing beard and the whiteness of his hair making him appear as old as time, and then there was Mother Rhea, full-breasted and ripe with milk, opening her arms to me.

"Suddenly Dionysos danced around me, laughing, laughing, and gulping clusters of grapes. He kept circling me. Then everything became quiet. It was if it were only him and me. 'Take courage,' he said. 'You have found favor in my heart.' And the vision was over."

Ariadne said, "Thank you, Ben. I am done."

There was a long pause, as if everyone was taking in my vision, seeing what I had seen or remembering visions of their own. Then Cynthia spoke up and asked, "Are the Protectors ready to proceed?"

In turn each of them said "Yes" and Casey came over to me, gently pulled me out of the chair, and led me back into the antechamber.

When we got there, he said "Well said, Ben. Now, wait here. I am sure it will only be a few minutes before we will proceed." With that, he went back into the temple, shutting the door behind him.

As he had said, it was only two or three minutes before he returned and brought me back to face the small congregation of Dionysians. Cynthia smiled at me as I entered and Casey told me to stand in front of the Protectors. Cynthia then said "How do the Protectors answer his request to continue his journey?"

"Let him proceed," Stephanie said, as did each of the others in turn.

At that the Protectors stood, and taking turns, chanted ancient verses that recalled the Titans and their cruel murder of Dionysos, Zeus's child:

Let us recount that tragic day
When our toddling Lord was at play
Midst the crests and waves of sea
Besides the shore in happy glee.

When from the depths of Tartarus prison
Did come the ghosts of Titans risen,
Spurred on by hateful Hera
Who to the child would bring her terror.

With those words Thomas and Casey donned terror-inducing masks of hideous faces, and stood in front of me.

Spying there the young god-man
They devised their devious plan.
With toys to woo the young lad
They enticed him to come to land

And having the child in their grasp
They now laughed at what would come to pass
They ripped the child from his play
And there determined him to slay.

At which point they pulled me to the altar, binding me to its hard cold surface.

Zeus's son and Semele's child
Would now suffer their hatred wild
With hands and teeth the kid they'd rend,
With evil passion his life they'd end.

They began flogging me, thankfully only softly, though as the stanzas went on they increased their beating and at some point, they exchanged floggers for whips and then whips for single tails. I felt them cutting the flesh on my back. I began to writhe with pain. I could feel the Titan's hatred in the slashing of my skin.

And when the child lay dismembered
Sweet meat they saw, ever so tender
And gathering the pieces into a cauldron
They built a fire to boil god's son.

Only the heart did they set aside
The rest they ate by the rising tide,
Not knowing that Zeus's ire
Would soon send down his wrathful fire.

Pain. It was searing pain. I began crying and screaming, yet my tormentors were relentless. I knew they were going to kill me. In panic I yelled for them to stop. Still the whipping continued. Drops of blood, my blood, splattered on the floor around me. What did they want, I asked myself. How far will they go, I wondered. The pain was exhausting me. My screams ceased; my sobs stopped. I could only lie there, as if dying. Still the beating and the chanting continued.

Lightning came and the villains it smote

And from their meal rose the smoke.
Holy son, we mourn your death
And wail as children left bereft.

With the lash we feel your pain
For joining you is our gain.
Knowing full well that life returns
For your power none can burn.

Mighty god-man risen you'll be
And enthroned for all to see.
Lord proclaimed as is only right
God of all, both day and night.

Thrice-born god we worship you.
Though you the Titans thought to slew
From Hades you returned
Risen now and power renewed.

So thy holy fate we choose
With thee our mortal bonds to lose.
Make us one with thee
And from death set us free.

With gladdened hearts to thee we sing
Let these walls with thy praises ring.
By many names we thee adore
And worship thee forevermore.

And then there was quiet. Deep tranquil quiet. No chanting.
No whipping.   No movement. I closed my eyes and felt the
darkness of the moment and when I did I saw the gentle face of
Dionysos.

Chapter 20

The Pastor Visits

I begged off going to Stephanie's the next afternoon as my back, though it seemed to glow with pleasure, was in no shape for a meeting. Instead I slept at Cynthia's that night, alone in a guest room. After the initiation Thomas had applied a soothing and healing herbal mixture to me, so I had slept well.

When I woke the next morning I knew I had been dreaming, though I had no idea about what. Cynthia and Thomas insisted that I stay with them for the day, which we passed quietly.

Stephanie called us at about two in the afternoon to say that after the Sunday service Pastor Horton had told her he would like to come over for a visit. She had delayed it until Wednesday and converted the visit into a dinner party with her, the pastor, and Rebecca and Joseph. "I'll be damned," she said, "if I let that rogue visit me alone."

"OK," I answered with a smile, "Let me know what happens."

On Tuesday afternoon, Stephanie called me at work to discuss their plans for Horton's visit. Simply put, they'd let him talk about his plans for the ministry. Stephanie would encourage him to go into the need for cleaning up the neighborhood and Joseph, too busy to do missionary work for the church, would see if they might help out financially. She was convinced that the quickest way to that pastor's heart was with cash. I regretted the idea of spending the Alliance's money on getting rid of prostitutes, but I knew that if it led to a conviction it would be money well spent.

239

On Thursday, Stephanie and Rebecca came down to the office to give Sebastian and me all the details of their last night's dinner party.

Although Stephanie had told Horton his wife was welcome to come as well, he had said, "Thank you, sister, but the Lord saw fit to take her to Himself eight years ago, and since then I have had to labor in the vineyard alone."

When Stephanie related that tidbit to me, she added "I'm not sure if I should believe he is really a widower or not. If it's true, then she sure was lucky to be freed from the likes of him. How these Bible-believing women can put up with that misogynist crap is beyond me."

Reverend Horton had arrived at six p.m. as planned, and Stephanie told the doorman to let him in. He was wearing a blue suit and tie, Stephanie told me, though the tie was more than a decade out of vogue. He carried what looked like a well-thumbed Bible, which, of course, they were sincerely hoping he would not open.

"Why, Reverend Horton," Stephanie had gushed, "you look so nice this evening. I am really so pleased that you've come to dinner. Now make sure that when you say grace for us, you ask the good lord to bless this home. You know, I've only been here a short time and it never hurts to have a man like you ask the Lord's protection, especially these days in a city like this one.

"Lord only knows I wouldn't have left my home in Ohio if it weren't that it's so much easier for Joseph to be here to watch over our investments. He and Rebecca are all the family I have now, since my husband Jordan passed on, and it really was lonely living alone. I'm alone now, too, but at least they're nearby when I need them."

"Well, Mrs. DiCarlo," said the reverend, "I sure hope you're not lonely for long. We'd be really happy to know that you've found a second home with us at Broadway Community Church."

"That's so kind of you to say, pastor," Stephanie told me she had said, "I have to say that I am delighted to have found real Bible teaching so close to my condominium. Of course we did have to look high and low before the Lord led us to your preaching."

"Thank you for saying that, Mrs. DiCarlo. I pray daily that Christ-filled people like you will join in our work."

"Now, pastor, please call me Stephanie," she had gone on. "There's no need for formality among brothers and sisters in the lord."

"Well, I will, Stephanie, if you insist. Please call me Jeremy."

"Thank you, but I think not. It's one thing for the pastor to call a sister by her first name, but I'm going to call you pastor because I know the lord's anointing is on you, and I want to recognize it.

"Now enough of chatter; Rebecca, you and Joseph talk with the pastor and I'll get us something to drink. Will sparkling grape juice suffice, reverend? I thought it might add a festive touch to our dinner."

"As the Bible says, Stephanie, I'll eat whatever you set before me with a humble heart. You know it is nice that we can have bubbling grape juice and avoid the evils of wine." With that "Mrs. DiCarlo" left the other two to fend for themselves with Reverend Horton.

"Tell me, Rebecca," he asked her, "how did you find the Lord?"

It was a question we all knew would be coming, so Rebecca told him the story we had planned. "Mom raised me in the church, and during a revival when I was high school I gave my heart to the Lord."

"Bless the lord for that, sister. So many children are departing from the ways of their forefathers. I can only take heart in that the Bible says 'Train a child in the way he should go, and when he is old he will not turn from it.'"

Stephanie returned with the grape juice and appetizers and the four of them toasted to the Lord. Although the odds (three for Dionysos, one for Jesus) were on their side, that didn't make the juice taste nearly as good as a glass of monastery wine would

241

have.

Horton grilled them on Joseph's work and they told him how Dad had built up a number of factories around the country, mostly doing higher-end machining and specialized metal work. Now that he was gone, it was Joseph's job to make sure everything ran smoothly and that the family fortunes continued to grow and were protected. We had hoped it was a subject that the pastor would know little about. We were wrong. Horton told them that he had been a welder before the Lord had called him "into the vineyards of his service."

With that they decided it would be better to keep him talking about himself, so they asked him how he found the Lord, how he had received his calling to the ministry, and when he had come to Broadway Community Church.

It turned out that Horton had been invited to a revival meeting some ten years ago in southern Illinois where he found the Lord. That led to his joining a small white board church where he eventually became a deacon. He had first come to Chicago some five years ago to work on a construction site, where he had discovered the filth of Halsted Street and Broadway. He went on to tell them that "It was then that I knew the good Lord wanted me to come back here someday and bring the message of salvation to this neighborhood."

"He was pretty livid," Joseph added, "about cleaning up this den of vipers and ridding the city of the demon forces of alcohol, drugs, and promiscuity. The Bible made it clear, he told us, that God's wrath would and must come down on these prostitutes and blasphemers."

We wondered what had brought him to this neighborhood in the first place, but they had decided not ask the question, though he would have probably just told me that it was the Lord. "Finally," Rebecca told me, "I was relieved when Stephanie began to put food on the table. In a few minutes dinner was ready and we made our way to the table.

"Joseph usually says grace for us when he's here, reverend,"

Stephanie had explained, "but we'd be really pleased to have you ask the Lord's blessing for us."

"My pleasure, Stephanie," the pastor said, and immediately began a long oration, blessing the food, the people, and the house. It was a good long prayer and one that guaranteed that the vegetables would be cold by the time they began eating.

When they had said "Amen," Stephanie thanked him and began passing around the roast beef and potatoes. She guessed that the long prayer had really worked up the pastor's appetite as he dug right in, not that they could blame him. Stephanie was quite a good cook. I wondered how he'd like the meat if he knew it had been offered to Dionysos.

Stephanie took over the conversation from there, prompting Horton to tell the story of how he had founded Broadway Community Church and what plans he had for its future. The pastor didn't need much encouragement and before long, he was explaining in detail his grandiose expansion plans to buy another old church near Broadway and Montrose "as soon as the Lord gives us the wherewithal to do so."

"Shouldn't you wait until the current store front is bit more crowded?" Rebecca had asked. "I'm not sure the current number of believers could support a building of that size, at least not yet."

"Well, sister," he said, "you're right about our numbers, but I know that a better looking church will bring in more sinners. You've just got to believe that the Lord will provide what we need to do his work. After all," he added, "God would smite evildoers as part of His plan to restore holiness to the world."

With that Stephanie went into a long narration about her husband Jordan and how that was what he had said about our prosperity, once he had found the Lord. Rebecca and Joseph let the two of them carry on for the rest of the meal. For their part, they'd rather have been having dinner with Cynthia, Thomas and me.

243

On Friday, Stephanie called me to insist that I drive her to church on Sunday as she wanted to be sure to tell Horton how much she had enjoyed his visit. Since Rebecca and Joseph had taken a quick trip back to Florida and the weather forecast was for clear skies and mild temperatures, and my back was fully healed, I didn't have a way out, so I did.

There weren't any parking spaces in the block before the church, so I had to drive past it, hoping to find a spot not too far away. "Oh my god," I said, just as I drove past the church door.

"What's wrong, Ben?" Stephanie asked.

"Don't look now," I said, "but I think I know the two people who just went into the church." With that I sped up, hoping that they hadn't seen me or my car.

A half a block away there was a spot, but I just kept on driving. A block later, I found another spot and pulled into it. I turned to Stephanie and said, "I think I just saw a couple I met at the theater walk into the church. They're not Dionysians. If they are who I think they are, I met them at the Bacchanalian play the thiasoi put on. They knew Thomas and invited us to their home for dinner."

"Well," said Stephanie, "we can't take a chance on their seeing you, but they won't know me. I'll walk back to the church and see if I can meet them. What do they look like?"

"He's a slightly over-weight guy with a rather petite wife who dresses like a librarian. Their names are Mark and Beth. They're in their late fifties and attended Stacie's book club. I recognized her by the church-lady hat and long coat with fur trim."

"Leave it to me, young man. I'll call you after the service is over."

"Yes, Ma'am," I said, kissed her on the cheek and added "Be careful. We don't need another dead priestess in Chicago."

"You never mind me, Ben. Our lord has got more on the ball than theirs."

As it turned out, Thomas and Sebastian were having coffee in Cynthia's kitchen when I arrived there. Cynthia was in the shower

244

but joined us shortly, her hair in a towel and wearing a terry cloth bathrobe. "Well," I said when she came into the kitchen, "you sure look like someone's wife this morning."

"I'll 'someone's wife' you," she smiled, giving me a kiss on the cheek. "Don't I get one?" Thomas said with a whine.

"You got plenty last night, big boy," Sebastian answered.

"So what brings you out this morning, Ben?" Cynthia asked, pouring herself a cup of coffee and taking the last chair at the table.

"I drove Stephanie to church and I think I saw Mark and Beth going into Broadway Community. I'm not positive, but I think it was them."

"Who are they?" Cynthia asked.

"A couple from Skokie who I know from the book club," said Thomas.

"What do we know about them?" Sebastian asked.

"Not much," Thomas answered. "As best I can tell they have been regulars at the book club for about six months or so. I do know that Mark had asked Stacie a lot of questions and she had met with him privately once or twice. I don't know if his wife was there or not. She had told me that he had questioned her about the group, had figured out that we were somewhat religious, and seemed to want to know more.

"Stacie had told me she had been cautious at first in telling him much about the Brethren, but both of them seemed enthusiastic about studying the classics."

Sebastian turned to Thomas and asked "Has either of them asked to join?"

"As far as I can tell, Mark asked Stacie about it and she had told him about learning about the faith, but that if he was to join, then Beth would have to join as well. You know, it's the 'single people can join singly but partners have to join together' rule. I guess that Beth was more reticent about joining."

"Do we know their last names?" Sebastian asked.

245

Cynthia volunteered an answer: "I think I saw them listed on Stacie's book club list. I'll go look," and in a few minutes returned with Stacie's address book, turned to the back of it and read "Mark and Beth LaForge, Kedvale Avenue, Skokie," and a phone number.

"I'll be right back," Sebastian said, hurrying out of the room. The three of us sat around mostly just looking at each other, and Sebastian came back in about seven minutes. "He's got a record," he said, "but it dates back more than ten years and it's only for petty behavior. Not enough to make him a murderer."

"I think we'd better go over to Stephanie's," I said. "This isn't much to go on, though it's a lot more than we had yesterday. Thomas, you'd better see if you can get in touch with Richard and have him meet us at Stephanie's if at all possible."

"Will do," Thomas said, and went to the nearest phone.

It took a short while for Thomas and Sebastian to get ready to leave and a longer while for Cynthia to get dressed . I drove Sebastian over to Stephanie's in my car and Cynthia and Thomas followed along a little later. On the way, Sebastian quizzed every detail I could remember out of me about the LaForges. "I haven't gotten to interviewing the book club attendees yet, and it might be a good thing that I didn't," I said. "I might have scared them off, if I had. I'll have to get back to Clark, Michael, Marjorie, and Christine, though, to see what they can tell us about these two."

Stephanie hadn't yet returned from church when we let ourselves into her apartment. I called the front desk and told the doorman that we were expecting Thomas, Cynthia and Richard and to let them come up. The three of them arrived about half an hour later and Stephanie walked in right after them. I was pretty hungry by this time, but Cynthia had had the good sense to stop at the Swedish bakery on Montrose for pastries. Stephanie brewed a pot of coffee and we eventually all settled around the dining room table.

246   "Thomas filled me in a bit on the elevator on the ride up,"

Richard began. "It sounds like the investigation is heating up."

"It is, Richard, but it's only really just beginning."

Turning to Stephanie, Sebastian asked "And what do you have to add to today's discovery?"

"The music had started by the time I got there," she answered, "but I spotted the two of them near the back of the church. There was an empty chair right next to the woman, so I sat there.

"They joined into the singing rather exuberantly and the woman followed the pastor's text in her Bible. He gave another rip roaring hellfire damnation sermon about bringing righteousness to the land.. On the way out I positioned myself right in front of them in the line to greet Reverend Horton and I made it a point to thank him for his visit. For his part, he made it a point to introduce me to the couple right behind me. You were right, Ben. Their names are Mark and Beth LaForge, at least I think that's what their last names are. Pastor Horton gave them a rousing endorsement of me and asked them to make sure that I felt at home in the congregation, since, he told them, I had only recently moved to Chicago."

"'Sure will,' Mark told the pastor, and after the introductions we moved along to the sidewalk. The two of them spent some time talking with me, or should I say that Mark spent time talking to me. His wife was pleasant enough but hardly forth-coming.

"'It was a distance for them to drive from Skokie, Mark told me, but they 'were glad to have found a preacher who knew what sin was and who wasn't afraid to preach against it. Too many preachers,' he said, 'are watering down God's word, and it was the likes of them that had led our country away from the true gospel of repentance from sin.'

"His wife only said that she was glad to have met me and hoped she'd see me at the Bible study on Tuesday night. By that time I'd had more than enough of Mark's preaching about preachers so I thanked them for making me feel welcome and said that I hoped I would see them again soon. Then I hailed a cab and came here."

"Well, what do you all think?" I asked.

Richard said. "Having two suspects and a motive isn't enough to make a case in court. We'll need a lot more evidence than this before we can go to the police."

"Anyone have any ideas?" Sebastian asked.

"It looks to me that we're going to have to get closer to Mark and Beth than we might like, and that looks like a job that I'm going to have to do," said Cynthia.

"That may be true," I said, "but you're not getting close to them without a chaperone. If Stephanie needs one to have dinner with Horton, you're not getting away with anything less."

"OK," Sebastian said. "Come on folks, brainstorm some other ideas."

"Well," said Stephanie, "it wouldn't hurt if I began attending Bible classes with Beth."

"Alone?" I asked. "Yes, alone, my dear boy," she answered. "After all it's only Bible class and I can take a cab both ways."

"I can start up the book club again," Thomas volunteered. "As much as it's controversial among the Brethren, it might help our investigation of Mark and Beth. And I certainly think that Clark, Michael, Marjorie, and Christine might shed some light on this as well."

"Yes," I said. "Asking them about these two is on the top of my to-do list."

"If you do start up the book club, Thomas," Richard said, "it needs to be somewhere other than at the Temple. Having unbelievers allowed there so freely was one of the more common complaints. I know that clients are usually unbelievers as well, but at least there's more than a passing chance that they'll neither ask questions nor talk about where they've gone."

"Don't worry, Richard," Thomas replied. "I hear you loud and clear on that one."

"Any chance of tracking down where those mickey pills came from?" I asked.

Not until we find an actual pill," Sebastian answered. "If we did find some, that would be evidence, but you can't track its source once it's been digested. Without fingerprints, the murder weapon, or a witness, the only thing we have to go on is the DNA. With the amount of time that has passed and the number of people that have come and gone from Stacie's since the murder, we can really only go on whatever evidence the police have already found."

"Then, maybe," Thomas said, "it's time for you to have a talk with the police detective."

"Yeah," Sebastian said as he shook his head, "that's a good idea. Unfortunately these guys are very territorial and my experience tells me that if they thought we were intruding on their turf, they wouldn't be very happy about it."

"So where does that leave us?" Cynthia asked.

"It means," said Stephanie, "that we have our work cut out for us, which is certainly no surprise. I'll go to Broadway Community on Tuesday night; Thomas will look into reviving the book club; Cynthia might want to meet Mark and Beth to talk about their interest in the Alliance; and Thomas will have to get another invite to dinner at their home."

"I can see that we can't keep you away from Broadway Community Church," Sebastian said to Stephanie, "and Ben certainly has to talk to the four others who might shed some light on the LaForges, but other than that, don't do anything else until we have time to mull over the other ideas for a few days. Let's plan on meeting here again on Wednesday night. Is that OK with you, Stephanie?"

"Of course it is, my dear, and I'll make sure I have dinner ready at six."

"I guess that's enough for now," Sebastian said.

"Yeah," I said. "I could use something to think about other than murder or verses from the King James Bible."

"Then we'll have to take you back home with us and distract you from both those topics," Thomas said.

"No!" Richard said sharply. "We can't keep Ben away

from the temple completely, but if the wrong people see him coming and going in and out of it regularly, they might become suspicious. There's nothing to say that only the LaForges are in on this caper and since it's obvious now that there's a connection between Broadway Community and the Chicago thiasoi, we have to be even more careful. If you young people want to party, then go somewhere else to do it."

"OK," I chimed in, "then it's my place. The last one there is it. Come on, Cynthia, let's beat Thomas to my bedroom."

With that she and I said our goodbyes and left. Thomas was quick to join us in the elevator before the door closed behind us. "Besides," Cynthia said on the way down, "it's time that Richard, Sebastian, and Stephanie had some time without us young people watching."

"Well, what did you think of that meeting?" I asked Cynthia on the car ride to my place.

"I think we're all tired of the topic. We also can't help but feel more threatened and more fearful as we get closer to discovering the murderer. Richard's right. There's really no way to know how many people are in on the crime. A place like Broadway Community and a preacher like Horton can create quite a horrible nest of pro-Jesus hatred.

"Ever read any of Jonathan Edwards's sermons? The one called 'Sinners in the Hands of an Angry God' was reputed to have started the Salem witch hunts. Take a dose of fundamentalist, sectarian doctrine, bolster it with good old-fashioned Bible quotes, mix it well with negative human emotions, and in no time at all you're burning women at the stakes. The Hebrews, too, were, after all, out to commit complete genocide against the Canaanites who lived in what they called 'their promised land.' The Pilgrims thought nothing of murdering or enslaving the native tribes of New England. And in the name of racial purity, eight million people were murdered by the Nazis.

"Each of those persecutors thought they had God on their side and were purifying the land in order to create for themselves some kind of a new and better society. For better or for worse, Ben, there's a direct link between Dionysians and Canaanites, just as there is between Joshua's invading army of Hebrews from Egypt and the likes of the self-righteous members of Broadway Community Church. Read Edwards and you'll see what I mean.

"For now, though, honey, when we get to your place, pour me a stiff drink and rip off my clothes. We've spent too much time playing detective and way too little making love."

I breathed a deep sigh and said "You're right about that, Ma'am. If I rip off your clothes will you punish me for it?"

"Only if the punishment includes you fucking me," Cynthia said laughingly.

In the meantime, I had forgotten my race to get to the house before Thomas and made the mistake of stopping on the way home to pick up some steaks and trimmings for dinner. When we finally got home, Thomas was cooling his heels on the front porch with his notorious brief case in hand.

"What did you all do," he asked, "stop at the nearest rest area for a quickie?"

"Hardly, minion," Cynthia replied. "We were buying some nice red meat to feed the savage lust in your heart."

"Good," he said. "I'll take a double serving. Just make sure it's dripping with blood."

"You're on, pagan," Cynthia promised. "Shall we offer it to idols first?"

"Only if there's enough left over for the three of us when they're done with it," Thomas said.

By then the three of us were in the kitchen and Thomas asked for some wine glasses and opened his brief case.

"Wine?" I asked. "No hard stuff?"

"Wine," he answered. "A good monastery pressing, at that." 251

Let's have a real Dionysian celebration. After all, if the lord of the vine can't gladden our hearts, who can?" With that he took out two bottles of wine and asked for a corkscrew.

"Sure," I said, opening a kitchen drawer. "Just remember you're going to get more than just a corkscrew today."

"I hope so," he grinned. "You know you're not the only one who's tired of all this detective work." He opened both the bottles, poured wine into the three glasses which Cynthia had gotten for him, and gave each of us one of them. "To Dionysos, lord of the vine and lord of the glad heart," Thomas said.

"To Dionysos," Cynthia and I said, raising our glasses.

In no time at all we were sitting stark naked on my bed and drinking wine right out of the bottle. "Do you really offer meat to idols?" I asked.

"Ah," said Cynthia, "the man on the journey wants his next lesson."

"No time like the present," Thomas said. "Here goes."

"Well, Ben, you've just popped one of the most often asked questions in the initiation process, and to be frank about it, the answer is yes. I mean we are pagans, after all, and whatever you remember from either the Old Testament or from classics classes probably has some semblance of truth to it. So let's put the cards on the table: we sacrifice animals in our worship to the gods."

"Really?" I asked.

"Really!" Thomas answered. "Now before you get all bent out of shape, let me ask you a question."

"OK," I said, " go on. I'm listening."

"Where do you think those steaks you brought home from the store come from?"

"From a butcher. Where else?" I answered.

"Exactly. From a butcher. And if you're a kosher-keeping Jew, it would have been from a rabbinical butcher. And if you lived your life according to the Koran, it would have been a Muslim butcher who did it according to the sacred precepts of his faith. Hell, if you were a good Catholic, when you went to communion, you'd be eating the flesh and drinking the blood of Jesus.

"Sacrifice and eating what is sacrificed is as common as can be. We ritually slaughter animals as part of our Dionysian recognition that everything, red meat included, comes from the bounty of the gods -- that is, by whatever name or theology you use to hold the concept of creator and provider sacred. Doing so is among the most primitive and the most holy of human actions.

"Now as to the idol part, we Dionysians do things a little differently than some others, even if some people think we worship a phallus in a basket as an idol.

"I suppose, like the rest of our doctrines, there are all sorts of interpretations of our sacrificial rites. You know, the 'many paths' philosophy I talked about a couple of weeks ago. Cynthia and I haven't ever discussed what we believe as individuals, so I'll let her tell you what she believes about it after I tell you what I understand it to be. When we're done, you'll just have to figure it out for yourself -- or else become a vegetarian.

"I see it two ways. First, the meat I offer to the gods I offer to you and to Cynthia and to the god that I am. Each of us, as I've said before, is divine and the offering means that we offer it to each other. Yeah, sometimes and in some places there is a representation of that god-in-us, but for the most part we are the gods that we worship. It is the recognition of all that is good in life and so we nurture and feed life.

"The other side of that equation, so to speak, is that we recognize the opposite of life, by which I mean death. We acknowledge that only by the death of the living, such as plants and animals, is life, our life and the life of all living things, sustained.

"That is the completeness of the Dionysian mysteries. Dionysos, god and man, the one who died and yet cannot die.

The one who cares and nurtures and, as I said in our toast, makes us glad, but who is also the wrathful angry god, who drives men mad. We have, I hope you see, no choice in life but to take in all of life, the good and bad, the beautiful and the ugly, the living and the dying, and celebrate it as life, all of life."

"Very good, Mr. Theologian," Cynthia said. "But just because I have some wine in me doesn't mean I'm going to continue this heady conversation. Ben, I agree with everything Thomas just said. Now kiss me, you two fools, and when we're done with loving you can both go back to the kitchen and cook the steaks."

Stephanie's apartment reeked of sautéed onions when I got there at about 5:45 on Wednesday. I'd had a busy day at work and since the Howard "L" train that brought me from the Loop to Addison was as slow and crowded as usual, the aroma was even more appetizing and encouraging. I wondered if Stephanie had gotten the idea out of Marabel Morgan's book, *The Total Woman,* or if instead Marabel had gotten the idea from Stephanie.

Thomas, Cynthia, and Sebastian had arrived there before I did, and two minutes after I arrived, the doorman rang to say that Richard was in the lobby. Stephanie had already told Thomas to serve drinks and Cynthia was putting out appetizers. I figured that the Alliance might not be the only religion to serve salvation with good food and drink included, but that even Episcopalians couldn't have it this good.

The party-like atmosphere hid the fact that the gathering was of a group of quasi-amateur detectives trying to find Stacie's murderer. There were cut flowers in a vase on the coffee table, and the views of the Chicago skyline and Lake Michigan made me feel like it really was a party. Obviously no one wanted to discuss a plan. "How's everyone doing?" I naively asked.

"Don't ask," Cynthia said. "We're not going to talk business until after dinner. Stephanie said so."

254

"OK," I said. "I always do what Mom tells me."

Stephanie walked into the living room, a fancy apron protecting her usual attractive attire. "You'd better do as you're told, son," she said with a grin, "or I'll have Sebastian take you over his knee."

"Really, Sebastian?" I asked. "Would you do that for Stephanie?"

"That and more," he answered.

"Well, I'm glad to hear that. When do you want me to misbehave?"

"Careful what you pray for," Cynthia said. "Even a masochist like you couldn't handle what Sebastian dishes out."

"Don't get your hopes up, lover boy," Thomas said. "I know for a fact that Sebastian's wife has told him that men are off limits."

"Even Dionysians have to make sacrifices to keep peace in the family," said Richard.

"Yes," said Sebastian, "it's true. To be honest about it, you men are good looking but, sorry, you're not my type."

"Come on, Sebastian, even straight men like blow jobs," Thomas said.

"That's true," Sebastian admitted. "That's why my wife makes sure she gives me really good ones."

Stephanie started dinner service with crab cakes, and to look at the size and quantity of crab meat, you would have thought she owned a fish store. She followed that with spaghetti, meat balls, and Caesar salad, ending dinner with vanilla ice cream drowned in rum-soaked raspberries. Of course it was all lubricated with monastery wine.

Thankfully, the wine lubricated us as well, so when Sebastian, drill sergeant that he is, said we needed to talk, it didn't feel any way near as bad as I thought it would. Cynthia suggested we should help Stephanie clear the table before we got down to business, but Stephanie wouldn't hear of it. "James," she said, "will be here in the morning, and cleaning up will distract him enough that I'll be able to get some reading done."

With that, Sebastian stood up and we all went into the living room. When we were all seated, he said "Why don't you start, Stephanie? What did you learn last night?"

"It's no wonder," she said, "that Beth LaForge read those Homeric hymns so well. She must have read the KJV every day since she was weaned. If you'd listen to her quote the Bible, you'd think she'd never leave Skokie, much less come to a Dionysian party in Rogers Park.

"The Bible study group had nine people in attendance, a few of whom I have seen at church. I was familiar with Beth, who was there without Mark, and with Pastor Horton, of course. Horton introduced me to the others at the beginning of the meeting: Chris and Marian, Jeff, Elizabeth, Theresa, and Colleen. The group had chosen to study parts of the Book of Revelation, so Horton began with these verses: 'But I have a few things against thee, because thou hast there them that hold the doctrine of Balaam, who taught Balac to cast a stumbling block before the children of Israel, to eat things sacrificed unto idols, and to commit fornication… Notwithstanding I have a few things against thee, because thou sufferest that woman Jezebel, which calleth herself a prophetess, to teach and to seduce my servants to commit fornication, and to eat things sacrificed unto idols.'

"It seems to me that it was a diatribe aimed directly at us. In fact, the whole Bible study worries me a great deal, as it appears to be more of a terrorist cell than anything that leads to holiness. There wasn't, of course, any way to find a direct reference to the Alliance, but it was certainly anti-pagan and if you read between the lines, there were a great number of hidden references to Dionysians. In that regard, it seemed a lot like what our classical book club would be, a recruiting mechanism. On the other hand, we're hardly out to find soldiers for Dionysos that would destroy Christians."

256   "Did you get any idea of where these people lived or

what they did for a living? How about their last names?" asked Sebastian.

"I didn't want to appear too nosey so I kept rather quiet," Stephanie admitted. "As far as I can tell, it sounded like most of them were commuting in from the suburbs, people who were rabidly anti-urban and thought that cities were dens of iniquity. I do remember that Chris and Marian were a married couple with the last name of McGregor, and that Jeff's last name was Davidson. I found it interesting that Davidson lives in Rogers Park and I wondered if he lived near Stacie."

"So," Thomas remarked, "we have one of those end times groups that thinks the Book of Revelation is God's plan for the end of the century. For some, the last two thousand years has been nothing more than waiting for Jesus to appear in the sky and rapture self-righteous Christians off the face of the planet."

Sebastian said to Thomas, "That doesn't make them any less dangerous."

I turned to Stephanie and said "Good work. I hope you're up for some serious acting. To be honest I really don't like the idea of your going into that hornet's nest alone, week after week."

"I've been thinking about that as well," Cynthia said. "Rebecca had better go with her."

"That'll work," said Sebastian.

"I had a good meeting with Clark, Michael, Marjorie, and Christine on Monday night," I said. "I went over Stacie's list of book clubbers name by name, and they were helpful in adding details. None of them felt good about the LaForges, and Christine had actually gone to Stacie to complain about Mark. She found him rude and crude and more sexist than sex-friendly. Stacie assured Christine that her intuition was correct and that she was keeping close tabs on both of them.

"From what Stephanie has said about the Bible study, though, I think we have bigger problems than we think."

"How so?" Richard asked.

"I'm sorry to say so, but it seems that Mark and Beth aren't the only infiltrators. Chris and Marian McGregor's names were on the list as well. Marjorie remembered them as having come to the book club. The four of them agreed, though, that they had only been seen there once."

"It's beginning to look like this book club idea was a bad one," Thomas said, "a really bad one."

"Well," said Richard, "there are a lot of Brethren who are saying 'I told you so.' But Monday morning quarterbacking isn't going to solve our problems. As a matter of fact, I think it's important that we revive the book club."

"Why do you say that?" I asked. "Isn't that asking for more trouble?"

"I say it because we've got to keep our enemies close enough to us to maintain nearly constant surveillance. It's obvious they're doing that with us. What we have to be clear about is that we keep them out of the temple and, just as importantly, that we're very careful as to who among us we allow them to meet. I'm beginning to think that Sebastian, Stephanie, and I ought to go down to Eagle Ridge ASAP. What we've learned so far doesn't paint a very good picture as to the level of security we have in Chicago. "

"I think that's a wise move, Richard," said Thomas. "I know that the monks are very concerned about the current turn of events. Having Reagan in the White House is only one of the signs of the times that the right wing is on the march. It's as if you can hear fundamentalists across the country singing 'Onward Christian Soldiers' and they're neither 'Marching to Pretoria' nor going to a St. Patrick's Day parade."

"So, Thomas," asked Sebastian, "what conclusions have you come to about the book club?"

"Well," Thomas said, "without throwing caution to the wind, I think that Richard makes a good point about keeping an eye on our enemies. Though most of the Brethren I've talked to don't have any desire to revive the book club, Clark and Michael thought that it was a good way, perhaps the only way, to keep tabs on Mark and Beth, since those two attended with regularity, and now we can see why.

"The Chicago Public Library has a branch on Belmont, called the Lakeview Branch, close enough from here, and therefore to the Broadway Community Church, to attract some of them to a classical book club meeting. They have a meeting room we could use, and a library is a good place to have a book club meet. Besides it's far enough away from the temple that we'll have improved security. As an added bonus, the library will help us promote it. The reference librarian that I met with was very encouraging, especially if we could bring in a speaker once in a while. For that matter, I think some of the professors at Chicago Theological might be willing to show up, even if their scholarship denies the reality of our existence."

"Well," said Cynthia, "denying our existence, though it wouldn't pass muster with the Broadway Community crowd, wouldn't hurt the rest of us right now."

"Nice work, Thomas," Sebastian said. "I think, though, that we ought to clear this with the folks in Eagle Ridge before we proceed."

"I certainly agree with you," Thomas said. "I'm in no rush to get this started again, though I do think it would be helpful to do so."

"Well, we certainly have our work cut out for us. I'll see what I can find on the McGregors and this Davidson guy. Richard, will you make arrangements for the three of us to go to Eagle Ridge?"

"Certainly," he said. "When would you like to go?"

"Give me a day or two to dig up some more data. Would Saturday work?"

"I'd rather not miss church on Sunday," Stephanie said. "Let's leave later on Sunday and hope we can get back in time for Bible study."

"Geez, Mom," I said, "you're sounding more like a Bible lady every day. Are you sure they're not getting to you?"

"Don't underestimate the power of a priestess," Cynthia interjected. "Believe me, none of us want to mess with Stephanie DiCarlo and soon enough the Broadway Community Church will wish that they hadn't, either."

Orders from **21**
Eagle Ridge

Since Cynthia was becoming increasingly busy with distraught and increasingly alarmed members of the Chicago thiasoi, Thomas and I planned to have dinner without her on Friday night. I stopped at the Smoque BBQ on Pulaski, just south of my "L" stop, on my way home from work and picked up some ribs and chili for dinner.

Thomas was waiting for me when I got home. "I'd better give you a key," I said as I unlocked the front door.

"Thanks for the offer, lover boy," he said back to me, "but be careful, you just might be getting more than you're bargaining for."

"How so?" I asked.

"I'll tell you after I get a proper kiss and a drink," he answered. I set the food down on the sofa and did my amorous duty. Then, picking up dinner, we went into the kitchen. "Help yourself, Thomas. You know where everything is."

In the meantime I went into my study and fetched a house key out of the desk drawer and returned to the kitchen. "With this key, I thee wed," I said, handing it to him.

"Thanks, buddy," he replied, putting the key into his pocket. With that he gave me a kiss and a hug. The hug lasted a whole lot longer than the kiss and I felt Thomas begin to shake.

I held him there for a few minutes until he seemed he to relax. When he moved away I could see that he was crying. "Lord, Thomas, you're not that sentimental, are you? What's wrong?"

He took a deep breath and wiped his eyes with his hands. I grabbed some tissue out of the box on the top of the refrigerator and handed it to him. "Here," I said, "these will work better." Then I added "Sit down. I'll get that drink for you."

I got him his double and myself the usual. "I'm not sure whether this will help or not. What's going on? Why the tears?"

He took the drink and gulped down a big swig. "It's worse than we thought. Sebastian did some research on that Jeff Davidson guy. He lives in Rogers Park, all right. In fact he lives across the street from the temple. He moved in about a year ago. Sebastian did a careful scan of the building and found a surveillance camera aimed at our front door.

"It means that Davidson has a video record of everyone who's come and gone from the Temple, documentation of who is part of the Alliance and therefore who they can target for their next kill. There'll be hell to pay when that news gets out."

"Well, don't let it get out," I suggested.

"Easy for you to say, Ben," Thomas replied. "You don't know how much this will freak out the Alliance. My guess is that the temple will be shut down, at least for the time being, and then everyone will want to know why. The best answer is the honest one, but the publicity could cause panic. Maybe I'm wrong, but that's what I think is going to happen.

"Richard, Sebastian and Stephanie are flying to Cincinnati on Sunday, after the church service. From there they'll drive to Eagle Ridge. I expect the shit will hit the fan when they give their briefing to the monks. I'm glad I'm not going."

"Well, none of you guys did any of this," I said.

"That's true," Thomas responded, taking another swig of his drink. "I guess I mostly feel really bad about the folks in Chicago. This is going to upset everyone. We are, after all, dealing with a group of religious fanatics who we already know will commit murder.

"It's a Dionysian's worst fear. After all, our religion isn't exactly the kind of faith that makes martyrs into saints. It may be a few decades out-of-date to say it, but we'd still rather make love than war. Unfortunately it looks as if, whether we like it or not, we're at war."

"I guess you're right. It's serious," I said, and was quiet for a minute, "I don't suppose you're hungry. Are you?"

"Not really," Thomas said, finishing his drink, handing me the empty glass. "Here, I'm still thirsty."

"You're not getting drunk on me, are you?" I asked.

"Maybe," he said. "Got a better idea?"

"I do," I said, grabbing his hand and pulling him up. "Let's go upstairs. Let's make love, not war."

"OK," he said, "you win."

I took him to my bedroom and we both undressed, fell onto the bed and began kissing. "You're right," he said. "What I really need is a good fuck."

"Me fuck you or you fuck me?" I asked.

"You go first, Ben," he muttered. "I just want to feel your arms around me and your cock in my ass."

Forty minutes later we both felt better. I heated dinner in the microwave and we ate it in front of the television. I guess giving him a key to the house did make us feel married. I wondered if Cynthia would want a key as well.

On Tuesday Stephanie called from the monastery and asked that I meet James at the apartment at eight o'clock that night. She wanted me to let him in so he could get dinner ready for us on Wednesday night. "Tell him to make dinner for nine, himself included, but to keep it simple, since this might be a long meeting.

"Ben," she asked, "can you make sure the others are

there?"

"Yes," I answered. "Is six o'clock OK?"

"Yes," she said.

"Sure. Is everything OK? Thomas was worried about the monks' reactions."

"Yes, dear, everything is fine. There were some ruffled feathers but nothing that a mother hen like me can't handle. Besides, it's not as if we haven't lived through this stuff before. Relax. It's going to work out just fine.

"If the Broadway Community Church thinks that there's fire and brimstone coming down from Heaven, they're going to be surprised that it's not coming from Jesus. They'll see it all right, but Zeus will be the one sending it."

This plot just keeps getting deeper, I thought, and wondered what in Hell was coming next.

Wednesday night couldn't come fast enough for me, so I left work on the early side, getting to Stephanie's by 5:15. When I got there I walked into a confab in the living room. Stephanie, Rebecca and Joseph were already there. As might be expected, Stephanie greeted me with a big, wet kiss. The others all arrived well before six.

As Stephanie had ordered, James had dinner ready at six and in no time at all we were practically done. It was a simple repast of Swiss steak, mashed potatoes and green beans. There was wine but no appetizers or cocktails. We quickly got the idea that this was a business meeting.

Rebecca and Stephanie kept the conversation going.

There was ice cream for dessert but no one wanted any, so we adjourned to the living room before seven, leaving James and Joseph to clean up after us. Even that job didn't take very long and the two men joined us in a few minutes.

I found myself comfortably seated on the couch between

Thomas and Cynthia. Richard and Sebastian each sat in an over-stuffed chair while Stephanie and Rebecca sat together on a love seat, their "slaves" comfortably sitting on cushions at their feet.

Sebastian quickly took charge of the meeting. "I'll start," he said, "and the rest of you, I trust, will help on the details. In no particular order, the agenda from the monastery is surveillance of the church, the future of the temple, protecting the Brethren, ending this threat against us and bringing criminals to justice.

"The meeting with the abbot and his executive staff went well," Sebastian assured us, "given the severity of the situation. We spent all of Monday and Tuesday in discussion and, though our conclusions and plans might seem drastic to some, they do set a good course for us. The abbot assured us that we have the full resources of the Alliance and that the world-wide Dionysian community backing us. I don't think we can ask for anything more, though prayer, patience, and courage certainly won't hurt our cause.

"Richard and Stephanie, do you want to add anything to that?" he asked.

"You said it very well, Sebastian," Stephanie said, "so there's no reason for me to add my two cents."

"I agree," said Richard, "though I do want to say that you're only hearing the conclusions. The meetings were long and arduous and not without a great deal of emotion. To say it felt like a war room is an understatement. The abbot had called in several experts, namely two experienced detectives from Scotland Yard, a psychiatrist from Columbia University, and two forensic experts from the FBI. You couldn't have asked for a better team.

"As for resources, as Sebastian just said, the abbot pledged unlimited (but reasonable) funding and each of the experts agreed to be on call for us and they were willing to come to Chicago whenever we felt it necessary."

"That's good news," Thomas said. "I was expecting the worst."

"Well," Stephanie said, "in fact, they were not only supportive but commended us for what we've done so far. They view these developments, on the other had, as extremely serious and it's obvious that we had better take their recommendations seriously as well."

"All right," Sebastian asked, "are there any questions so far?" There were none, as everyone was anxious to know what plans had been proposed. "As you can see, we've been told to ask for more help if we need it.

"The first priority is to protect the Brethren. Therefore all official Alliance gatherings in the Chicago area are to be cancelled until this threat is over. The Brethren in and around Cook County will be seriously encouraged to go into hiding and even to relocate, if feasible. The abbot assured us that those willing and able to move elsewhere would be assisted financially as well as given job and relocation assistance."

"Does that mean everyone?" Cynthia asked.

"Well, not exactly," Richard answered. "First off, they know that there are those who cannot or will not leave the city. Secondly, of course, some of us have to remain to serve their needs, even if it's in a very covert way. And we're not going to retreat. The monks were unanimous in that conclusion as there will be Dionysians here to oppose our persecution, eliminate this nest of fanatics, and ensure the future safety of a prospering thiasoi in Chicago.

"As a matter of fact we're liable to have to create a larger task force than the nine of us gathered here. Since we have no idea of how many of the local Dionysians are known to Horton and his henchmen, we may have to find able-bodied Dionysians to join us from other areas.

"I just want to assure you all, and I hope you'll pass this on to the other Brethren as well," said Rebecca, "that the Dionysians in Florida are acutely aware of your sorrow and share your anxiety. We've seen a frightening increase in intolerance and bigotry in Florida as well. The Anita Bryant anti-gay fiasco is only one sad example of what I mean. I'm happy to remind you, too, that we're here with the full support of the Brethren back home.

266

At that point Sebastian began talking again. "Another change the monks insisted upon is that we re-structure our team, replacing our current large-size team with cells of three, as many insurgent and counter-insurgent groups do.

"This is the last meeting of its kind that we're going to have. Ben and I will meet with each of you to assign you a new place in the structure and to tell you with whom you can communicate. I know that you might think that's extreme, but it's the only way can be sure to protect the integrity of our plans. Obviously there will be some cross-communication, but we need to keep it at a minimum. When there is crossover, you're all going to have to be really discreet as to what you tell even one another. It's not that we don't trust each of you, but that we can't be sure that the murdering Christians we're fighting won't resort to kidnapping and torture to find out what they need to know. The less each one of you knows, the less you can be forced to tell."

"We know," said Stephanie, "that breaking into small cells is difficult, but it's also safer, just as going underground is difficult, but it's the only safe way to proceed."

"Sebastian," Cynthia asked, "how does going underground affect the temple?"

"Well," he said, "I'm sorry to say that it means we have to shut it down and shut it down soon."

"I saw that coming," said Thomas, "but how do we do that?"

"Don't feel too bad. It will only be a shell game," Richard said. "We're putting it up for sale. In fact, one of our real estate holding groups will put up the 'for sale' sign tomorrow."

"Tomorrow?" Cynthia asked.

"Tomorrow," Richard answered.

"Now before you get all bent out of shape, this is what will happen. The sign goes up. As soon as we can arrange it, we'll have an architect come in to draw up plans that will conceal and protect the assembly hall and anterooms in the basement. That will happen this week. By the weekend, a Dionysian work crew will come in and seal off access to the actual temple and do so with all our tools of worship protected within it. The area itself will not only be impossible for the uninformed to find, but will be protected in such a way as to prevent harm through fire or, the gods forbid, explosion. In about ten days a moving van will show up and everything in the house that can't be stored in the hidden basement will go into storage.

"Very soon afterwards the house will be sold to another Dionysian real estate holding company and a nice Christian family will move in, a family that will have nothing to do with either Dionysians or detective work.

"In the meantime, Cynthia and Thomas, we'll relocate the two of you to a safer part of Chicago, since your expertise and your ministry to the Chicago Brethren are still needed here."

"That's no problem," I said. "I already gave Thomas a key to my house. Both he and Cynthia can move in with me."

"Thanks, Ben," Cynthia said, grabbing my hand and squeezing it. "I just may take you up on that offer."

"Not so fast," Sebastian said. "It does sound like a good idea, but we ought to sleep on some of this before we decide."

"I suppose you're right," I said, "but can we sleep on it together?" Despite the seriousness of the evening, that raised a little chuckle.

"James, you're going to have to help me with surveillance. We're going to have to rig up some cameras around Davidson's, to see who comes and goes. We're also going to have find out where Horton lives and do the same with his place.

"Richard, can you get another warrant to wiretap Davidson's?" I asked.

"We're already on it. Our man at the FBI says we'll have it in the morning."

"You can see," Sebastian said, "that we've got plans in place for the Brethren's safety and to infiltrate the church. The monks nixed the idea of starting up the book club. They thought it was too dangerous for any of us, or anyone else for that matter. On the other hand, getting into that nest of fundamentalist hornets will give us quicker access to their plans."

"I can see that," Thomas said. "The only base we haven't covered is Stephanie, Rebecca and Joseph's parts. I don't think any of us like the idea of them going to church, and now with the discovery of Davidson taping the comings and goings at the front door of Stacie's home, we can't even be certain that any of them is safe."

"That's true," Sebastian said. "Looking back we should have shut down the temple when Stacie was murdered, but we didn't. There's no use crying over what we should have done. In their case, we'll just hope for the best and not make the same mistakes again."

"Those are good suggestions," Richard said. "The monks were very clear that we couldn't endanger anyone who might have been known by the Broadway bunch as a Dionysian. Obviously that means that we may have to find auxiliaries who haven't been seen at the temple.

"We're not going to be very open about who joins the team, but rest assured there are reinforcements that are not only on their way, they're already arriving. You're not fighting this war alone by any means."

The evening didn't last very long after that. Sebastian, Richard and I would form the top cell and then we took each of the others into the bedroom, gave them the names of the two others who would be in "their cell" and sent them home with the strong admonition not to share information about the investigation with anyone outside of their cell.

When we were done telling each of the others what we

wanted them to know, we told them to say goodbye and leave. Doing so felt creepy, to be sure. At least I'd still be seeing Cynthia and Thomas as they were the other two in my second cell.

It worked this way. Each of us was in an "upper cell." In my case it was the top cell with Richard and Sebastian. Each of us also was in a "lower cell," so that information could be passed cell-to-cell in either an upward or downward direction.

About fifteen minutes after I got home, the doorbell rang. It was Thomas and Cynthia who were, they told me, spending the night with me.

I quickly learned that when Dionysians decide to do something, they do it quickly and well. As Richard had said, the "for sale" sign went up on Thursday morning. That evening Richard and Sebastian met Thomas, Cynthia, and me at The Drake to talk about their moving in. The three of us had talked about it more seriously after Wednesday's meeting and had come to the conclusion that it was something that we wanted to do. The house was certainly big enough, and since we got along so well it seemed a no-brainer.

Richard was insistent that there be no other Dionysians at my place, if Cynthia and Thomas did move in. "Your location is far enough and discreet enough that it will work fine, but from now on whatever happens has to happen as covertly as possible. We can't afford to have your home known as a Dionysian gathering place."

"We'll also have to beef up electronic security there," Sebastian added. "Would it be all right if we put in security?" he asked.

"Fine with me," I said. In the final analysis they agreed that the move would be a good one.

That night I gave Cynthia a key to the house as well. Thomas moved in two days later but Cynthia, having packed her things, went to Florida. It was hoped that if she were out of town for a few weeks, it would be harder for the church-folk to pick up her trail when she returned. She would sell her car and buy a different model when she came back to Chicago. She'd also come back from Florida with differently-colored hair and a new hair style.

Thomas spent most of the weekend, first at the Hyatt on East Wacker and then at the Palmer House in the Loop, meeting with as many of the Brethren as possible to break the news of the security breach to them and to help them develop their own Alliance-assisted plans to go underground. He came home on Sunday at about three in the afternoon, frazzled to say the least.

"You've got to give Chicago Dionysians credit for being a stubborn bunch, that's for sure," he said once he had a double scotch in hand and the two of us were comfortably seated in the living room.

"OK, Thomas," I said, "I know when you want to talk, so just spill the beans, will you?"

"Now that I'm with you, I will," he replied. "I met with 32 of the 43 Dionysian family units who've attended something at the temple in the last two years. Casey, Ariadne, and I decided that, as far as we can tell, that's how many have done so. There are some who show up often, some only occasionally, and some, like in any church, who never show up except for a funeral service or wedding."

"You had weddings and funerals at Stacie's?" I asked.

"Not as you might think," Thomas answered. "Those kinds of ceremonies are held in other places, such as a funeral parlor or a banquet hall, but we do have special blessing ceremonies for the dead, and sometimes couples like to have their marriages blessed in a temple ceremony as well. Fortunately, we've had none of those recently, not even for Stacie, so we're not as concerned about the rarely-come folks as we are about everyone else.

"For the most part everyone took the information without too much drama, though when the realization hits them they may 271 feel otherwise. A few, of course, reminded me that they had told Stacie 'I told you so,' but most saved me the trouble of listening to their bitching. They all promised to think seriously about what they would do, but some were just glad that the Alliance was going to help, since they had already decided to leave.

"As you can imagine, a few, like Clark and Michael, were insistent that they weren't going anywhere and wanted to know how they could help. I told them we'd try and find a way, but that since we were pretty sure that Horton's henchmen had their names, and probably a lot more information than that, they really had to stay out of sight. I suggested that Clark talk to his father about our recent developments. I hope his dad is able to talk some sense into them, since I don't think they get the idea that they're probably on the church's death list.

"On top of that the monks were insistent that since Ben, Clark and Michael were not yet fully initiated they would have to be and soon. That applies to you, too, Ben, so I hope you're ready."

"I am and I'm looking forward to it. When and where?"

"You'll probably be glad to know that it's going to be at Eagle Ridge. We'll book a flight for you, Clark, and Michael for a week from next Thursday. I think you'll enjoy a few extra days there and I know the monks will want to get to know you."

"Cynthia and a monk from the monastery will meet you at the Lexington airport and from there they will drive you to the monastery. It's the best we can do under the circumstances. In the meantime I will help you and them prepare for the ceremony with a couple of meetings in the evening next week." With that he handed me an old hard-bound book called *The Eleusinian and Bacchic Mysteries*, by Thomas Taylor." I want you to read this book before then. We'll probably arrange to meet at one of the hotels in the Loop. That will make it easier for you to get there after work."

"Why not have them come here?" I asked.

"Because," Thomas explained, "we can't take any risks in exposing where you live. For all we know they're watching this place. Sebastian doesn't think they have the manpower to do so, nor that they've followed Cynthia or me here to learn of its whereabouts, but he's not sure.

"When the word is to go underground, that's what we do. It should be painfully obvious that we've really let our guard down. What might seem to some as a simple Bible-believing church is proving to be a death squad of remarkably high sophistication. Don't forget that they were able to infiltrate us, perpetrated a murder leaving almost no clues, and had us under surveillance for only God knows how long.

'We just can't take any more chances. The monks think that we're lucky that Stacie has been their only victim. Face it. We really don't know how much they know and we can't take any chances on giving them opportunities to learn anything else.

"In the meantime plans are being drawn up to secure the temple's worship areas.

"I'm sorry to say that even though I've moved in, you're just not going to see much of me in the next two weeks. I'm up to my neck in things to do and I certainly intend to get them done. Enough talk, let's go somewhere quiet and get a good dinner. I think we both deserve that much."

"Fine with me," I said. "The Gale Street Inn, Anna Maria's, or do you have another suggestion?"

"Which is closer?" he asked.

"Well if you want close let's go down Pulaski to The Villa. I think you'll like it. It's just south of the Kennedy."

"OK," Thomas said, "can I clean up a little before I go?"

"Sure," I said. "Can I stop you from washing your face and hands? I don't think so. On the other hand, don't shower. I want to smell every bit of your manliness when we get back."

The Initiate 22

Thomas was right. Even though he had moved in, I didn't see much of him except at the Monadnock office as Alliance business kept him well-occupied. It was strange not to see Cynthia around, either. Richard didn't give me any news about his trip to Sarasota. I didn't hear anything directly from Stephanie, which was a really strange turn of events, but Sebastian relayed her information to me regularly.

Taylor's book was a heady mixture of Platonic philosophy and Orphic myths. It was also remarkably devoid of any discussion of sexuality. There was some mention of Dionysianism in it, of course, but hardly anything that sounded like the religion I had joined. The only value I could see in it was the recounting of myths, especially Aeneas's journey into Hades and his return.

I met with Clark, Michael, and Thomas twice, as Thomas had asked, and he prepared us for the last initiation. Clark and Michael did tell me that they had gone out of the city to receive their next initiation into the taxidiotis status, but I didn't get any details.

On Thursday morning a cab pulled up in front of the house, as Thomas had told me it would the night before. I was surprised to find out that I was going alone. He handed me tickets to Atlanta. I looked at them and said "To Atlanta?"

He smiled and said "It's a Dionysian protection scheme. Don't worry. You'll be met at the gate. I love you. Have a safe trip."

This, I thought, was odd. Where are Clark and Michael and how come Thomas isn't coming with me?

I puzzled about this all the way to Atlanta, when to my surprise Cynthia met me at the gate. "I thought I was supposed to go to Lexington," I said after we had exchanged kisses.

"We are," she said, "I've got our tickets right here." That meant we had to rush to another gate and board another flight. It wasn't even on the same airline.

"Why didn't I get a direct flight from O'Hare?" I asked. "After all, there certainly are flights from there to Lexington."

"Honey," she said, "I love you but you've still got a lot to learn about protecting Dionysian secrets. It's a ruse to make sure that no one is following you. Dionysians often travel separately, especially when we're under attack as we are now."

"I'm not complaining," I said. "In fact I'm glad to have time alone with you."

"As I am with you. But remember, no talk about the Alliance or anything about it until we're safely in the van."

"Yes, Ma'am," I said.

We made it to the boarding gate just in time and the flight to Lexington went without a hitch. I was surprised to find a limo waiting for us, but no Clark or Michael. I kept my mouth shut and the driver drove us through the city to I-75. It would have been a lot easier to take the outer loop around the city, but I wasn't going to make a fool of myself by saying so. It must be evasive maneuvers, I thought, just like in the movie "The In-laws," where Peter Falk yells to Alan Arkin, "Serpentine, Shelly, Serpentine."

We rode about twenty miles south of the city and onto a secluded back road. I thought we must be almost there. I was wrong. What was there was a van, another driver, and Clark and Michael waiting for us. Cynthia and I got into the van and she introduced me to George.

"Yes," I said, "I remember you. Weren't you at
Richard's?"

"That's right," he said. "It's nice to see you've come this far.

"I'm sorry guys," he continued, "but I'm going to have to ask you to sit in the back and I have to blindfold you until we're safely on monastery land. It's a ways from here, but we have to work to keep its location secret. I hope you'll understand." We said we did, of course, but that didn't make the ride in the dark any easier.

I have no idea how long we rode, nor in what direction. They were doing a good job of keeping the location of Eagle Ridge hidden. Once I thought about what had happened to Stacie, I had to admit that I understood why.

The ride was long and certainly boring. There was, after all, literally nothing to see and not much conversation. At least it was comfortable and I may have even fallen asleep. Eventually it was clear that we had pulled onto a little-used dirt road, as the ride became bumpy to say the least. After what was probably twenty minutes of bumps, Cynthia took off our blindfolds. "Welcome to Eagle Ridge, guys," she said.

Once my eyes adjusted to the light, all I could see were forests and glens. "I don't see a monastery anywhere," I said.

"Oh, we're not there yet," Cynthia explained, "but we will be in about 25 minutes."

When we finally did arrive, I have to admit that it was a beautiful and tranquil spot. There was a rather large stone house, several out-buildings and two large barns. These were surrounded by fields on all sides, some with crops, some fenced in as pasture land, and some with vineyards, pruned and sending out fresh green shoots.

The landscape was impeccably groomed and everything

had the sense of peace and new growth, as you would expect in late May. I'd say "late May in Kentucky" but honestly I had no idea where I was, and wondered if I ever would find out. To my surprise there was a paved road to the place. We just hadn't taken it.

Two men, in their forties or so, welcomed us and introduced themselves. They were dressed in the bib overalls and work boots that you'd expect on a working farm. They picked up our luggage, and said "Follow us, please."

From there we were shown to our rooms. Clark and Michael had their own and I had mine, with a double bed in it. Sitting on the bed was Thomas, who hugged me and gave me a big kiss. "Sorry, Ben," he said. "I took the shorter route. I tried to argue that it was safe for you to travel with me, but the abbot wouldn't hear of it. Wartime security and all that."

I broke into a big smile. "No problem, Thomas," I said. "I'm just glad you're here."

"And I'm glad you are too. Come on," he said. "We've got a date with the abbot. He's anxious to see you."

It was no simple farmhouse that Thomas led me through. The inside décor of the building was lush and warm, paneled and trimmed with red cedar and white ash and birch. Murals of the gods at play and at rest adorned the walls. Rich tapestries lay on the marbled floors. The furniture looked both comfortable and inviting, richly covered in fine cloth of pastel hues, greens and browns with accents of embroidered flora and fauna. A rich estate to say the least.

The house was obviously bigger than it had looked when I first saw it. We left the second story, where we were to sleep, walked down a wide staircase to the foyer and then back into the recesses of the house, past a dining room, library, sitting room and kitchen. At what must have been the rear of the house there was a large sun room, and off to one side a hallway. I followed Thomas a short way and he knocked on a door.

"Come in," the voice of an older man said.

278   Thomas opened the door and said "You first." I entered to

see a man, elderly but hardly infirm, rising from a mahogany desk, The room was bright and airy with windows that overlooked the farm. The office was every bit as lush with plants as the outdoors would be in a few more weeks.

"Ben, Ben, Ben," he said. "My how you have grown. But then we all do, don't we?"

I stood there rapt in wonder. The face was familiar, as was the voice. The man was perhaps in his eighties, a bit stout or rather husky, like an aged football player who hadn't gone to seed. He was bald and bearded, with the brown eyes that ran in our family. "Uncle Jonathan?" I asked. "Are you my Uncle Jonathan?"

"That I am, son, and I'm not even back from the grave. You can't imagine how happy I am not only to see you but to know that you've finally come to Eagle Ridge. Now, enough chatter, boy, if I may still call you that; give your uncle a hug while he holds his niece's son."

It was a strange surprise, to be sure. After all, there were all these indications that he had died, though in all honesty no one had ever told me so. On the other hand the fact that he was still living and that he was "the abbot" was certainly information that no one, not even Thomas, had come close to revealing. Did my mother know? I wondered.

As we stood there, I felt his body begin to shake slightly and I held on to him more tightly. He backed away, his eyes glistening with tears of joy. "Thomas," he said, "Richard has told me how carefully you have taught my great-nephew and I am grateful for your ministry to him."

With that he grabbed Thomas's hand and pulled him close to himself in a warm greeting. "It's good to have you home, young man. I know you've been working way too hard in Chicago and have done that under great stress. Even so, you've done us proud. And me, you have made me doubly happy since it was you who have brought one more of my family into my life."

"Come, gentlemen," he said. "There are people waiting to

greet you both."

With that he led us through another door to a greenhouse and thence to a sitting room. As if one surprise wasn't enough, there were three more: my mother, my brother John, and his wife Beth. There were hugs and cheers and tears all around. A real family reunion. Then I remembered that they hadn't (or had they?) met Thomas, so I quieted everyone down and introduced them to the man who had grown to mean so much to me.

"Thomas," my mother said, "I'm so glad to meet you. I have heard such wonderful things about you from Cynthia."

"Likewise, I'm sure Mrs. Kramer," he said. "I've heard great things about you, too."

"I hear it's time to welcome you to our family, Thomas," my brother said. "They tell me you've moved in with Ben. It's about time he settled down with a godly man."

For the rest of the afternoon, we talked and talked, our conversation only interrupted when Thomas took us for a tour of the farm. As the tour began, Uncle Jonathan begged to be excused. "I've things to do and had better do them and get in a nap as well. I'll see you all at dinner."

The evening passed like a joyful party too soon over, a celebration akin to a wedding or a baptism. There were cocktails and a plentiful feast. "Enjoy the night," Thomas told the three of us, "for tomorrow you will be required to fast and prepare yourselves for Saturday's initiation."

Friday morning I slept late, though Thomas had risen early without me. I remember waking as he was dressing. "Stay in bed, Ben," he said. "There's nothing for you to do today. When you do get up, come downstairs and I'm sure you'll find me." The day passed quietly but, as Thomas had warned, Clark, Michael, and I were not allowed to eat. Water was available, but nothing else. Fasting was a new experience for me and when I went to bed that night I was starving.

Thomas wouldn't even make love to me that night. I tossed and turned in the bed for a while but eventually dozed off.

By noon on Saturday I was famished and felt a little faint. Thomas brought the three of us to an anteroom in the barn where the ceremony was to be held. With John and Clark's father, they washed us and then dressed us in white togas. "Here," Thomas said, handing each of us a rope. Then he explained what would be required of us and that this first part of the ceremony included the sacrifice of a bull.

"A bull?" I asked.

"Yes," Thomas replied, "but it is only a bull calf, so don't worry, you'll be able to handle it without a problem."

When the preparations were done, we waited for a signal to enter the temple. From within, we could hear singing and tambourines. Then a monk opened the door to the worship area and said that all was ready and we could enter.

We walked into the room and circled the room in pairs, my brother John with me, Clark with his Dad, and Michael with Thomas.

Uncle Jonathan hardly looked like an uncle, dressed as he was in splendid attire. Fawn skins, red velvet, and a golden crown, holding a thrysos in his hand. He looked like a king or emperor. "Your great-uncle," Thomas had said, "is not only the abbot, but a hierophant, the highest order one can attain in our midst. He is revered throughout the Dionysian world. Today you will see why."

The hierophant began with an invocation: "Come, Brothers and Sisters, Let us celebrate the mysteries. Let us call the gods into our midst," and a long prayer. There were many "Amen's" and lots of songs, until finally, he turned to us and said, "My Brothers, and so you are if only partly, I will now conduct you on the most important journey of your life, from which if you return successfully, you will have gained immortality. As you undoubtedly know, many, no, a great many, have gone before you on this path and few have returned to what we call this mortal life. None, I dare say have returned unchanged, except that they were divine before they started.

"Now therefore in imitation of his deeds and his example, you will follow the path made sacred by our Lord Dionysos, who though born of god was bound to the flesh of his mother, Semele. Happily twice-born, he is divine through springing from Zeus' holy thigh. Even thrice-born, having survived by Athena's grace the death the Titans would have sent him to.

"Let us begin, then, as did god's holy son. Let us seek first the blessing of the divine Father of us all. Kneel in holy supplication and repeat after me, with sincerity of heart and supplication real, so that which you seek might be found, that for which you knock may be opened to you, and that for which you ask will be given. For in all certainly, the gods look not on the outward appearance of man but on the condition of his heart.

"Most high Zeus, I implore you…"

"Most high Zeus, I implore you," I repeated, as did Clark and Michael with me, and as we all did for each phrase as we were prompted.

"That," continued Jonathan, uncle, abbot, hierophant, "I may be found worthy to descend the steps to the throne of your brother Hades and from him, with your sacred permission and by the power of your mighty word, redeem my soul to everlasting life, be made worthy to live eternally in joy, becoming as a god by the grace of your permission and the power of your sovereign will. Grant this boon, I implore you, Mighty Zeus, highest of the gods, that with your most blessed children I may live to praise and honor you forever.

"Look upon this unblemished calf, my gift to you, and his blood in which I will be washed. His life is offered that, made worthy through your help, I might live forever. Amen."

282   "Now, my brothers, do as you have been instructed. Bind

the calf and carry it as one to the altar, that your prayers may be heard and your requests granted."

I looked at Clark and Michael and each of us took the ropes we had been given, and gently laying the bull calf on its side we bound its legs. First, Clark bound the front legs, then Michael the rear, and I, with their help, bound front and back together. We lifted the frightened animal and carried it to the altar.

"Now, therefore," we were told, "place your hands on the calf and repeat after me.

"Holy bull calf, animal most sacred to Dionysos, I thank you for your life. I beseech you that you permit me to make of you an offering to the Holy Zeus. Take upon yourself my sins that I might be forever freed from the mortality of my flesh. Take upon yourself my sins, that Divine Minos might judge me just, that the scales of Justice might show me worthy of eternal life, and that I may join the company of the saints in ever-lasting bliss.

"Holy Zeus, giver and taker of life, take this spotless calf as our gift, as our supplication, and as the offering who takes our place. Amen."

"Now," the abbot, continued, "you, too, must be bound."

In like fashion, then, the monks bade us lie on the floor and, taking cords of silver silk, tied our hands and feet and laid us around three sides of the altar. Those watching began softly chanting to the gods. From my vantage point I could see Cynthia and Thomas, their eyes fixed on me. They held each other as they chanted. I had been told the words would be in Greek and that the gist of what was sung would ask Zeus to hear our prayers and accept the sacrifice.

Three priestesses, dressed in what I knew was the garb of maenads, that is, in singlets of leopard skin, barefoot and with their hair pulled back, stepped up the altar, each holding a dagger by both hands and said in unison: "Bull calf, we thank you for your willingness to die in Clark's stead. Mighty Zeus receive this sacrifice that Clark's prayers may be heard and answered, that you grant him a safe trip to the throne of Hades, a blessed return, and permission

283

to receive from your divine brother life everlasting.

"Bull calf, we thank you for your willingness to die in Michael's stead. Mighty Zeus receive this sacrifice that Michael's prayers may be heard and answered, that you grant him a safe trip to the throne of Hades, a blessed return, and permission to receive from your divine brother life everlasting.

"Bull calf, we thank you for your willingness to die in Ben's stead. Mighty Zeus receive this sacrifice that Ben's prayers may be heard and answered, that you grant him a safe trip to the throne of Hades, a blessed return, and permission to receive from your divine brother life everlasting."

With that, as one, they plunged their knives into the calf's chest. It let out a loud roar and twitched violently in its bounds. Blood burst forth from its pierced body and seemed to flow everywhere at once.

I could feel the hot liquid pour off the altar onto me and saw the same happen to Clark who lay in front of me. I was drenched in the blood of the bull. I felt its life bathe me even as it ebbed away, running onto the floor and into the drains that encircled the altar.

With that the women in the room clamored up and over us, pulling at the dying beast, screaming and shouting. "Dionysos! Dionysos! La! Lo! Lo! Lo! Euloi. Euloi." In moments there was hysteria and the banging of cymbals and the clapping of tambourines. They were lapping at the blood and pulling at the now dead bull, ripping with bare hands at the carcass. It was the madness of Dionysos. It was the death of Pentheus, his mother ripping off his head, as if it were a beast and not her son. I couldn't believe their strength to do as they did, tearing and ripping the young bull's flesh.

Then the men began singing. The clanging ceased, replaced by a simple beat of one tambourine and the quiet strum of three or four lyres. It was a peaceful lullabye of some sort, a cooing, and a calming. The woman ceased their frenzy, almost as quickly as it had begun.

"The omens are good," said the priestess who stood in the center of the three. "Let us prepare our brothers for their journey. Loosen the ropes that bind them. Prepare the sacrifice for the holy fire."

My brother John came forward and untied me, as Clark's father did the same for him, and Thomas for Michael. John held me, for a moment and cried. "Thank god," he said. "Thank god."

It made no difference to him that I was drenched in blood and that now he was too, I thought. Now we are, in a real sense, blood brothers. Then he stood up and pulled me up with him. "Follow me," he said, "the ceremony must continue."

All three of us were led into a shower room, stripped and placed under a cleansing shower. We weren't allowed to do anything. "Just stand there," John said. "It's our job to cleanse you, since you are the sacrifice. It is your journey and our privilege to help you on your way."

When we were clean and dry, they dressed us in what looked like lion skins, with long manes covering our necks. "What are these for?" I quietly asked John.

"Shh," he said. "Did you forget? You're supposed to look like Hercules when you trek through the underworld. Now stand still so I can give you your royal crown."

The crown was metallic, and looked like if was made of gold, even if it was only gold plate. It was fashioned, as I knew it would be, in leaves of myrtle, like the gift that Venus had given Hercules. All this preparation took less than half an hour, as everyone seemed to move quickly and with practiced steps.

When we had been readied, we were led to within sight of the small pond near the entrance to the cave that Thomas had shown us during our tour on Friday. There we were met by Uncle Jonathan. "And now," he said, "Dionysos, you begin your quest. See here comes the worthy Polymnus. He can show

285

us the way."

"Worthy, Polymnus," Clark said, "it is said that you know the place where we can find the gate to Hades. Is this a certain truth?" They were the words that Thomas had told us during our preparations for initiation in Chicago.

Luckily there wasn't much to remember and we had been told we could prompt one another, if necessary. With Clark doing all the talking for us, we didn't really expect to have to prompt him. but Michael and I were both sure we could. Thomas had been pretty strict in making sure we had memorized our part of the script.

"Yes, oh man of beauty, I certainly can and certainly will. What might you give me in return for such a favor?"

"It is," Clark as Dionysos said, "of great importance to me and therefore of great worth. What might you seek in return?"

"I ask that you let me know you as a man does a woman. Yield to me your ass, its beautiful flesh a feast for my prick. Its dark hole, I desire to penetrate, that I may know you man to man, in love and worship."

The thought went through my mind that Polymnus was asking the wrong person. Michael and I were more likely to offer ourselves to ass fucking than Clark was. Then I thought of my brother John and what he had to go through to become a Dionysian. All of a sudden I had to think differently of him.

"This, Polymnus, I promise, to you when I return from my sacred quest," said Clark, "I will gladly offer you what you seek."

"Then," replied Polymnus, "follow me." With that we went to the shore of the pond, the rest of the congregation following us closely. "Here is Alcyonian Lake and to its center I will take you in my boat. From there descend and you will find the gate you seek."

The abbot approached us when Polymnus had finished his lines and led us up the hill a short way to the entrance of the cave wherein was the local temple. "Let us proceed, brothers," he said, "to pray and take some nourishment. You must first break your fast before you enter the gate to Hades."

So we entered the cave and a large cavern, exquisite in its details and its murals. The floor was covered in bright mosaics. Golden chandeliers with candles brightly burning hung from the ceiling. In the center of the underground room was a large and ornate altar. On it was a simple meal of bread and wine.

"Eat this bread, the gift of Ceres, the goddess of grain, and drink this wine, which Lord Dionysos has given us. Let these simple gifts strengthen you in your quest," the abbot said. We ate and drank as he bid. And after the quick meal returned to the daylight.

"Let us now go with Polymnus in his boat. But first, take off your crowns lest the gift of a god be polluted by contact with the dead." We did so, placing them on branch of a nearby tree.

As the three of us returned to the boat with the hierophant, the crowd of on-lookers began cheering us on with shouts of "Go with the blessings of the gods," "May the gods grant you success," and other such phrases of good wishes.

The boat was a simple row boat, hardly big enough for the five of us, but we managed to get into it and Thomas and Clark's dad pushed us from the shore. I felt dizzy and light-headed in no time at all. I suddenly felt drunk, though the wine hadn't tasted exceptionally strong. On the other hand I had drunk it on an empty stomach.

As we neared the center of the pond, I saw a low platform, not more than an inch above the water line. Polymnus steered to it and carefully brought the boat to its side. "Here," he said, "is the way you seek."

"Come brothers," my uncle said. "I will lead you on your quest."

With those words he slowly stood up. Polymnus offered him a hand as he stepped onto the platform and did the same for each of us. "Don't rock the boat," he said, "and don't fall into the water either." The platform was barely large enough for the four of us.

"Now," Polymnus said, "I will take my leave. And from

you," he said with a big grin and a wink, "most beautiful god, I will wait to receive your ass."

As our boatman rowed away, my uncle, the abbot, said, "Now help me lift this door." And there, in the middle of the platform was a handle cut into the rock of the platform. Clark and Michael leaned over it, grabbed it, and lifted it with ease. "This isn't heavy at all," Michael said.

"Yes," commented Jonathan, "the way into Hades is easy. It is getting out that poses problems."

The door, once opened, revealed a narrow set of steps. "I'll go first," said the hierophant. "Now follow closely." The downward path was quiet and grew darker with every step.

It was difficult to walk since I felt dizzy and couldn't see well in the darkness. I could feel the walls on each side of me and used them to balance myself. Down we went. I hadn't thought to count the steps, but they were many. Deeper and deeper the steps wound their way.

The deeper we went, the wider the steps became. "Take my hand," said my uncle, offering it to me, "and Clark you take Ben's and Michael you take Clark's. This is no place for us to lose one another."

Then I heard hissing and screaming and sounds that made me fearful. It's only some kind of dramatic effect, I said to myself, or the effect of some drug that Uncle Jonathan gave you. Shadows appeared as the darkness lifted slightly, under the thinnest sliver of what looked like the moon. But they were strange and eerie shadows, moving and darting as they did. Your whole family has done this, I thought, even your younger brother John. Get with the program. Get with the program. Thomas wouldn't betray you. Cynthia loves you. Look how glad your mom was to see you go.

The steps ended and we were on a slight incline of moist earth. Beneath our feet was a well-trod path. "This way," Jonathan said. "We go to meet Charon, who will ferry us, if we can convince him to bring us across the river Acheron."

288

With that I saw the shore of a surging river. Its waters were black, brackish, and smelled of death, of poison. That was it. Poison. Like Pastor Horton had read somewhere from the Bible, "Their wine is the poison of dragons, and the cruel venom of asps."

There was a boat and a boatman, too. Gruesome, he looked, and forbidding, with his ferry man's pole in his hand, a haggard beard and filthy clothes. "Who are you?" he growled. "You look not dead to me."

"I am a guide," my uncle said, "and these are men on a holy quest to Hades."

"Mortals, I see," said Charon. "I cannot let them pass."

"These you must, as they have the permission of Zeus and the required coins." With that, the earth beneath our feet shook as lightening struck nearby.

"I see, old man, that indeed you do. Give me my due and you'll be on your way."

"Give the boatman your coins," Jonathan said to us. In awe, we did so.

"Now hurry into the boat," the ferry man said. "There are souls waiting and they ought not be delayed."

We did as he bade and with his pole he launched us into the devilish waters. On he rowed until at length we came to the far shore where no light of day is seen. It was an eerie darkness, only faintly lit by the same crescent of a moon, casting ghostly shadows upon the mist that rose from the cesspools of Hell itself. We landed upon a slimy shore, where grew blue sedge.

Barking filled the air. "What is that sound, uncle?" I asked.

"Cerberus, the three-headed dog, as he lies stretched at prodigious length in the opposite cave," he answered.

"Fear not, for like Sibyl when she conducted Aeneas to Hades, I have treats for him that will subdue his wrath and let us pass unharmed." Before us were three paths and a profound and hideous cave, with wide yawning mouth, stony, fenced by the black lake, which we had just crossed.

"Now," yelled Charon, "take the path to the right and be gone from these shores, traveler, as others await their passage to the realm of the dead."

Into the gloom of woods Jonathan led us, and this was no familiar forest, devoid as it was of green. No birds did we see as we tread among its trees. I remembered now what Thomas had said about the journey to Hades, how no bird could fly over it unhurt and therefore the Greeks called the place by the name of "Aornos," without birds.

I saw Tityus lying on the earth, and a vulture devouring his liver; Sisyphus was there, too, continually rolling a stone up a hill. And, lastly, I saw Tantalus extended by the side of a lake, and that there was a tree before him, with abundance of fruit on its branches, which he desired to gather, but it vanished when he reached for it.

Was it a dream?, I asked myself. But, I thought, my feet press upon the ground. I smelled the stench of death and heard the sounds of misery. I knew, somehow, that this was real, even if surreal, and that my destiny awaited me.

Past the road to Tartarus we went and saw the souls of children and innocents, as I had been taught. There were Rhadamanthys, Minos and Aiakos sitting in judgment of the newly dead. We passed those who had committed suicide, and then recently slain warriors, men in uniform who had been slain in Viet Nam, or so they seemed, both American and Viet Cong.

Onward Jonathan led us 'til at last we came to Elysian Fields, a blissful place where the righteous dead dwelled in peace amid plenty, and thence to the walls of Hades' palace. We entered through a foreboding gate. Unbowed the hierophant brought us to the very throne of Hell.

"Who comes here?" a thundering voice asked.

"The hierophant of Dionysos," Jonathan replied, "with three mortals who seek the blessing of immortality."

"And why should I grant them this blessing? With what

power do you appear before me to rob me of their presence in my domain?"

"By the word of your brother Zeus." With that the abbot stamped his foot on the floor before the throne.

Lightning flashed and thunder roared, giving assent to his request. "So be it," Hades said, "and leave."

"We will praise you with the slaughtered sheep," Jonathan said, and turning to us, said, "Bow now before his royal highness and let us depart."

And so he led us by another route, upward, upward, and though the path was steep and we saw many threatening things, none came near. The way grew lighter, the air cleaner until at last we trod steps of granite. Before us was a door and Jonathan told each of us to knock on it three times, which we did.

The three priestesses who had sacrificed the calf opened it and we found ourselves back once more in the sanctuary in the cave. "Speak to no one," Jonathan warned us, "until you have fulfilled your promise to Polymnus."

Exiting the cave, we walked down to the place where we had first met our guide. He was not there but looking around the area, we found a tomb with his name engraved above the portal and entering it we saw the crypt in which Polymnus had been laid. "He is dead," Jonathan said, "but his shade awaits you to see that you perform what you have promised. Find an olive tree and from its branches carve a phallus, that the rites might be performed and your journey ended."

Leaving the tomb we found an olive tree nearby and knives that had been laid at the base of its trunk. Each of us did as commanded and whittled a small dildo. When that had been done, we returned to the tomb, and knowing what came next, the three of us took off our lion-skin robes.

"Here," said Jonathan, "this will make it easier," and handed us a jar of scented cream. It was Dionysian lubricant, which each of us used lavishly, coating both the olive-pricks and our ass

291

holes. One by one each of us began fucking ourselves and saying what we had been taught: "Polymnus, we keep our word."

As I did so a certain joy came over me, which has never passed. The ritual was no big deal for either Michael or me, but I could see Clark wince, if only a bit.

"And now," said the abbot, "let the sacrifice continue."

We left the tomb and walked back to the grassy area near the barn. Three barbeques had been set up and hot coals were burning in them. Nearby, over a propane burner, some kind of liquid was boiling as well. The congregation of Dionysians were gathered and as we approached, naked as jaybirds, a huge cheer went up. Thomas, Clark's father, and John brought us white robes that were trimmed in silver and gold.

My mother came over to me and gave me a big hug. "I'm so happy, Ben," she said. "This is one of the best days of my life." Over the hill, the sun was beginning to set and a monk went around the assembled thiasoi lighting torches.

Beth handed me a goblet of wine and said "Here, brother-in-law, you've earned this. Welcome to immortality."

Chapter 23

Celebration

The abbot led us to three throne-like chairs that faced the barbecues and, as if on cue, a monk began banging a tambourine at the door of the barn where the calf had been slain. The crowd, now silent, formed a semi-circle facing us, with the sacrificial fires burning between us.

The monk walked toward us, now leading a procession that included the three priestesses who were carrying our crowns, followed by three fawn-skin clad maenads who were carrying trays of meat. The monk joined the small group of musicians, each maenad placed the tray she had been carrying on the ground near a barbecue, and the priestesses approached us, bowed low, and began a chanting "Dionysos, we adore you. Dionysos, we praise you. Dionysos, we worship you." In no time at all, the entire gathering took up the chant with them and as they did the priestesses placed the crowns that we had left at the entrance to the cave on our heads.

Next they gave each of us a thrysos, the long rod of Dionysos that was capped with a bunch of grapes and leaves. "Hail, Lord Dionysos," they said as they did so. "Now sweet lord receive our offerings."

"Hail, Lord Dionysos," the crowd repeated. "Now sweet lord receive our offerings."

Then each priestess went to a grill and placed pieces of meat on the fires. Smoke soon rose from it as flames, feeding on the drippings of the recently slain calf, licked at the meat.

"Great Dionysos," said the priestesses in unison, "we offer 293 this calf to you. Let the smoke bear our gift to you above, seated as you are on your Olympic throne. Let the smoke bear our gift to you here present, seated on the thrones before us. We offer the calf in praise, in adoration, and in worship of you. Accept our heartfelt thanksgiving for the safe return of these men, devoted to you and now joined to you in death and in life for evermore."

In a short time, each priestess cut off a small piece of meat of the roasting calf and threw it into the flames. Then they cut off another piece and brought one to me, one to Clark, and one to Michael. "We offer the calf in praise, in adoration, in worship of you, Holy Dionysos. Accept our heartfelt thanksgiving for the safe return of our brother Ben, devoted to you and now joined to you in death and in life for evermore." As she handed it to me, she said "Take this, Ben, and eat it. It has been offered to our god." I did as she bid and another cheer arose from the congregation.

The same was done for Clark and Michael and then the priestesses returned to the fires and each took a piece of meat from the grill and carried it to the now boiling cauldron.

"Holy calf, you who have given your life that eternal life may be bestowed on our brothers Ben, Clark and Michael, be now united again with your mother. See, here is her milk that it might refresh you on your journey to life everlasting as well."

They threw the meat into the boiling milk and, when a few minutes had passed, they drew out a piece of it, cut it into small pieces and offered each of us a piece of it. We took and ate it as well. Soon, the whole congregation was eating roasted calf and calf meat boiled in its mother's milk.

When it seemed that the last of the assembled Dionysians had eaten, the Hierophant asked, "Are there any more? Are there any more? Are there any more?" and there being none, he said "Amen. I pronounce the ceremony over. Let the party begin."

The congregation yelled their own "Amen," and thronged around us to wish us well.

With the Help of 24
Our Friends

The trip home on Sunday was thankfully less convoluted. We took leave of our families and newly-made friends and a monk drove us back to the Lexington airport. We rode on paved roads the whole way and without blindfolds. It really was pretty country, but the four of us were anxious to get back home, although to be truthful I regretted having to leave Cynthia behind.

The flight was smooth, with no delays, and the weather in Chicago was spring-like. As we landed at O'Hare we debated as to what to do about dinner and were about to decide on Anna Maria's when Thomas reminded us that we were still at war.

I had almost forgotten about the gruesome state of affairs in the Windy City and wondered what we had missed. So Thomas and I took a cab back to our place and Clark and Michael went their own way home.

Once we got home, I took in the mail and checked the answering machine for messages while Thomas made us both a drink. When I had gotten all the messages, I went into the living room where Thomas was waiting for me with our drinks. "It's a call from one of the detectives; let me call him back to see what he wants," I said to Thomas.

"Yeah," he said, "no rest for the wicked."

The conversation was short and to the point. He wanted to meet with me now. I told him to call Sebastian as well and I would meet them at the office.

"Things are heating up," I told Thomas. "It's best if you just stay here." With that I kissed him quickly and left before he could protest.

I drove downtown as fast as I could and two of the three detectives were there waiting for me to let them in. Sebastian arrived a few minutes later.

"The phone tap on Davidson's place has been ringing all weekend," said Victor, one of the guys who had been keeping an eye on the church and an ear on the wire-tapped phones.

The Broadway Church crowd was planning arson. Their conversations made it clear they want the world to know that God hates sinners and will smite evil-doers such as us. What they were going to do, they were going to do soon, very soon, on Thursday to be exact. Fortunately they were sloppy about what they said on the phone. We were going to be ready for them.

The next morning we met to make our plans: Sebastian, the three detectives, two bomb squad technicians from the FBI and I would station ourselves in the dark shadows around Stacie's home, ready for whatever our Christian friends might be up to. We would also alert the Chicago Police Department so that they could have a paddy wagon ready when we needed it.

The wire tap had worked even better than we might have hoped. It was obvious that Horton was egging them on to violence and that Davidson was the ring-leader of the group when it came to implementation. The Forges were in on it as well. The four of them would meet at Davidson's to pray for what they called "God's Justice" and then Davidson was going to plant the bomb at nine p.m. and they would set it off remotely shortly thereafter.

On Thursday afternoon, Thomas and I went home from the office early. He seemed to know something was up, but I hadn't shared any details with him. At about 4 p.m., I told him I was going out on some business and that he ought not to wait up for me.

From what I had learned about the Davidson and the rest of his murderous crew, this would be no easy task. Sure we were skilled and had the backup of both the FBI and the Chicago police, but we might have just as easily been ensnared in their plot to kill us. I didn't want Thomas to worry, even though I knew that he would.

I went upstairs, changed into dark clothes, donned a bulletproof vest, and tucked my gun into a side holster under my arm. It all reminded me of my days in the military police. I grinned to think that I felt like a hero again, only to shake my head remembering that being a hero isn't all that it's cracked up to be.

We had scouted out the nooks and crannies around the Alliance's mansion and each of us quietly and singly took our places. We were connected with private channel CBs. It was high-tech as only the government could provide. Each of us hunkered down in anticipation of what was coming next. We were early, we were prepared, and we hoped that having set the trap we could make this the last night that the thiasoi had to worry about its safety.

On schedule, Davidson's front door opened and he stepped out into the darkness, carrying a shopping bag. As he crossed the street, I came out of the shadows.

"Stop right there," I said. "Don't move. I'm armed and I'm not alone." With that Sebastian and one of the federal agents walked into the light cast from the telephone pole in front of the house. Davidson, lucky for him, did as I ordered.

"You're under arrest," the agent said. "I'm Captain Orsino with the FBI," pulling out his badge. While he was doing that I grabbed the bag out of Davidson's hand. It was heavy and full of what looked like dynamite. Davidson dropped the bag and struggled to get something out from his coat. Orsino was too fast for him and the other agent grabbed Davidson's arms, pulled them behind his back and snapped on handcuffs.

He took a small CB out of his pocket and said "Close in, guys. We've got the goods. See who's in the house." In minutes they had converged on Davidson's, knocked quickly, burst through the front door and swooped in to arrest the others.

The others, as we expected, were Horton and Mark and Beth LaForge. There was a remote control in the living room, just waiting to set off the charge. Five minutes later a police van rolled down the street. The investigation was over; now justice could be served.

I snuck into my place at 3 am, exhausted and delighted. Thomas was in bed, asleep, so I decided not to wake him. "The morning headlines will fill him with enough questions for the whole day," I thought. "No need to wake him now."

I was right. The Friday morning headlines read "Police Foil Bomb Attempt." The story lacked a lot of details but said all Thomas needed to know: "A pastor and three members of his congregation were arrested in an alleged bombing attempt late last night in East Rogers Park. Jeremy Horton, the pastor of Broadway Community Church, and parishioners Jeff Davidson, Mark LaForge and Beth LaForge, were charged with attempting to bomb a home at 6129 North Lakeview Avenue. In January Stacie Sherman, 27, was found murdered in the building. Police are withholding further details pending a search of the suspects' homes and the Broadway Community Church."

"Holy Shit!" Thomas yelled. "Look at this."

"What?" I asked, looking away from the kitchen counter where I had been making coffee for the both of us.

"Here's what," he answered, shoving the headline under his nose.

"Oh yeah," I smiled. "I forgot to tell you what happened last night."

298

Just then, the phone rang. It was Richard, inviting himself over for coffee. "Come on over," I said. "See you in half an hour."

"Who was that?" asked Thomas.

"Richard. He's coming over to get the story. I guess we don't have to go into the office today. You'd better make a full pot of coffee," I told Thomas.

"Sorry I didn't say anything last night," I said, with a Cheshire cat grin on my face, "and I'm sorry that we had to keep you in the dark about what was going on, but the guys from the FBI were insistent. It was out of my hands."

"So what happened?" Thomas asked.

"I'll tell you when Richard gets here."

"Well," I said twenty minutes later, "we got a lucky break because the Broadway crowd did too much talking on the phone and the taps on Horton's and Davidson's phone lines gave us exactly the information we needed.

"Victor actually got the details over the weekend. Lucky for us, they were sloppy about their level of secrecy, or they would never have been so lax as to say what they were going to do over the phone. Once we heard their plan, it was easy to station ourselves and the bomb control experts just out of range, but in sight of the temple. Last night, as Davidson was about to put the bomb under the front stairs of Stacie's house, we nabbed him. The LaForges and Horton were in his home. They never knew what hit them.

"The police are combing the church now, as well as Horton's, Davidson's and the LaForges' houses. With our FBI friends helping them, you can rest assured the problem is solved."

With the Broadway Community Church effectively 299

shut down, it was safe to re-open the Temple in Rogers Park. Cynthia returned home on Monday and workmen began un-sealing the basement worship space. On Wednesday, the movers brought back the furniture and things really began to return to normal.

We were all excited and relieved. Yet when I finally saw the furniture back in place and knew the temple was ready reopen, my heart suddenly sank. It was hard to explain, and I was unusually quiet that evening, even though Cynthia and Thomas spent the night at my place.

The next morning as the three of us drank coffee and read the paper, I decided to tell Cynthia and Thomas what was bothering me. It was too important for a casual announcement. "How about I treat the two of you to dinner tonight?" I asked.

"Anything wrong?" Cynthia asked. "You look serious."

"No," I said, "I just think a little celebration with the three of us is in order."

"Sounds good to me," Thomas said. "Where?"

"Where?' I said. "At Anna Maria's. Is that romantic enough for the two of you?"

"You're on," Thomas said, and Cynthia added "Count me in, too."

With glasses of wine in our hands and appetizers ordered, I told them I had something I wanted to say. "I'm sorry that the investigation is over," I admitted. "You see, I don't want you to move out. I like having you both living with me and I don't want this to end."

Cynthia and Thomas both broke out into big smiles. "Well, Ben," Cynthia said. "I'm glad to hear you say that. Thomas and I were going to ask you if we could stay."

"Could stay?" I said. "Of course you can. I don't want it any other way."

"Then," said Thomas, "that's how it's going to be."

We three clinked wine glasses, Dionysian style, in a toast to our friendship and love.

300

Chapter

Epilogue 25

Early the next year, Jeff Davidson was convicted of murdering Stacie Sherman and of attempted arson. Mark and Beth LaForge, with Reverend Jeremy Horton, were convicted of being accomplices to both crimes. Broadway Community Church ceased operation and the Chicago thiasoi returned to its secretive normalcy.

This manuscript, filled with forbidden revelations, was sent to Eagle Ridge for safe-keeping, lest I be accused of violating my sacred oath not to reveal Dionysian secrets.

Notes

In case you're interested in knowing more about Dionysos, here are some of the sources that I've used in my research:

Religions of Rome, Volume 2, A Sourcebook, by Mary Beard, John North, and Simon Price, Cambridge University Press, 1998.

The Ancient Mysteries, A Sourcebook, Marvin W. Meyer, Editor, Harper & Row, San Francisco, 1987.

A History of Religious Ideas, From Gautama Buddha to the Triumph of Christianity, by Eliade Mircea, pages 277-284, The University of Chicago Press, 1982. For those interested in a factual understanding of shamanism and mystery cults, Dr. Mircea is an excellent reference.

Dionysos, Archetypal Image of Indestructible Life, by Carl Kerényi and translated from the German by Ralph Manheim, Princeton University Press, Princeton, New Jersey, 1976.

There are no ancient manuscripts that retell the complete story of Dionysos's descent to Hades. Mythology tells us that he did so to redeem his mother Semele and then to bring Ariadne back to life, whom he then married. There are the tales of Aeneas's descent to Hades and of Odysseus's and Hercules'. Both Virgil and Homer recount some portion of these journeys and there are references as well in the writings of early Christian authors, though these are of a disparaging nature.

For a complete and very readable retelling of the life of Dionysos, read *Bacchus, A Biography*, by Andrew Dalby, Getty Publications, Los Angeles, 2004.

For a very good translation of Euripede's play, *The Bacchae*, see *The God of Ecstasy, Sex Roles and the Madness of Dionysos,* by Arthur Evans, St. Martin's Press, New York, 1988.

Acknowledge-
ments

Fiction though it is, a novel arises out of an author's life experiences and is crafted with skills that others have shared with him. Authors don't live in vacuums and neither do I. So it is only fitting to acknowledge those without him this book could not be.

I am grateful for my parents, Rose Marie and Joe, who labored to provide my brother and I a loving home and an excellent education; for Patrick my friend and partner who has encouraged, supported, and advised me without fail; and to my good friend Lynn who has done the same.

I also want to acknowledge the editors and artists in my life: James Gaynor, Christine Pfeiffer, and Michael Tallgrass. You have all done much to improve this book. Thank you.

Jack Rinella
August, 2011

About the Author

For more than seventeen years Jack Rinella wrote LeatherViews, a weekly column about his favorite topic: kinky sex. The acclaimed author of the best-selling book, *The Master's Manual*, as well as *The Compleat Slave, Partners in Power, Toybag Guide to Clips and Clamps, Becoming a Slave, Philosopphy in the Dungeon, The Dictionary of Scene-Friendly Terms*, and *More From the Master*, is a free-lance writer and college instructor. A sought-after lecturer, Jack has presented seminars on BDSM history, techniques, and relationships across the country including the Leather Leadership Conference, Black Rose, Bash at the Beach, Beat Me in St. Louis, TES, Headspace in Bloomington, IN, and the Arizona Power Exchange.

Born in Albany, New York of Italian-American parents, he's been a high school and college teacher, a drug rehabilitation counselor, a cook, a computer salesman, a Catholic seminarian, a Pentecostal minister, an advertising copy writer, a graphic designer, and has done stints at printing, publishing, telemarketing, head-hunting, and computer consulting. He has a Bachelor's degree in Philosophy and a Master's Degree in Business Administration.

He has been active in the Leather scene since 1983, is a member of the Chicago Hellfire Club and is a past board member of the Leather Leadership Conference. He has written extensively about the kinky lifestyle as a weekly columnist for Gay Chicago Magazine. His writing has also appeared in Drummer Magazine, in The (San Francisco) Sentinel, and in Philadelphia Gay News, and is available on-line at his website at http://www.LeatherViews.com and through his free weekly newsletter which can be subscribed to on his website. 307

He lives on the North side of Chicago with Patrick, his partner of more than fifteen years, where he passes the time writing, cruising, and falling in love whenever he can. You can contact Jack at mrjackr@Leathermail.com.

Other Books by Jack Rinella

The Dictionary of Scene-Friendly Terms
Rinella Editorial Services, 2008.
ISBN:0940267136 $7.95

Did you ever wonder what someone meant when he used a strange word at the munch? Did you ever want to know what a certain fetish really was? Have you ever been embarrassed to ask that top or bottom what he was talking about? Finally here's a handy Dictionary of Scene-Friendly Terms.

Philosophy in the Dungeon
Rinella Editorial Services, 2006.
ISBN:0940267101 $17.95

From devout Roman Catholic, to Pentecostal minister, to Transcendental Meditation student, and finally to a national position of leadership in the BDSM community, writer and teacher Jack Rinella is fully able to discuss spirituality in relation to sex, and in particular kinky sex. Jack carefully leads the reader through the oftentimes circuitous journey of sex and spirit to both an balanced view of human purpose and richly kinky view of sexual ecstasy. In his easy-going way, Jack encourages all his readers to embrace their life as having the potential of being a profoundly spiritual experience that is well-grounded in common sense and filled with lots of fun.

Becoming a Slave:
The Theory & Practice of Voluntary Servitude
Rinella Editorial Services, 2005.
ISBN:0940267209 $21.95

The complete guide to creating a master/slave relationship. Does domination of another turn you on? Or do you dream of submitting to the lord or lady of your life? There aren't many books to get you started or keep you going. Here's a solid resource on D/s that is safe, fun, and responsible.

The Toybag Guide to Clips and Clamps
Greenery Press, 2004.
ISBN:1890159557 $9.95
A "workshop in a book" on clips and clamps- including:
- clothespins and beyond: types of clips and clamps
- where to place your clamps
- zippers, weights, nets and other advanced techniques
- psychological issues in clamp play
- a special section on getting to know and love your tits
Plus there are a lot of tips and anecdotes that bring practicality and humor to the topic... just like a good workshop leader should do!

Partners In Power: Living In Kinky Relationships
Greenery Press, 2003.
ISBN: 1890159530 $16.95
Respected scene leader Jack Rinella has carefully explored how BDSM relationships fit into the lives of real people of all genders and orientations. From that research, and his own two decades as an active leatherman, he has assembled this sensible, readable manual about how kinky relationships really work.

The Compleat Slave:
Creating and Living an Erotic Dominant/submissive Relationship
Daedalus Publishing, 2002.
ISBN: 1881943135 $15.95
In this highly anticipated follow-up to The Master's Manual, author Jack Rinella continues his in-depth exploration and discussion of Dominant/submissive relationship with his latest

book, The Compleat Slave. This informative overview of the leather scene features Rinella's guidelines, tips, and personal experiences in creating safe and sane Master/slave relationship. Whether you are a novice D/s player or an experienced Master or slave, this insightful and forthright volume will prove to be a great read and a valuable reference guide.

The Master's Manual: A Handbook of Erotic Dominance
Daedalus Publishing, 1994.
ISBN:1881943038 $15.95

The Master's Manual examines various aspects of erotic dominance, including SM, safety, sex, erotic power, techniques, and much more. Even if you're into submission rather than domination, this book will give you insights that will lead you to a more fulfilling sexuality. I've written the book clearly, frankly, and without judgment so that any man or woman, regardless of sexual orientation, can find the info they need to make their dreams come true.

More from the Master
Rinella Editorial Services, 2010,
ISBN: 0-940267-12-8 $15.95

In the acclaimed tradition of Jack Rinella's best-selling Master's Manual, here is his newest collection of essays on BDSM. Compiled from essays written over the last 15 years, these popular columns have never before appeared in book form.